# DANCE WITH DEATH

Also by Will Thomas

*Some Danger Involved*

*To Kingdom Come*

*The Limehouse Text*

*The Hellfire Conspiracy*

*The Black Hand*

*Fatal Enquiry*

*Anatomy of Evil*

*Hell Bay*

*Old Scores*

*Blood Is Blood*

*Lethal Pursuit*

# DANCE WITH DEATH

WILL THOMAS

MINOTAUR BOOKS
NEW YORK

First published in the United States by Minotaur Books, an imprint of St. Martin's Publishing Group

DANCE WITH DEATH. Copyright © 2021 by Will Thomas. All rights reserved. Printed in the United States of America. For information, address St. Martin's Publishing Group, 120 Broadway, New York, NY 10271.

www.minotaurbooks.com

Library of Congress Cataloging-in-Publication Data

Names: Thomas, Will, 1958– author.
Title: Dance with death / Will Thomas.
Description: First Edition. | New York : Minotaur Books, 2021. | Series: A
    Barker & Llewelyn novel ; 12 | "First published in the United States by
    Minotaur Books, an imprint of St. Martin's Publishing Group"—
    Title page verso. |
Identifiers: LCCN 2020047620 | ISBN 9781250624772 (hardcover) |
    ISBN 9781250624789 (ebook)
Subjects: GSAFD: Mystery fiction.
Classification: LCC PS3620.H644 D36 2021 | DDC 813/.6—dc23
LC record available at https://lccn.loc.gov/2020047620

Our books may be purchased in bulk for promotional, educational, or business use. Please contact your local bookseller or the Macmillan Corporate and Premium Sales Department at 1-800-221-7945, extension 5442, or by email at MacmillanSpecialMarkets@macmillan.com.

First Edition: 2021

10  9  8  7  6  5  4  3  2  1

To my dear sisters, Sherry and Denise

# DANCE WITH DEATH

# CHAPTER ONE

I heard him before I saw him: a thick, rich, two-toned baritone voice. Just the two notes, sliding up and down like a trombone: up, down, down, down, up, down, up, down, up, down, down, down, down.

"'Scuse me, sir, I'd like to speak to Mr. Barker, please."

He was American, our visitor; no one irons a sentence like an American. Yet there was something musical about the cadence that I didn't quite recognize.

"Or Mr. Llewelyn, if he is available," he added.

My desk is to the right as one enters our chamber from the waiting room. Our clerk, Jenkins, has his to the left just before one enters. One must get past or through both of us to get to Cyrus Barker. Being an enquiry agent is dangerous work. There was a pistol in each of our desks, an old Adams revolver in Jenkins's right drawer, and a Webley No. 2 in the cubby of my roll top. There's also a British-made Colt suspended on a hook under Barker's desk, within his immediate reach.

"Have you got a card, sir?" Jenkins asked the man. From where I sat, our clerk looked dubious.

"'Fraid not, but I can wait if it's not too long."

"Show him in, Jeremy," Barker called in that basso rumble of his.

Our visitor entered, removing his top hat and running a hand over his short hair. He nodded his head and did not offer to shake in greeting. He wore a tight suit coat and even tighter trousers. Gas pipes, they are called. He was well groomed, fashionably dressed, and polite. He was an American Negro. The only time I had ever laid eyes upon one was at an outdoor concert in Hyde Park. The band had come from a town named Dixie, if I recall correctly, and were anxious to return.

"Are you Cyrus Barker?" he asked.

The Guv stood, bowed his head, and then waved him to one of the visitor's chairs. "I am, sir. And you are?"

"Jim Hercules," he said.

"That is an interesting name, Mr. Hercules," my employer replied. "This is my partner, Mr. Llewelyn."

Hercules nodded as I quietly observed him. The first thing I noticed was that when he sat, his feet spread apart until his heels hooked around the edges of his chair in a defensive position. He could spring to his feet immediately, if necessary. That led me to look at his hands, clutching the brim of his hat. The knuckles were marble-sized, and the skin well battered. I hazarded a guess that his ears were also a little thicker than average. He was a boxer.

Looking up, I saw that Barker was making observations, as well. I couldn't help but wonder if we were getting the same impressions of the man. The Guv sat back in his oversize chair and tented his fingers.

"How may I help you?"

"My boss is in trouble," our visitor said. "All sorts of trouble, I suspect."

"You require a bodyguard?"

For the most part, the Guv is stone-faced behind his thick mustache and black-lensed spectacles, but I could read his face easily enough. He hates bodyguard work. He refers such work to the hungrier agencies in our court whenever it arises.

"Oh, no, sir. I am his bodyguard—of a sort, anyway—but when a man is putting out one fire, he cannot put out all the other fires around him."

"What duty would you like us to perform, specifically?" the Guv asked. I could see the interest behind his stony expression. He was as curious about the true nature of this visit as I was.

The man shrugged his shoulders. I was still taking impressions. He was approaching forty. There were two or three gray curls among the black.

"I don't know, exactly," he replied. "I suppose I would like my boss to not be murdered, for a start."

"That is an admirable sentiment," my employer continued. "Has he been threatened?"

"He has, and there was an attempt on his life a year or so ago, a very close call," Mr. Hercules said. "My employer still has a scar on his forehead from the incident. I was across the room when it happened. I'm afraid I cannot protect him every moment. For one thing, it isn't my job."

"What is your job?" Barker asked.

"I am a guard," he replied, "but it is only a ceremonial position."

"There are professional bodyguards watching him, then, I assume?"

"There are, but I find it difficult to trust them. There are some within his own family that covet his position. They already have money and power, yet they always need more. They are ruthless. My boss is just learning the family business, and he is young and callow."

"If you are a mere ceremonial guard," the Guv asked, "why do you care so much what happens to him?"

Hercules resettled his top hat in his lap nervously. "I consider him a friend. He certainly needs one. He's out of his depth and the vultures are circling. I wish he hadn't come to London at all."

Barker nodded as if he understood. "What other problems is he facing?"

"His father's been sick and my boss might become head of the family before he is properly trained. If I were one of his uncles, I believe I'd feel justified in thinking him a poor choice, but his father insists, and the old man generally gets his way, things being as they are."

"Is that all?" the Guv asked.

"What? Ain't that enough?" the man replied, smiling. "All right, then. He tends to go on benders from time to time, and risks his own life."

Barker and I looked at each other. We didn't understand the word, so Hercules mimed lifting a bottle to his lips.

"The boy's not happy," he continued. "He's under a good deal of pressure and he's young. I'm worried about his nerves. He's high-strung. Could snap at any minute."

"Who is this man, and where does he work?" I finally asked. I couldn't stand it anymore. Barker and Hercules glanced at each other.

"We are expected to deduce that, Mr. Llewelyn," Barker said. "That is how Mr. Hercules will know that we are worthy to take the case."

Hercules smiled. He had good teeth for a boxer.

"Obviously he is an American," I said. "A young heir to a large business, perhaps, a name even I would recognize."

"Nope," our guest said, shaking his head.

"The son of a senator, then?" I persisted. "The president's son? No, then he could not be an heir."

"Strike two," Jim Hercules said, enjoying the upper hand. "Mr. Barker, would you care to try your luck?"

Barker looked down at his blotter, as if it would tell him the answer. I watched him closely. It must have happened, for when he looked up again, there was a smile playing at the corners of his mustache.

"I believe your employer is the tsarevich of Russia."

Hercules slapped his knee and laughed. "I knew I came to the right fella!"

"What?" I exclaimed. "How does an American boxer find himself guarding the son of the tsar of Russia?"

"Here now. I never said I was a boxer," Hercules replied, shaking his head at me. "Good for you, Mr. Llewelyn."

I was slightly mollified, having given two wrong answers already. Curbing my tongue has always been difficult for me. The flippant remark comes easily to my lips. Not so to my senior partner's. Some days he does not speak above a hundred words.

Barker couldn't think without a pipe in his mouth. He crossed to his smoking cabinet, a rather nice one, with stylized carvings that always remind me of owls. He opened one of the doors and took down a pipe from an inset atop it, since most of his meerschaums are outsize. His smoking had mellowed the white pipe to a deep honey color. It was dimpled like a golf ball in a swirling, teardrop pattern, like paisley. He stuffed it with his personal blend, lit it, and returned to his chair.

"I'm sorry, Mr. Hercules, but under such conditions we cannot take your case. You have presented no actual proof that the tsarevich's life is in danger, merely an assumption that it is. If I may borrow your analogy, we would be expending our energy running about with buckets of water waiting for a fire that might never come. Unless you have more information forthcoming, we must decline."

Our guest nodded. "I know he's in danger, but I can't prove it."

"How came you to choose our chambers over others'?" Barker asked. "This court is lined with detective agencies."

"I heard you own a boxing school and that you were the sparring partner of the late Handy Andy McClain, heavyweight bare-knuckle champion of Britain," Hercules said. "I always admired him."

"Andrew," the Guv murmured.

Andrew McClain had been one of Barker's closest friends. He'd given up the sporting life, having reached the pinnacle, and opened a mission in Mile End Road, redeeming the worst dregs of humanity: beggars, streetwalkers, the maimed or disfigured. It was his habit on many nights to choose a public house and vocalize the dangers of drink until inevitably a fight ensued. I admit it was a novel method. I had become his friend, as well, and he had given me the occasional boxing lesson before his death. He'd been gone awhile now but he wasn't the kind of man one forgets. Once I'd called him Saint Andrew, and it actually made the Guv smile.

"That is an odd nugget of information to be found floating around Saint Petersburg," I remarked.

"I didn't get the information there," he answered. "I found a club in Stepney and they recommended you."

Stepney, I thought. Dirty and down-at-heel. That sounded right. Jim Hercules would not be allowed in any "respectable" sparring club or gymnasium in the West End. It must have been an odd predicament for the friend and employee of a tsarevich to find himself in.

"You must be pretty good to keep up with old Andy himself," he continued.

Barker made no comment, but then, he wouldn't.

I answered for him. "He is."

Jim Hercules leaned forward. "I'd like to spar sometime with a man who McClain thought good enough to train with."

"Perhaps you shall," Barker replied. "Are you a Russian citizen, Mr. Hercules?"

"No, sir. I was born in British-owned Tortola and rose in Alabama, U.S.A." Our visitor scratched his forehead and gave a small sigh. "Sir, I have a secret. I hope you both will keep my confidence. I speak Russian. That is, I've learned it while working for the tsar. Everyone speaks English to me because the royal family has been taught it. All of them assume an uneducated Negro from Tuscaloosa is unable to master the intricacies of the Russian language. Now, I admit I can't speak it well, and I can't write Cyrillic, but I understand what is said well enough."

"Tuscaloosa," I repeated, savoring the strange word.

"That's in Alabama, what we call the Deep South."

"You speak Russian," Barker cut in, trying to shorten the conversation. "And?"

"And I overheard two members of the secret police, the Okhrana, talking about an assassination warning they had received."

Barker took his pipe out of his mouth. "Tell me the exact words that were said, as well as you can remember."

"Well, sir, they passed in the middle of a conversation. The first one asked, 'Why the tsarevich and not the tsar?' And the second said, 'There won't be as many people to protect him in England.' And it's true. There are about thirty of us in the delegation, but that includes maids and cooks and valets. There are a dozen mounted soldiers for show, but for the most part, Nicholas will be protected by the Queen's Guard while he is here."

"Anything more?" Barker asked, still not ready to commit us to the task.

"Would the name of the assassin help?"

Barker chuckled in that grim way he has. "It might."

"He's a Russian, I assume, but with a French name. Russians do like to kick up their heels in Par-ee."

"The name?" Barker asked, with a trace of impatience.

"La Sylphide."

"You speak French as well?" I asked.

"I've boxed there before. A lot of Negro musicians from the U.S. work in Paris. Better work, better pay, and far better treatment. We're considered exotic down there."

"I'm sure."

"Got to watch those French boxers, though. Ankle-kickers."

"*Savateurs,*" the Guv said. I wasn't the only one sampling words that morning.

"Have you heard of this assassin, Mr. Barker? La Sylphide?"

"I have not, but then I'm sure his name would only reach those few wealthy enough to afford his services. You were fortunate to have overheard it."

"I've become as much a fixture in front of the imperial family's private quarters as the ornamental gong I stand beside. The secret police talk as if I didn't even exist, as if I were a statue, or a painting on the wall. I could reach out and tweak their noses. Or punch them."

I heard in his voice the rancor that he must have felt.

"I say, you didn't answer my question," I said. "How did you come to work for the tsar?"

Jim Hercules shrugged his muscular shoulders.

"I was in Paris, just walking about the Rue de la Paix one morning looking for a café, when I was stopped by some rich-looking youths in sailor suits. The oldest was Nicky, that is, the tsarevich, who was no more than fourteen years old at the time. I shook hands with him. His little brother thought me some kind of black giant. Anyway, a fellow—a tutor or advisor, I supposed—told me to move along, but the woman I assumed was their mother shook my hand and offered me a job. She was the tsarina. Apparently they'd had trouble hiring Ethiopians as guards at the Winter Palace, and there had only been one guard to fill several shifts. That's like one salt shaker all by itself. Two doors require two guards. Anyway, I'd grown tired of the itinerant boxing life and standing about in eight-hour shifts sounded safe and easy. I've been there ever since. Ten years."

"What are your duties, Mr. Hercules?"

"I guard the tsar's private family quarters. I am what is officially known as an Abyssinian Guard. Two such guards were given to Peter the Great by the king of Abyssinia, and there have been three pairs guarding the imperial family in three shifts every twenty-four hours since. We wear outfits out of an Arabian fantasy: tasseled hats, embroidered jackets, and turned-up Persian slippers. In an age of howitzers and Enfield rifles, my colleagues and I guard the household with a spear, a scimitar, and a scowl, although I carry a derringer in my pocket. I've learned to lock my knees like a horse to stay upright. I'd call it dull, but I've developed a close relationship with the tsar's family. One is part of the household and hears a good deal of private family business. When I first began work in Saint Petersburg, I found it absurd to think that my duty would be to give my life before allowing anyone access to the family quarters. Now I would not hesitate, even for a second."

"It sounds to me as if your work is analogous to the Swiss Guards who safeguard the pope," I said.

"I'll have to take your word on that, Mr. Llewelyn. I don't reckon the tsar and the pope will ever break bread."

"How did you come to be the tsarevich's favorite?" Barker asked.

"I believe it's because of guava jelly, sir."

There was a pause in the conversation as we considered this information. Both the Guv and our guest regarded the other.

"Sir, I believe you are enjoying the upper hand too often," my employer remarked. "Very well. Explain, please."

"Once a year I get a holiday and go back to America to see my family. While I'm there, I visit my grandmother, who is famous for her guava jelly. It's won several ribbons at county fairs. I generally come back with several jars. One is always to be found in the icebox of the palace kitchen. Well, sir, I began to notice somebody was dipping into my jelly. I assumed it was one of the other guards, so I set a trap. It had to be one of the late guards who would sneak in after his shift when the kitchen was closed. I hid behind a table, and when someone sneaked in around one o'clock in the morning, I pounced. It was the tsarevich himself, about seventeen then, a growing boy who'd developed a taste for it. He didn't know it was my own private reserve. Since then, the whole palace has developed a hankering for Grandma's jelly. She makes two boxes for me to take back every year and it still ain't enough. We run through it by Christmas. Foreign foodstuffs are contraband in Russia, gentlemen, but the tsarina pays the penalties. She indulges her son."

Barker turned his face toward me as if he wondered if it were a tale the man had spun for our benefit. I shrugged. I had no idea, either.

"To how much information are you privy, Mr. Hercules?" he continued. "Do ministers come to the chamber and discuss important matters?"

"Not often, sir, no. However, things are discussed in the quarters among the family and are circulated through the servants to me. There is quite a lot of gossip there, as I'm sure you might guess."

"You must overhear a good deal," I said.

"I do, but it's none of my business unless it concerns the family's safety."

"Why have you not become a Russian citizen, Mr. Hercules?" my employer asked. "Or have you?"

"If I did, I wouldn't be able to leave the country freely. I'd never see my relatives again. No, sir. I'm still as American as blackstrap molasses and hush puppies."

I wondered if the imperial family had more luck interpreting what this man said than we did. I also wondered if there were such a thing in the Reading Room of the British Museum or the holdings of the London Library as an American English dictionary.

"Is my citizenship significant, Mr. Barker?" he asked.

"I'm merely collecting facts," the Guv replied. "I shall interpret them later."

"An actual assassin," I said to no one in particular. "The Hashishin, an ancient sect of killers in . . . where? Arabia? Turkey?" I'd have to look it up later.

Our visitor put out a hand.

"I know what you're thinking," he said to the Guv.

"Mr. Hercules, I assure you, you have no idea what I am thinking."

The American looked at me in alarm. I knew as well as anyone that Barker can be thorny with the best of them.

"There are no such things as assassins," Hercules replied.

"On the contrary," Barker said, crossing his arms and leaning back in his seat. "Anytime an out-of-work soldier of fortune with marksmanship skills meets a wealthy man with an obstacle in his path, there is an assassin."

"But not a professional one, who hires himself out for pay."

"Mr. Hercules, the fact that you know what one is and how he operates is at least a small proof."

"Does that mean you'll accept the case?" our guest asked, sliding to the front of his seat.

Barker shook his head. "No. However, I shall look into the matter. It is the most I can promise."

"I'll take what I can get," the American replied. "Thank you for seeing me. We are staying at Kensington Palace."

He jumped to his feet, bowed to Barker, then awkwardly shook my hand. He clapped the top hat onto his head and was gone.

I waited for the Guv to say something. Hercules was one of the most unusual visitors we'd ever had in our chambers. Of course, my partner said nothing. I don't know why I expected he would after all these years. I had no more idea what he was thinking than Jim Hercules.

# CHAPTER TWO

He seems an affable fellow," I said, when he was gone.

"Newspapers," the Guv said, ignoring my assessment. "Bring the newspapers."

Sometimes in our profession, the strangest on earth, I have thought more than once, one has no idea how to begin an enquiry case. At other times one does. Jenkins has a small table by his desk heaped with newspapers, *The Times, The Daily Telegraph, News of the World, The Courier,* and *The Pall Mall Gazette.* Sometimes *The Times'* afternoon edition. The Guv purchases them in Northumberland Avenue, or rather, he has me purchase them for him and keeps them for a week, so that one had thirty newspapers from which to draw information. I say thirty and not thirty-five because we do not go to the offices on Sunday, and if we did Cyrus Barker would not be so pagan as to read a newspaper on the Sabbath.

I brought them in two stacks and put one on each corner of

the Guv's desk. Then we tucked in, like tenants at dinner in a boardinghouse. I had read all this information before but it did not have the immediacy it did now.

The tsarevich; no, wait. He is the tsarevich, to use the proper term. The first is any son of the tsar, but the second is the heir. However, I have trouble pronouncing and even spelling it, so I shall call him the tsarevich.

The tsarevich was in town to attend the wedding of Queen Victoria's second son, George, to Princess Mary of Teck. From what I read, Mary had been engaged to Prince Albert Victor, George's brother, but he had died abruptly of influenza a few years ago, though there were rumors it was something worse. George and Mary had been thrown together during the funeral and an unexpected attraction sparked between the two of them. It was just in time. Really, what was one to do with a leftover princess? It was embarrassing. This settled matters all around and I'm certain Her Majesty was delighted with a wedding in the family, the first in a generation. She wasn't alone. Half the nation looked forward to it.

Not all citizens were as eager. A group calling itself the Socialist League had begun protesting the rising cost of the wedding. It must be admitted that the royal family does not do things by halves, but one cannot please everyone, even if one is empress of nearly half the world.

"What is the Socialist League, Thomas?" Barker asked. "Do you know?"

In fact, I did, but it still felt novel to be asked. At times it seems as if my employer knows everything, but since our partnership, he'd lowered his guard ever so slightly, to allow me to participate more.

"Yes, sir," I replied. "It is a group of politically radical men and women who feel a strong need to alter the norms in our society, including the monarchy, the class system, the aristocracy, and the Church. As I recall, some began as former followers of the late Mr. Karl Marx. I believe its leader is now William Morris."

Barker looked at me as if I thought he should know who that was, which I did. One brow rose above his dark spectacles.

"I suppose," I continued, "were one to create a list of people who might wish the tsarevich harm, one might put the Socialists at the top of the list of people to question."

"They have not threatened Nicholas, merely the Prince of Wales," the Guv said, drumming his fingers on the table.

"True, but many members of the Socialist League are Russian exiles. I'm certain there is no love lost between them and the tsar. Most escaped imprisonment or were purged."

"Add them to the list," he said.

I had not started a list, so I reached for my notebook and began one. Cyrus Barker allowed me to participate in conversations, but we both knew which one of us was running things, not to mention paying for them.

"Who else?" I asked.

"The Okhrana, the Russian secret police. I know whom they are secret from, but I wonder, lad, whom they are secret for. I have heard they are corrupt and violent. In the previous generations they were Cossacks."

"How did you come by that information?" I asked.

"It is helpful to know the various police forces around the world, as well as their reputation," he replied.

I wrote *Study international police forces* on a separate page.

"There are the various uncles Mr. Hercules spoke of," he continued. "The Russian grand dukes. I wonder how many of them have come with the imperial entourage. Not that they need to be here, of course. They could merely bribe the Okhrana, to arrange an accident or conceal themselves among the Socialist League members. That is just the sort of tactic the secret police would use."

"That's three," I said. "The Socialist League, the grand dukes, and the Okhrana. Anyone else?"

We sat for a minute, thinking furiously.

"Who is this Morris fellow you mentioned?" he asked.

"He's a poet and painter," I explained, wondering how he didn't know. "He's very successful. I believe he is designing textiles at the moment. Fabrics, wallpapers, that sort of thing."

Barker sat back and crossed his muscular arms. "Why should a successful poet start a league dedicated to altering society?"

"Well, sir," I answered, "I assume it started with feeding the homeless and clothing the naked."

The Guv laughed, a rare occurrence in our chambers. He slapped his desk so hard I feared for the glass atop it.

"Touché, lad. You have delivered a good deal of information in the last ten minutes. Well done. Now, could you explain to me how you come by it?"

I coughed. I had been dreading this question for years, my conservative Baptist employer asking me if I were a Socialist. To a degree, I was.

"Well, sir, some of my friends are politically radical, but then they tend to be an artsy and intellectual crowd. It is practically expected of them."

He frowned and I feared storm clouds would form. Then I realized my mistake. It wasn't my politics. He disapproved of slang terms.

"Artistic," I corrected. "Anyway, the Socialists tend to discuss everything under the sun and hold the most utopian views, as if the world would fix itself if only governments would listen to them. They—we—are young and a trifle idealistic. I'm sure even you must have been idealistic once."

He looked at me in that blank but somehow menacing way of his. Suddenly I wasn't as sure as I thought I was.

"How familiar are you with the Socialist League?" he asked.

"I told you all I know," I admitted. "I'm not especially political."

"Who might know more?"

I considered the matter. "My friend Israel Zangwill, I suppose.

He is a member. In fact, name any East End organization these days and he is a member."

"That's the teacher from the Jews' Free School, isn't it?"

"Well, he was for a time. Then he became a reporter for *The Jewish Chronicle*. Now he's a novelist. He sheds his skin every few years."

"Do you think he'll see us on short notice?"

"Yes, he seems to stay in one spot these days, far more so than when he was a reporter. He is generally home writing during the day, sir. It's at night that he goes to coffeehouses and Socialist meetings."

Cyrus Barker likes to be about in the mornings. Sitting in offices is lollygagging. There are things to accomplish and one cannot accomplish them if one is lazing about in chairs. We clapped bowlers on our heads and removed sticks from the stand. Barker told Jenkins we would be out while I stepped into Whitehall Street and whistled for a cab.

Yes, Israel had been a teacher and then a reporter for a time, then he became a popular novelist. I tried not to be jealous, since he was my best friend, but I only nearly succeeded. He was being hailed as the Jewish Dickens on the strength of his book *Children of the Ghetto,* a novel that was not only interesting to those unfamiliar with the private Jewish community, but also allowed him to air his political convictions in a way that was not too political. He was invited to speak at dinners and for public events. He had become the darling of the Jewish community.

His second book was even more interesting. It was called *The Big Bow Mystery*. The victim in the novel was a man found dead in his bed in a locked room. No one could work out how he was killed. Israel claimed to me that even he did not know. It was written and printed in installments, and whenever such-and-such wrote to him demanding to know if someone was the killer, he'd cross that suspect's name off the list. That was brass, not to mention talent, writing a book chapter by chapter with no idea who the murderer was. Or did he? I wondered.

*The Big Bow Mystery* was written in such a way that one was not in the detective's thoughts, which was genius because in the end the killer was the detective himself, being the last on Israel's list of suspects. That intrigued me, you see, because I wondered if he actually did know who the culprit would be, and had planned accordingly. The letters from the public may have been merely a publicity stunt. I thought it possible he knew who he wanted the killer to be from the outset.

Israel, from the very first, was terrified of my employer. My friend is a small, bony fellow, with long, aesthetic hands, thick spectacles, and very little chin. Barker is large and imposing. Perhaps very large and very imposing. I'd grown used to it, but my friend, having met him infrequently, had not. He called the Guv a golem, a magical giant built of clay. He called him a dybbuk, a Jewish demon. Zangwill could never understand how I would willingly work for such a man and always urged me to find "proper employment," by which he meant anything that did not involve the danger and trials of working for the singular monolith that is Cyrus Barker, Private Enquiry Agent.

He now lived in a good Georgian house in Bethnal Green, which had some nice streets tucked in behind the warrens and the workmen's housing. He rented all three floors, one bachelor knocking about in what could house many families, as this semi-Socialist has told him on a few occasions.

As I said, I was jealous. He made money at writing, and I did not. My single publication, a volume of poetry entitled *Poems for Nobody,* had lived up to its name. I never thought I was in competition with my best friend, but apparently I was, though I would not trade lives with him, a poor bachelor alone in his house. But an article in a magazine would be welcoming.

"Here we are, then," I said when we arrived at his door in Old

Ford Road overlooking Victoria Park. "Perhaps you should wait in the hall while I speak to him. You tend to make him nervous."

"He is a timorous young man, as I recall," the Guv said.

"He has his moments."

A manservant answered the door. There hadn't been one before. I gave him my card and we stepped inside. I was led into Israel's writing room, a large, airy chamber with a good-sized desk and a small owner.

"Thomas!" he cried, standing, a pleased look on his face. "Thank the Lord of all Creation. I couldn't gather two sentences today with a net. Do you want to have a spot of lunch and go buy some books?"

"Sorry, Israel," I answered, cocking my head toward the door. "This is not a social call. I'm afraid 'Mr. Groban' is in the hall."

My friend started as if given an electric charge. He stood behind one edge of his desk, hands and carpet slippers spread, looking for a way to escape. Groban was the detective and murderer in his book, but Barker had no knowledge of it and would not have read it if he did. Any book published after 1700 held little interest for him.

"I never realized that there was only the one exit in this room," he said. "Why is he here? What does he want?"

"Answers," I replied. "You are something of an expert in the field that currently interests him."

"Me?" he exclaimed. "What, pray tell, is that?"

The door opened and my employer crossed the threshold. The manservant had taken his hat and stick. Barker bowed.

"Mr. Zangwill," he began. His voice boomed in the oversize room. "It is good to see you again. Mr. Llewelyn informs me that you have enjoyed some success at novel writing. You have my congratulations."

"Thank you, sir," he replied. It was more of a squeak, the kind one emits when one is a thirteen-year-old boy and one's voice is changing. "How may I help you?"

Barker looked meaningfully at the chairs in front of the desk and our host waved us to them, if a bit reluctantly.

"We have been asked to look into a matter we cannot currently discuss, but in which you may be of service," the Guv said as he settled into his seat and placed his bowler on his knee. "It concerns the Socialist League."

"The League?" Zangwill repeated, glancing at me. "What about it?"

"Some of the members have been making threats about the royal wedding," Barker said. "Placards, wheat-paste posters plastered to walls, and the like. I shall not ask if you are a member. That is not my concern. I wish to know if you believe they might go beyond protesting to actual violence."

"It's odd that you should ask about that, sir," Israel responded. "Last night I considered resigning. The club has become politicized. The membership has become a mixed bag, many of the foreign members not long in this country. We still print the magazine *Commonweal,* but the mood has definitely become more somber at our meetings. Morris has stopped coming and Eleanor Marx, daughter of the late founder, is trying to keep peace between the factions in order to preserve her father's name. The meetings have become acrimonious. We all agreed to protest the wedding politically, but I've heard some mutterings there about a revolution."

"Is William Morris still the leader?" I asked.

"Not officially," Israel answered. "Oh, he still pays for everything, but he is no longer technically in charge."

"The placards around London seem like his style," I remarked. "Not his artistic style. Let me call it his method."

Zangwill shrugged. "They are, I admit. You should understand that just because someone identifies themselves as Socialist does not necessarily mean they are ready to blow up the House of Lords. We have the same philosophies for the most part, only different ideas about how we should express them."

"How many members of the Socialist League are there?" Barker growled at my friend. I could feel it in the floorboards underfoot. In his nervousness, my friend began fidgeting with his pen.

"That is a good question, Mr. Barker. Officially, membership is around five thousand, but that is grossly exaggerated, and includes Britain as a whole. The last annual meeting had about three hundred and twenty men. Excuse me. Men and women, I should say. Socialist, Communist, and anarchist."

"Anarchist women?" I asked.

"They exist."

"Of this membership, Mr. Zangwill, how many would you say were anarchists?" the Guv asked.

Israel set down his pen, as if suddenly aware he was holding it.

"I would say, Mr. Barker, that there are currently one hundred and fifty avowed anarchists in and around London. That is a conservative number. You must understand that most would not know a pistol from a pineapple, but they might be willing to give money to fund a political activity that they would not participate in themselves for various reasons."

Barker and I took that number in. It was far higher than either of us had anticipated.

"Are these numbers mostly foreign born or domestic?" I asked.

"Foreign, for the most part," Israel answered. "Russians, Poles, Germans, French."

"Jews?" Barker asked.

"Oh, most of us are Jews, sir. Remember the pogroms. You would be surprised how easily having the door of your home kicked in, your grandparents beaten, your wife and daughter savaged, and your children slapped about for sport will make an anarchist of you. I am East End born, but even I am traumatized from the stories I have heard by survivors of the Russian pogroms. The women are silent and the men impotent. They are angry, and the anger will not go away. It may never go away."

"Mr. Zangwill," the Guv said in a low voice, "has anyone spoken of the arrival of the tsar's son?"

"They have, yes, in no uncertain terms. One would think the boy had driven their families from Russia all by himself. They hate him, Mr. Barker. They hate him passionately. He represents all they have endured and may yet endure in the future. Oh, the West Enders may fawn over him, but it would be well if he did not travel east of the City."

It did not surprise me when Israel refused our offer of lunch. He had too much work in front of him, he said. Barker was not especially put out, and we gave our adieus. My friend looked visibly relieved.

# CHAPTER THREE

So that was that; for the time being Barker had at least momentarily satisfied his curiosity. However, we were already at the end of another case and we expected our client later that afternoon. He came, we gave him the information he had been searching for unsuccessfully, and he gave us a cheque on the Bank of England. By that time it was late and our own bank, Cox and Co., had closed.

The next morning I deposited the cheque in the bank and typed the notes for our files. The case finished, we went out for a well-deserved lunch.

The Goat Tavern in Kensington is one of the oldest public houses in London, having opened its doors in 1656. It stands across Kensington High Street from the entrance to the palace itself. It's a beautiful old building, gleaming white, and I could picture it when the public house and the palace stood alone a century before Kensington became popular.

I like The Goat. The furnishings are authentically quaint and they make the best Welsh rarebit in London. Barker ordered the fish-and-chips. I've always thought of trying them but just as always decided on the rarebit.

Being professional men, we were acquainted with most of the public houses and restaurants within a mile or two of our offices. The Guv was distracted while we ate. I thought about Jim Hercules. The only way the Guv would take the case was if he found a way to receive an introduction to the tsarevich, and that seemed an unlikely prospect.

When we were finished with lunch, we crossed the High Street into the Palace Gardens. I generally ride my bay mare, Juno, in Battersea Park, but once or twice in the days before Rebecca against all logic agreed to be my wife I rode nearby in Hyde Park and viewed the pretty girls along Rotten Row in their glossy top hats and side saddles.

It was a good day. The cool had lingered past noon. Children passed us with toy boats in their hands, while their nannies pushed prams. Two boys nearby were trying to coax an obstinate kite into the air. A young gentleman trotted by on a shiny black gelding that must have cost a fortune. I was wondering what one had to do to get the kind of life in which one could spend an afternoon riding a thoroughbred in Hyde Park when I heard a pop nearby. A pistol had been discharged.

We'd entered through the gate at Palace Avenue and had just turned into the Dial Walk when we saw a man brandishing a pistol at an open landau. I did not wait for Barker's permission. My professional instincts took over and I was off like a hare. Something flew over my shoulder and I looked up to see bits of copper gleaming in the noonday sun: Barker's sharpened coins, which he kept in his pocket as weapons.

"Kill the tsar!" the man bellowed just before he was struck by the coins.

I tackled the fellow about the knees and we both went down.

Then two men fell atop us as if it were a rugby scrum. Someone tried to push my face into the dirt, but before he did, I saw a red sleeve lined in gold and a white glove grasping the fellow I'd taken down. What in blazes? I wondered.

"Your Highness!" another man called in a loud voice. "Are you safe?"

"I—I think so!"

"Go, man! Go!" one of the men shouted in my ear as he held the squirming shooter by the tie. There was a crack of a whip, the sound of wheels kicking gravel behind, and the landau rattled off. Meanwhile, I discovered that the two guardsmen in their uniforms and bearskin hats who held me down were not particularly concerned about which of us was the shooter and which the rescuer.

It was suddenly pandemonium all about us. Women were screaming, horses reared, in danger of throwing their riders, and the guard tried to sort out which limbs were mine and which were the assailant's by tugging on them.

The shooter was perhaps forty-five, with a thick beard and a cloth cap. One of his cheeks had been laid open by Barker's coins, and another coin was partially embedded in the back of his hand. Meanwhile, the Guv had arrived at a more leisurely pace and was watching the four of us wrestling in the grass.

The man was still struggling in my arms, but he was no match for two burly soldiers and a man trained in bar-jutsu. His pistol was jettisoned onto the lawn and one of the guards succeeded in pinning him to the ground. We soon had him safely in hand, but we were all puffing like racehorses after a steeplechase. He looked crestfallen that his murder attempt had not succeeded. Something told me this poor blighter in his cap and threadbare clothes was not La Sylphide.

"Did he say 'His Highness'?" I asked Barker.

"Who are you gentlemen?" one of the guards demanded, still pinning the assailant to the ground.

"Cyrus Barker and Thomas Llewelyn of the Barker and Llewelyn Agency," the Guv answered.

"What sort of agency is it?"

"We are private enquiry agents."

Together the four of us hauled the suspect to his feet.

"I believe you gentlemen should come with us," the guard said.

The two guards looked about. Their horses had bolted. One was cropping grass a few hundred yards away and the other was probably down by the Serpentine by then. I think we were all trying to work out how to transport the man and where to take him.

"What's your name, you?" the second guard asked the shooter, shaking him. "Out with it!"

There was a sudden buzz, a whine in the air. It made me think of a dragonfly zipping over a pond or a fat horsefly as it circled a stable. We didn't hear a shot, but something happened all the same. One second, the shooter's head was there, and the next, it wasn't. A spray of blood, a pink mist, drenched the guards and me. The body in our arms sagged and fell. Then bits of bone and teeth rained upon us like hail.

"Down!" the Guv bellowed, and we all complied. On the ground again, we listened for a second buzz. Blood dripped from my chin. It was in my eyes and hair. My white collar was now stained crimson and the guardsmen's spotless uniforms were sullied. Barker had been just far enough away to remain unscathed. We waited perhaps two minutes, though it seemed like an hour. Everyone in the park had fled in an instant. There were no children, no kites, no perambulators, no blades looking to impress young ladies. There were no young ladies there to impress.

Barker stood as if daring a second bullet to come. The fact that he was in mortal danger either didn't occur to him or didn't concern him.

"An expanding bullet," he remarked. "It was from an air rifle or we would have heard the report."

"What do we do now, sir?" a guard asked, as if the Guv were his superior officer.

We all looked about. It was midday in the middle of the West End. We were in a park, near a popular thoroughfare in front of a palace, and three of us were coated in blood. There was a horse nearby with which to summon help, if he could be corralled, but as a rule, horses are skittish around men who smell of fresh blood. We were miles from a hospital or a barracks, and Scotland Yard was farther still.

Barker pulled a handkerchief from his pocket and handed it to the first guardsman.

"Wipe your face the best you can and go to the palace, young man. Help can be summoned from there."

"Yes, sir," the guard replied, taking the handkerchief before he hurried away. He was tanned and blue-eyed and looked as if he'd been rose on a farm. I hadn't realized at first how young he was.

"Who did this fellow attempt to shoot?" the Guv demanded of the second guard.

"His Royal Highness, the Duke of York."

"You mean George, the one that's getting married next week?" I asked.

The guardsman frowned. One did not call an heir to the throne by his Christian name. It was bad form.

"Forgive me," I said, when I realized my error.

"Thomas, find out who the dead man is."

"Yes, sir. How, exactly?"

"Go through his pockets, of course."

It was a punishment, I decided. I had committed a verbal faux pas by not showing respect to an heir to the throne. I told myself I would not look at the man's destroyed head, so of course I did, and regretted it at once. Poor blighter. At least it had been over quickly, but then, people say that because there is no one left to argue otherwise. I went through his pockets and pulled out the contents.

"No papers, sir. A twist of tobacco, a box of Swan Vestas, a clay pipe broken in the struggle, and two shillings in his pocket."

"Thomas, do you think you could create a likeness of his face as you saw it? Perhaps these gentlemen can help."

"I can try."

The three of us sat on a nearby bench and I began to sketch a likeness from memory in my notebook, while the afternoon sun baked the blood onto our faces.

"We just saved a royal's life," the second guard remarked. "That should mean a commendation!"

"I need a bath," I muttered as I sketched. "Two baths."

People began to pass by again as if nothing had happened, but gave us a wide berth. People looked away, looked back to make sure what they saw was real, then looked away again. The trees overhead shaded us, and there was still a hint of a breeze. It was like pieces from two different puzzles. A beautiful sunny day, a headless corpse.

There was movement from the palace and manservants began to trail out like a line of ants from an anthill. The servant in front carried a bowl and ewer, with towels neatly hanging from his forearms. The second carried blankets. The third brought brandy and glasses. I didn't notice what came after. I finished the sketch, ripped it from the notebook, and passed it to Barker. My thumb mark had stained the edge red.

We washed our faces and hands in the bowl, outside by the trees. There were bits of bone in the bottom when we were done. Blankets were wrapped about our shoulders, and another laid upon the body of the assailant.

"What's going on here?" a young man asked, stepping among us and looking about. He wore an ornate military jacket and a short beard. He looked familiar. Just as his face registered the sight before him I heard an intake of breath from Barker's lips. Then I recognized him. It was Nicholas, the tsarevich of Russia, come to see what the fuss was all about.

"Your Highness," my partner said coolly. "Your life is in grave danger this very instant. Pray, keep your head lowered as much as possible. Everyone! Circle around him! We must walk His Imperial Highness back to the palace without drawing attention. Don't panic. Don't run. Keep together. His life depends on it."

The tsarevich's eyes widened, but he did as the Guv instructed. We huddled close to him and Barker spread out his arms and leaned over him. If there was a second attempt, it would be his head that was lost. We approached the glass doors of the palace, past the statue of William of Orange. As we arrived, the doors flew open and three men jumped out, armed with pistols. I reached around for the revolver I kept in the back of my trousers but my employer's hand came down to stop me. The men began shouting in Russian and turned their pistols away from us and toward any possible threat. They must have been bodyguards.

It had been a tense few minutes for all of us. Once inside, people began to disperse, but not before I took command of the tray with the glasses and bottle of brandy. I poured a glass and nearly gulped it before I thought. Then I moved through the crowd and offered it to the tsarevich.

"Thank you," he said, before downing it eagerly. Someone had just explained how close he had come to losing his life. His face looked ashen.

"What is your name, sir?" Nicholas asked the Guv.

"Cyrus Barker, Your Highness, of the Barker and Llewelyn Agency."

"Barker. Are you the fellow Jim Hercules mentioned yesterday?"

"He did visit our offices yesterday morning."

"*Detektif,*" one of the Russian guards muttered into the tsarevich's ear.

"I know, Olgev. Someone get me a chair."

One was brought immediately. He sat, or, rather, fell into it. He put his hands on his knees and began to breathe rapidly.

"A fine way to start a state visit," Nicholas remarked.

"The man who died believed it was you in the carriage," Barker said.

"No doubt. George and I, we look alike," the tsarevich answered. "And while I am here I am forced to wear English Army colors. Protocol, you see. How did he . . . Who killed him?"

"A second shooter, I would presume," the Guv said. "One who was not pleased that someone was poaching on his territory."

"Did he have identification?"

"No, sir. My partner made a sketch from memory, but it will be difficult to identify him now."

"The English don't like me," the tsarevich said, looking forlorn.

"Russia has been England's enemy since the Crimean War," said the Guv. "Feelings still run deep, sir."

"The Russians don't like me, either, but what can one do?" Nicholas answered. "Olgev, help me up. We've got things to do."

He took two steps, then turned back. "I had intended to leave earlier, but I was delayed, and Georgie left for a fitting. He wants to look impressive on his wedding day. He took my carriage. I was waiting for a second. How did that fellow know my plans so closely?"

"The shooter? I assume he was milling about outside," the Guv said.

"No; the second man who shot the first. That could have been my brains dashed out on the lawn. I mean, it was intended to be."

He stood and walked off without a word. He looked as if his knee-high military boots were the only thing holding him up. Then he was surrounded by his entourage. One of them was Jim Hercules, who gave me a nod and a knowing look as if to say "I told you so." Then they all passed through a door and were gone.

"Interesting," Barker said.

"Brusque," I replied. "Perhaps even rude."

"Lad, you'll never hear a tsar thank his servants. And to his way of thinking, we are all his servants."

A fire-pumper came, though there was no fire. An ambulance

vehicle arrived, though the patient was beyond help. Scotland Yard followed, but they had no real jurisdiction on the grounds of Kensington Palace. Not that they didn't try.

The inspector from the Metropolitan Police was named Langton. I didn't much care for him, but then I don't believe he would be crushed if I told him so. He was stocky with a paunch so heavy he had to spread his feet when he sat. He led us outside again to question us about our involvement in the shootings.

"So, Mr. Barker, you stopped an attempt on the life of Prince George, the Duke of York, and then a few minutes later you saved the son of the tsar. You have been a busy boy."

"So it would appear, Inspector," Barker said.

"How did you happen to be in front of the palace at just that time?" he asked.

"Mr. Llewelyn and I had just eaten at the Goat Tavern."

"Oh, out for a stroll after lunch, were you?"

"We were," the Guv replied, handing him our card. "The day is pleasant."

"Not for the poor blighter in the drive. Lost his head, didn't he?" He chuckled.

Barker did not respond. Nor did I, although I would dearly have liked to.

"What is a private enquiry agent?" Inspector Langton asked, studying the card. "Some kind of detective for toffs?"

"Something like that."

"And what is this?" he demanded, tossing a coin in the air and catching it.

"A penny," Barker replied.

"Oh, is that what it is? Sharp edges. Ground them down, did you?"

"As you see."

Langton squinted at him. "What for?"

Barker growled. "Self-protection."

"That's the only form of protection you got? Don't you carry a knife?"

Barker nodded. "I do."

"And a pistol?"

"And a pistol."

The inspector frowned. "So you were in the presence of the tsar, armed with a knife and pistol?"

"He is the tsarevich," Barker corrected. "Yes, I was, and yet I did him no harm."

"Admit it, Inspector," I said. "You have nothing with which to charge him."

A man had come down the path toward us while we were talking. He was tall and lank, and extremely elegant. I recognized him at once. His name was Hesketh Pierce and he came from the Home Office.

"What's this?" Langton asked. "Pierce, what are you doing here?"

"The case is ours," Pierce told him. "National matters. Be off."

The inspector said—well, never mind what the inspector said. He blustered and said his fill, then he retrieved four constables he had brought with him, and left.

"Inspector Plankton," Pierce said. "Always good for a laugh. Hello, gentlemen. You do have a knack for being in the thick of it. Mr. Llewelyn, tell me what happened here. I know if I asked your governor it would be boiled down to ten words or less."

I told him, while the ambulance drivers carried the tarp-covered body to a litter and wheeled it away. A gardener came out carrying two large buckets of water, and soaked the blood into the ground.

"Assassins." Pierce scoffed when I had finished explaining the situation to him. "They are a myth."

"Yes, well, that myth just blew off a man's head," I replied.

"Did you hear the shot?" Pierce asked.

"No bang," I said. "A sort of whizz, as if you could hear the bullet coming."

"How far away was the shot, would you say? Where do you think it originated, in one of these trees?"

"We'll have to investigate," Barker answered.

Pierce knew his man when he said "ten words or less."

"Where did the second shooter go?" the Home Office man asked.

"Another good question."

"Why do you think he shot the first man?" I asked.

"Competition," Barker and Pierce said in unison.

# CHAPTER FOUR

I felt almost sorry for the cabman who picked us up. My hair was sopping wet, my suit and shirt soaked in blood, and I was wrapped in a blanket. However, and this is an important however, the cabman recognized Barker, who had a reputation among cabmen all over London as an excellent tipper. His greed overcame his fastidiousness and within half an hour we were home in Newington.

Once inside, I went to my rooms and stripped everything off, consigning them to the rubbish bin. Even my shoes had been sullied beyond redemption. I put on a cotton dressing gown and went outside to the bathhouse in Barker's garden. The water in the giant tub was not yet heated, but that from the faucet was, so I nearly scalded myself washing my hair over and over on a stool nearby, getting rid of whatever was left of the poor blighter who had been killed in front of me. Then I climbed down into the pool and poured in some bath salts. I floated for half an hour until I began to feel human again.

Our butler, Mac, brought fresh towels and asked if I needed anything. I did not and so he departed. Occasionally he is not a bad fellow. Afterward I entered the house and went upstairs to change. It was a mercy that my wife was receiving visitors at our house in the City and did not have to see me in my dreadful condition. A full hour after we arrived, I came down the stair to our hall and met Barker by the door. We walked to the Elephant and Castle, where we took the Underground to Charing Cross. I assumed we were returning to our offices, but Barker passed them as if he'd never even heard of Craig's Court. I had no idea where we were going, but I still held my tongue. When we reached Great Scotland Yard Barker turned into it. *Ah*, I thought. It made sense now.

"Well, well, gents," the desk sergeant said, looking up from some paperwork he was filling out for an old woman standing in front of him. He smiled. "Hail, hail the conquering heroes. You've been punted upstairs. The commissioner is waiting for you. Do you know where his office is?"

"Only too well," I muttered.

We climbed the stair. The office was on the third floor, closer to God. The door was open and there was no constable or secretary sitting at the desk.

"Is that you, Cyrus?" a voice called from within.

"Aye."

"Bring your man with you."

Man indeed. I was a partner now. I hadn't come to whisk Barker's suit.

We entered and sat. Commissioner Munro was a stocky fellow in his late fifties with a brushlike haircut and an equally bristly mustache. He had almost no neck and his head reminded me of an overturned bucket. He and Barker had an adversarial relationship going back to the days when Munro ran the covert Special Irish Branch. Their relationship had warmed a little since they had begun sharing the responsibilities for a secret society the Knights Templar, no less. *Sigilum Militum Xpisti.*

"Barker, you might have warned me before you put us both in danger of treason. Who was the man who was shot this morning?"

I looked from one of them to the other. *What?*

"His name was Joseph Bayles," the Guv answered. "He was a patient at Colney Hatch. Some members of our society convinced him to leave voluntarily, gave him a wooden pistol, and drove him to Hyde Park. He did the rest. He is a committed anarchist, subject to delusions, generally inspired by newspaper accounts."

"How many were involved?" Munro demanded. "You understand. The fewer who know, the better."

"Three, including the director at the asylum, who is a member," the Guv replied.

"That was close, Barker, too close. Don't ever come that close again without informing me. We have an agreement."

"Still," he continued, "I believe we inadvertently saved the prince's life."

I noticed when there was trouble it was "you" and when some good came out of a situation he said "we."

"What about the assassin?" the commissioner continued, drumming his fingers on his desk. "Where was he? Where did he go?"

"We never saw him," Barker growled. "He came and went like a ghost."

"Have you a client?" Munro asked.

"I do, but I have not officially taken the case."

"Explain."

The Guv gave him a limited description of our encounter with Jim Hercules, which caused the commissioner to raise a brow.

Munro shifted uncomfortably in his chair. His office was spare and devoid of bookshelves, which I consider essential. The room was large, however, and appointed with a table and chairs made of red mahogany. I suspected it was used for meetings and guests. Wealthy guests. Barker was one of them, come to think of it.

"The thing that concerns me," my partner said, "is that the tsarevich will have public appearances while he is here, culminating in a procession during the royal wedding in an open carriage. It almost invites an assassin to try his luck. Something shall have to be done, but to be frank, Commissioner, I have no idea what that is, yet."

Munro nodded, putting his hands upon his waistcoat, which could have been cut a little larger around the middle. But then the commissioner of the Metropolitan Police was not a fashion plate and probably never should be.

"Agreed. It shall have to be a joint effort between the palace, the War Office, the Foreign Office, and the Home Office. I may need to bring in the lads from Special Branch to keep an eye on the East End radicals. You know, the Socialists are poor to a man, but if they pooled their resources they could hire someone to shoot the tsarevich. The assassin might even be one of them himself."

Barker nodded. "You might see if there is a way Thomas and I could be attached to the imperial delegation."

"The Okhrana would not like that, but then you just saved Nicholas and they didn't. Let me take a meeting with them. It certainly warrants one.

"Is there anything else?" the Guv asked.

"Just stay out of trouble," Munro said, giving us both the gimlet eye. "If you force me to toss you into a cell, you can't be saving the boy. Remember, if the tsarevich is shot, it would cause an international incident, possibly even war. Try to be more circumspect than usual. No more treason. I cannot protect you or the Templars should that happen again or if the word gets out. Tell no one."

"We won't," we agreed.

"Who did you speak to at Kensington Palace?" Munro asked, raising a brow. "Which inspector, that is?"

"It was Langton, sir," I replied. I nearly said Plankton. The commissioner put a hand to his face.

"Ruddy hell," he muttered.

"You have a problem with him?" Barker asked.

"He's not the sort I want to represent the Yard in front of royals," Munro answered. "He can club a sailor in Dockland with the best of them, but royalty is another matter. There's no telling what he said."

"I saw him speaking to the tsarevich," I said.

His shoulders slumped. "I shall speak to him later. Perhaps an assignment to the marshes east of London is in order."

I made a sound in the back of my throat. It wasn't triumph or celebration. I merely cleared my throat, but Munro jabbed a finger in my direction.

"That's enough out of you, Prisoner 7502. The truce between your employer and me does not extend to you. I've got a cell and a pillow waiting whenever you cross the line."

"Yes, sir," I said. Then I grumbled. Sometimes I am my own worst enemy.

"Javert, is it?" He actually chuckled. "I've read that book. Thomas, you are no Jean Valjean."

Barker turned and looked at me. I was a little behind him, so he had to turn around almost completely. I sank into my chair, attempting to avoid his questioning look. Unfortunately, one cannot evade his stony gaze forever.

"Gentlemen, I will ask you again," Munro said. "Could you wear kid gloves this time? This is a delicate matter. There is more than a royal wedding going on here. There are delicate negotiations between our two countries. There is also some speculation concerning whom the Russian heir should marry. Her Majesty has decided opinions, I understand. She has a horse in that race, if you take my meaning."

He sat back and looked out the window at the river below, which wound snakelike along the Embankment.

"Nicholas doesn't need another bodyguard," he continued. "He's got the Okhrana. However, you know this city as well as anyone. You've got more resources and more time than my men. We have close to a quarter of our constables at the disposal of the palace. There is a royal wedding next Thursday, and there are anarchists who are none too happy about the cost, if you haven't been paying attention."

"What would you have me do?" Barker asked.

"Investigate quickly, but avoid the tsarevich as much as possible. We have diplomats for that."

Barker nodded. "We shall do our best."

"Try not to kill anyone this time, Barker. Oh, and do your best to stay out of the bloody newspapers!"

We stood and bowed. Then we left the Yard and walked up Whitehall Street in the direction of Trafalgar Square.

"Who, pray tell, is Javert?" Barker demanded.

"He's a character in a French book, *Les Misérables,* by Victor Hugo, an inspector who unjustly hounds the protagonist, Jean Valjean, throughout his life."

My employer said nothing more, but his hands were behind his back, reminding me that he was once a ship's captain. One wrong word and I'd be keelhauled, whatever that was.

# CHAPTER FIVE

Excuse me, sir, but did you just commit treason in the name of the agency?"

"I would not call it treason," Barker replied.

"Was a member of the Royal Family not shot at?" I continued.

"A bang went off and there was a puff of smoke, but no projectile. It was a stage prop."

"But in a way it was an assault upon the Duke of York. And you let a madman out with the express purpose of attempting to shoot the tsarevich, just so you could meet him. And the poor fellow died!"

"Yes, I regret that, Thomas, but there was no intent to kill him. He was let go from Colney Hatch, he shot a popgun, and he would have been returned to the asylum. Mr. Bayles was insane. Of course, I regret the death."

"Really, sir," I said as we stepped inside our chambers. "I don't know how you can work with—"

We knew immediately that something was amiss. Jenkins was not in his chair. Jenkins is always in his chair. It may look like he's doing nothing, but while we are on an enquiry he is guarding our offices, the base of all our operations.

I reached behind me and tapped the Webley tucked into my trousers in the small of my back. Barker resettled his coat, feeling the weight of his Colt. I could sense a kind of pent-up energy in the room as we stepped through the threshold into our offices.

The first thing I saw as I entered our chambers was our clerk tied to a chair with the swag from our curtain and a handkerchief stuffed in his mouth. He looked moderately miserable, but not panicked. Two men stood on either side of him and I saw he had a bruise on his cheek.

There were four other men in the room besides the bookends that propped up Jeremy Jenkins. One had the gall to sit in Barker's chair. I didn't recognize him, but I did one of the men standing beside Jeremy. It was Olgev, the Russian who had been unsuccessfully protecting the tsarevich in the park. Even a poet can add two and two. This was the Okhrana.

"Welcome, gentlemen," the leader said.

"You are in my chair, sir," the Guv replied, crossing to the center of the room by the visitor's chair. I gripped my stick, but I was ready to pull out my pistol if required.

"Am I?" the fellow asked. He looked about fifty years old, with a thick mustache and a spade-shaped beard. He was stocky, but hard looking. His black brows looked like they had been applied with a paintbrush.

"Get out of my chair," Barker warned.

"You are in no position to give orders, Mr. Barker."

Then Barker did the last thing they expected, which is always the best place to start. The toe of his boot hooked under the visitor's chair, and he launched it over the desk. It careened off the pristine glass top, shattering it, and struck the man full in the face. He really shouldn't have sat in Barker's chair.

It all went mad after that. The Guv punched one of the book-ends in the face. Olgev he kicked in the side of the knee, possibly breaking it.

I'd perfected a trick of my own. I slipped the brass cap of my stick through my fingers until I caught it at the very tip and then drove it into a man's face. Then I turned and brought it down on another's wrist. A third seized me by the shoulders, but I drove my knee up between his legs and most of the fight went out of him. That took care of the men within my reach.

I pushed aside my coat with my left hand and drew my revolver from my waistband, but as I did I heard simultaneous clicks in the room. When I looked up, everyone was pointing pistols at each other, except the man I had incapacitated, who was occupied being sick near one of the bookcases.

"Put down your gun, Mr. Barker," the Okhrana leader said. He held a pistol, but also a handkerchief to his nose, which I'm sure had been broken.

"Get out of my chair," my partner demanded. "I have told you twice."

"You are in no position to give orders. It is seven against two."

"Six," I replied. "Your lackey there is busy soiling our carpet."

"Lad, when I am going down," Barker said, standing firm, "shoot our visitor between the eyes."

"Yes, sir."

"It's been a good life."

I turned and aimed at Barker's chair, at the head of the Okhrana, at the spot where his brows met.

"Wait!" Our visitor vacated the Guv's seat. "It's just a damned chair!"

"He won't even let me sit in it," I said.

"We didn't come here to die or to kill anyone," he persisted. "We only wanted to talk to you."

"Most conversations do not begin with tying up a man's clerk."

"Olgev, untie the man."

He had an odd accent. It was English strained through Russian, and then strained again through French. To be kind, I'll call it Continental.

"You've broken the glass atop my desk," the Guv said.

"You broke it yourself, Mr. Barker. I must say your priorities are strange." He muttered something in Russian and the men put away their pistols. We did the same.

He came around the desk and sat in the other visitor's chair.

"Jeremy," Barker said, seating himself in his chair. "Go to the Silver Cross and bring beer."

Our clerk's eyes opened fully at the word.

"Yes, sir," he answered.

"You're sending for Scotland Yard," the man stated.

"And ruin our new alliance?" the Guv replied. "That will hardly do. Now, whom do I have the pleasure of addressing?"

"I am Pyotr Rachkovsky, the bureau chief of the Okhrana. You made us look like fools today."

"On the contrary," the Guv replied. "I saved the tsarevich's life, with the aid of the Queen's Guard and a few servants. Your men made themselves look like fools without any help from me."

To a man, they looked at the floor.

"Idiots," Rachkovsky said. "Go. Go sit in the lobby there, all of you."

They slunk out like whipped puppies licking their wounds.

"We can be civilized about this, Mr. Barker. I'm glad you understand. I'd like to know who hired you, please."

"No one hired me. My partner, Mr. Llewelyn, and I had just come from lunch across the street and were reluctant to return to the office on such a fine day."

Barker stood and walked to his cabinet table. A moment later, he offered the box of cigars to Rachkovsky.

"Excuse me, sir, is that brandy there? I do not drink beer."

I went to the table behind the Guv's chair, under the ancient coat of arms of the Barker clan, and poured a glass. I handed it to him.

"Armagnac," I said.

"I must say I am impressed, gentlemen. I have been too long in Paris, you see."

"You are the bureau chief there?"

"I am, but I am not here to discuss me. The tsarevich is young. It is difficult to contain him."

"I understand."

"I believe you have broken my nose," he said, dabbing it with the handkerchief.

"Regrettable," Barker answered. "I should not need to mention it, but the third in line to England's throne was nearly killed today. What is happening, sir? Who means to take your charge's life?"

There was a long pause. I thought it perhaps fifteen seconds, which seems interminable in a conversation.

"There is an assassin attempting to kill the tsarevich."

"So I assume," the Guv replied. "Do you know anything about him?"

"He is called La Sylphide."

"Who is he?"

"We don't know," Rachkovsky replied. "He comes and goes like a ghost. He has an air rifle, which we suspect he can break down and carry in pieces. We assume he is Russian. He reads and writes it."

"Has he sent a message to you?"

"Just once," he replied, setting his glass on the table. "Before we left Saint Petersburg, he shot out a window in the Winter Palace, simply to cause trouble, I believe. It kept Nikolai Alexandrovich secluded until we left. The boy was petulant, wanting to go out and meet his friends, but we would not allow him to go. Two weeks later, we found a hole in the new glass, in the exact same spot as the last, and a rolled length of paper inserted in the hole. It read: 'You cannot keep him safe forever.'"

"He's toying with you," Barker said.

A few minutes earlier Barker and Rachkovsky were ready to fight to the death. Now they were comparing professional notes.

"Oh, yes. I think he could have shot the tsarevich a half dozen times if he went to much effort. The man is very talented but he seems to be a dilettante."

"How can we help you, sir?" Barker asked.

"Help me?"

"Help you find the man attempting to assassinate the tsar's son."

"I need no help."

"No? How many of your men speak English? I regret to inform you there are few people in London who speak Russian. Also, you aren't familiar with the City, whereas Mr. Llewelyn once sat for a cabman's exam and knows every mews and back alley in London Town."

"What are you suggesting?" Rachkovsky asked.

"If I learn a piece of information that I believe you require, I shall give it," Barker said. "The same applies to you. Someone shot at a future sovereign this morning. Very nearly two."

"How could he mistake the Englishman for the tsarevich?" the Okhrana leader asked.

In response, the Guv reached to the edge of his desk where a newspaper lay. It was *The Pall Mall Gazette,* known for having illustrations and photographs within its pages. He placed the copy in front of Rachkovsky.

Prince George was on the cover, along with his future bride, Mary of Teck. I could see the light dawn in Rachkovsky's eyes. Despite growing up on two different continents, the two royals were nearly identical.

"The assassin shot at the wrong man."

"It was a stage prop," Barker replied. "The other bullet was not."

"Why shoot at the assassin and not George?" I asked. "The prince was still visible. Was it accidental? Did the assassin just get in the way of firing at Prince George?"

"No," Barker stated firmly. "The sharpshooter wouldn't have missed. It was vexation. It was hubris, which says one thing about him. He is emotional. He considers himself a professional. The other fellow blundered about with his prop, spoiling his chance, and made him angry. He wasted the only chance he had to kill Prince George and spent the bullet on his rival instead."

"I'm sorry, sir," I said. "It was my fault."

Barker turned his head in Rachkovsky's direction.

"Mr. Llewelyn has a habit of taking blame for everything he cannot control," the Guv explained. "I'm not sure if it is a Welsh trait, or something peculiar to himself. If you will recall, Thomas, there were three of you tugging on the one man and two of them were guardsmen. I do not believe you can take full blame. On the other hand, you were the first to tackle him, which goes to your credit."

"It would be difficult to identify a man with no head and no identity papers," I said, wanting to change the subject.

"Does your Scotland Yard use the Bertillon method of identifying criminals?" Rachkovsky asked.

"It does, but I do not consider it conclusive," the Guv said. "It would be difficult to gauge how tall he was."

"You have impressed the tsarevich," the Okhrana leader said, frowning at Barker. "He wishes to meet you."

"You do not approve," the Guv stated.

"I most certainly do not!" Rachkovsky answered. "I suspect you are a spy yourself. Suppose this entire matter with the dead assassin was a charade to place you close to Nikolai and you are an assassin yourself. What is a detective but a soldier for hire, willing to do whatever is expected of him?"

"Codswallop," Barker said. "We're in the business of saving lives, not taking them."

"We have wasted our time coming here. However, His Imperial Highness has asked to see you. I believe he wishes to thank you."

"Just how large is the Russian delegation?" Barker asked.

"Forty-five, according to my list."

The Guv and I glanced at each other. Forty-five people. Rach-kovsky made no attempt to apologize or explain. Forty-five servants to accompany one man in order to serve him or save his life. But they had failed, twice if one counted an assassination attempt in Japan.

Suppose every monarch attending the royal wedding requires fifty servants, and all need lavish rooms? The hotels of London will be swollen with them.

"I can make no promises, Mr. Rachkovsky," Barker said. "I have certain duties to my country. However, I have no wish to join your camp. There is an assassin loose in London, and I need to stop him, and I cannot do so if I am nursemaiding a boy. There is unrest, and Mr. Llewelyn and I have our duties to perform."

"We are perfectly capable of protecting him," Rachkovsky said, though the handkerchief stuffed in his nostril did not inspire confidence.

"Of course you are," Barker answered. He was being diplomatic, maybe even magnanimous.

We had just bested his men, the two of us.

The Okhrana leader stood. "We are guests in your country, gentlemen. However, we do not brook interference."

"That is your duty."

"It is," he said, nodding. "Nikolai wishes to see you now. He is awaiting you. I suspect he wishes to offer you a temporary position. You will, of course, refuse."

*Oh no,* I thought to myself. He'd been doing so well until that order. One doesn't tell Cyrus Barker what to do. It only makes him more determined to do as he pleases.

# CHAPTER SIX

Our cabs formed a procession all the way to Kensington. Rachkovsky rode with Barker while I was made to go with Olgev. He was nursing a bruised eye, which would be purple by morning. Luckily, I hadn't given it to him. I could very well have found myself sharing a cab with the fellow I kicked in the cobbles. Olgev was sullen and so we traveled in blessed silence.

*What does one say to the tsarevich of Russia?* I wondered. I hoped I would not be noticed. Barker takes over a room, so it was possible I would not have to speak at all. If pressed I could say how glad we were to have him in our country. But after that, nothing came to mind. I am creative, but not spontaneous.

Soon we found ourselves in the drive in front of Kensington Palace. A few people stopped to watch us alight, but when they realized we were actual people and not royalty, they melted away like snow on a warm day. We were marched to the Orangery and taken inside, then led through innumerable halls and finally into a gold-lined chamber with a very high ceiling. The tsarevich was there. When we entered, he shooed the guards and the Okhrana away. He looked us up and down as if wondering what we were there for. Then he broke out in a grin that almost made him look like a youth.

"I say," Nicholas said, with almost no trace of an accent at all. He turned to Barker. "You're that fellow, the one that turned me about and herded me back into the palace."

"I am," the Guv rumbled.

"If it weren't for you, I believe there would have been a second bullet. And you," he said, looking at me. "The last I saw you, you were covered in blood."

"Yes, Your Highness. I seem to recall the incident."

"Ha!" he said to the room, as if wherever he stood embodied the imperial court. "Very droll. I like this fellow."

I spotted Jim Hercules in the back. He wore the outfit he had warned us about: a tasseled fez; a long, frogged jacket of a fiery red; baggy harem trousers; and Persian slippers. Not to mention he carried a scimitar. I'd have been embarrassed to wear such an ensemble in public, but I supposed it was better than being an itinerant boxer. One goes where the work is.

"So, you two are . . ." He paused and looked at Hercules. "What was that, Jim?"

"Private enquiry agents, sir."

"Yes, that. It was awfully good for me that you arrived when you did."

I glanced at my partner. "Yes, wasn't it?" I murmured.

Barker merely nodded in reply.

"It's dreadfully dull around here. Would you care to be a part of the imperial delegation? I imagine you have some stories to tell."

I could tell one or two but I wouldn't without the Guv's permission.

"Alas," Barker said, "if we guard you here, how can we track whoever is menacing you with an air rifle?"

"An air rifle?" he repeated, frowning. "I do not believe I have heard of that. What is it?"

I looked askance. The fellow was at least a major in the Russian army but had no knowledge of military weapons. I wasn't particularly surprised, however. It would be an honorary position given to him so he could dress up like a soldier.

"An air rifle," Barker explained, "is a rifle that uses compressed air instead of gunpowder."

"How is it compressed?"

"Mechanically. It is often pressurized by cranking a gear."

"Does it take any bullet?" the tsarevich asked. "Or only the kind that busts open a skull like a melon?"

"It can use a regular bullet of the proper caliber. The shootist, if I can call him that, took the time to scratch an $X$ in front of the bullet, which causes it to fragment when it reaches its target."

"In effect, it is like a tiny bomb."

Barker considered the question. He is not obsequious. If he objected to the idea he would have said so. "That is an apt description."

Nicholas shrugged. It was nearly a convulsion. "I hate bullets and I hate bombs. I saw my grandfather, Alexander the Second, carried into the Summer Palace, legless, his face disfigured by a bomb that blew him apart. I had to watch him die, you see. It is imperial protocol. He choked on his own blood. Pints of it soaked into the sheets and mattresses until it dripped on the floor beneath the bed. I held my father's hand and tried not to cry. I was thirteen."

I murmured in sympathy.

"I have nightmares, you see. I am being carried legless, leaving a trail of blood along the Persian carpets. Or I am in front of a firing squad of peasants, surrounded by cheering rabble. I don't imagine I shall end well. It is a bad time for monarchs."

"'For what is your life? It is even a vapor that appeareth for a little time, and then vanisheth away,' James 4:14," Barker quoted.

"You sound like the patriarch of Saint Petersburg, Mr. Barker," Nicholas said. "He has a verse for everything. I am to be tsar. Surely there are enough men in the Russian Army to see that I live to a ripe old age. Jim here makes a better attempt at protecting me. He recommended you, and it angered Rachkovsky to no end, so of course, I summoned you."

"You have no use for the Okhrana?"

"One has the rabble on one side and the secret police on the other, and neither allows one to sleep at night," the tsarevich said, flexing the muscles in his shoulder. "I suspect the Okhrana is a puppet in the hands of my uncles, the grand dukes, each of whom would very much like to be tsar himself."

"I see," my partner said, although I suspected he knew the fact already.

"I thought I might be safer in London, but apparently you have Socialists and anarchists of your own."

"They arrived after the pogroms," I replied. "From Russia."

The tsarevich nodded. "I have seen the shtetls burning, set on fire by the Cossacks. I had no quarrel with the Jews, but too many people owed them money. It was easier to drive them out than pay them back."

Nicholas shook his head. He was very melancholy, this young man.

"Mr. Barker, you know this city," he said. "The Socialists must congregate somewhere. Surely you can track them and this madman with the air rifle. Aunt Victoria is plotting my wedding. I should like to be present for it. Go, stay, whatever you see fit. Do whatever must be done to keep me alive. Oh, and keep Cousin George alive as well. I'm rather fond of my English twin."

"Yes, sir."

"Keep Jim posted about your activities. May I assume you have no problem reporting to an Ethiop?"

I glanced over. Hercules tried to preserve his sangfroid, but it is not easy when one is dressed like a djinn from a tale by Burton.

"None whatever," Barker replied.

"Good, then."

"And one more thing," Nicholas added. "Gentlemen, I have a delicate matter to discuss with you. The Okhrana refuses to let me see Mathilde. Mathilde Kschessinska, I mean, the famous ballerina of the Imperial Mariinsky Theatre. She is my mistress. My cousin, Sergei, brought her here from Paris to see me, but that pig Rachkovsky won't allow me to get near her. I need to speak to her, you see. She knows the Queen is scheming to create an alliance by marrying me off to Princess Alix of Hesse and she is madly jealous. Mathilde wants to be tsarina. She has a temper. If I can't see her she will take it to mean that I refuse to see her. I was wondering if perhaps you might get a message to her from me, to tell her I haven't forgotten her and will get away as soon as I can."

"Get away?" I asked.

"Well, not for very long. An hour, perhaps two. She's difficult to convince. Ballerinas are sensitive creatures. Oh, I cannot describe how she dances. It's as if she will take flight at any moment!"

"Hmmph," Barker said. He did not approve of mistresses.

Nicholas didn't need a pair of private enquiry agents following him about. We were hired to take messages to Mathilde. Whenever the time was right, we were to secret him away for a tryst. *Yes,* I thought, *a tryst.* I did not fall for the statement that he required two hours to "calm her nerves."

"In fact, that is the perfect thing," Nicholas continued. "You go off and deliver my message to Mathilde and bring her answer on the pretext of giving me a shooting lesson. Yes! I'm so clever sometimes. You will do that, won't you, gentlemen?"

"I don't think—" I began.

"I don't think that sounds too onerous, Your Highness," the Guv said. "We will be glad to do so. Write your letter, and I suggest a long one if you are going to mollify a young lady. Have Jim here deliver it to me and I will see that she gets it."

Nicholas grinned like a naïve schoolboy. "Wonderful. I've got a letter to compose tonight. At last, something to do in this wretched old pile!"

"Your Highness," I said.

Nicholas turned and frowned. "Yes?"

"Are we to defend you, deliver your letter, or give you a shooting lesson?"

"I thought that was obvious," the young royal replied. "All three."

Jim Hercules cleared his throat.

"Getting a cold, are we, Jim?" the tsarevich asked.

"You have an appointment, sir," Jim drawled. "Lady Wagstaff."

The tsarevich harrumphed. "Another dinosaur, no doubt. They've trotted them through here hourly. Lady this, Viscountess that. I gather their husbands are intelligent enough to hide. Most of them have bad teeth. I want to go riding. I want to talk to people my own age. I'd like to sample English ale and walk about Whitechapel incognito, like cousin Albert did. You know, to see the guttersnipes your Jack the Ripper slaughtered. London is no Paris. It is such a dull place."

"It has its moments," I said.

Nicholas pointed a finger at me. "Now, that's what I'm talking about. Let me go about with the two of you. I'll bet that will be jolly. I could be a private enquiry agent for a day."

Barker shook my head. "I'm sorry, sir, but you can't fear being assassinated one minute and then want to ride about in unprotected cabs with us the next."

"I could wear one of those sets of false whiskers and spectacles like yours, Mr. Barker. They'd think I was an anarchist trying to kill the tsarevich. That would be . . . what would that be, Jim?"

"Ironic, sir," Hercules supplied.

"The very word."

Hercules had made it sound as if he and the tsarevich were the best of friends, but he seemed more Nicholas's lackey. Just how did a former boxer turned harem guard get put in charge of a baby tsar?

"I fear that is not possible, Your Imperial Highness," Barker insisted. "It is far too dangerous, and the Okhrana will demand to know where you are at all times."

Nicholas pointed to me again. "Can he stay? He seems sardonic enough. He could keep me entertained, I'm sure."

"Alas, I need him. He takes notes, asks questions, stays armed."

"Are you armed?" Nicholas asked. "Really? Have you got a pistol?"

I nodded.

"Teach me to shoot a pistol," he said, smiling. "That would be marvelous and I could defend myself. Take that, you swines! Bang! Bang!"

"The very thing," Barker said, clapping me on the shoulder.

"Well, that's something like. That's the English expression, isn't it? I read it this morning in the newspaper. Something like?"

"You speak the vernacular like a native, Your Highness," I said

"It's settled, then," he replied. "We shall squeeze a lesson in between old cows of the aristocracy. Surely Kensington Palace can create a makeshift shooting range on the property. There's plenty of room in this old pile. It's dull here! Dull!"

I thought the tsarevich was an enfant terrible. It appeared no one had told him no before and he was spoiled. For once, I felt sorry for whoever was in charge of him. Just then another young man entered in a military jacket and looked about.

"What is all the rumpus?" he asked.

"Georgie!" Nicholas cried. "You're back."

"Hello, Nicky. Whom are you torturing now?"

"These are the men investigating the shooting," Nicholas said to his cousin. "This one is going to teach me to shoot."

"That will be entertaining," George said, stepping forward. "Gentlemen, how do you do? I am George, Prince of Greece and Denmark."

"Your Highness, were you not the one who defended the tsarevich in Japan?" the Guv asked.

"I am."

"Oh, let's not dwell on that!" Nicholas said. "He was in the perfect spot to step in, but really, I could have defended myself."

Prince George, not to be confused with England's prince of the same name, was a good-looking young fellow, blond-haired and mustachioed. He looked particularly fine in a pale blue military jacket. The prince bowed. This fellow was every inch the royal.

"You failed last night, George," Nicholas told him.

"My apologies, Nicky. I hadn't prepared for guzzling an entire bottle of port."

"You cannot go by halves, you know," Nicholas said. "It's all or nothing. You'd better prepare for next time. Where have you been, sport?"

"I inspected the barracks and stables of the Queen's Own Guard. Such beautiful horses, and I love the Guard's shiny helmets and scarlet capes. I'll have to have a word with the army when I return to Athens."

"Where's Sergei?" the tsarevich asked.

"Oh, you know, looking after his bit of stuff."

"That's my bit of stuff, remember," Nicholas interjected. "He'd better remember it, too."

"I'm sure he will."

I felt sorry for George, having to keep Nicholas occupied. A full bottle of port. I'd have choked after one glass.

"Did you just get in, Georgie?" the tsarevich continued.

"I did."

"Have you eaten?"

Prince George shook his head. "No."

"I'm starved. Let's raid the kitchen."

"Dinner is being prepared, sir," Hercules said.

"Oh, bother dinner. I don't want to wait until Aunt Victoria deigns to spoon her wretched pheasant consommé. I want some real food. Let's go down to the kitchen and see what we can liberate."

The two young men walked out and we watched them leave.

"You have our deepest sympathies," Barker said to Jim Hercules.

"You have to understand," Jim said. "Nicky is trying to show Russian strength in front of English imperialism. It's a complicated situation."

"What are you here for, precisely, Mr. Hercules?" the Guv rumbled. "Why did you come?"

"I'm trying to keep him calm. It is the opinion of the doctors in Saint Petersburg that the tsarevich is having a nervous breakdown. This is all too much for him."

"You are surprisingly patient, considering how he treats you."

"But you see, he only treated me that way because the two of you are here. When we are alone, we are very nearly equals. My boss has little personal esteem and feels he must show bravado, especially in front of men such as yourselves."

"You are saying he is only pretending to be a tsar," Barker said.

"Exactly!" Hercules replied. "It doesn't come naturally to him."

"This is your regular work outfit, then?" I asked.

"It is. I have one that's worse. A short vest with no shirt and a large turban. They even oil my skin for effect. I look ridiculous."

"Why do you do it, then?"

He shrugged. "It's a living. If I were back in the States, I'd probably be a sharecropper by now. I'm no longer young and there are a lot of new boxers out there. Grammy's proud of me. I've done the best of all her grandchildren."

"You have a very unusual occupation, Mr. Hercules," I noted.

"Well, yours is not exactly shining shoes, now, is it, Mr. Llewelyn?"

The last was said a trifle tartly.

"My apologies," I said.

"Sorry. You're not the first person who's told me that. How are things coming along?"

"It is still early days yet," Barker replied. "But I now have an idea of what is required. We will start by interviewing various factions of the Socialists."

"Have you ever heard of an agent provocateur?"

"Of course."

"The Socialist parties all inform on each other, mainly for money to run their own organizations. Some join other groups to encourage them to do something that will get them arrested, or even executed. I'm from America, gentlemen, and I have seen my share of lynching. Doing it for money or to make your political society a little more powerful is the basest of reasons."

"I agree," Barker rumbled.

"Oh, and some of the radicals are actually Okhrana plainclothesmen burrowed deep inside the organizations."

"What you're saying," the Guv replied, "is that we can't trust anyone."

"Yep. Everyone lies. You've just got to figure out why."

"This is quite a little drama you've brought us into, Mr. Hercules."

"Now you know why I asked you gentlemen for help."

"I believe I now fully understand what is required and what it entails, so I accept your case," Barker said, shaking our new client's hand. "Come along, Thomas."

We left him then, standing in front of a door, though there was no one inside to guard. As we walked out through the glass doors of the Orangery I heard a sound coming from Barker, a kind of grunting noise. It took me a moment to place it. He was humming to himself.

"You seem quite pleased with yourself," I remarked.

"I am pleased with myself."

"Now we're in for it. Three separate assignments and none of them aligns with the others."

"Aye, lad, but it gives us freedom to do whatever we wish. It is another fine day, is it not?"

# CHAPTER SEVEN

When Cyrus Barker ruminates, he nestles back against the buttoned leather of his green chair and turns it on its casters toward the window as if seeking inspiration, crosses his meaty arms at the peril of his suit coat seams, and then he scratches under his chin with the backs of his fingernails, flicking them forward without being aware he is doing so. That could go on all day. I recall a particular case once involving the old Spring-Heeled Jack legend, where he sat for two days entire. Generally speaking, however, he might do so for an hour or two, at the expense of my nerves. Once or twice I've taken a walk, giving him time to think without his partner squeaking a chair or typing correspondence. That was out of the goodness of my heart, mind you, and had nothing to do with any personal impatience of my own.

I was dying to know the particulars of Mr. Bayles, and how

he went from a cell in Colney Hatch to shooting at the Duke of York in one hour. However, he was expecting me to ask, so I held my questions until a proper time. I knew the subject would arise eventually.

He'd lingered deep in thought for the next hour and a half. I dared not move or interrupt his train of thought. The mantel clock ticked as if regretful for the interruption, and there was a wheezing, almost whistling noise I eventually tracked to our clerk's desk. He was asleep. This was another danger of prolonged inactivity.

Suddenly, I heard our clerk jump to his feet. If Jeremy Jenkins has a gift beyond forgery, it is the ability to become totally awake at a moment's notice when it is required.

"Good day, sir." His voice carried from the next room. "Welcome to the Barker and Llewelyn Agency. How may I help you?"

"I wish to speak to Mr. Barker on a private matter," an elite upper-crust voice replied. "Mr. Llewelyn as well, I should imagine."

An old duffer who'd got himself caught in a problem he couldn't get out of, I supposed. There is no fool like an old fool, save perhaps a young one.

"Have you a card, sir?" Jeremy enquired of our visitor.

"I do, but I do not wish to give it."

"Ah," Jenkins replied, looking put-upon. I could just see his face from where I sat. He would not get to deliver it to the Guv on his beloved silver salver. I don't know how that tradition began, because it started before my time. Certainly Barker would never require such a thing. I suspected our clerk purchased it in a stall in Covent Garden in order to give our agency a certain tone.

There was a squeak of the chair and Jeremy entered our chambers and came to the desk.

"A gentleman to see you, sir."

"Hmmph?" Barker did not move. He still stared out the window.

"A visitor," I repeated. "We have a visitor."

"Do we?" the Guv asked. "Where is his card?"

My partner can be brusque when interrupted. In a near-silent room he had not heard our visitor utter a word. That is concentration.

"He prefers not to give it," Jenkins replied. "A private matter, he said."

"Well, show him in."

Our clerk looked disgraced. I didn't blame him.

The visitor entered. He was a duffer, just as I suspected. Sixty if he was a day. He was immaculately dressed, however, from his glossy top hat down to his shiny pumps. He was slender and the waxed tips of his gray mustache were bent at the ends as if they had been caught in a mousetrap.

Barker did not rise, as if longing to go back to his thoughts.

"How may I help you, sir?" he growled.

"I wish to speak to you privately, sir. You and Mr. Llewelyn, that is."

"Is that necessary?" the Guv asked. "Mr. Jenkins is the soul of discretion."

"I fear it is."

It wasn't what he said, but the way he said it. He, too, could be frosty, and there was a degree of authority in his voice. Perhaps he was a solicitor ready to lay a summons to the Old Bailey, or a general in Her Majesty's Army, requiring his services.

The Guv nodded at Jenkins. "Jeremy, go have a pint."

I tossed him a shilling and he blew away like smoke from a chimney. One did not need to tell him twice.

"Now, sir, again, how may I help you?"

Belatedly, the man pulled a card from a silver case in his waistcoat pocket and handed it to Barker, who scrutinized it carefully. Then and only then did he rise and offer the man a seat.

I reached forward and snatched the card from his desk. It read:

*Col. Henry Francis Waverly*
*Equerry*

Equerry. There weren't a great lot of equerries about, and those that were generally worked for Victoria Regina, our gracious queen.

Barker's brows rose above the twin circles of his black-lensed spectacles. Not in astonishment, but in irritation. He'd already asked our visitor how we could help him and he was damned if he was going to ask again.

"I've been sent by the palace, gentlemen," the colonel said. "Is it true that you were present at an assassination attempt on the life of Prince George?"

The Guv and I looked at each other as if to say we seemed to recall such an event, but weren't certain. Finally, we nodded.

"Did you in fact apprehend the man who shot at the prince's carriage, with the aid of two guardsmen?"

"That was Mr. Llewelyn," Barker explained. "I was injured last year and am not as swift off the mark as he."

"But you threw, what? Some pocket change at him?"

"Aye," the Guv replied.

The equerry turned his attention to me. "You subdued him?"

I looked at the Guv and back at the colonel. "I did."

"Good fellow. But he was then shot from somewhere on the grounds?"

"Yes," I answered. "Yes, he was, sir."

Waverly glanced at Barker. "According to servants, the Russian tsar's son came out of Kensington Palace then to see what the commotion was about. You then convinced him to go back into the building, using yourself as a shield, Mr. Barker. Is that correct?"

It dawned on me that the palace was keen to find out precisely what had happened that put the Queen's son in danger.

"It is," Barker replied. "But I was only to hand, and it was the briefest interval before the guardsmen surrounded us and helped him back to the safety of the palace."

"Why were the two of you in front of the palace in the first place?"

"We'd just finished eating at the Goat Tavern in the High Street," I answered. "We felt the need to stretch our limbs in Hyde Park. The sun was out."

"Do you dine there often?" Waverly asked.

"From time to time," I said. "Their chef is Welsh and I like the rarebit he makes. It's difficult to find a good rarebit in London."

"I dare say," Her Majesty's equerry said. I suspected he wouldn't know a good rarebit if he were standing in it. "You visited the restaurant randomly, then."

"We did," Barker replied. "Can you tell me your purpose in coming here, Colonel Waverly?"

"All in good time, sir, if I may intrude a few minutes longer," the equerry continued. "I'm sure you have other duties and so do I. I have a point and I must eventually come to it. May I continue?"

The Guv held out a palm. "The floor is yours."

"Thank you," Waverly replied. "Was there not a time several years ago when you defended the Prince of Wales against a bomb-maker?"

My mind went back immediately to that day. Maire, her name was. Maire O'Casey. She was a pretty Irish girl who fell among the Irish Republican Brotherhood. She blew the two of us off the Charing Cross footbridge hard by Scotland Yard. I survived. She did not.

"She was running past the prince with a Fenian bomb in a satchel," Barker explained. "I'm not certain she recognized him. He'd just come out of one of the clubs."

"You're being modest, Mr. Barker. Did he not give you an engraved pocket watch in appreciation?"

"He did," I said, pulling it out of my waistcoat pocket by its chain, and opened it to read the inscription:

*To Cyrus Barker, from HRH the Prince of Wales*
*for services rendered to the Crown*

"That was years ago," my partner said.

"His Highness recalls it," stated Colonel Waverly. "Why shouldn't you? You must understand, gentlemen, that Her Majesty is very concerned about these events. She nearly lost a son, only a few days from his wedding. She has also been attempting to arrange a marriage between the House of Romanov and the House of Hanover from which the royal family springs. This is of unimaginable importance, an alliance between the two most powerful families on earth, sworn enemies since the Crimean War. It is also extremely complicated. Dozens of ministers are involved and hundreds of missives sent between London, Saint Petersburg, and Germany. It is a very delicate business. Dowries must be considered, spheres of influence balanced. There was a time when the tsar refused the match and another when talks broke down completely because Alix of Hesse refused to become Russian Orthodox. Had the tsarevich died this morning, all of Europe and most of Asia would have fallen out, diplomatically speaking. Many countries have sent their leaders and emissaries here. It is to be the first royal wedding in over thirty years."

"I am glad we were there to help," Barker said.

"Yes," Waverly replied. "Very fortunate there. Very fortunate."

The equerry reached into the inside pocket of his coat and retrieved a small notebook. He began to thumb through it. "Now, yesterday morning you were approached by an employee of the imperial household. Some sort of guard."

"Jim Hercules," the Guv supplied.

"Yes. What did he want?"

Barker frowned and sat back in his seat. "The gentleman was concerned that the tsarevich was not being adequately protected."

Waverly rose a brow. "With the combined services of the English and Russian armies?"

"Now, sir, we know the Russian delegation is largely ceremonial," the Guv replied, tenting his fingers. "As for the English, all eyes are on the wedding. The Queen's Guard did excellent work safeguarding Prince George and disarming his assailant. However, Nicholas strolled out onto the lawn of Kensington Palace alone. I conveyed him to safety with the help of a few servants."

"This was the day after you were hired to protect the tsarevich."

Barker held up a hand. "I was not hired. I refused the enquiry."

"Why did you refuse it?"

My partner reflected on the question. "I have accepted the duties of a bodyguard in the past and have regretted doing so. A determined killer will always find a way. It is difficult for one man—excuse me, Mr. Llewelyn—two men to predict all contingencies in order to save a man's life. It's too difficult an operation for our agency."

"Yet the two of you found yourselves in front of the palace in time to stop an assassination," the colonel said.

"No, sir," I said. "We did not stop an assassination."

Waverly nodded. "You are correct, young fellow. Forgive me. It was a poor choice of words."

Waverly pinched one of the bent tips of his mustache in apology and harrumphed. He was a trifle embarrassed.

"Yes, but the two of you were there. Are you telling me that it was a coincidence that you should be in Kensington Gardens at such a time?"

"We do eat at the Goat Tavern now and again, Colonel Waverly," the Guv said. "But I'll admit I was mulling over having refused Mr. Hercules's request. I felt guilty, in fact. I thought I might see under what conditions the tsarevich was being protected, even if it were but a glance from the front gate. Of course, I did not expect anything to happen. The assassination attempt was as much a surprise to us as it was to everyone else."

The equerry began sifting through pages in his notebook. "We've been collecting information about you in the past few hours. It made for interesting reading, but there are gaps, and I must admit some of what we have seems difficult to believe."

Cyrus Barker leaned forward and rested his arms on his desk. "Name something and I'll tell you if it is a fact."

"Very well. You helped the Empress Dowager in Peking."

"Aye, she was being poisoned. I discovered the culprit. In gratitude, she gave me one of her prized dogs. He still lives with me. Doesn't he, Thomas?"

"Or we with him," I replied.

Waverly consulted his notebook again. "You were born in Scotland and moved to Foochow with your missionary parents, who passed away."

"Of cholera," Barker supplied.

"Yes, and the next bit of information we find is that you were in the civilian army at Shanghai during the Taiping Rebellion as a youth."

The Guv nodded. "True."

"Then you came to London, tried to become a police constable but were refused, and opened your own agency here in Craig's Court."

"All of it true."

"You own a house on the Surrey side of London," Waverly continued.

Barker nodded. "I do."

"A very nice house."

"It is."

"How does a detective own such a property?"

The Guv cleared his throat. "I prefer the term 'private enquiry agent,' and my fortune was made as a sea captain in China."

The man nodded, then made a notation in his notebook.

"The various branches of government are undecided about you," he said.

"I prefer it that way, Colonel," the Guv replied. "On one hand, I wish to be helpful, but on the other, I don't wish to make them complacent. I prefer to remain private. It gives me freedom to do as I like."

"No doubt," said Waverly. "Pray forgive my numerous questions, Mr. Barker. I shall be asked about you at both Buckingham and Kensington Palace. I wish to be ready to answer any question they might ask. For example, is it true you have a boxing and wrestling school in Glasshouse Street?"

"It is."

"And an Asian garden that was shown to the Japanese delegation two years hence."

"I am proud of that garden, if anything," Barker answered.

"And you . . . You keep . . . That is, you are acquainted with Mrs. Philippa Ashleigh."

Barker tilted his head to one side and I heard a click in his neck. He only did that before a fight, if I recall.

"Sir, I would prefer that her name not become a part of this conversation."

Waverly stared into the notebook a final time. "That seems to be all the questions that I shall pose, Mr. Barker. Thank you, gentlemen, for your patience."

# CHAPTER EIGHT

My partner and I did not go to the office the following morning. The Russian ambassador had sent a message and was coming to speak with Barker. Baron Egor de Staal would be given a tour of the Guv's garden, a sight to behold this time of year, and be ushered into the library to have a discussion about the tsarevich. Afterward, in the dining room, we would be served a light lunch catered by Etienne Dummolard from his restaurant, Le Toison d'Or.

"Let us consider Miss Kschessinska," the Guv rumbled from the chair in his private chamber. "We must question her before she meets with the tsarevich."

"We don't know where she is staying," I pointed out. "I assumed Nicholas would tell us how to find her when he gives us a message for her."

"We must speak to her first," the Guv said. "Perhaps we can

persuade her to leave London and to go back to Russia or Paris, wherever she is going next."

"How shall we find her?" I asked.

"Go get Miss Fletcher," the Guv replied. "I think she could be useful in finding Miss Kschessinska."

"Yes, sir," I answered.

I went out to find a cab and instructed the driver to head for our offices in Whitehall. While the cab bowled along, I thought about Nicholas's mistress, Mathilde Kschessinska. I was eager to get a look at her myself. What sort of beauty would turn the head of a future tsar to the point of flouting the rules of society? I also wondered what she would say when confronted by Cyrus Barker, a man who intimidates powerful men, not to mention delicate young women. Just now Russia balanced on the head of a Polish ballerina.

When we arrived in Whitehall, I jumped from the cab and paid the driver, walking past the door of our chambers. Miss Fletcher's office was across the alley from ours and deeper into the court. She had rented a room on the first floor over the offices of J. M. Hewitt, a detective who handled some of the enquiries we were too busy to undertake. There was a sign over the door in black letters:

*S. Fletcher, Enquiry and Typing Services*
*Female clients only*

The sign notwithstanding, she occasionally worked for Cyrus Barker when he had some matter involving women, such as finding a Russian ballerina in London. I had never visited her office before. It was small and narrow. There were rugs on the floor, one in particular taking up a good amount of space around her desk, but otherwise the room was Spartan. She was not the sort of woman who studied decorating or read *ladies' magazines*. I suspected she'd never heard of such things.

"Come in, Mr. Llewelyn," she said, looking up from her typing machine.

"Good afternoon," I said, removing my hat.

I suppose Miss Fletcher was attractive to some men, but she dressed plainly, fixed her hair plainly, and most definitely spoke plainly. I had yet to detect a sense of humor from her, and there was a constitutional difference between us. The reason I enjoy my work is because of the places I go and the things I do. Seeing the hidden places of London. Standing in a makeshift mortuary one minute and buying a dozen roses in Covent Garden to send to the missus the next. The changeability, the danger, the spark. The bullet that missed. The one that didn't. Above all, the thought that there was a poor blighter somewhere in London who wished he could trade places with me. That was the life I wanted. Something told me Sarah Fletcher was in the business for a different reason entirely. For her, it was a crusade.

"Mr. Barker would like to see you," I stated.

She looked up from the document she was typing at her desk. The Guv paid well and I knew she was interested.

"I am finishing a case that took me to Wapping," she said, covering the paper she was typing as if it were a state secret. "Can it wait until tomorrow?"

"He would very much like to speak to you as soon as possible," I answered, tucking the hat under my arm.

She frowned and looked at me as if she suspected I had no idea what was entailed in the running of a detective agency. "That does not surprise me in the least. Tell him I shall be along directly."

"Mr. Barker is at his residence today, taking meetings," I told her. "I have a cab waiting outside if you're agreeable."

"Together?" she asked.

"I suppose we can take two if you are concerned about propriety."

"No, that's fine," she answered primly. "Let me get my hat."

She donned a tan mackintosh and a boater hat and I led her out into Whitehall and hailed another cab. I was uncomfortable and wondered what to say to her in the confined space all the way to the Elephant and Castle, but I need not have worried. She turned her face away from me and did not speak during the journey. We reached Newington without incident and when I opened our door, Mac was there as usual, attached to the inside handle. He looked surprised when he saw my visitor.

"Miss Fletcher, this is Jacob Maccabee, our factotum," I said. "Mac, this is Miss Fletcher. She is here to see Mr. Barker."

"A pleasure," Mac said, bowing.

She gave a small curtsey. We climbed the stair, where we were met by Rebecca. I introduced Miss Fletcher to my wife. Sarah bobbed again, but Rebecca was having none of it. She stepped forward and took her hand.

"Miss Fletcher," she said. "It's so nice to meet you. Have you been to Mr. Barker's residence before?"

"No, ma'am."

"My mother is 'ma'am.' You may call me Rebecca."

"Sarah," she replied.

We continued upstairs to Barker's loft. Miss Fletcher looked dazed when she beheld it. It is a sight, to be sure: sloping red walls from the apex, covered in weapons from his travels, low bookcases lining the room, sturdy tables with chairs that were old and stained and purchased from a library somewhere, books and souvenirs from his travels, two large brown leather chairs, much worn, in front of a fireplace, and the grandest sight of all, Mr. Barker himself. He wore a crisp wing-tipped collar and maroon tie under his jacket.

"Ah, Miss Fletcher," he said, rising and bowing to our guest. "It is good of you to come on such short notice."

"Yes, sir," she said, curtseying again. Everyone had received a curtsey except me, but then I had no desire for one.

"I have an assignment for you, if you choose to take it," the Guv continued, offering her a chair. "There is a young ballerina in town intent upon encountering the Russian tsarevich, but we don't know where she is staying. Her name is Mathilde Kschessinska. His Highness said he thought her hotel is called the Imperial, but he wasn't certain."

"There is not a hotel in London named the Imperial, sir," she replied, clutching her reticule tightly.

"Precisely," Barker answered, nodding his head. "After you find her, I want you to follow two men. Both of them work in Kensington Palace, but I need to know where each of them goes. I want you to follow them, but under no circumstances speak to them. Here are their names and descriptions."

He scribbled on a bit of paper at his elbow for a couple of minutes. Miss Fletcher and I waited without a word until he handed it to her.

"Three assignments, then, sir?" she asked, trying to make heads or tails of the paper in her hand. His handwriting is practically illegible. "I don't generally get hired to follow dangerous men about."

"Do you find three assignments beyond your abilities, Miss Fletcher?" Barker was suddenly at his most imperious.

"Oh, no, sir," she replied, looking uncomfortable. "I like to keep myself occupied with work."

"A noble sentiment," he said, which was a swipe at me, of course. "That's all I have for you, then. Thank you, Miss Fletcher. Give her a tenner, lad."

"Yes, sir," I answered. I took out the wallet I carried for my partner and handed her a ten-pound note. She stared at it and then put it carefully into her reticule.

"That will be all," Barker intoned.

We stood and I walked Miss Fletcher to the staircase. She looked stunned as we went down.

She wasn't prepared to meet Cyrus Barker, Esquire, in his lair. My wife was waiting for us at the landing.

"You look as if you could use a cup of tea, Sarah," she said. "Come down to the kitchen with me."

I thought Miss Fletcher looked reluctant, but my wife would brook no refusal. She ushered her along and I bobbed behind in their wake.

The meal for the ambassador was in a state of preparation; those dishes that did not arrive fully cooked from Etienne's restaurant, that is. As Rebecca, Sarah, and I entered the kitchen, I saw that Mac had doffed his jacket and put on a starched apron. He had rolled up his sleeves in order to aid the chef who had been sent to prepare lunch, but froze and stared at the three of us when we entered the room.

"Would you care for tea?" he asked.

Without waiting for an answer, he filled a kettle with water and set it to heat. He was caught between performing a duty and being a good servant.

"I'm so glad you came," Rebecca said to Sarah. "I've heard your name mentioned once or twice and was curious who you were. It is so nice to put the name to a face."

Sarah Fletcher attempted a smile. It did not look natural on her, I thought.

"Are you the only female detective in London?" Rebecca asked.

"To the best of my knowledge, yes, ma'am," Sarah said, nodding.

"Please call me Rebecca, remember?"

I was hanging about when suddenly the chef thrust an apron into my hand and ordered me to chop carrots. Then Rebecca and the chef began a conversation in rapid French. She had worked for a while in Etienne's restaurant after we were first married, in order to improve her cooking skills. Soon all of us, even Sarah Fletcher, were put into service. Rebecca didn't stop asking questions of our guest, however.

"Do you have relatives in the area, Sarah?" she asked.

She had thrown dough onto a flour-strewn surface and began kneading. Meanwhile, Sarah was stirring a mixture of sugar, cream, and strawberries in a bowl.

"I am an orphan," Miss Fletcher replied. "When I was dismissed from school at seventeen, I went into service for a few years, first as a char and later as a lady's maid."

"Did you always want to be a detective?" Rebecca enquired.

Sarah Fletcher looked reluctant to answer, but my wife is very good at winkling secrets out of people.

"It wasn't my original plan, no, but the downstairs maid collected journals and I read a story once about a female detective and I thought it sounded intriguing."

*"Non, non!"* the chef suddenly scolded me. "They are too large. You must chop carrots much finer than that."

"Very well," I replied.

Mac was stirring mashed potatoes in a pot under his arm, watching the conversation between Rebecca and Sarah with endless fascination. I wondered what was going on in his head.

"Have you worked at another agency?" Rebecca persisted.

"No," Sarah answered. "I applied for one once, but the position was taken."

"Ah."

"Too small! Too small!" the chef insisted, pointing at the vegetables in front of me.

"I have a knife in my hand," I told him. "Step away."

Rebecca turned her attention back to Sarah. "And what do you do for entertainment, if I may ask?"

"Entertainment?"

"Yes, dear, in your off time."

"Oh," Sarah said, coloring slightly. "I have a typing machine in my flat. I always have work to do."

My wife turned to me as if I were responsible, as if I cast her out to type until her fingers bled. At that point in the preparation of the meal, the chef no longer trusted us, so he shooed us out the door. We heard the kettle whistle as we left the kitchen.

"We never had tea," I observed.

I walked Miss Fletcher to the cab stand near the Metropolitan

Tabernacle in Newington Causeway, a few streets from Barker's home. The day was blustery and we both pinched the brims of our hats. She looked troubled for a moment and finally broke her silence.

"Have I done something wrong?" she asked, glancing at me. "Mr. Barker seemed angry with me."

"Miss Fletcher, I believe you have an inflated view of my partner," I replied. "He is wise, he is the best enquiry agent in London, and he can be very generous and kind. However, he can often be brusque. I am a full partner now and married, but he is still 'sir' to me while he calls me by my Christian name. I believe he is a great man, but that doesn't mean he is always easy to work with. He is complicated."

"I did not realize," Sarah Fletcher murmured. "Thank you, Mr. Llewelyn."

"Not at all, Miss Fletcher. You've done nothing wrong, by the way. The Guv has a great deal on his mind. The case that you're helping us with is both complex and delicate. He'll be speaking to an ambassador within the hour."

"I see."

A hansom arrived and I waited until she was settled. She looked away, deep in thought, as the cab pulled away from the curb.

When I returned, I heard a murmur of voices in the library, Mac's included. The door opened and Rebecca came into the hall. She took my arm and we went upstairs to our room, where she sat down on a sofa beside me.

"She's such a darling," Rebecca said.

I shall never, ever, under any circumstances, understand the mysteries of the female mind.

"Perhaps Miss Fletcher is more charming to women than to men," I replied.

"Jacob Maccabee doesn't share your view," she said.

There was no mistaking the sparkle in her eye.

# CHAPTER NINE

When the ambassador arrived I waited as Mac stepped out of the house, followed by Barker. The carriage came to the curb, its side door displaying the two-headed imperial eagle, and a driver in livery climbed down and opened the door. A short man in a large hat stepped out of it. I was reminded of Tenniel's sketches of the Mad Hatter. He had small features, thick, dark brows, and pendulous side whiskers. He looked like a child next to Barker; however, he carried the weight of almost an entire continent on his shoulders.

De Staal bowed solemnly and the Guv bowed back.

"Thank you for coming, Baron," Barker said. "Welcome to my home, such as it is."

"I hear great things about your garden, sir. I took this opportunity to see it. Then we have international matters to discuss."

"Indeed," Barker said. "Won't you step this way."

The tour of the garden went well. As it happened, de Staal

was an amateur gardener. They discussed seedlings and seasons, costs and compost as I wandered about the garden, letting them finish this part of the visit, trying not to show that I was beyond bored. I don't like tea, and I don't like gardens. I'd have made a poor Englishman.

The two finally finished their tour and we went inside to talk. Mac had lit a fire in the grate. Baron de Staal sat and turned away offers of drinks, coffee, or cigars.

"You must understand," he said. "I have come to the match late. Let me see if the facts I have are correct. The two of you gentlemen were walking by the palace after lunch yesterday in time to see a man shoot at Prince George, the Duke of York. You, Mr. Llewelyn, tackled the assailant almost immediately, an anarchist named Bayles. Then Bayles was shot by persons unknown. Is that correct so far?"

"Yes, sir," I answered.

He didn't know about Jim Hercules or about the coincidence of our arrival in front of the palace, but neither Barker nor I was about to reveal it to him.

"The commotion attracted the attention of the tsarevich, who, not knowing of the danger, stepped out to see the commotion. You, then, Mr. Barker, escorted him back to the palace. Is that not so?"

"It is," the Guv replied.

"Later, you had a meeting with the tsarevich at his request. What did he ask you and Mr. Llewelyn to do?"

Barker rose a brow. "I am not at liberty to say. It was a private conversation between the tsarevich and me."

Of course, Hercules hired us, but the baron didn't know about it. Where did he get the notion Nicholas had? Had he inferred it, or had someone told him?

A thought occurred to me then, a thought so strong that I lost the gist of their conversation for a moment. What if Nicholas had sent Jim to hire us in order to protect himself? Hercules would do anything for his boss. Would an employee, an Abyssinian Guard, hire agents to stop an assassination attempt?

"In effect, gentlemen," de Staal continued, "you may be under the assumption that you are now working for the Russian government, but unfortunately, you are not. The tsarevich had no business hiring you, if that is what he has done, either to protect him or to investigate possible suspects in his name. It was rash of him to speak to you without discussing it with his government, which is to say me."

Barker gave a hint of a smile. Telling a horse no when the bit is between his teeth accomplishes little.

"I spoke to Rachkovsky last night. The two of you had a serious altercation in which his nose was broken and two men were so severely injured that they were taken to a hospital. He said the two of you set upon the three of them unprovoked."

"Baron," Barker said, "do you believe Mr. Rachkovsky is in the habit of reporting things exactly as they happen, or does he give you the Okhrana's version of the truth? He claimed we attacked three men, hardened agents of your secret police, just the two of us. Thomas, do you have any wounds on your person?"

"I nicked myself this morning under my chin here," I said, "but that's all."

"Cheeky to the end, Mr. Llewelyn," the Guv replied. "As you can see, I am without any sort of injury myself. If we emerged from a fight in which three men were wounded while we remain unscathed, either they are no better fighters than a women's badminton team or they are lying. Which do you believe more likely?"

De Staal stared at him, one arm crossed over the other, cupping his chin. He was trying unsuccessfully to make out my partner. The key to understanding Cyrus Barker is to know that whether in conversation or altercation, his first step is to get one off balance.

"Let us set that aside. You are private detectives."

"Enquiry agents," we both said at once. It had become automatic.

"Whatever you wish to call it. I understand you have offices by Scotland Yard. How do I know you do not work for them? Or for the Home or Foreign Office? I would be a fool to allow foreign agents to get close to the future tsar of my country. In particular, two men with a propensity for violence."

"Sir," I replied, "I only weigh thirteen stone, and I am a published poet. What sort of violence would I inflict upon anyone?"

De Staal pointed a finger at me as if I'd been caught out. "Ha, sir! Admit it, Nicholas has asked you to teach him to shoot."

"Yes, sir," I admitted, "but it was not done on the strength of any marksman ability on my part. He hired me because of a remark I made and the fact that we are of a near age. He hired me on the spur of the moment for no other reason than the novelty of it. And speaking of that, how does a young man who must hold rank in the military not know how to shoot a pistol? Or am I mistaken?"

The ambassador shifted uncomfortably in his chair.

"You must understand," he said. "The tsarevich is headstrong. He plans things without permission, but rarely completes them. He is spontaneous, and being young, he does not think things through. He must be protected from himself. That is why I am here. Naturally, the tsar is concerned about his heir. We thought it best not to give him a pistol. I'm afraid there is no more polite way of saying this, gentlemen, but we must dispense with your services, such as they are. Protecting the tsarevich is no longer your concern. We appreciate what you have done and you will be compensated. We understand that you saved Nicholas's life as well as the Duke of York's, who was mistakenly believed to be him, and we are grateful. However, we cannot have foreign agents among our staff wandering about, listening to all that is said and done. The Okhrana are here to protect our future tsar, which I'm certain they shall do successfully."

"No doubt, sir, no doubt," the Guv replied. "So, to be clear, what you are saying is that we are sacked."

"I would not use such rough terms, Mr. Barker," de Staal stated, "but the effect is the same."

Barker leaned back in his chair and crossed his arms, studying the ambassador. I'm certain he wished he were in his large green leather chair in our offices. The ones we were using in the library were a more proper size for Rebecca.

"Alas, Baron," the Guv continued, "I don't expect you to understand the protocols of private enquiry work, but a person cannot order us to quit a case if he did not hire us in the first place. It isn't done. I can refuse a case, if I so choose, or I can resign and be done with the matter. My client can ask us not to pursue actions or he can sack us. But no third party, no matter who he is, can insinuate himself into the agreement."

De Staal looked at him, unimpressed with his argument. "What shall happen then? Shall you bring suit against the Russian government?"

"No. I will not consider my duties discharged, and shall continue as before. Or rather, we shall."

"That's right," I said.

"You are a stubborn man, Mr. Barker," the ambassador said. "I see no reason why we cannot discuss this like gentlemen. The tsarevich does not understand protocol when one visits a foreign nation." He waited a moment, but got no reply. "Very well. I shall meet with Nicholas today. If I take you to Kensington Palace and he says he no longer requires your services, your services will be discharged."

"Why should they be discharged?" Barker argued.

"Obviously, because the man who hired you no longer desires your services according to your precious code. That is, unless you believe we are forcing him under duress."

I looked at the Guv. When he became a Baptist he gave up

such things as cards, but as a ship's captain, I believe, he was a dab hand at gambling.

"That is immaterial to me, Baron de Staal. He didn't hire me to protect him. Another member of your delegation did."

The baron leaned forward and frowned, clutching the arms of his chair. For a moment he reminded me of Napoleon. "Who, then?" he demanded.

Barker smiled. "I am not at liberty to say. Protocol, you understand. Tell me, Baron, what do you make of the assassin who shot Mr. Bayles in front of the palace?"

"What assassin?" the Russian ambassador demanded. I saw the veins in his neck begin to distend.

"La Sylphide," I replied.

"He is a rumor," he growled. "I don't know who invented him. Perhaps it was the two of you."

"That rumor blew a man's head off his shoulders," I pointed out.

"It was probably a guard who for one reason or another refuses to come forward. Or a coconspirator meaning to shoot Prince George, who missed and killed his partner instead. Afterward, he escaped."

"I see you have considered this," the Guv said, sitting back.

The ambassador jumped from his chair and began to pace. "La Sylphide is a bit of fiction," he stated. "A heavy-handed one, at that. I don't doubt that the Duke of York was in danger, but it was more likely from one of your anarchist gangs who have been pasting placards all over London. It has nothing to do with us. There was no obvious attempt upon Nicholas's life. I suspect you helped him back to the safety of the palace for no reason. The only man in danger was the prince."

"And what of the cry 'Down with the tsar!'?" I asked.

"Hearsay," the baron replied.

"But we both heard it," I countered.

"Perhaps, but you are not expert witnesses. In fact, your

employment would be groundless if you could not supply—or invent—a villain to threaten His Imperial Highness."

"Ambassador," Barker said coolly. "You dismiss La Sylphide at your peril."

"Mr. Barker, I have been an ambassador for most of my professional life. I know when I am being hoodwinked. I do not believe anyone hired you but the tsarevich and you cannot convince me otherwise. There is no point in continuing this conversation. I have many other matters to attend to. Good day, gentlemen."

Baron de Staal stalked from the room. I imagined him putting on his tall hat and taking his stick. We heard the door slam behind him.

"I assume he's not staying for lunch," I said. "Etienne will sulk for a week."

"It is a mercy he sent a chef and is not here to throw pots at the windows," the Guv replied.

"I agree."

"I don't really think the baron knows much about gardening," he continued. "He couldn't recognize a yellow azalea."

"No!" I said.

"We're leaving in half an hour."

"Yes, sir."

My partner went upstairs. I heard a sound a minute later and turned back in time to see Rebecca leaning out into the hall, her hand on the banister.

"He's gone, then?" she asked.

"The Baron? Yes," I answered.

"He seemed a disagreeable man."

"I would say so."

"He all but called the two of you spies."

"How do you know?" I asked. "Could you hear our conversation?"

"Almost as clear as a bell," she replied.

"Did you drill a hole or something?" I asked. "I never noticed one could hear what was being said in the library. But then I wouldn't. I'm generally the one holding conversations there."

"You defended yourself rather well, I think," she said, taking my arm.

"Thank you. You can hear us talking in Barker's room and down in the library. Can you hear in the kitchen?"

"Well enough," she admitted.

"And the back garden?"

"If the window is open."

"Oh, yes?" I enquired. "Prove it."

"Last night you were humming *Peer Gynt* in the bathhouse."

I smiled. "Off-key?"

"No," she answered. "It was in tune, for the most part."

"That's good to know."

Rebecca frowned. "Was the conversation with the ambassador significant?"

"It opened a few areas of enquiry," I replied as we walked to the staircase.

"Such as?" she asked.

"It would be good to know for whom we are actually working."

# CHAPTER TEN

We arrived at our offices after noon, having tried to do justice to Etienne Dummolard's meal. When we opened the door we found Jenkins alone, buried in a crime journal. Unfortunately, he had forgotten to purchase the newspapers for the day.

"I'll be back in a few minutes," I said after offering to get them myself. "Is there any newspaper you'd like me to purchase while I'm out?"

"The usual will suffice, I think," Barker replied.

I stepped out into Craig's Court and was turning into White-hall Street when my hat blew off. I turned and ran after it. It was my best top hat, from James Lock and Co., a Christmas gift from Rebecca. I sprinted down the alleyway, but the wind rushes through the court at a tremendous volume and I had to run like the dickens. I could not lay hold of it until I reached the telephone exchange at the far end.

Rescuing it from the ground, I glanced at it for a moment, and there seemed to be no damage, so I clapped it on my head, trying to remember what I was doing. Newspapers. I grasped the brim and began to walk in the wind. Reaching Whitehall Street, I was aware of a whistling sound from somewhere nearby. I looked about. Whitehall can get blustery sometimes.

There was that sound again, a wheezing noise. It seemed to be coming from somewhere around me. I pulled the topper off my head. There were two neat holes in the fabric, one in front and the other in back. My hat had not blown off. It had been shot off. La Sylphide had returned and it was the second time he had missed my cranium by mere inches.

I turned and hurried back inside our offices. Jenkins was smoking a cigarette and reading the *Police News,* and he looked up when I returned. I crossed to Barker's desk and sat in one of the visitor's chairs. The Guv looked up and rose his eyebrows.

"No newspapers, Mr. Llewelyn?"

I placed the spoilt hat on his desk. He examined it as if it were some kind of relic, turning it about this way and that and then finally lifting it from the new glass that had just been installed. He inspected the trajectory of the bullet. He tried to get one of his thick fingers through the holes, but it was impossible. He set it back down on the desk and pushed it my way. He didn't want it, nor did I. I supposed it could be re-silked, but I preferred not to place it on the counter of James Lock and Co. in such a condition. They might ban me from ever setting foot through the door again.

"Someone doesn't like you, Mr. Llewelyn," my partner said.

"It would appear not," I answered. "That was my best hat and it was attached to my best head. Who wants to kill me?"

"No one is trying to kill you," he replied. "If they were, you would be dead. If they missed, they would try again immediately. Someone is merely trying to vex you."

"Whistling vexes me," I said. "Shooting at me I take exception to."

"From which direction did the bullet come?" Cyrus Barker asked.

"From across Whitehall Street, sir."

"The angle is steeply downward. You were shot at from the roof or a window."

I felt a chill go through me and flinched.

"Shock," he observed. "Do you need some brandy?"

"No, sir. Thank you," I replied. "Should I go back out and get those newspapers?"

"Wait awhile," he said. "Or I can send Jeremy. I presume he has not angered any assassins lately. Have you, Jeremy?"

"No, Mr. B.!" our clerk called from the outer room.

"This is serious, sir," I protested. "I was just shot at, nearly murdered. I'm a married man. There is nothing I have done that deserves this. I go to church, I say my prayers, I do unto others. Don't cheat, don't swear, try to be a good husband, and someone wants to blow my bloody head off anyway!"

"You are shouting, Thomas," Barker said.

"Am I?" I asked. "The question is, why me? I'm sure there are plenty of other people in Whitehall who deserve a bullet more than I."

"Have you done anything to anyone that would cause them to bring a hired assassin all the way from Saint Petersburg in order to frighten you?"

"Frighten me! It's done more than frighten me!"

Barker rose, crossed to the bow window, and looked out at the traffic in Whitehall. A man had been shot doing that very thing a few years before, but the Guv seemed little concerned.

"It might be in the realm of possibility that you were the target at Kensington Palace and that some move on your part or someone else's resulted in Mr. Bayles taking the bullet meant for you.

It's highly doubtful in a seasoned professional, but possible. Are we agreed?"

"I suppose so."

"But on the street in Whitehall," he continued, "were you walking at a steady pace?"

"I was," I admitted.

"Was the street crowded?"

I shook my head. "Not particularly."

"Were there vehicles that might have shielded you from a random shot?"

"No, I don't believe so."

"There you are, then," he said, looking triumphant. "No professional assassin of any reputation misses twice in their entire career. You could scarcely avoid being killed under those conditions. Ergo, someone is trying to vex you."

"He's doing very well at it, too."

"But you are perfectly safe. If you were meant to be dead, you would be dead. Isn't that a relief? You could jump about, you could try to get shot, and it would not happen. You are, what is the expression? Safe as houses?"

"Well, that's a relief," I replied. "If bullets start flying all about me I need only remind myself that none is meant for me."

"Exactly."

"Step away from the window, then, sir," I said to him. "Nobody claimed you are safe."

A couple of hours later, Sarah Fletcher arrived in our chambers. As usual, she was neat as a pin, carefully coiffed and prim. She sat on the edge of her seat, her hands on her reticule, a straw boater perched on her head. Pulling a small red notebook from her bag, she opened it and looked at her notes.

"I've discovered the location of your ballerina, Mr. Barker," she said, the consummate professional. "Mathilde Kschessinska is the principal dancer at the Mariinsky Theatre in Saint Peters-burg. She is staying at the Metropole Hotel, trying to work out the best way to meet the tsarevich."

"How did you come by this information?" Barker asked. I could almost hear the approval in his voice.

"I questioned some of our own dancers in London," she re-plied. "Apparently, the affair is a royal secret, so everyone knows of it. In Saint Petersburg, she has actually sat on the edge of the imperial box during a performance. She is beautiful and talented and every theater in Europe wants her. Personally, I found her petulant."

"You met her, then?" the Guv asked, surprised.

"She called for someone to do her hair and I happened to be lurking in the lobby, so I volunteered."

"What were your other impressions of her?" he asked.

"She is pretty enough, if that matters. However, she is self-important, ambitious, vain, mercurial, and perhaps a bit frightened," Miss Fletcher replied. "The little thing is but one-and-twenty. She doesn't understand that mistresses cannot be tsarinas."

"Some have, as I recall," I noted.

Miss Fletcher shot me a glance for interrupting her narrative and then she continued. "Rumor has it the tsarevich is under orders to find a suitable royal bride and marry her as soon as possible. Poor Mathilde is not in the running, I'm afraid, and she knows it. She is staying with a grand duke who must care very deeply for her to put up with her shrill outbursts. One second she is crying and the next elated. I think it is impossible for her to conceal a single thought. However, there was only so much time I could spend dressing her hair before I got my face slapped for poking her with a hairpin when she moved. She knows me now, so I cannot follow her openly."

"Is there any more information you can give, pertinent or otherwise?" Barker asked, tenting his fingers on his desk.

Miss Fletcher consulted her notebook, winnowing the pages. "Let us see. The literati of Saint Petersburg are watching the affair as if it were a grand opera. Each day brings new intrigue. She is here on her own, you know. She is not with a corps de ballet. She came from Paris incognito. Well, as incognito as one can be with a Russian borzoi."

She flipped more pages. "Miss Kschessinska is the favorite of the imperial librettist, a fellow named Tchaikovsky. He is writing a ballet especially for her, they say. She is to appear as the Sugar Plum Fairy in his newest work, *The Nutcracker*. She was the principal dancer in *Sleeping Beauty* last season. And of course, her first role, which brought her to the attention of Saint Petersburg, was the title role in *La Sylphide*."

The Guv and I both froze. Miss Fletcher's brows lowered in puzzlement at our response. Barker cleared his throat as if to say to me "We must keep this to ourselves."

"Thank you, Miss Fletcher," he said. "You have done very well in such a short time. Send me a bill for your services."

"That is all you require?" she asked.

"Follow the two gentlemen I described to you. That will be all."

She rose, clutching her bag, and looked slightly embarrassed. There was a red spot on each cheek.

"Very well," she said, suddenly brisk and professional. "I'll be off, then."

And she was, paying no attention to me as she did so. I didn't need her approval, but somehow her outright disapproval rankled me.

"Very well," I repeated when she had gone.

"The Metropole," Barker said, the slip of paper still in his hand. "Excellent. Let us go speak to Miss Mathilde Kschessinska."

"Sir, may I make a suggestion?"

Barker turned his head and looked at me. "Yes, Mr. Llewelyn. Of course."

"Sir, I do not think you should go. Let me go instead."

"And why would you going alone be better than our going together?" he asked.

"I fear you might intimidate a young ballerina," I said, choosing my words carefully. "She would close up like an oyster and tell you nothing, whereas if I spoke to her, I would draw her out and get her to reveal her plans. Perhaps they already have a rendezvous in the offing and she'll give me the day and place. I'll play to her vanity. I'll claim to be a liaison from the palace sent by Nicholas. In a way it's true."

"You don't think she will see through the subterfuge, lad?"

"If she does, what harm would it do?" I answered. "She doesn't know me from Adam."

"You believe women find me intimidating?" he asked.

Kodiak bears found him intimidating, but now was not the time to tell him.

"No, sir, not under normal circumstances. You are polite, even chivalrous. However, she may be expecting some kind of interference from the palace and you have the look about you of some sort of agent, which in fact, you are. Whereas I do not look in any way like a government agent."

"Perhaps," he said, mulling the issue. He did not sound convinced.

"How would you have me go, sir?" I pressed. "Am I to be sympathetic or not?"

He sat back in his chair and looked over my head in thought. "Have her . . . have her believe you are sympathetic to her plight, one of a small contingent within the palace. However, the queen is aware of her existence and is adamant about splitting the two of them apart so Nicholas can marry her niece. She does not approve of immorality."

"Or of mistresses, ballerinas, assignations, or impropriety . . ."

"Which of course she does not," the Guv said, "and for good reason, as is so obviously illustrated here."

"That seems simple enough."

"There's more," he continued. "Tell her that the entire matter is political. There is an alliance between our countries and the tsarevich is to be the sacrifice. No one cares how the boy feels. He's just a pawn."

"Excellent. And if she presses about some sort of rendezvous?"

"Blame the Okhrana. They sense something is in the wind and are circling him like jackals."

"I rather like that, sir," I admitted.

"Most of all, you must make her believe that the tsarevich is cracking under the strain. There is a rumor afoot that Princess Alix is coming here so the two can meet."

"I assume there is no such rumor."

"About Princess Alix?" he answered, shrugging his beefy shoulders. "No, the last I heard, she is still holding out against conversion. She is a steadfast young woman and her piety does her credit."

"Whereas Mathilde is a mere flibbertigibbet," I remarked.

The Guv nodded. "You are correct, sir. Whatever sort of tsar he will prove himself to be, he is no gentleman."

In Barker's mind there could be no greater indictment.

# CHAPTER ELEVEN

I hailed a cab and made my way to the Metropole, near Oxford Street. The hotel had been built within the last twenty years, but had already endured a scandal or two. Lady Something-or-Other had tried to corner her philandering husband with a pistol but had chosen the wrong room, thereby firing at a curate from Brixton. The hotel seemed an obvious choice for an assignation between Mathilde and the tsarevich.

I climbed the stair and knocked at the door. I expected a maid, if not the ballerina herself, but in her place was a severe-looking Russian aristocrat in a braided uniform. He was losing his hair although he was not yet thirty. He looked cut from the same cloth as the tsarevich, but there seemed to be a lot of that in London these days.

"Good afternoon, sir. Is Mathilde Kschessinska in residence at the moment?"

"I don't—" he began, but I stepped by him just as a woman who must be my objective entered the room.

"Miss Kschessinska," I said. "I am a liaison sent from Kensington Palace by the tsarevich. He has enlisted my services to get a message to you."

She looked even younger than twenty-one or twenty-two. She was a small woman, and more curvaceous than expected for someone who spends half her life en pointe. Rebecca was far more beautiful in my eyes, but this woman was attractive enough to have a future tsar of a good portion of the globe entranced with her.

"Who are you?" she asked.

"My name is Thomas Llewelyn. My partner and I have been hired by the tsarevich to do some duties for him while he is in London." I turned to the gentleman who was standing next to us, observing our conversation.

He nodded and bowed. "I am Grand Duke Sergei Mikhailovich, sir, and I am not aware of your employment by Nicholas."

"I was the one who saved him during the shooting in front of Kensington Palace. He called me and my partner in to discuss some matters, including the matchmaking by Her Majesty, who is negotiating a marriage between the tsarevich and Princess Alix of Hesse, who was left behind by the late Prince Albert Victor."

The dancer's nostrils flared. "That scarecrow isn't going to marry my Nicky. It is a damnable lie! That harpy had better keep her pointed nose out of our business or we shall cut it off."

"I never cared much for the princess myself," I fibbed. In truth, I had no idea what Alix of Hesse was like. "She's as cold as a herring and not particularly bright. Bit of a dullard, in my opinion. Certainly not as lovely as you."

"At least somebody in this country has some sense," Mathilde said, sitting down in a chair and smoothing the pink folds of her dress.

Just then the strangest animal entered the room. It looked like a fur-covered greyhound. Its face and neck were so long and thin they looked like another limb. As soon as it saw me it came over and stuck its cold, wet nose in my face. Then it tried to climb into my lap. In an instant I had become his deepest friend.

"Kostya, leave the man alone. Go away!"

The dog climbed down again, gave me a look of abject regret at our parting, and slunk away.

"The tsarevich has been raving about your dancing," I continued. "He called you the Queen of Dancers. Your Sugar Plum Fairy was dainty, he said; your Sleeping Beauty divine. I understand you also danced La Sylphide."

"I don't think . . . ," the duke began.

"Silence, Sergei," Mathilde ordered. "Let the young man speak."

I was blathering, I'll admit. I hadn't won over Grand Duke Sergei yet, but I could see Mathilde Kschessinska wanted to believe my story.

"Please sit with me, Mr. Llewelyn. Galina!" she called. "Bring some water! Or would you prefer wine?"

"Water will do, thank you very much. The wine here in London leaves a good deal to be desired."

A maid appeared with a goblet of water. I used the time to think of the next stratagem.

"This man is a popinjay and a mountebank," the grand duke insisted. "You should throw him out into the street!"

"Sergei, a fine way to treat a man who has my interests at heart," she protested. "Leave us to speak!"

"Mische . . ."

"Leave us!" she screeched. It was so high and shrill, it made both of us jump. The little ballerina had claws. Silently, Sergei Mikhailovich stood, the very picture of wounded honor, and left the room. He'd fared little better than the dog.

"You must forgive him," she said, smiling. "Sometimes he gets jealous. He wants me all to himself."

"As any man would, I'm sure."

She tried to hide a smile, but she was susceptible to flattery.

"Why haven't I heard of you?" she asked.

"I've only known the tsarevich for a short while, but it is my pleasure to make his first stay in our country enjoyable."

"Quite right," she replied. One could say she was little more than a petulant child, but so far she had done well by herself. She wanted more and nothing less than to become the first tsarina of Russia without royal blood, and it was still possible that she might succeed.

"Have you seen him yet?" I asked.

"No, not yet," she admitted. "I've been waiting for him to call me. He has promised to slip out of the palace at the first opportunity and send word."

"He's been pining for you," I said.

"Nikolai asked me to come here so he may visit when he can," she replied. "Russian society understands such things, but you English. Such a scandal! I think you are all hypocrites!"

I tried not to smile and nodded, commiserating with her. Her English was good, with a slight French accent. Paris is the Riviera of Moscow. All the wealthy visit there when it turns too cold.

"Is there anything I can do for you?" I asked. "Perhaps I could get a message to the tsarevich."

"Could you?" she asked, clapping her hands together. "Could you tell him how desperately I wish to see him? Tell him he must be strong, so that we can be together. My Nicky is not so forceful. He bends with the wind. He must be reminded to stay strong or that fat toad Victoria and her niece will have their way."

"I certainly will. You could write a note now, mademoiselle."

"Mische, I am, to all my friends, and you are my newest one," she replied. "Tell me, Mr. Llewelyn, why is it that your climate is warmer than mine, yet it is wet and windy in a way that not even Siberia experiences?"

"England does not bend to anyone's rules. It makes up its own."

"It does not know any better," she said. She put out her lips,

still a petulant child. A girl that age should not be allowed to influence would-be kings.

"So you wait here daily, hoping he will call?" I asked. "That
must be terrible for you."

Mathilde nodded. "That and shopping. I must look my best.
Since I cannot eat much due to my training, it is my only vice.
Except for cigarettes, but Nicky insists they are not feminine."

"What do you intend to do if the rumor about a match with
Alix of Hesse is true?" I asked, playing with the ferrule of my
walking stick.

"It will never happen. It's impossible."

"But if it does?"

"I will have no choice but to write to the scarecrow herself."

"What do you mean?" I asked.

"I will fight to keep what is mine," she said. "What woman
wouldn't?"

The woman rose the back of her hand to her forehead, a sign
of anguish. A sign, that is, in a cheap melodrama. I began to
wonder if the Russian arts crowd had any discernible taste. Did
Nicholas actually like this little prima donna? Was it some sort of
youth's fascination for his first paramour?

"And what of him?" I persisted. "Surely you would not allow
him to cast you over for that German princess. You can't."

"Darling, if I can't have him, Russia cannot have him, either."

"What do you mean?" I felt a moment of alarm.

She crossed to a fainting couch in a corner of the room, opened
a reticule, and withdrew a small pistol.

"I shall shoot us both if I cannot have him," she said. "She will
never be his bride. He is my Nicky, or he is no one else's. It's that
simple."

"You would do it yourself?" I asked with a morbid fascination. "With so much at stake? Why, you could become the prima
donna of all Europe."

"I will become a martyr to love," she said, waving the pistol around as if she might use me for target practice. "What better way to die?"

She was such a child, I thought. She'd had a taste for finery and infamy, and was being spoiled and cosseted by almost everyone. She was desperate and willing to take risks.

"Mademoiselle, I feared when I heard an attempt had been made upon the life of the tsarevich that you had heard the bad news and might, with your broken heart, have hired someone to kill him."

She looked at me frankly, with no pretense in her voice. "What are you talking about?"

"The attempt upon Prince George's life yesterday at Kensington Palace was supposed to have been upon Nicholas. It was kept from the newspapers, but there is the truth of it."

"You are talking nonsense. If it were true, Sergei would have told me."

"Mademoiselle, I assure you it is true."

She rose her pistol. "Sergei! Come out so that I can shoot you!"

"Miss Kschessinska, I implore you!" I cried. "Put away that pistol. You will cause a scandal."

At that moment, Grand Duke Sergei walked into the room. "I am going out for a drink, Mische. You can shoot me when I return."

She stomped her foot when he left and then turned to me. "You cannot forbid me to shoot Nikolai. Remember Meyerling? I can do no less. I head to my doom and he to his. You must go now. Go, Mr. Llewelyn. It's a pity you didn't get to see me dance."

She looked away pointedly. I rose, nodded, and left.

"She means Nicholas mischief," I said to the Guv when I returned to our chambers.

"You don't think her threat was an attempt to gain sympathy?" he asked.

"The pistol looked real enough," I replied. "She's like a child who breaks a china doll rather than share it with her sister."

"Meyerling," Barker repeated. "That name is familiar."

"A few years ago, the prince of Austria killed his young mistress and himself in a hunting lodge when his family tried to force them to separate. I believe it was initially claimed that she had an aneurysm of the heart, but word soon spread. The girl was seventeen, I think."

"Royals can do stupid things sometimes, Thomas," the Guv said. "I suppose all young men can."

"And not a few older ones."

"You are referring to Sergei Mikhailovich?" Barker asked.

"Yes. He is the one delivering messages between Nicholas and Mathilde. And he is a grand duke, one of the suspects on our list."

"Those are valid points," Barker replied. "He deserves to be on the list."

"Meyerling. She wants them to die as a sort of romantic gesture."

"While thumbing their noses at the world," I added.

"Do you consider her a true romantic, or merely opportunistic?"

"If you are asking if she's more in love with Nicky or with being tsarina of Russia, I would tend toward the latter."

"That's good, then," the Guv said. "She is practical."

"Practical, sir?"

"Yes. The problem with a romantic gesture is that you're not alive afterward to enjoy the notoriety."

# CHAPTER TWELVE

Barker was seated in a barber chair the following morning, his face swathed in a hot towel. My face was being lathered with a brush.

"We have fallen behind," the Guv said. "The wedding is a few days away and we have people to interview and questions to answer. I have not time to lie about when a man's life is at stake, whose death could throw us into a war. I'll not be accused of fiddling while Rome burns."

I'd have said "Yes, sir," if there wasn't a razor at my throat and my face full of suds, and really, he wasn't speaking to me.

"Suspects," he continued. "Name the suspects, Mr. Llewelyn."

"William Morris, Eleanor Marx, Pyotr Rachkovsky, Mathilde Kschessinska, and the grand dukes of Russia. And an assassin named La Sylphide."

When our shaves were completed, I paid our barber and we left.

"Tell me about this Morris fellow," Barker said as we stepped into the road. "You appeared to be familiar with him."

"I'm rather surprised you haven't heard of him before, sir," I replied. "He's a true artist in many fields. He's a great poet, a mystic, and a philosopher. He was known as a painter for several years but his latest fascination is textiles. He hopes to drape drab London sitting rooms in textile prints."

"He makes pretty pictures. He is a poet," Barker grumbled.

"Not just any poet. He was offered the position of poet laureate after Tennyson died, but he refused it because it took him from his political work."

"He is a Socialist."

We were south of our home in Newington Causeway, walking to the Underground.

"One could call him The Socialist," I continued as we descended the stairs. "He speaks at rallies. He debates and lectures at universities. He edits and writes for a Socialist journal. He supports his political activities from the coffers of his own printing company. At least that's what I've heard."

"From whom?" Barker asked.

We stepped out onto the platform and watched a train speed by, heading toward Kensington. The tunnel was momentarily full of smoke.

"Israel Zangwill," I replied. "Remember, he used to be a reporter for *The Jewish Chronicle*. Much of his writing was political."

"Do you know where this Mr. Morris lives?"

"Yes, his publishing press is in Hammersmith," I answered. "A mansion called Kelmscott House."

"A writer in Hammersmith?" Barker asked.

"Stranger things have happened, I'm sure."

We arrived in Hammersmith thirty minutes later, that bastion of middle-class morality.

Kelmscott House was a mansion of Georgian brick at its least imaginative, a brick box held together by English ivy. I'd have thought Morris would have chosen something stylish.

I had suggested to the Guv that more people were having telephones installed these days and we should consider calling those we wished to question. His response was that he preferred to catch them unprepared and doing mischief. There is some logic in that, I suppose.

A seedy-looking butler answered the door at Kelmscott House and led us through a dusty house, most of the wall space taken up with paintings or lengths of tapestries Morris had designed. There was a painting over a fireplace that I recognized as a Burne-Jones. I nodded my head at it.

"Mrs. Morris," I murmured. "First name, Jane. A celebrated model of her time. That is, the 1860s and '70s."

Barker grunted, either docketing the information or rejecting it as irrelevant. We passed through an iron-studded door that appeared reclaimed from a medieval keep.

"Mr. Baker and Mr. Lelland, sir," the butler said. I let it pass. We had been called worse.

The room looked as if it had been damaged by an anarchist's bomb. The mantelpiece, the chairs, the floor, were littered with books, lengths of fabric, half-finished speeches and poems, busts of famous men, and objets d'art. Each of them would do a study proud if properly presented and cared for, but most of the poor fellows were facedown on their noses or being used as paperweights. Papers drifted in the corners like leaves. In the very center sat the man himself.

"May I help you, gentlemen?" Morris asked. He looked like he had just woken up from a nap, disheveled and gruff.

Stepping forward, I presented him with a card from my waistcoat pocket. I have them tailored to hold business cards.

Morris reached out a hand and took it. He was very nearly as much of a mess as his room. His silvery hair and beard looked as if no comb or brush could penetrate them. There was something almost biblical in his appearance, a modern prophet, save that he was stuffed into a brown suit, and one bootless foot was resting on a chair.

"Sit, gentlemen," he said, studying our card. "Private enquiry agents?"

The Guv and I looked about for a place to sit, but it was impossible. Every chair was piled high with stacks of books and papers so precariously perched that one touch would either tip the chair or knock the stacks of papers and books onto the floor, so we remained standing.

"Yes, sir," I replied. "We have been safeguarding the tsarevich of Russia while he is here at the royal wedding. There have been threats and at least one attempt on his life."

"Mr. Morris, we understand there have been protests about the upcoming wedding of the prince by the Socialist League," Barker said, taking in our host. "Are you involved in any such demonstrations?"

"I understand that demonstrations have been organized and are now occurring around London, but I have not been personally supervising them. It's my gout, you see. I rarely leave the house unless it is to visit my press, which is just down the street."

"I see," Barker rumbled. "Who would be in charge of such demonstrations, then?"

"This person or that might have made the decision to hold an event, but it would be Eleanor Marx who organized and implemented the plan. She is the drive behind the movement these days. She's Karl's daughter, you know. Karl Marx. He wrote *The Communist Manifesto,* which we consider our Magna Carta, so to speak."

"What is a Communist, and how does that compare to a Socialist?" Barker asked.

Morris scratched his mane of hair and considered the question.

"It's rather complicated," he answered, "but if I were to boil it down to its essence, I would say that Socialists believe in helping the poor and meeting their needs, while Communists want all moneys shared between everyone in society, regardless of sex, race, or occupation. They want to eliminate aristocracy. None in particular, just in general."

He pointed toward a photograph nearly buried on his desk, of an equally bearded wild man, but with a sterner look. The image seemed familiar, and it took a moment to recall who it was. It was Marx himself. I thought I recognized him. He used to have a desk and table near mine in the Reading Room of the British Museum. He was probably writing his manifesto then.

"That is certainly revolutionary," the Guv said. I had no doubt I'd discover his personal opinions later.

"It's time for a revolution," Morris answered, warming to his subject. "The monarchy has been unsuccessful in feeding and caring for its own people, as a two-minute walk in Whitechapel at any time of day will tell you. Her Majesty is willing to spend three million pounds to impress the world and keep the colonies in subjugation, but it is blood money. How many infants will die this winter from diphtheria and whooping cough?"

"Which are you, sir," the Guv asked. "A Socialist or a Communist?"

"More the former than the latter," the poet/printer/painter/playwright/publisher said. "I believe in the tenets of the Communist teachings of the manifesto, but it seems impractical because of man's basic foibles and selfishness. What incentive, for example, would a man have to work hard if he would receive the same salary for being lazy?"

"I see," Barker murmured. "And which group constitutes the largest of the protesters and demonstrators?"

William Morris sighed. He leaned back in his chair and repositioned his aching limb.

"Neither, I'm afraid."

The Guv gave me a look of exasperation. A good shaking was being considered if this famous man was not more forthcoming.

"Anarchists, sir," he finally answered. "The majority of the Socialist League is no longer strictly Socialist. We have been o'erwhelmed. Great Britain is the only country willing to take them in."

"Anarchists," my employer rumbled, savoring the word. Here was an ideology he understood. He had once moved among them in Paris in order to stop their plans. He still had the letter *A* scar burned into his shoulder, an initiation of a secret organization.

"They're not all bad," Morris replied. "But they've been through pogroms and other trials and driven from their countries. They have reason to be angry."

"But not reason to harm a future sovereign or a visiting monarch."

"Ah," Morris said, shaking his head. "But you see, many of the anarchists—the largest part of them—are from Russia. It was the government's Cossacks who destroyed their houses, killed their families, and drove them out of Russia. Russians have long memories, Mr. Barker. Something as trivial as moving to a different country would not change how they think or act after so much suffering."

The Guv crossed his arms, which always makes him look larger than he is, if such a thing is possible.

"Are you suggesting I let the Russians settle their own differences in public in the middle of a royal wedding?"

"Good heavens, no," Morris replied. "Mr. Barker, it is vitally necessary that you and whomever you are working for stop the threat. If the tsarevich is shot, the government and possibly the citizenry shall blame London's Russian population. There will be blood in the streets, gentlemen. That's what will happen."

"Then we must see that Nicholas remains safe."

"And Prince George while we're at it," I inserted. "His bride, as well. Any assassination would throw the country into turmoil."

Barker cleared his throat, a signal he was changing the subject. "Could you tell me, sir, what Miss Marx's opinions are regarding the change of position of the Socialist League?"

Morris took a drink of the dregs of a cold cup of tea at his elbow. "When last we talked, oh, three months or so ago, I believe, she was on the fence. As famous as I am, and as many issues of *Commonweal* have been published with my editorials, I am expendable. Eleanor, however, is the daughter of the founder of Communism. Her leaving is unthinkable. Therefore, she must compromise."

"If Miss Marx is holding the society together," Barker asked, "who is trying to tear it apart? Is there anyone who is banging the drum, either against the wedding or the tsarevich's arrival? Who is the most vocal critic?"

"That would be Kazimir Chernov. He's a dyed-in-the-wool anarchist from Moscow. It is rumored that he had a hand in the assassination of Alexander the Second. He escaped and fled to France, but he made enough of a nuisance there that the Sûreté suggested he leave the country or cool his heels in prison."

The Guv crossed his arms and looked grave. "I thought I knew most of the prominent anarchists in Europe, but I haven't heard of him."

"Well, I wonder if perhaps he exaggerates," Morris admitted. "I don't know, but he is a firebrand. He has attracted more members to the League and converted some of our more conservative members. I suspect he has reached the point where he has to do something to prove his abilities, to show that he is more than a braggart. I certainly believe him capable of doing something that will put himself in jail and cause the Socialist League to disband, something more than putting up placards. I know the man carries a pistol. I've seen it myself."

"Do you know where this man Chernov lives?"

"In the middle of one of the worst warrens in Spitalfields," Morris replied. "It's in Woodseer Street, off Brick Lane."

The Guv nodded. "I know it."

Barker had begun pacing, or attempted to. He brushed a stack of books with his elbow and sent it all slipping sideways like a stack of cards. Morris did not bat an eye.

"We are familiar with that kind of gentleman," the Guv said.

He placed the emphasis on the last word as if he was being generous with the term. "I presume he has little money."

"Not a sou."

"Do you think him likely to have access to a rifle?"

"Not if he owned it," Morris said. "He'd have pawned it for cheap beer by now."

"No doubt."

"The man's a menace. As for the rest of the League, they support my movement financially."

*There it is,* I thought. *My movement.* He was proud of what he had done years before, but now it had been wrested from his hands. He was too old, put to pasture. I'm sure that must rankle.

Barker bowed. We had run out of questions, and Mr. Morris, the Great Man of Art and Poetry, had run out of answers. We rose and bowed, and the butler led us outside into a dissolute-looking garden. Barker stopped and began pruning a rose bush with his bare hands, twisting the faded roses and removing them. He hates a thing undone.

"I have a hard time imagining Mr. Morris on the roof of Kensington Palace with an air gun," I said.

"Mr. Llewelyn, I imagine he knows several men just waiting to kill the tsarevich."

The Guv was right, I had to admit.

# CHAPTER THIRTEEN

Barker and I were back in our offices; I to transcribe some of my shorthand scribbles into typed notes, he to play a kind of chess with London as the board and humans as chess pieces. He was so deep in thought that he didn't hear the clacking of my Hammond typewriting machine or the sound of a visitor.

Jenkins looked pleased with himself as he brought the salver in with a card upon it. His small world had been restored to normal. I envied the fellow, rather, and not for the first time. He led a simple life, uncomplicated and satisfying to him. Isn't that all a man requires?

Barker took a glance at the card and stood immediately. I did as well, but only because he did.

"Colonel, come in," he said as Waverly crossed the threshold into our chambers. "Would you have a seat, sir?"

"It is good to see you gentlemen again," the colonel replied. "I hope I didn't overtax you with my little inquisition yesterday. I have come with good news."

The colonel was smiling at us. When he last saw us he chewed our private histories as a beaver does a log. Now his expression was nearly beatific.

Barker frowned. Like me, he became suspicious when someone smiled. Anything could happen. Sadness and anger we could brace for, deal with, but smiles? In our business we don't trust smiles. Generally they are masking something.

"Mr. Barker, I am here to tell you that Her Majesty's government would like to present you with the Order of British Merit. Not only have you saved the lives of two princes, but you helped England avoid what could have become an international incident."

"Would you care for a cigar, Colonel?" the Guv asked.

Waverly took one from the proffered box. After lighting it, he turned back in my direction and blew smoke above my head.

"Mr. Llewelyn, it is not the government's policy to offer such an honor to so young a person. However, the palace shall decide upon some sort of medal or honor for you, as well. Do not believe we will leave you without a suitable recompense for your heroic service. You well deserve one. I understand the assassin was in your very arms when he was shot."

"Yes, sir," I said.

I've said it before. Our bodies are simple mechanisms. Several stimuli will produce the same response. I suddenly felt as if someone had thrown a bucket of water down my collar. *Me? A medal? Me, Tommy Llewelyn, the coal miner's son? Won't Rebecca be excited?*

"Well, Mr. Barker, what say you?"

"It is a great honor, Colonel," the Guv said, sitting down in his chair. "I am flattered. However, I cannot accept."

Waverly blanched. "Cannot accept?"

"I did not save the life of Prince George and I did not protect the tsarevich for more than ten seconds. That hardly deserves an OBM. Thomas was in the thick of it both times. Give it to him if he wishes."

The colonel sat back, looking winded. Then he looked at me. "What say you, young fellow? It's unprecedented, but would you care for an OBM?"

That old rascal. Cyrus Barker, I mean. He knew I couldn't accept a medal if he didn't. It would be bad form. Perhaps at one time when I was in prison, I might have grasped for all I could attain, but I had been living with my employer for going on ten years and had unknowingly adopted his way of thinking.

"Thank you, sir," I answered, "but no. It is indeed an honor, but I fear I must refuse."

The words tasted like ashes in my mouth.

"You see, Colonel, it is helpful in our line of work to be as anonymous as possible," Barker explained.

"I understand. But, hang it, it's a great honor, Mr. Barker!" Waverly insisted.

"It is indeed, but you must realize that when we protected the prince and the tsarevich, we had no idea they were royalty. We were merely looking out for fellow citizens. I only recognized Nicholas when he stood at my elbow."

Waverly pointed a finger at him. "But your lives were in danger. Admit it!"

The Guv put out his cigar in the large glass ashtray upon his desk. "I do, sir, but our duties frequently place us in danger, as you might surmise. A twelve-month does not go by in which one of us is not shot."

"Or stabbed," I said.

"Or blown up," he continued. "We had these offices repaired just a year ago."

"Well, I never," Waverly replied.

"Our agency should always be here to safeguard Their Majesties whenever it is required. Mr. Llewelyn and I have worked years to make private enquiry work an acceptable profession, free from the taint of the underworld. It is why we opened our doors in Whitehall Street, in the shadow of Scotland Yard itself. To protect the royal family is our duty and our pleasure. It is also our business. I am certain you will warrant there isn't another agency like ours in London." Barker knitted his thick fingers together on the glass top of his desk. "Please do not think that we are slighting the government in any way, Colonel Waverly. We are proud to live and work in this city and to call ourselves Londoners."

"Then accept the honor, Mr. Barker!" Waverly insisted.

"Alas, I cannot," the Guv answered. "I try to avoid the fanfare of public recognition in my work. An image of myself in the newspapers, for example, would reveal my identity in some circles and hamper my work."

The colonel blinked. Barker might as well have spoken Urdu as far as he understood the words.

"And anyway," the Guv continued, "as you are aware, Mr. Llewelyn has a criminal record—trifling as it is—which would preclude such an award. Is that not correct, Mr. Llewelyn?"

I rose a brow, unable to reply.

"Well," Waverly blustered. "Yes, both of your pasts are shady, but together the palace thought we could push it through."

"You need not bother on our accounts," the Guv said. "Now, was there something else you required?"

"Required?" the colonel parroted.

"Did you have any more questions for us?"

"No, I—"

Barker stood, came around the desk, and shook his hand. "Then you'll appreciate we have work to do. The wedding hasn't even started and we have much to do. But it has been a pleasure talking with you again."

He put a hand on the old soldier's shoulder and steered him into the waiting room. Her Majesty's equerry could find his own way into Whitehall Street. I followed him out into Craig's Court and watched him go. It felt as if he were taking my precious medal away with him.

It's strange. I had never thought of a medal before the man darkened our door and now I was bereft. No medal at all! No medal to wear on my lapel or display on a table, none to polish and admire. None to show to my friends while boorishly gushing over the events. Blast it. I sulked, which only makes the Guv pugnacious, which in turn made me sulk all the more. There he sat, scratching his neck. Who knows what he was thinking. He could be considering dinner for all I knew. Finally I could take no more and stood.

"I think I'll take a walk," I said.

He didn't answer yea or nay. He made no comment, no comic retort, no wise aphorism. He scratched his chin while I left.

It was hot in London that afternoon. I wandered to Trafalgar Square, waved a foot at a few pigeons, and looked for someplace cool to sit. I found a public house not far from St. Martin-in-the-Fields, went downstairs to the basement, and nursed a Pimm's. It was dark and quiet and cool and as good a place as any to lick one's wounds.

I'm not the sort to be heaped with honors and praise. To be truthful, I never ask or expect it, because I find that a high in one area of my life often produces a low in another. Now, granted, lows can come by themselves and lows can even generate other lows, but so far I'd never had a high generate another high. Don't put on airs or raise your chin, or as my grandfather used to say: don't give the devil a shoe to kick you with.

Poor old Waverly. He'd have to go back to the palace and tell the queen's secretary that the grand honor bestowed had been refused. Would the queen have to know? I don't know why it mattered if she did. She wouldn't be disappointed to find out two fellows she had never met had refused an honor, if she'd even be told at all. But still, I could picture her shaking her head in disapproval.

It would have been amazing, though. It could have changed everything. It would have balanced that blot on my record and I wouldn't care a fig if Munro called me Prisoner Number 7502. I'd just rattle my medal in his ugly face.

I would have to explain to Rebecca why I turned down an honor and she wouldn't understand. The whole subject of Men's Honor gets very complicated and is nearly impossible to explain. I could have said, "Yes, please," to Waverly, but my partnership with Barker would have dissolved before I even received it. He cannot work with a man he doesn't respect.

The Pimm's tasted like gall. I don't even drink Pimm's. I don't know why I ordered it. I suppose it sounded cool on a warm day.

Outside the public house, I rose an arm and summoned a cab.

"Kensington Palace, please," I said, climbing aboard.

"The palace?" said the cabman. "Oh, lawks. Give Princess Mary a kiss from me."

He clicked his teeth and the gelding began to move. A quarter hour later, I was where it all began, squatting over a spot of grass until I found what I was looking for, a minute fragment of bone gleaming among the blades. I'd been standing right there when Joseph Bayles's head came off. One minute I was thinking about how nicely full of Welsh rarebit I was, and the next I was wrestling with an assassin. With my finger I pushed the bit of bone deeper into the ground, giving it a burial of sorts. Then I stood and looked about.

There were dozens of trees from which a man could shoot. However, he would have to crawl down in broad daylight where he could be easily spotted. There were rows of shops and restaurants across the street, but there was also a wrought-iron fence in the way. Even a professional assassin—if such a thing exists—would have trouble siting a moving target through a grid of iron bars. Some of the buildings across the road were taller than others, a few providing a commanding view over the fence, but it was a good distance and the trees along the avenue were in the way. That only left one possible location for the assassin: on the roof of the palace itself, which was just as Barker suspected, drat the fellow.

"Sir?"

A guardsman from the palace was standing a dozen feet away, holding a rifle. Not brandishing it, mind, merely holding it, but that was menacing enough.

"Yes, sir?" I replied.

"Sir, you are moving about in a very suspicious manner. I must ask you to leave."

"I was just . . . Wait, I know you," I said. "The last time I saw you we were both covered in gore."

"You're right," he replied. "It is you. What are you doing out here?"

I handed him my card. "I'm still enquiring."

"You and Scotland Yard and the ruddy Home Office and the Russian police."

"Oh?" I asked. "Not you guardsmen yourself? This is your plot of land. I'd have thought the lot of you would be over this place inch by inch."

"It's ours," he agreed. "And we have."

"They looked down their noses at you soldier boys, didn't they? No one can tell a Scotland Yarder anything, and as for the Home Office men, they'll think nothing of you unless you read history at Cambridge."

"You're right there, sir," he answered. "Butter don't melt in their mouths. I hope they choke on it."

"You lads know every inch of this park, and I'm sure you've talked among yourselves. By the way, I didn't get your name."

"Corporal Alan Dinsdale."

"Pleased to meet you, Corporal. Thomas Llewelyn. Did you come to any conclusions?"

"Only that he was a bloody ghost. Comes in, goes out, makes no noise, leaves no sign. We climbed every tree from here to

Hyde Park looking for scratches. Nothing. We climbed to the roof of every building within sight of this spot. Nothing. A ghost, I tell you."

"What about the palace itself?" I asked. "A man could shoot from the roof."

Dinsdale smiled. "You don't know what you're saying, sir. Every door is locked and secured. We tug on them or check the lock each time we pass. I don't think—"

I held up a hand. "Tell me, are you free anytime tomorrow to speak to my partner, Mr. Barker? He was the big fellow with the dark spectacles, if you recall. He's very good at asking just the right questions."

"Well, I'm off guard duty at six o'clock every night this week. Then it's back to the barracks."

"Mr. Barker has a chef who can cook anything you might want. He also has a butler who makes the best porter in London. Could you do with a good meal at a rich man's expense, a strapping lad like you?"

He considered the matter.

"Anything you want," I continued. "Beef Wellington to bangers and mash, you name it. I can get you fancy French food. I can even get you Chinese food, if you like. Where are you from?"

"Whitby."

"Seafood, then? A couple of lobsters?"

"I am uncommonly fond of lobsters. And oysters!"

"A wise choice," I agreed. "My partner does like his oysters. Answer some questions for him and you'll have a meal your comrades will think you invented."

"There are some things we are not allowed to talk about."

"Well, of course. Yours is a very important occupation, protecting the most famous family in the world."

"I suppose I could come, then."

"We're in Newington, by the Elephant and Castle. Number three Lion Street. Every cabman knows it. We'll see you then."

"I'll be there."

We'd been walking toward the palace as we talked. He was on duty, after all. As we reached the portico, two men came around the corner from the east entrance. One was Jim Hercules. The other was Cyrus Barker. He nearly smiled when he saw me.

"I assumed you were off for the day," the Guv rumbled. "Holding packages for Mrs. Llewelyn."

"There is a case to solve, sir," I said. "One can't traipse about London with an assassin on the loose."

"Agreed."

"Hello, Mr. Hercules," I said. "How is the tsarevich?"

"He's fit to be tied," our client said with an easy grin. "The only women he's being introduced to are more than three times his age."

Barker nodded. "Mr. Hercules believes that the tsarevich is chafing under his confinement. It appears the palace should remain vigilant. As should we."

He turned and regarded the guardsman beside me.

"Mr. Barker, this is Corporal Alan Dinsdale. I have taken the liberty of inviting him to dinner. Corporal, this is my partner, Cyrus Barker."

"Have you, indeed?" the Guv asked.

"I have. He is a Yorkshireman with a fondness for oysters."

"I am fond of them myself," Barker said.

"May I join you gentlemen?" Jim Hercules asked.

I happened to glance up in time to see the corporal's eyes widen. I believe he found the idea of sharing oysters with an American Negro alarming.

"I'll be happy to invite you to my home another time, Mr. Hercules," the Guv said. "However, for the moment, you have an amorous royal to protect, if only from himself."

Hercules nodded, but he looked hurt, as if doubting he would ever be invited to our home. Barker put out an arm, directing Dinsdale forward. Just then, my employer turned his head and looked down at the tree-lined path leading to the palace's Orangery. Halfway down the row there was a woman sitting on a bench. He watched her for a second, no more, but I noticed it. Barker doesn't make casual gestures. I would have looked closer but Barker hurried me along.

That evening, the Guv and I went to our bar-jutsu class. The night was fine. There was a cool breeze and night descended with a steady calm and air of peace. It seemed to not understand what was going on under its very nose. No one shot at me that night, either coming to Glasshouse Street or leaving, but a thought occurred to me. The assassin had to have known my destination in order to shoot at me. He'd fired at me in Craig's Court because he was already there. It would take more than a minute or two to set up the air rifle and aim. That was good to know, because as Barker would say, forewarned is forearmed.

# CHAPTER FOURTEEN

The next morning after services, we went to Kensington Palace for my shooting lesson with Nicholas. Barker accompanied me knowing that he would be excluded. I was sure he would find Hercules or wander the halls looking for information.

When we arrived, we met a servant in the hall. I believe servants should display an insignia of some sort on their uniforms, so one can know a first footman from a second. This fellow could have been anyone from head butler to silver polisher.

"Sir," Barker called to him.

"Just Bingham will do," the fellow replied. "How may I help you gentlemen?"

"My name is Cyrus Barker. This is Mr. Thomas Llewelyn. He is here for a shooting lesson with the tsarevich of Russia."

"I am aware, sir. It is on the schedule."

Bingham was approaching fifty. He was clean-shaven and going gray at the temples in a manner most men would hope for.

"Is Grand Duke Sergei Mikhailovich here today?" the Guv asked. "I'd like to speak to him at his leisure."

Bingham's brow rose. He was very good at the cold disdain business.

"All the royals and dignitaries are in the ballroom for a rehearsal."

"Of the wedding?" I asked.

"Of the parade, Mr. Llewelyn. It is where each dignitary learns where his or her carriage will be. In what order, I mean. Some will be disappointed, I fear."

"I hope we will not be among the disappointed," Barker answered. "Mr. Llewelyn and I shall wait in the Orangery until the tsarevich requests us."

"Very good, Mr. Barker."

He left us and I watched him go. For the first time it occurred to me that Nicholas was only one of the palace's problems.

"I notice he stopped calling you sir," I remarked. "Servants make the worst snobs."

"Aye," the Guv said. "But I don't care how I am treated as long as I can speak to the grand duke."

"I wonder how long we will have to wait."

"I assume that will be determined by whether he is satisfied with his position in the procession."

It proved to be a brief wait by royal standards. We were there no more than thirty minutes before we heard boots echoing in the chamber nearby. They almost seemed to be running. A moment later, the door burst open and two men entered, chuckling to each other. One was the grand duke, but I did not recognize the other.

"Oh, my soul," the young man said. "Thank you, gentlemen. You have saved us. We were in there over two hours. It's straight from the Bible, you know. The least will be first, but the first want to be last. The further behind, the more important you are, until there's Aunt Victoria all by herself."

"Sir, we are Cyrus Barker and Thomas Llewelyn," my partner said. "Mr. Llewelyn is here for Nicholas's shooting lesson."

"Forgive our manners," Sergei said. "This is Prince George of Greece and Denmark. We are cousins of Nikolai Alexandrovich."

Prince George bowed.

The duke sat, or rather fell, into a chair, and ran a hand over his bald pate. He looked at me and I saw a bit of confusion on his face and then he recognized me.

"You're that cockalorum who was conspiring with Mathilde the other day."

"Yes, sir, I was."

"And you're here now to teach Nicholas how to shoot? You seem to be everywhere."

"There is an enquiry going on," I pointed out. "A man was killed."

"I thought a tramp was killed," the duke insisted. "A madman."

"It was in fact an attempt upon the tsarevich," I replied. "The shooter confused his identity with Prince George of England."

"The similarity in appearance between the two men is remarkable," said Barker.

"It is," the prince answered, smiling. "Even we get confused at times."

Barker cleared his throat. "The assassin was in Mr. Llewelyn's grip when he was killed."

The prince shook his head. "Wait. The assassin was assassinated?"

"That is correct. Your Highness, did you come to England as a representative of Greece and Denmark for the wedding or as support for the tsarevich?"

"Both, actually, Mr. Barker. There was no need for either country to send an ambassador if I could go in their stead."

"Very wise, I'm sure," Barker replied. He turned to Sergei. "And you, sir?"

"Nikolai is my cousin," the grand duke said. "This is his first visit outside of Russia since that unfortunate incident last year in Japan. He wanted his friends with him for support. I was in Paris at loose ends so I agreed to join him and here I am."

"It is helpful to have cousins upon whom you can rely," my partner replied. "And how are you acquainted with Miss Kschessinska?"

The grand duke looked uncomfortable. He ran a hand over his head as if to cover it from Barker's harsh gaze.

"I escort her, provide for her, ferry her through governmental and legal regulations, and see that she trains vigorously, for she is the greatest dancer in the world."

"She is also the mistress of your cousin," Barker said.

Sergei shrugged. "We are not puritanical Englishmen, sir. Rulers keep mistresses and always have. Marriages are arranged between grand families for the sake of bloodlines and treaties and they rarely result in a love match. I wish they did, and I especially hope it will work out for my cousin."

"With a mistress?"

"Mr. Barker, this is a complicated situation. He loves them both, you see. He fell in love with Alix when he was fourteen, but she has refused to marry him because he is Orthodox and she is Lutheran. It hurt him greatly. Wishing to divert him, the tsar took him to the ballet and to a party afterward where he introduced Nikolai to Mathilde. She was meant to be a diversion."

"Quite," Barker answered, looking uncomfortable. "I assume the arrangement continues while the queen sorts matters with Princess Alexandra. What happens if the princess finally agrees to become his wife and tsarina of Russia?"

"Then the die is cast and he will marry her," Sergei replied.

"And what of the little Sugar Plum Fairy?" I asked.

"I will continue to meet her financial needs and offer support until my cousin decides whether he can remain faithful to Alix."

"And then?" Barker pressed.

"Then I will arrange a pension for her, which I hope will be provided by the government. Nikolai has no money and sweet Mathilde is bleeding me dry. We shall put pressure upon the Imperial Mariinsky Theatre to make her their prima ballerina and the toast of Saint Petersburg. I hope it will be enough for her. What are you laughing at, Georgie?"

Prince George had lit a cigarette and the remark had set him coughing.

"I'm trying to imagine Mathilde satisfied with anything," he said. "For a poor girl from Poland she certainly has a taste for finer things. How large was that ring you bought her last Christmas?"

"Three carats," Sergei admitted.

"I'll bet a thousand kroners it's still sitting in the box."

"I get the impression Miss Kschessinska would very much like to be the tsarina of Russia," I said.

"You noticed that, did you?" George drawled, taking another puff of his cigarette. "She's an ambitious little minx. Do you know what she just did? She wrote to Alix and told her to go away, that Nicky was hers."

Barker made a grunt that might have been a chuckle. One couldn't know for sure.

"A spirited girl," he said. "And what was the response?"

"Alix laughed," Sergei said, looking down at his boots. "There was no written reply, but word got back from her ladies-in-waiting. Mathilde was beside herself with rage. She smashed the contents of her hotel room to bits. More of my money to replace everything. Some nights she comforts herself by drinking absinthe and imagining her life as tsarina."

"Would the Church be so barmy as to accept a ballerina as the wife of the tsar?" George asked. "I hardly think so."

"She does have sway over Nicholas, you must admit," Sergei replied.

"My money is on Alix," George replied. "And the sooner he packs off his little dancer, the better."

"Unfortunately, my money is very much on Mathilde." Sergei sighed. "What's left of it, anyway."

I looked at Barker, waiting to ask a question. He nodded.

"When I spoke to her the other day, she mentioned something that concerned me," I said. "She spoke of Meyerling."

George rolled his eyes and waved at a servant to bring champagne. Meanwhile, Sergei looked like he had a toothache.

"She is obsessed with the matter," he admitted. "A young prince like Nicky and a common mistress like Mathilde go off to a cabin because they are not allowed to marry, and he shoots them both. Tragic. But it happened."

"Idiotic is what it is," George remarked. "Would anybody care for some champagne? Here you are, Sergei. You need this."

"Not an hour goes by that she doesn't mention a suicide pact," the grand duke continued. "He must be hers or they will die. She has planned a dozen ways to do it so far. You must remember, three years ago, she was a schoolgirl."

"Has she made threats against Princess Alix?" Barker asked.

"Of course. By the dozens," the grand duke admitted. "As he begins to slip through her fingers, the threats grow more ominous."

"What of Nicholas? Does she make threats to him as well? Of him alone, I mean?"

Sergei spoke in falsetto. "'If I can't have him, Sergei, then no one shall have him. I'll shoot him myself with my little pistol.'"

"She owns a pistol?" Barker's face slid my way, his eyes hidden behind his spectacles.

"Yes, sir," I admitted. "I'd forgotten. It was a little thing, hardly bigger than a derringer."

"I bought it for her in the Rue St. Louis," Sergei said. "She wanted a bigger one, but the shop owner insisted upon a so-called 'woman's pistol.'"

"Presumably, it shoots bullets and not powder puffs," the Guv said with frost in his voice. "Can she shoot?"

Sergei nodded. "Of course. She's quite the little marksman.

She plinks at crockery so often I have a man in to repair the holes in the walls."

"Tell me, sir," my partner asked. "In your heart of hearts do you believe she would shoot the tsarevich, her lover?"

"I don't think so," Sergei replied. "We are not in a Zola novel."

"Friends!" A voice came echoing down the hall. Nicholas's boots stamped on the marble floor. He scooped the delicate glass out of George's hand and downed the champagne in one gulp. Then he fell into a chair beside Sergei.

"I never thought there could be anything more boring than an Orthodox service, but congratulations to the English, they've done it! More champagne!"

The latter was addressed not to a particular servant but to the Orangery at large. While we waited he complained about the length of the ceremony, the ages of the women, the weakness of the English in overorganizing every minute of a man's life, and the uncomfortable tightness of English boots. I was never so glad as when the servant whom we had met first when we entered brought a tray of glasses and a bottle of Veuve Clicquot.

"To the Potato Club!" the tsarevich cried. *"Nostrovia!"*

They downed their glasses. Barker and I did not partake.

"What, pray tell, is the Potato Club?" the Guv asked. There was a ghost of a smile on his face. He found the little tsar-in-training amusing.

Nicholas tapped the side of his nose.

"Secret society, you know," Nicholas said. "Younger royals only. We only let Sergei in because he pays for everything. Sergei! You've left your hair in your other suit!"

I began to feel sorry for the grand duke, having to nursemaid a young crazed woman I was sure he must be weary of and placating her equally crazed lover. I hoped his government would cut him a substantial check someday after he was beggared and living in the streets. Mocking a man's baldness is bad form.

"Nicky," George said, "it isn't a secret society if everyone knows about it. It's merely a drinking club, gentlemen. We don't plan to invade Switzerland or anything."

"Switzerland!" Nicholas exclaimed. "Good cheese and chocolate."

George laughed. "Let's discuss invading Switzerland at our next meeting."

"How did your club get such an interesting name?" I asked.

"We discussed this and the three of us decided that we have no idea," Sergei replied. "We were blind drunk when we set up the rules."

"I think Nicholas got up to make a speech," George said. "It concerned the virtues of the humble potato. Of course, we'd been drinking vodka since midnight. Anyway, there you have it. The Potato Club."

"The Potato Club!" Nicholas echoed. "Look here! I had necklaces made."

They each unbuttoned the top button of their shirt and retrieved a gold chain from which hung a lump of gold that, if one used his imagination, resembled a potato.

"Impressive," I said.

"We are inducting Georgie into the club. Oh, not this Georgie, the English one. Stuffed shirt. He needs half a bottle poured down his throat as soon as possible. We're going to have a party for him the night before the wedding. One cannot go to one's marriage bed sober. You are invited. Oh, not you, Mr. Whatsis. You're too old and too disapproving. But my shooting teacher here can come!"

I supposed it mattered little that he never actually learned or remembered our names, though we were trying to save his life and ducking bullets in the process.

"It's time for lunch," Sergei interrupted, pulling a watch from his pocket. "We should limit ourselves to half a bottle of champers each. We might be forced to speak to the queen."

"Mind you," Nicholas said, "if the Prince of Wales arrives we can drink until dinner."

Barker frowned. It was true that Victoria's heir was proving to be a bit of a rogue, a lesser version of Nicholas. Much lesser since he had married. I'm not certain why that is. Young royals in line for the throne with parents who demand they toe the line seem to invariably rebel. Perhaps it is the only way to get their parents' attention.

"Lunch!" Nicholas cried, jumping to his feet. "We'll shoot afterward. I'm starved. But I don't know why everything is preserved in aspic here. What is aspic, anyway? Congealed fat? It's disgusting."

The other members of the Potato Club rose, bowed to us, and left. It looked as if they wanted to apologize for Nicholas's boorish behavior.

"They are a pair of royal governesses," I said when they were gone. "But the infant rules the nursery."

"Heaven help us all," Barker rumbled. "It takes all the composure I have not to put the boy over my knee."

# CHAPTER FIFTEEN

I was wondering about the advisedness of refusing both a guest of this country and a man who would eventually rule a tenth of the planet at the very least. Teaching Nicholas to shoot was the equivalent of giving a tot a knife and telling him to go play with his friends. Nothing good would come of it.

We sat once again in the Goat Tavern over a crust of bread stuffed with ham and a pint for our troubles while the royals dined in elegance with silver candlesticks and champagne.

"He's probably a major in his country's army," I complained to my partner. "Surely someone would have taught him to shoot a pistol by now."

Barker grunted in reply. He reached for a pickled onion.

"Why me?" I continued, aggrieved. "I don't work for Colt. I am not an instructor of firearms. I'm not even a particularly good shot."

"Amen," the Guv said.

I gave him a withering look. "Nicholas has his own secret police. Let them teach him. We have an assassin to find."

"You must take every opportunity to be at the tsarevich's side," Barker replied. "You're of a like age. That's why he asked you. As you know, I've been excluded."

"He wants to impress his little ballerina friend."

"It is a male trait. Lad, you know you are going to teach him to shoot. You are merely kicking at the goads."

"Yes, well, some goads need kicking. I still hoped that sound reason might give me an excuse to refuse him. Might I be considered a traitor if I agreed to teach a future tsar, our sworn enemy just ten years ago, how to kill someone? I mean, really, sir. He didn't ask so that he can stand on the lawn of the Summer Palace and shoot at targets. He wants the thrill. What will satisfy him? Shooting me in the leg?"

"You've got an assassin for that," the Guv said, giving a dour smile.

"My point exactly. I already have one person trying to kill me. Why would I invite a second?"

"As I said, the assassin is not trying to kill you," he reminded me. "He's merely trying to unsettle you."

"Perhaps he is just a poor shot."

"I think we both know better."

"Blast," I grumbled. "I can't get out of this, can I?"

"You never had the slightest chance, Mr. Llewelyn."

And so I reported to the Orangery after lunch. We British are very prompt. Corporal Dinsdale was there to open the door, but the second I stepped inside a hand seized my shoulder.

"There you are," Nicholas cried, clapping me on the back. "Where have you been? I've been waiting for hours!"

He pulled me down a hallway gleaming with marble and gilt. He led us through rooms and halls and down two flights of stairs so quickly I could not take the opportunity to look at the sumptuousness of the palace. I've retained a vague image of marble and carved hardwoods. Finally, we reached some sort of cellar, longer than it was wide, with large barrels stacked at one end. The walls were a humble plaster and the floors cement. There was no marble here. It might have been a cellar anywhere in London. It was probably the oldest part of the palace.

"With an assassin about, it's all the more reason to learn how to shoot."

"True, Your Imperial Highness."

"Oh, bosh. Call me Nicky when we're alone. I'm quite bored with bowing and scraping. You know, you may be the first fellow near my own age that I've met since I came here. I was beginning to think you were a nation of septuagenarians."

I tried to think of a response but I was bone-dry. The tsarevich continued as if he didn't really expect an answer, anyway. I gave him an excuse to hear himself talk.

"So, you were holding the blighter who tried to assassinate me, and his head exploded. How did that feel?"

"Feel?" I asked, shocked by the question.

"Yes, yes. I saw you," he said, sizing me up. "His brains were in your hair and clothing. Were you scared?"

"No," I answered. "I was more stunned and disgusted."

"But you did not recognize the fellow?"

"No, sir."

"He had a long beard, did he not?"

"He did," I replied.

"All anarchists wear long beards. They can't afford barbers, I expect. It's money better spent on dynamite and cheap vodka."

*Surely there must be a clean-shaven, teetotaling anarchist somewhere*, I thought. However, one does not argue with an absolute monarch. Or the son of one, anyway.

Two cases were open on top of one of the barrels. One was at least a hundred years old, an old French dueling set. The case had seen better days and looked particularly disreputable next to the other, which was so new it must have been purchased since the tsarevich's arrival. Two excessively long-barreled Colts lay in a gleaming black case with red silk lining. The contrast between the red and the faded aqua velvet was striking, but still, the antique set had a particular charm of its own. I confess I have an affinity for old things: books, knickknacks, curios, and detritus of a previous age. I ran my hand around the edges of the case and closed it. There was a small brass inscription set in the top, the Cyrillic letters rusted in green.

"What does it say?" I asked.

"Oh, that?" the tsarevich remarked.

He could not have been less interested. I imagined the case had been foisted upon him by the tsar's ministers. With a cap and ball, he might be less likely to shoot off an imperial toe.

"It's a gift presented to my grandfather by . . . what's the name? Georges Charles de Heeckeren d'Anthès. Yes, that's it."

I blinked. "Isn't he the one who shot the writer Pushkin in a duel?"

"Indeed he is. He donated the pistols in order to get rid of them, but we couldn't very well tell the public that we had possession of a pistol that killed the world's greatest living author, could we? It's knocked about the Winter Palace for decades. I think I saw it under a table leg once to stabilize it. But look here! This is what I want to know about!"

I could have talked about Pushkin all day. The man was a genius. However, one must acquiesce to a tsarevich, especially if he could attack one's country on a whim.

"That's a very good set," I replied. "Did you get it in London?"

"Yes, George smuggled it here for me."

"The Duke of York smuggled this in?"

"No, the other George. Prince George of Greece and Denmark."

I noticed for the first time a scar on Nicholas's forehead, near the hairline, where George had deflected an attack on his cousin in far-off Otsu, Japan.

"He bought this for you?" I asked. "It isn't easy to get permission to purchase pistols here, you know."

"He's a prince of two countries, no less. Who would tell him no? So, come show me how to shoot one of these things."

He lifted a pistol loosely in his hand and I leaned back out of the way. The gun was unloaded, but the way he waved it about still put an ache in the pit of my stomach.

"Where shall we shoot?" I asked before walking to the far end of the room.

There were many large barrels in a corner, one stacked atop the others. I found a piece of chalk and drew a crude ring on the top of the barrel. Then I lifted the other pistol, pulled the pin, and rolled out the cylinder. I began to insert rounds and then stopped myself. Two bullets would be enough, unless it was two too many.

The tsarevich took it from my hand and gave me the empty one. Hurriedly, I jammed bullets into the chambers, as Nicholas stamped about, waving the pistol at the target. *This was a terrible idea,* I told myself. *How did I get myself into this?*

"Shouldn't someone else be here?" I asked, feeling distressed. "Someone from your government, I mean?"

"George said he'd be outside, making sure we aren't disturbed. Now, come. How do I stand?"

"Turn sideways and hold out your right arm a little lower than shoulder height. Excellent. Now raise your left arm and grab your other wrist. You'll need the support, you see, because the pistol kicks backward when you shoot. You don't want to lose control and shoot wildly."

"Yes, yes."

"There is a sight you can look along at the end of the barrel here, see? You can use that or merely point and shoot. It's up—"

He shot. Twice. So much for restraint. I was glad I had only given him two bullets. He ran to the barrel to look for the marks.

"Here's one!" he shouted. "It's about a foot away from the center. I can't find the other one."

"That's excellent for a first shot," I said. "Mine was closer to a foot and a half. Depressing, isn't it?"

"A little," he admitted.

"It's a skill, not a talent, sir. Would you like to try again?"

I filled the cylinder on my pistol, then traded with him in spite of the foreboding I felt coming from deep inside me.

"Thank you," he said, shooting six times as quickly as he could squeeze the trigger. "This is great fun, isn't it?"

He had a lopsided grin on his face. I watched him run over to see how he did this time.

"Look!" he cried. "Two inches away with one shot! I am improving under your fine tutelage."

*Tutelage, my eye*, I thought. He hadn't listened to a thing I said. It was like teaching a puppy to sit.

"That partner of yours, Mr. Barker. He's a very interesting fellow," he said.

"He is that," I agreed.

"When I left the palace the other day and saw him I was certain he was another assassin sent to kill me."

He turned and fired off the pistol again. If anything, his shots were wilder and more erratic than when he began. This could quickly get out of hand. What if he shot himself?

Barker taught me something not so long ago. When one is in the middle of something that may get out of hand, try to calm yourself. Close your eyes for the briefest moment, then open them and observe clinically, without preconceptions or set conclusions. I breathed in. I let it out, closed my eyes, then opened and observed.

Nicholas was agitated. He was shooting at the target without aiming. It was as if he thought the assassin was in front of him and he was trying to defend himself. His face was perspiring, though it was cool in the cellar. He couldn't be still. He was almost in a frenzy.

It wasn't mere nerves, I thought. Nicholas did not seem like a born leader of men. I suspected he didn't want to be tsar, and even if he did, he wouldn't be any good at it. The thought of eventually being responsible for so many millions of people is too much unless one is a natural leader of men. In his first official duty, he'd nearly been murdered. This was his second time out of Russia and an assassin was already barking at his heels. He hadn't even made his first official speech and the people of his own country already hated him as a symbol of oppression. Not for himself, perhaps, but for what he stood for. He was a target, as much as the one I had crudely sketched on the barrel.

He held out the empty pistol and reached for the loaded one. Let's just suppose he did put a bullet in the old Llewelyn cranium. What then? We were alone. It would be his word against mine if I were shot. His word alone if I died. I switched pistols with him.

"Aim," I told him.

He did. At my head.

I lifted my pistol, my heart hammering so loudly in my breast I thought he could hear it. This was not how I pictured ending my life. I thought it likely my situation would not lead to longevity, but being shot by the future tsar of Russia? I hadn't anticipated that one.

We were both breathing hard, not moving. We aimed our pistols at each other, but we knew mine was empty. How would I defend myself? Throw it at him?

This may have been his plan all along. Shoot an insignificant person in a "safe" country, disgrace himself, and perhaps the tsar's title would pass to one of the innumerable grand dukes of Russia. Then he could move to Paris, marry his ballerina, and perhaps become a milkman or something.

"Your Highness?" I choked out, my mouth suddenly dry. Nicholas grasped the pistol so tightly his knuckles were white. His eyes bulged in his head. I felt like I represented everything that stood in his way.

Just then the door opened and a man walked in. The tsarevich did not hesitate. He turned and fired. The bullet missed
the man's sleeve by no more than a few inches and struck the
plaster of the wall behind.

"Have a care, there, Nicky," Prince George of Greece and
Denmark drawled. "You'll spoil my new jacket."

Now there was a natural leader, cool as ice when fired upon,
easily parrying a killing blow in Otsu, Japan, or the basement of
Kensington Palace.

"I brought some champers, old fellow," he said. "You look
parched."

A reluctant member of the palace staff entered with a small
cart containing a bucket of champagne and glasses. I put out my
hand. Nicholas considered for a moment, still not willing to re-
linquish his weapon, the only weapon he had.

Still nonchalant, George crossed to the tsarevich, traded the
glass for the gun, and tossed the latter my way. I opened the cylinder and emptied out three rounds.

George stretched and yawned, still holding the delicate glass.
Then he blinked.

"I'm bored, Nicky. Let's go to the stables."

He turned and walked out. Without a glance at me, Nicholas
followed him. When they were gone, I walked to a corner and sat
down facing the room. Then I held my head in my hands and
tried to calm down.

For a moment there, I thought I was as dead as Pushkin.

# CHAPTER SIXTEEN

We were traveling down Whitehall Street, having come from Kensington, and were nearing our offices when I noticed an open carriage at the curb. Barker was busy thinking, planning questions to direct at Corporal Dinsdale later that evening, so I nudged him on the side of the knee and nodded toward the cab. He stiffened. We recognized the vehicle at once.

"Philippa," I murmured. "I wonder what brought her to London."

Mrs. Ashleigh was the Guv's lady friend. Their arrangement was unusual because my partner was of a much lower class and unsuitable for society. His money made him slightly more palatable to some. She owned a large estate on the coast between Seaford and Alfriston and could afford all the creature comforts, and would allow him to purchase almost nothing for her. She enjoyed being self-sufficient. He visited her on alternate Fridays if we were not elbows deep in a case, or whenever she was in London at her townhouse.

We entered and found her in residence in our chambers. Jenkins had been shooed out, and was probably at a pub somewhere.

"My dear!" Barker said, coming through the outer office and taking her hand. It was as effusive as he ever was in public. He would never kiss her in front of a partner, but then her hat precluded such an activity, anyway.

"Sit, sit," he stated.

She did not sit; she merely subsided like a floating bubble into one of the visitor's chairs.

"I cannot stay," she said. "I'm seeing my solicitors in an hour."

"When did you arrive?" Barker asked, putting his stick in the stand and his hat upon the desk.

"Yesterday," she answered. "I'd have told you, but I've been quite busy."

"And how is your uncle?" he enquired. Mrs. Ashleigh's uncle had been unwell for some time and she occasionally came to London to look in on him.

"Oh, you didn't know! How could you? Poor Uncle Harold passed away two days ago. I've been dealing with all sorts of legal matters. They are dry as dust and go on forever."

"Then . . ." I began.

Barker turned his head. "Then what, Mr. Llewelyn?" he demanded, curious.

"Nothing, sir."

I gave Philippa a pleased look and she favored me with a dazzling smile.

"Yes, Thomas, I am now Baroness Philippa Ashleigh."

"Congratulations!" I said.

"Thank you."

Barker sat down in his chair, not like a bubble, more like a deflating balloon. He nearly missed the chair entirely. This was a moment he had been dreading for some time. Mrs. Ashleigh was titled. She might want things now, things he could not fully control. She had the upper hand in some matters. As linked as they were to each other for so many years, there was a struggle for power, as well. Barker is elemental, but he met his match in Philippa Ashleigh, who is impervious. It was only natural that like should follow like.

"Would you care for some tea?" he asked.

"No, no, thank you. As I said, I cannot stay long. I've come to tell you that you shall receive a visitor soon and I want you to be polite. Listen to him. Agree to everything and don't be stubborn."

My partner sat back in his chair and crossed his arms. "Colonel Waverly of Buckingham Palace, perhaps? He came this morning."

She wilted. Like most redheaded women, she is very pale, and the powder she wore to give her face color soiled her gloves as she pinched the bridge of her nose.

"You turned him down, didn't you?" she said in a small voice.

"I did."

"I worked all day yesterday to bring that about, wheedling and flattering and cajoling," she said. "I kowtowed to people I despise, lunched with old women who have great power but have never read a book. I compromised my principles. I practically begged, and you turned him down."

"I'm sorry, my dear," he replied evenly. "Apparently, you informed everyone but me."

"I was late from that dratted lunch. Countess Wynn-Scott tends to ramble. I came as soon as I could get away. Drat all colonels. They are so deucedly punctual."

Barker looked scandalized. "Such language, Philippa!"

"You have not heard the language I'm carrying in my head, Cyrus. It would blister your ears. We discussed this!"

"We did, but I made you no promises. You are not the only one floundering in deep waters. I have sworn to protect the tsarevich.

I consider the possibility of war between Russia and England to be of more importance than an OVM."

"That's OBM," Philippa corrected. "As you know perfectly well. Mr. Llewelyn, may we have the room?"

I stood, wondering where I should go. I could already hear her voice rose as I stepped out into the street. I was at sixes and sevens before I realized that she was a friend of Rebecca's now, as well. She stopped by our house in the City when she was in town, and might be planning to visit her next. I had to beat her to the punch if I did not want to find myself in Barker's situation. Frantically, I began waving my arms to attract a cab, in danger of knocking people's hats off.

An interminable half hour later I put a pound note in the cabman's hand and jumped down to the pavement in Camomile Street. There was no carriage at the curb and I hoped my wife was alone.

I stepped inside the front door. The maid did not see me until I reached the sitting room, where Rebecca was seated alone. She didn't rise and kiss me. That was the only sign I needed. She already knew. I held out my stick and hat to the maid, but I dropped them. The clatter of the stick on the parquet floor made me jump.

"You heard?" I asked. "She already came?"

"Philippa?" Rebecca murmured. "Yes, she called. Mr. Barker is going to receive an OBM! How exciting!"

I swallowed. She only knew the half of it. I had to break the news to her. I didn't know which would be more difficult, her knowing or her not knowing.

"Mr. Barker refused the offer, Rebecca," I said.

She rose, not in anger, but complete surprise. "He refused it? Whatever for? He earned it, Thomas!"

"I'm not completely certain why," I said. "He said he didn't want to draw attention to himself. For example, he never wants his photograph or a sketch of his likeness in the newspapers."

"But darling," she protested. "Mr. Barker is one of the most distinctive-looking men in London. I'm sure hundreds know who he is."

"He is," I agreed. "I wondered if he felt that others would think he was unworthy of the honor, being lowborn. Being wealthy doesn't make one part of the set."

"Does that even matter to him?" she asked.

"To him personally?" I replied. "No, but it does to Philippa."

"But Thomas, that is why she planned this, so he would be more welcome."

"I suspect he doesn't like to be got 'round."

Rebecca blinked and crossed her arms. "And you?"

"Colonel Waverly offered me some sort of medal. He didn't specify which it would be because I am so young."

"And?" she asked, holding her hands to her cheeks as if she were afraid of the answer.

"I turned it down."

"Why?" she asked sharply, crossing her arms.

"Because Barker did."

Rebecca breathed in and out quickly. "But you earned it, Thomas! You saved the prince's life."

"It doesn't matter."

My wife clapped her hands to her ears as if she didn't want to hear any more. "It would have made you more acceptable to my family. You'd be a hero."

"I'm no different than I was last week," I argued. "They can accept me or they cannot accept me. It's their choice."

She sniffed. I was in the untenable position of both wanting to comfort her and being the one who caused the need to be comforted. I pulled a handkerchief from my pocket and she wiped her eyes.

"It's about honor, isn't it?" she asked.

"Yes," I admitted. "I couldn't accept if he didn't. It would be disloyal."

"I don't understand," she protested. "What is honor but an

arbitrary set of rules made up by schoolboys? Why do men with wives and children suddenly rush off to war when there are plenty of unmarried ones to do it? What is that? What does it mean? What is duty and honor?"

"I did not make the rules," I said.

"I thought we make decisions together."

"We do. It was stupid. Honor is stupid, sometimes. But I'll abide by it all the same. I won't consider myself a man if I don't."

She sat down again on a hassock.

"Where's Philippa?" she asked.

"When I last saw her, she was in our office, giving my partner a few stern words."

"I wish I had that gift."

"I'm sorry," I said. "I came here immediately afterward."

"Could you do something for me?" she asked. "Could you go to the colonel and tell him you changed your mind? I'm sure he'd listen to reason."

"No," I said, shaking my head. "I can't."

"Think about it a few days. You needn't answer right away."

"It's still no."

"Let us begin again," she said. "I need to understand this. Mr. Barker saved the life of the tsarevich, and to an even greater extent you saved the life of Prince George mere days before his wedding. You both deserve the honor, yet Mr. Barker refused the honor. Do you know why?"

"I'm afraid I don't," I answered. "It was a complete surprise to me, but then the offer itself was a surprise. Her Majesty's equerry came earlier in the week to give us a good grilling. He certainly took us apart like a watch and studied every cog. We assumed that was that."

"You must have had some inkling," Rebecca said.

"I assumed he thought that ushering a foreign leader to a palace door did not justify such an honor. He may also have thought that my tackling an assassin who had already discharged his weapon was not worthy, either. Had it been a real gun the man was holding, the royal bridegroom would be dead, and I late to the party."

"Her Majesty's government did not believe so. I'm certain they discussed the matter thoroughly before offering such an award."

"Ah, yes, but Mrs. Ashleigh, that is, Baroness Ashleigh, has been using all the influence at her disposal to make the offer available. Mr. Barker might have felt he did not deserve it. He takes chivalry very seriously."

"Would he have become Sir Cyrus Barker?" Rebecca asked.

I shrugged my shoulders. "I don't know. It wasn't mentioned. However, that is thorny in itself. If he were made a knight—and understand, the Guv would like that very much in itself—it would forever separate him from all his East End associates and friends. He could no longer receive information from the underground network that he has long cultivated. There would be a wall between them. He wouldn't be 'Push' anymore. He'd be too grand, you see."

"What is 'Push'?" she asked, puzzled.

"It is his moniker in the East End. It's Cockney rhyming slang. Push for 'push-comes-to-shove,' which rhymes with Guv."

"I have no idea what you are talking about," my wife said, staring at me intently.

"The name doesn't matter," I replied. "If he became 'Sir' he could not perform his duties in the East End, some of which he could not complete a case without. That's all there is to it."

"Do you believe he would refuse such an honor and any similar ones in the future?" she asked.

"Perhaps."

"Therefore, you would be forced to do the same in perpetuity."

"I would hope not," I said. "If I earned it, he would say I deserved it. If I didn't, however, it would gall me whenever I pinned it on."

The maid brought in a tea tray and set it upon a table. Rebecca stared at the tea leaves as if they might predict the future. She wasn't seeing the tray at all. She was miles away.

"You do understand that many, perhaps most men would not care a fig as long as it would make their wives happy," she said. "That is another form of chivalry."

"I know. Chivalry, honor, duty; it's very complicated."

She gave a long, shivering sigh as if she were admitting defeat. "Sir Thomas Llewelyn would have been nice to present to my parents and friends. They don't care for you very much."

"I don't believe my being knighted would help, and anyway, there was no discussion of receiving a knighthood."

That was not strictly true. Colonel Waverly had made an offer, but it was off the cuff, because Barker had refused his.

"I don't like this case," she stated. "You are risking your life for little or no reward, for a young man you do not respect."

"You're right," I agreed. "I will most certainly admit to that."

"Mr. Barker's sense of honor grinds exceedingly fine," she added.

"On that we can agree. You know, I didn't have so much a sense of honor before I met him. I suppose it is contagious."

"Like a disease," Rebecca said.

I looked away.

"You are the loser here, Thomas. And Philippa, and I. Even Mr. Barker comes away empty-handed. What was he thinking?"

"I don't know, Rebecca," I answered. "He doesn't reveal his plans to me. Generally speaking, however, everything works out for him. I'm not sure whether he is incredibly lucky or if he leads a charmed life."

She sighed. "You're not the easiest person to be married to, Thomas Llewelyn."

"I suppose not," I admitted. "But if you'd married a man without honor, what kind of husband would that be?"

"I'm sorry," she answered. "I still don't understand, but I'm sorry if I hurt you."

I stepped forward, but she put out a hand as sturdy as a brick wall.

"Not yet," she said. "I'm still angry. Perhaps in a few hours I will forgive you. Perhaps not. We shall see by dinner. No medal, Thomas. What were you thinking? They aren't like daisies one can pick anytime. Now go."

I went, feeling like the total cad I doubtless was. I was also confused. If there is a choice between a wife and one's honor, how does one choose?

# CHAPTER SEVENTEEN

Later that evening I was sitting sprawled in my easy chair, an unread book in my lap, and one foot swinging slightly in the air to show I was thinking. Rebecca was reading Charlotte Brontë; I don't recall which book. I've long forgotten which book I was attempting to read, as well. I was too full of energy to read a book, which is saying something.

We had hardly spoken since that afternoon. She hadn't forgiven me, but she was too self-contained to express her feelings on the matter. If I asked her a question, I would receive the briefest response and she had not begun a proper conversation since I had returned. Dinner had been a quiet affair. Once or twice she gave Barker a scathing glance.

"What o'clock is it, dear?" I asked.

"A few minutes past seven o'clock," she replied. Then she frowned. "Why? Are you thinking of going out?"

"I am," I replied. "I've got a question rattling about in my head. How would you fancy a drive?"

She put down her book. "Really? Are you asking me to accompany you on an errand involving a case?"

"Thought I might."

"Is this a blatant attempt to cajole me into a better mood?"

"The most blatant."

"Is it dangerous?" she asked. "Is it in the East End?"

"No to both questions," I answered. "It's at the British Museum, actually. Or rather, he is. He's a friend of sorts."

"Does your friend have a name?" Rebecca asked.

"He does."

"Might I be permitted to know it?"

"You may, yes."

"You think you're so clever, Mr. Thomas Llewelyn. Very well, you've piqued my curiosity. Who are we visiting?"

"You'll never know unless you get ready," I replied. "Do you think you could manage it in a quarter hour? We need to be somewhere at the stroke of eight."

Rebecca jumped to her feet.

"I'll do it in ten," she said.

True to her word, she was ready early. She threw a white wrapper over a plain black dress, clasped with a brooch of jet.

"Move along, Thomas," she scolded. "We don't want to be late."

I nodded. "Perish the thought."

We made good time, but the evening service traffic slowed our progress and I feared we would be late. However, we arrived in front of the museum just as we heard Big Ben tolling somewhere in the distance.

"There he is!" I said, pointing at a man who had just left the museum and was in the act of donning his gloves. He was a dapper fellow of more than fifty years with a top hat and a white scarf around his throat.

"Who is he, this friend of yours?" Rebecca asked, regarding him curiously.

"He's a librarian of sorts," I said. "He works in a volunteer capacity for the Reading Room at the British Museum, you might say. His name is Liam Grant. He's a gentleman. That is, he doesn't work, and he spends all of his time here in the Reading Room studying and occasionally helping patrons find the information they desire. He inhabits the place. I honestly don't think he's left this square in five years at least. His passion is esoterica. I suspect the man may be a wizard. Come!"

We descended from the cab and mounted the stairs of the museum in time to meet him coming down.

"Liam!" I cried.

"What? Thomas?" he replied. "Thomas Llewelyn, where did you come from? And who is this extraordinary goddess?"

I made introductions. Grant adjusted his pince-nez spectacles the better to see my wife. There was something molelike about him, as if he'd been hiding in the bowels of the museum too long and had forgotten the outside world.

He bowed. "I'm so very pleased to meet you, Mrs. Llewelyn. We were about to despair of this fellow. He needed taming from a female of the species. How is that coming along?"

"He's a work in progress," she replied.

"I was just going to have dinner at the Alpha across the street. Have you any objection to joining me for coffee and cake? I'm in the museum all day, you see. They need me there at the Reading Room."

Rebecca looked at me. It wasn't done by her circle, a young woman visiting a common public house.

"I'd be delighted," she said, surprising me.

Grant smiled. "Excellent!"

He offered an arm and she accepted it, accompanying him down the final steps. When we were across the street, we entered the Alpha. That is, the two of them entered and I followed along behind like an afterthought. Once inside, Grant made a number of signals with his hand to the publican and sat down at a table covered in rings from ten thousand pint glasses.

Rebecca's eyes were glittering. She came from the tearoom set and being here was exciting, even daring. If someone she knew saw her here with this rabble, she might not live it down in the City.

"What brings you here, Thomas?" Liam asked. "I presume you require some piece of information. I hope your visit will be worth your while."

"So do I," I said. "I don't know if I caught hold of the wrong end of the stick, but do you recall a rumor or a fact or a legend, I'm not certain which, that there are tunnels under any of the royal palaces? That is, tunnels leading to other places?"

A pint of stout had appeared at Grant's elbow and he stopped to refresh himself. I had ordered a stout as well, and Rebecca held a dry sherry in one of those impossibly small glasses that look like they belong in a doll's house.

Grant let out a long, slow "Ahhhh" after his first gulp, which every man understands as the First Swallow, not to be hurried.

"Tunnels," he said, nodding. "I love tunnels. If you connected every tunnel under London they would stretch all the way to Rome, I believe. I've made a map of London tunnels. That is to say I purchased a map and drew in all the tunnels I've found in my research. Some I marked in red as solid fact. Some are in green, meaning completely disproven and fallacious. And some in sepia because I like sepia. It stands for 'not yet proven.' I saw your name in the newspapers this week at Kensington Palace. There is a line on my map at Kensington in sepia brown. Neither proven nor disproven."

"I'd like to see that map," I remarked.

Rebecca nodded. "So would I."

Grant's meal arrived then, simple sandwiches with chips. I saw what was in the sandwiches and glanced away. I don't eat tongue, under the theory that I won't eat anything that tastes me back. Undaunted, however, Grant tucked in.

Rebecca took the opportunity to glance at me, with a smile upon her lips. Eccentric, that smile said, but harmless. I looked down at his shoes and she did the same. There was thick wool felt glued to the bottoms, lest he should make noise in the Reading Room. She covered her mouth with the glass of sherry.

"I daresay you've been down one or two of those tunnels," Grant said after the sandwich was consumed.

"I've been down an even dozen, I should think," I replied.

"Are there any you would care to mention?" he asked. "I'm always looking for more."

"Not without permission."

"Of course not, dear fellow," Grant answered, holding up his hand. "I would not want you to get into trouble with such a man as Mr. Cyrus Barker."

Grant had never met the Guv, but had developed an exaggerated sense of his importance, his wisdom, and his saintliness. Goodness knows where he acquired it, unless my partner was giving regularly to the British Museum, which, of course, he might. I do our business accounts, but not Barker's personal or charitable ones.

"Fortunate you are, Mr. Llewelyn," Grant continued, "to have a fine employer and a beautiful wife. What more could any man ask?"

Rebecca smiled. "I like this fellow."

"I won't argue about the second, at least."

"Where was I? The map!" he exclaimed. "Would you really like to see it?"

"Certainly. I'd love to."

"We could look at it now if you wish," he said before draining the final gulp of his pint glass. "It's in my flat in Montague Place, across from the museum. You know. You've been there before." He turned to Rebecca. "That is, madam, if you are not affronted by the abode of an old bachelor who has more bibelots than sense."

"We wouldn't want to put you to any trouble," Rebecca replied. She knew me too well already. To see a man's nest is to know the man.

"Not a bit of it," Grant replied. "I'll make some tea and let you see the map."

He stood, paid for us all, and offered an elbow to my wife again like a courtier. She took it and the two of them stepped out into the balmy evening.

"That's the one," he said, cocking his head in the direction of a building at the far end of the road. "There on the corner."

"An agreeable spot," Rebecca murmured.

"I think so. What could be more wonderful than to awaken in this wonderful city every morning to the view of such a wonderful building? She is wife and mistress to me, if that is not being coarse."

"You never married?" she asked.

"No one would marry this old wreck, good woman, and I was so reticent a young man I could barely stammer out a greeting, let alone a proposal."

"You're doing well so far," she replied, smiling at Grant. "You do understand that there are a number of women of a certain age in this town that would like to meet a gentleman such as yourself."

"My blushes, madam. Now you're telling tales at my expense."

We reached the door of a respectable row of attached flats. He led us up the stairs and pulled an old key from his pocket in a way that somehow reminded me of Ebenezer Scrooge. Then he threw open the door.

The first thing we saw was the tall row of bookcases that completely blocked our view of the rest of the room. He led us along the wall until we came 'round to a fireplace near the window and a pair of old leather chairs. Then one noticed his library. They were not merely walls of books but cases coming out perpendicular to the room at intervals as like an actual library. Each shelf had some curio from ancient times and far-off places: statues of unknown deities, shrunken heads, prayer beads, Egyptian statuary, and rune-covered stones. There was an owl I assumed was stuffed until it turned its head and looked at me, and above us, suspended horizontally from the ceiling, was an entire Nile crocodile. Thankfully, that was stuffed.

"They were out of space at the museum, and I bought it for two pounds," he said, noticing our upward gaze. "Two of the conservators helped me carry it here. They claim Captain Speke shot it, but it's not proven!"

"This is quite a place," I said. Even though I had seen it before, it was still quite impressive. "Merlin would be very comfortable here."

"Thank you, Thomas," he answered. "That was the intent. I'll make some tea and then I shall find that map."

The tea was good enough, or so Rebecca said later, and Liam Grant did find the map after all. It reminded me of Henry Mayhew's maps of the London poor, colored in sections. Here was an extended crypt under a church, there was an unfinished railway tunnel, or a sewer shaft sunk by that engineering genius Bazalgette. The information from a thousand sources had been collected and plotted onto this one subterranean map, and I imagined a thousand people would like to get their hands upon it. My partner would be one of them.

"Do you see any glaring errors?" he asked. "I would imagine you know this city as well as anyone."

"Not from what I see here," I said, shaking my head. "According to this, London has an entirely different topography twenty feet below. It's honeycombed in every direction. There is a subterranean city below the city."

"That is why I made this map, to keep track of everything."

"How accurate is it?" Rebecca asked.

"That's the problem, Mrs. Llewelyn," Liam Grant said, pouring cream into his tea. "I rarely leave the comfort of this street, and I haven't been in a tunnel in my entire life, unless it was a railway tunnel. This map is all conjecture, I'm afraid. Speculations, legends, fairy tales, if you will. Oh, some of this information is bona fide, on the word of experts. Some of the tunnels existed once, but were later filled with rubble. Here, for example, are mass graves from the Plague years. And here is a mosaic tile from a Roman residence. This tunnel was begun and in an advanced state when the railway company went out bankrupt. Rather than sell to a triumphant competitor, the president of the railway blew up the supports and let it fall."

"Is that what you do all day?" my wife asked. "Research?"

"It is, and the British Museum is the ideal place to study. I came into a bit of family money several years ago, and have been living upon the residuals. Not a fortune, but enough to meet a bachelor's needs."

"Why, your rooms look like an extension of the library itself," she remarked. I had to agree with her.

Grant gave a small but satisfied smile. "The museum can't keep everything, obviously, and books arrive daily by the lot. Some have been purchased for the collections and others are donated. I'm able to lay hands on them before they are dispersed."

"So, you go there all day, and at night you bring a book or a piece of historical bric-a-brac home with you," she continued, amazed by what she had seen.

"He doesn't tell anyone that he isn't a librarian," I told her. "And since he knows the museum better than anyone, he answers questions as if he were. As a matter of fact, that is how I met Mr. Grant myself."

"The staff treats me with great tolerance," he admitted.

"Confess it, Liam," I said. "You pay for the privilege. I'm sure you help support the museum financially."

"In a small way. One does what one can."

"Exactly where is Kensington Palace on this map?"

"Ah, yes. The tunnel," he said, pointing. "Here it is. William of Orange and Queen Mary purchased what was then called Nottingham House in 1689 and hired Christopher Wren to design a castle on the premises, but he merely added to the original buildings. So, the tunnel could predate the castle by a century."

"What was the purpose of the tunnel?" I asked. "It looks like it leads to the Goat Tavern. Granted, the tavern has fine food, but the palace has its own chefs. And if a royal gets hungry for some fish-and-chips, he can just send a servant through the front gate should he so desire. Why a tunnel, then?"

"Why indeed? From time to time, especially in the evenings, members of the royal family—male members, that is—may feel the need to stretch their limbs without being recognized. Public scrutiny is the bane of royal houses. Kensington began to be filled with mansions and shops around the palace, stripping them of their freedom to . . ."

"To visit low women and drink vintage wines in houses of assignation," Rebecca supplied. "Bawdy houses."

Grant's face pinked. "Yes, ma'am. If you see a tunnel near a palace you may be certain it was for nocturnal purposes."

"You don't say," I remarked. I was not a little shocked at the turn of conversation my wife had instigated.

"Mr. Grant, do you believe the tunnel is there?" Rebecca asked.

"I do."

"And not destroyed?"

He shook his head. "It would be too much work and expense to remove it, not to mention the revelation would bring a scandal on the royal house. Really, it was only minor royalty who used the palace after 1760, so why bother destroying the tunnel, anyway? It may be bricked over or locked and chained, but I believe it is there."

I wasn't going to allow him to get by based on an opinion.

"Why?" I asked. "If I may play devil's advocate, why would you, a scholar, believe it without proof?"

"It rings true," he said. "If there were a tunnel, it would be to the closest property, which is the Goat. Public houses require licensing at the discretion of the king. Also, any public house would be glad to help His Royal Highness or his progeny."

"No, no, that won't wash, Liam. That's a very long distance in a tunnel merely to step out to a private house on a Saturday evening. I don't believe it."

"Very well. Then consider this. Let us suppose there is some kind of danger to the royal family. An insurrection or a war. The royals would need to reach safety while people outside the palace think the family is still trapped inside."

"Now *that* I might believe," I said. "It's likely that every royal residence has some kind of tunnel to protect the heirs."

"Of course, the existence of a tunnel is a classic sword of Damocles," Grant murmured, nodding.

"True. One cannot build a tunnel that only goes in one direction."

"Precisely."

I mulled over that thought—several thoughts, in fact—still trying to work out what I was thinking.

"One could not build a tunnel that leads to nowhere; that is, open-ended."

"True," our host said again. "The palace had no idea what might be built upon the other entrance over time."

"That leads me to infer that the Goat Tavern has had a relationship with the palace for centuries. It could not be purchased by a third party without royal consent. It may be a functioning public house, but it is also an extension of the palace in a way."

Rebecca looked away, lost in her own thoughts. On the other hand, Liam Grant looked keen as a knife's edge.

"Thomas, you came here for a reason. Are you going to trust me? You don't need to, you know."

"Forgive me, Liam. I was occupied, and not seeing how things might look from your end. I don't trust many people. Few have given me reason to, but you appear to be the sort of fellow who understands the importance of discretion."

Liam Grant said nothing, but nodded, as if in thanks.

"When Cyrus Barker and I were walking toward the palace two days ago, having just finished eating at this selfsame Goat Tavern, there was an attempt on Prince George's life within only a few hundred yards of where we stood. I grassed the assassin who tried to shoot him, but he himself was shot by a second and killed. Now Barker and I have walked about the grounds again and we came to the same conclusion: the second assassin shot the first from the roof of the palace itself. After that he completely disappeared. The roof is not easily accessible for obvious reasons. We have not even been given access to it ourselves."

"Whereas," Grant continued, "if the assassin had access to a tunnel so old the current residents have no knowledge of it, he could leave the premises unseen."

"Completely unseen."

"Of course you have no proof, but it is an enquiry worth investigating. And in fact, you are an enquiry agent."

"That works out neatly, doesn't it?" I asked.

"There is one thing that puzzles me," he said by the light of the fire, which played along the lines and seams of his wise face.

"Oh?" I said. "Just one? Well, out with it, then."

"What was Cyrus Barker doing there before the event even began?"

"Aye, there's the rub."

We said our adieus and I hailed a cab as it passed the dark exterior of the museum. Rebecca was silent and I wondered if one of us had done something to put her off. Normally, I know what bone-headed mistake I make as soon as I make it, but not this time.

"What's wrong?" I asked, after waiting a few agonizing moments without either of us saying a word.

"I'm stupid," she said as she began searching through her clutch.

"What do you mean?"

"I mean, I'm uneducated. I was taught at the Jews' Free School, where a girl learns how to be a good Jew, but it doesn't prepare one for living in a world of Gentiles. I don't know what a sword of Damocles is. I can't participate in a conversation between two highly intelligent gentlemen. I thought I could, but I was wrong."

"Of course you did. You were wonderful!"

"Don't humor me, Thomas. I understand if I am going to be your wife that I shall have to learn a few things, and I don't mean sewing and piano playing. I must study, and I am out of practice."

"I could help you."

"No, I'd prefer not to be your pupil. Do you suppose Mr. Grant might be able to suggest some books for me to study?"

"That's like asking a dairyman if he could suggest a place to get milk. I'm sure he'd like to help you, and you know where he is to be found most nights from nine in the morning to nine at night."

"He seems a gentle sort."

"Yes. Obviously, he is something of a recluse," I replied. "His circle of friends could not form a circle at all. It would be good for both of you."

"He's very old-fashioned and courtly."

"I suspect he got his manners from a book, probably one a century old. I don't believe the chap's had much experience with the fair sex."

"I would need to study at the museum occasionally, I think, or find some titles to purchase."

"I'm sure he could suggest a few, and I have a membership at the Reading Room."

We rode on for a few minutes.

"Oh, very well," she said. "What is a sword of Damocles?"

"There once was a king . . ." I began.

# CHAPTER EIGHTEEN

Once we were safe and sound in Lion Street again, I excused myself and knocked at the corner of Barker's staircase.

"Come," his voice rumbled.

I went aloft. The Guv was in a nightshirt and robe, his large feet in slippers.

"How was your visit?"

"Interesting," I answered. "But then Liam Grant is an interesting fellow."

"Were you safe?" he asked. "You did not put your wife in any danger?"

"We were not followed, sir," I replied. "And there was no way the assassin could have known I was visiting the museum. We returned by a different route, and I do not believe there was a spot high enough in Newington to shoot from, save perhaps the Metropolitan Tabernacle, and the assassin wouldn't dare."

"He would. Assassins are not a pious people. Was it worth the effort?"

"I'll leave that for you to decide," I answered. "Mr. Grant informed me that there is an old legend of a tunnel between the palace and the Goat Tavern. I saw his map for myself."

Barker scratched his head. His hair was disheveled. He had been asleep in a chair by the fire when I knocked.

"A tunnel?" he repeated.

"Yes, sir. Times were dangerous when William of Orange was brought in to restore the monarchy in 1689. The palace was being enlarged."

"A good time to build an escape tunnel, then," he remarked.

"Indeed, unless it was already in place."

"You believe it possible that La Sylphide will return and use the tunnel to kill the tsarevich," the Guv said.

I nodded. "It's possible, certainly."

Barker considered the matter. His pipe lay on a round table at his elbow, I noticed, atop a copy of Gibbon's *History of the Decline and Fall of the Roman Empire,* volume 2.

"If one has a bucket, and there is a hole in it, it must be plugged."

"Agreed, Thomas. We shall look into the matter in the morning. Did Mr. Grant appear to find the legend believable?"

"He has made a subterranean map of all London, sir. The tunnel is on it, inked in sepia, which means he believes in the veracity of it, although there is no proof without investigating it."

"A map?" Barker asked, his mustache bowed in a small smile. Most people's countenances brighten when they smile. His became more devilish. "I should very much like to see that map, lad."

"Should we enquire about the tunnel tomorrow, then?"

"It is worth the effort, even if we prove the legend false. Good work, lad."

"Thank you, sir," I said. "See you in the morning."

"Good night, Thomas."

I was on the stair when he called again. "How did Mrs. Lle-welyn find your friend?"

"I believe she preferred him to me."

"Ah," he rumbled. "Sensible woman."

I grumbled on the way to our rooms. Rebecca was in front of her vanity, unpinning her hair.

"Sensible, indeed," she said.

"There is no privacy in this house. Henceforth, I shall be as silent as the tomb."

We arrived in Whitehall the following morning at seven-thirty precisely. The Guv is nothing if not punctual. He examined the morning post and attacked the first newspaper. It all concerned the royal wedding: who would attend and in what order they would appear in the procession, what the bride would be wear-ing, and whether the service would be long or short. The book-makers said long.

"When are we going to the palace?" I asked the Guv.

"No earlier than ten, I should say," he answered. "Most royals sleep late, then dawdle over their breakfast. I thought we might beard Mr. Pierce in his den first and put the matter before him."

"It seems as good a plan as any," I replied.

"I am pleased it meets with your approval, Mr. Llewelyn. Let us go and see if we can roust him from his chair. It is a good day to walk."

It was, indeed. The sun was out in Whitehall Street, but there were pockets of cool air in the shadows. Once we reached the Home Office we climbed the stair and asked for directions to Pierce's office.

Hesketh Pierce was in shirtsleeves with a cup of coffee in his hands when we arrived and knocked upon his door. He looked rumpled. I couldn't help thinking the man kept almost royal hours.

"Gentlemen," he said, running a hand over his slick, pomaded hair. "To what do I owe the pleasure?"

I looked about. Every inch of his office was taken up with maps—large ones of London, small ones marked with the parade route in red ink. One in particular caught Barker's attention, a map of Kensington Palace itself.

"Mr. Pierce, Mr. Llewelyn has come across a piece of information that you might find useful," Barker said. "We wish to trade it for a letter giving us official permission to investigate this case. We cannot go about claiming to be working for the tsar or Her Majesty's government or the Home Office if we have no proof. It slows the process."

Pierce looked down his patrician, Cambridge-educated nose at us. "No."

"Very well. When I find whoever has hired an assassin to kill the tsarevich, I will be certain to tell *The Times,* the *Daily Mail,* and every other newspaper who asks how the Home Office was not in any way helpful to our enquiry."

Pierce took a sip of his coffee and retrieved a silver case, extracting a cigarette. It took three strikes to get his Vesta lit, which is always demoralizing. Finally, he lit his cigarette and drew the smoke into his lungs. He was using the time to consider the request. The Guv did have an impressive record.

"How viable is this information?" Pierce asked.

"Not very, I admit, but it is necessary for you to investigate since we have no permission to do so."

"I will consider it."

"Very well," Barker said. "I will give you the information and rely upon the Home Office to do the proper thing. Have you ever heard a rumor about a tunnel connecting the palace to the Goat Tavern across Kensington High Street?"

"A tunnel?" Pierce repeated, sounding surprised. "Good heavens, no. Do you mean a recent one?"

"No," I answered. "One from the days of William of Orange, when the building was being renovated. At that time, it was dangerous to be a royal."

"It still is, Mr. Llewelyn," he replied. "Which is why I assume you are here. Who claims there is a tunnel there?"

"A scholar I consulted," I replied. "An amateur."

"Interested in tunnels, is he?" Pierce asked, sounding unimpressed.

"He works for the British Museum," I said, stretching the truth somewhat, "and is a collector of out-of-the-way information about London."

"Quite," Hesketh Pierce replied.

I began to feel foolish.

"Nevertheless," Cyrus Barker said, "the palace must be searched. The tunnel must be found, if it exists. You are charged with protecting the tsarevich. You must also protect the Duke of York, his fiancée, and the other royals who live there. It is your duty."

Pierce sighed. The Guv draws out one's better nature, whether one wants him to or not. The Home Office man was just learning that.

"Please do not lecture me about my duties, Mr. Barker," he replied. "It is too early in the morning. Very well, but we must search ourselves. The Queen's Guard, that is. We cannot have amateurs crawling all over the palace."

"Why, Mr. Pierce," Barker said, bristling. "We are not amateurs. We are professional enquiry agents. We have been hired."

"No doubt, but you cannot search the palace yourselves," Pierce insisted. "I'm afraid that is final."

My partner bowed. "We understand. What about the letter?"

"Oh, ruddy hell. If it will get you out of here."

After the Home Office man scribbled a note on a piece of official stationary, the Guv led us outside. I could see the frustration on his face.

"This could all be for nothing," I reminded my partner.

"It could, indeed."

"A good number of my ideas come to nothing all the time."

"I've noticed that," Barker answered.

"But still," I replied.

"Aye, still," he said. For a moment, he paused, deep in thought. A moment later, he spoke. "If we cannot examine the palace cellars, let us try at the other end."

We hailed a cab and Barker ordered the driver to take us to Kensington. We stopped in front of the palace, but the Guv did not enter the gate. In fact, he turned away.

"The Goat Tavern, of course!" I said, realizing at once what he was up to. There are two ends to every tunnel. "What incentive shall you offer the publican to have a look 'round his establishment?"

"Let us see. One is bound to come to mind."

Barker grasped his wrist behind him and walked with his head down, pondering things. I liked when he pondered things. It was a good sign.

We crossed the street and stepped into the shade of the entrance. Despite the warmth outside, it was cool inside the building.

"Two porters, please," I said to the barman. There were empty tables everywhere, but the Guv hooked his boot on the rail in front of the bar. I watched the ale being poured into pint glasses. The barman took his time, pouring slowly, which is the proper way to respect a dark ale. Good stout should never be rushed. Barker took a long draught, put his glass down, wiped the foam from his mustache with a crooked finger, and spoke.

"Sir," he said to the man. The latter was as burly as my partner, with a curling mustache and thinning hair. He looked a no-nonsense sort of fellow. He would not take it nor give it. "We would see your cellar, if you please."

The man's eyes narrowed. It must have been a while since anyone challenged him, and in his own mansion, so to speak.

"The devil you say."

"I am working with the Home Office," Barker said, and pulled the folded paper from his pocket.

"I don't care if you bring a note from God Almighty. You're not seeing my cellar," the man replied.

"You're retired navy, are you not?"

As the Guv spoke, I noticed the anchor tattooed on the man's forearm.

"What of it?"

"Mason?"

"Don't have no truck with secret societies."

"Ah," Barker said. "Churchman?"

"Nor them, neither."

"Payment, then. Would twenty pounds suffice?"

"Here now, clear off."

"Fifty pounds, then, just to look about your cellar."

"Hop it!" the man said, lifting an ugly-looking club from under the bar. From the scratches and dents in it, it looked well used.

"No self-respecting publican would refuse fifty pounds to look about an empty storeroom," Barker said to me. "Our friend here is hiding something."

The barman rose his club and brought it down on what he hoped would be Barker's head, but the Guv rose his left arm and caught the blow with his forearm. Had it been my arm it would have snapped like kindling, but my partner's arm was all sinew and muscle from running a sailing vessel in the South China Sea. Also, I heard the clang of metal, and remembered that he always kept a knife in a leather sheath strapped to his wrist.

The Guv reached forward, curled a hand around the man's thick neck, and slammed his head forward into the edge of the bar. It sounded like the thump of a melon. I leaned over the bar and watched as the fellow slid down to his knees and fell over onto his side. The club made a rattling sound on the stone floor as it rolled and came to a standstill.

We were not alone. There were perhaps ten people in the room, enjoying a pint and an early lunch. A cook came out of the kitchen wiping his hands on a rag, and looked at his employer lying insensible on the floor.

"I suggest you bring a constable and an ambulance, sir," Barker said nonchalantly. "This poor fellow has injured himself."

The cook looked at us, glanced at the prone publican behind the bar, and then studied the people in their chairs, who had turned to look at us with their pints in their hands.

"Go!" Barker growled.

The cook dropped his rag and ran out the door. We walked around the end of the bar and looked at the barman. There was an angry welt above his brow.

"His skull looks thick enough," he said. "I shall stay here, but you've got perhaps three minutes to inspect the cellar."

I crossed to an unmarked door and opened it. It was a public water closet, but there was a curving stairwell at the far end. I descended it quickly. The stair continued down two flights, but I expected that. The lower the basement, the cooler the temperature to store ale barrels therein.

The stair opened onto a square room lined with old timbers and crumbling plaster. There were shelves containing glasses, plates, and equipment of the restaurant trade. The rest of the cellar was taken up with barrels of all sizes, brands, and types, some stacked haphazardly upon the others. I tried to push one and found it near impossible to move, but I heard the slosh of beer within. I climbed on top of it and worked out which direction the palace was in relation to the Goat. I was facing a wall. There was no tunnel that I could see. I looked about, tried to move the smaller barrels, and poked my nose anywhere I could put it. I hunted for spring catches that might suddenly reveal an opening. There was nothing.

Coming up the stair, I cursed under my breath. *No tunnel*, I thought. Why had I trusted Liam Grant? He was a friend, of course, and I had few of those, but he was a bit of a one-off, an eccentric even by Barker's standards.

Returning to the bar I found a constable already in residence.

"You're saying this fellow burst in here and demanded to see your cellar?" the officer asked, writing in a notebook.

The publican was seated in a chair, looking both angry and dizzy. The redness extended to his entire face.

"Yes," he shouted. "Stop making me sound like an idiot!"

"Well, stop sounding like one. Why would a stranger demand to see your cellar? And if they burst in, why are there two half-finished pint glasses here on the bar?"

"There was a difference of opinion, Constable," Barker said. "Blows were traded, but no one was permanently damaged."

"Mr. Barker, is it? Did you want to see this man's cellar?"

"I did."

"I see," the constable said, taking in Barker's size and generally threatening appearance. "And why was that, sir?"

"I cannot tell you."

The constable, who was a stout veteran with gray in his mustache, eyed him as if he, too, was thinking of clubbing him. "And why not?"

"It is palace business."

The Guv reached into his coat again and pulled the letter from his pocket. The Met officer took the letter and read it, studying it for some time. I don't believe he spent his evenings in libraries.

"Home Office," he said, looking at the publican as if to say "Quit wasting my time." "So, are you going to inspect the cellar?"

I spoke up. "I already have."

"And who are you, sir?" the constable asked.

"I'm his partner," I replied, handing him my business card.

"Nice card. Did you find what you were looking for, sir?"

"I'm afraid I did not. There was a rumor about a tunnel leading to the palace, but it seems to have been a prank from the newspaper. Still, we had to investigate it."

The publican pointed at us both. "I demand this man be arrested!" he said. "Both of them."

"As many in this room will attest," Barker said, "you were the one who struck the first blow. I merely defended myself. I'm a good friend of the commissioner, by the way. He is aware of my connection in this matter. The wedding, you know."

As a private enquiry agent, one is often called upon to invent a story on the spot and make it sound convincing. However, nothing can improve upon the unvarnished truth. The constable didn't care about tunnels and altercations in public houses, which happen too frequently to mention. He had a beat and he had to maintain it according to schedule.

The constable bent over and spoke to the publican as if he were hard of hearing or perhaps simpleminded.

"I'm sure you won't be pressing charges, sir," he said. "That would require shutting down your establishment for the day and questioning each and every person in this room over and over again."

The barman turned. Every patron was now glaring at him. They had come in for lunch. They had no intention to stay for dinner also. And of course, if the Goat Tavern closed for a day, a great deal of revenue would be lost.

"No harm done, I suppose," the man grumbled.

"What was that, sir?" asked the constable, who was near enough to hear every word.

"I said no harm done!"

The officer smiled. "You heard the man," he said to the crowd. "No harm done."

Everyone looked relieved and hurried out the door before something else happened. The publican looked sulky. The constable looked genial, like a father after his daughter's wedding. And Barker? He just looked like Barker, expressionless behind that mustache and those black spectacles.

"Good day, gentlemen," the constable said, tugging at his helmet.

"We'll be on our way then, Constable," Barker said. "May I have that letter back?"

The officer handed it over, and the Guv slipped it into his pocket again.

It had been dim inside the Goat, and stepping out into the day was dazzling. Hansoms and goods vans bowled by and the street was thick with pedestrians. It was an ordinary day, at least for them. There are no ordinary days for private enquiry agents.

"I'm sorry, sir," I said. "I shouldn't have trusted Grant."

"No, it was right to find out for certain. I'm glad the theory came to light, if only to disprove it. This is far better than finding out there was a tunnel that we didn't know about. Not every clue is helpful, but each must be investigated. I almost wish you had found it. A secret tunnel is always of interest, and as Mr. Grant pointed out, London is honeycombed with them. I really must make your friend's acquaintance. And congratulations."

"For what?"

"You have got yourself a Watcher."

Watchers. It was Barker's term for those with particular information or skills that might help us that only they could provide. Every Watcher could be relied upon to help us move a case along.

"So I have."

"That is two during this case, in fact," the Guv continued. "Mr. Zangwill provided the information about the Socialist League."

*My own Watchers,* I thought to myself. *Imagine that.*

# CHAPTER NINETEEN

It was another warm day. Soon the wealthy would begin fleeing the city for ocean breezes or cooler climes. The rest of London, and those of us there to defend them, would swelter in the heat and long for the cool of the evening. I wanted to go to Lion Street and stand in the kitchen pantry with the icebox open. It would be the coolest spot in a mile.

We had fled our steaming chambers and were standing on the Victoria Embankment in the vain hope that a breeze would come across the water. We were standing by Cleopatra's Needle, an obelisk that was carved in this kind of weather and should be accustomed to it.

"Do you think your friend Mr. Zangwill could provide information on Miss Marx of the Socialist League?"

"I should say so," I answered. "The man's been half in love with her for a while."

"Oh, really?" Barker said, smiling. "Your friend is a little Lothario, eh?"

"He falls in love at the drop of a hat, but it never works out well. Generally, he loves women who are far too good-looking. Israel is very intelligent, as you've seen, but he shall never be a matinee idol. He's a modern-day Hans Christian Andersen."

Barker looked at me blankly. The immense number of things he knows is balanced by the sheer number of things he doesn't.

"He was a storyteller from Denmark," I explained. "He was in love with Jenny Lind, among others. Do you recall Amy Levy?"

"That was the friend of Miss Potter in one of our old cases, as I recall. You told me she was a poetess."

"She was prone to melancholy and killed herself. Israel was cast down about that for a long time. He's a sensitive fellow, you know."

"Back to Miss Marx. Can Mr. Zangwill help us?" Barker said, trying to sound patient, but not completely succeeding.

"We need not bother him," I answered. "I know nearly as much as Israel even without going to her meetings. She's something of a marvel. She's a distinguished actress. Israel and I saw her in *A Doll's House* and *Hedda Gabler*. She's also a translator of novels and plays: *Madame Bovary. An Enemy of the People*—most of Ibsen's works, in fact. She writes monthly articles for Morris's *Commonweal* magazine, the mouthpiece of the Socialist League. And I've heard she used to play under her father Karl's desk while he wrote *Das Kapital*. She has the mind of an economist, as well. William Morris brought his illustrious name to the organization, but she has done all the work."

"You sound enamored of her, lad, and you a married man."

"Oh, no," I said, laughing. "She's too good at everything. It's intimidating."

"I should like to meet this person," Barker continued. "Tell me, does she strike you as a person who might hire an assassin?"

"I would not put it past her. In one play, she performed Hedda Gabler, the character who shot her husband for his brutishness. It was . . ." I stopped as a thought occurred to me. "Oh my word. 'La Sylphide' in French is feminine. Do you suppose our assassin is a woman?"

Barker considered the matter, crossing his arms. "It does not take brute strength to pull a trigger. In fact, the pistol is a great leveler, I find."

"Yes," I agreed. "Especially as far as murder is concerned."

"You are the wordsmith, Thomas. Tell me, what exactly is a sylphide?"

"It is a spirit of the air, a creature untethered to the land, a fairy of sorts. I believe it is Greek in origin."

The Guv stared at the river before him, his mind working. "Spirit of the air. Air rifle. Someone shooting down on his or her victims from a height. From a distance. Yes, it all fits together rather well."

"That doesn't mean it is Eleanor Marx."

"No, lad," he replied. "But it doesn't mean it isn't."

Eleanor Marx lived in Sydenham, far south of commercial London, not far from where Prince Albert's Crystal Palace stood. It was a leafy suburban neighborhood bordering on the bucolic to those of us familiar with the hustle and bustle of Whitehall. Miss Marx's house was an attractive redbrick home with a large white bow window. As we arrived, I seized the knocker first and rapped. When Barker does so, it sounds like an assault upon the house.

A very proper-looking maid answered the door and looked at us primly down her nose. She did not approve of our appearance, I think. We did not pass muster.

"Yes?" she said, but it was more of a challenge.

Barker presented her with his card, but she seemed no more impressed.

"I'll see if Miss is taking visitors today," she said, closing the door in our faces. Barker looked at me and shook his head as if he found our treatment amusing. I decided to be philosophical as well. There did not appear to be any men about and suddenly a pair of toughs appear at the door uninvited. I wouldn't have invited the Guv in myself under such circumstances.

The door opened again and the maid said, "Come this way, please," in a tone that showed that what she was doing was altogether beneath the dignity of her office and she was only trying to please "Miss." We were led through a tastefully arranged house that was decorated with a mix of Regency and Art Nouveau. At the end of a hall was a sort of study that made me think of William Morris. Not because it was messy, which it wasn't, but because, like his, her room was designed to be used for a number of purposes. She wrote manifestos here, translated books from various languages, memorized lines from a play, and wrote speeches.

As we entered, Eleanor Marx stood in the center of the room holding the card between her fingers. She was taller than I expected her to be and quite a handsome woman.

"Which of you is Cyrus Barker?" she asked.

"I am he, miss," the Guv said, bowing.

"And what may I do for you?"

"We have a few questions to put to you, if we may," he replied. "We've already spoken with Mr. Morris."

"Dear old Morris," she murmured. "How is the dear?"

"Gouty," I said.

"Yes," she answered, nodding. "He suffers so. May I call for tea?"

"Not on our account, Miss Marx," Barker replied. "This is my associate, Mr. Llewelyn. He saw you perform in *A Doll's House*."

"Did he?" she asked, raising a brow. "Imagine that. You have questions for me, then? About what?"

"No doubt you are aware of the recent attack upon Prince George in Kensington," he said. "We are working in conjunction with the Home Office to hunt the individuals responsible for the attack."

"And the trail led you to my door?" she asked.

"Aye, but merely to find information. Mr. Morris suggested that there has been a growing division in the Socialist League in the past few years between the Socialist and anarchist factions."

"Has he?" she said. "Well, Mr. Morris is mistaken. There is no division in our organizations. We are unified toward a common goal. They are our brothers and sisters in the fight against capitalist oppression. I assume you are looking for the anarchist Kazimir Chernov."

"His name is on our list, but we are not hunting him especially. We do wish to speak with him, but he is one among others."

"I shall not turn him over to the calloused hands of Scotland Yard."

"Miss Marx," I said. "We are not from Scotland Yard."

"Worse, then. Were you not seen speaking to Pyotr Rachkovsky the other day? Your appearance is unmistakable."

"I was," Barker admitted. "We speak to people. This is what we do. I am no more a crony of the Russian secret police because I spoke with them than I am a translator because I speak with you."

"In fact," I interjected, "Mr. Rachkovsky had a difference of opinion with us that resulted in some damages to our chambers."

"And yet I see no sign of it upon your faces."

Barker gave a low smile. "The day a Scot canna down a simple Russian would be a day of mourning in auld Edinburgh. The gentlemen were of little consequence."

"You're a strange man, Mr. Barker. I don't know whether to take what you say seriously. Surely you do not expect me, the leader of the Socialist League, to turn over one of my members to you? I don't even know what a 'private enquiry agent' is. I don't know you, yet you want me to produce Mr. Chernov, as if he were hiding behind my apron."

"We demand nothing, Miss Marx," Barker replied. "This is England. We are not Cossacks. Our aim is to verify his innocence if possible, and get on with our enquiry. Should he indeed be behind your apron, then produce him that we may be on our way."

She put her hands on her hips and frowned. The woman was formidable.

"Hand him over to you?"

"I don't want you to hand him over," the Guv replied. "A civil conversation with the man is all I ask. You may be present. It can be in this very room if you wish. I'll not hide plainclothes detectives in the bushes. I'm trying to keep the prince and the tsarevich from being assassinated."

"But they are nothing," she answered with contempt in her voice. "Less than nothing. Pampered members of the aristocracy, being trained to oppress others out of a sense of entitlement. There is no difference between the prince inside his palace, drinking champagne from a golden goblet, and the man outside tending his royal garden."

"I agree with you, Miss Marx, but as human beings, neither young man deserves to have his skulls punctured by an assassin's bullet. Aristocrats are no better, madam, but they are no less."

The two of them stood and stared at each other.

"Would you care to sit down?" she asked. "And do you still refuse tea?"

"Thank you, ma'am," he said, taking a seat opposite our hostess. "Miss Marx, Mr. Llewelyn tells me that you possess a nimble mind. Let us play a little game, if you will humor me. An intellectual exercise. I shall build up a case against you, spontaneously, and then you shall tear it down again. Will you play?"

She looked at him, trying to decide, and finally nodded.

"Miss Marx, your organization is composed, in large part, of men and women who fled the pogroms in Russia. The tsarevich, who represents the tsar of the future, has arrived here on this soil. Prince George, also a future leader of his country, is in London as well, whose wedding costs would have been better spent feeding the poor or providing medicine for the infirmed. The Okhrana has been informed that an assassin has been hired to kill Nicholas. There is no available information about this assassin save an odd name, La Sylphide."

"The Sylph," she murmured.

"Aye," Barker continued. "Mr. Llewelyn and I were hypothesizing no more than an hour ago that this assassin might be a woman. The moniker is feminine. Any woman can lift a loaded pistol and pull a trigger, particularly if she has been properly trained."

"In *Hedda Gabler*," I said, "you gave a very realistic performance of a woman who shoots her husband due to his terrible behavior. You handled a pistol very well, Miss Marx. I wondered if you might own a revolver yourself."

She had reclined on a black velvet fainting couch and now watched us both with some degree of fascination. Her dress was of a vibrant blue. She hugged a cushion to her breast, but laid it aside and sat up.

"Mr. Barker, surely you can do better than this," she said. "Your reasoning is flimsy, connected with a tissue of coincidence and conjecture. You create a straw man, or rather, a straw woman, then try to connect her to me. I don't know who she is, but I assure you I am not stalking London to kill a visiting royal. Royals are ridiculous, and from what I have heard so far, he is not going to improve the bloodline."

"Continue," the Guv said.

"Just because I have played a woman who shoots her husband does not mean I contemplate killing the tsarevich myself or even paying someone to kill him for me," she replied. "The young man is already living in a country on the verge of revolution. I needn't do anything. He will meet an assassin soon enough. It will soon be the twentieth century. That boy staying in Kensington Palace has done nothing yet, but the anarchists would hang him, shoot him, or throw a bomb under his carriage, as they did to his grandfather. He represents something, the poor thing.

"And yes, Mr. Barker, I was trained to use a pistol," she continued. "I insisted upon learning how to use one. There is nothing in theater that I despise more than an actor who has not taken the trouble to learn something that his or her character is supposed to do. I could shoot Nicholas myself but I choose not to. It is not the way to win hearts. It makes us an enemy, taking on a fledgling tsar. It makes us bullies. That will not bring people to our cause. I would argue, therefore, Mr. Barker, that we are the last ones in London who want the tsarevich killed, because no matter who has been hired to kill him, we shall receive the lion's share of the blame."

Barker nodded. "Very good, madam. You argue well. Tell me, do you fear for your people? Do you feel as I do that something shall happen in the next few days?"

She stared at him solemnly. "Mr. Barker, I believe I do. I have not slept in two days. Perhaps I should send the members of the League away, to Liverpool or Manchester, I thought, but I decided not to. If a bullet took down a royal or a foreign dignitary, it will be viewed as an attempt to provide an alibi. Wouldn't it be ironic if the assassin were paid his thirty pieces of silver, while our ragged members receive the blame?"

"A churchgoer, ma'am?" I asked.

She laughed. Her voice was a rich alto, perfect for the stage. "A figure of speech. One must speak in terms that one's audience understands."

"Tell me, Miss Marx," Barker continued, "is it that you fear your flock will be blamed for something they did not do, or that among them there is one who will fix the blame on all of you?"

Eleanor Marx regarded the Guv. "I cannot answer that, sir. If

I say no, then I am a fool. If I say yes, but it were not so, then I have become jaded and should pass the reins to someone else."

She rose a palm to her eye and her shoulders slumped. "I am so tired, gentlemen. Are we done with the questions?"

"Come, Thomas," my partner said. "Let the woman rest. Thank you for seeing us, Miss Marx."

We rose and nodded and were seen out the front door by the prim maid.

On the way along the stone path to the street I said to the Guv, "She is an actress. A professional. There is no way to say whether she is lying or telling the truth."

"She argues well, but she made a fatal mistake, lad. I said that there was an assassin. I never said that someone had been hired to kill the tsarevich. 'Save me, Lord, from lying lips and deceitful tongues.' Psalms 120:2."

# CHAPTER TWENTY

I heard the outer door of our office open and a brush of fabric sweep along the floor. It made me stop writing, although I did not look up from my paper.

"Hello, Miss F.," Jenkins said a trifle loudly.

She turned with another rustle and would have disappeared if the Guv hadn't called her back.

"Miss Fletcher!"

Sarah Fletcher entered our chambers. I tried not to stare. She was dressed like a Salvation Army matron with a blue bonnet, a tightly corseted dress of the same color, and a small red shield pinned to her bosom. It was an actual uniform. *Ah,* I thought to myself. *Very good, Miss Fletcher.* A Salvation Army worker would be the only genteel woman brave enough to travel easily in the Tower Hamlets of the East End.

"Mr. Barker."

"Come in," he said, waving her to a visitor's chair. "Would you care for some tea?"

"Thank you, no," she said, perching on the very edge of the chair.

Barker turned to me and explained her presence. "I asked Miss Fletcher to watch Jim Hercules, and see what he is about."

"Has he given you any cause to suspect him of something?"

"No," he answered. "I am merely being thorough. Report, please, miss."

She folded her hands over her reticule and spoke. "Mr. Hercules left Kensington Palace at approximately ten o'clock this morning. He had a shave and haircut near Dover Street, then went into a tobacconist and purchased a small cigar, no larger than a cigarette. He lit it in front of the door. He looked in shopwindows, and was particularly interested in a display of ties and pocket handkerchiefs, then he went into a public house for either a late breakfast or an early lunch. Then he hailed a cab. I followed."

The Guv nodded, knitting his fingertips together on the glass-topped desk. "Continue."

"We stopped in Oxford Street and went into a building," she said. "It was a house, really, built perhaps early this century. At first, I thought it was a residence. I paid the cabman and alighted. Then I waited, walking back and forth as far as I could go in either direction and still view the premises. I reasoned if he left the building and found a cab I could do the same and not lose him."

"Sensible."

"Thank you," she replied. "He was in there an awfully long time, three-quarters of an hour before he left. I saw an Asian man leave and suspected it was a gentleman's club that catered to foreign guests."

I could picture him, a single man in a strange city. He gets his hair cut and a shave. He buys a cigar, then has a meal and an ale. Then he stops into a club to read the newspapers. It was a satisfactory way to spend an afternoon off duty.

"He called for another cab and it took him to a second public house, the Cromwell Arms in Exhibition Road."

"How long was it after his previous meal?"

"An hour and a quarter."

My partner leaned back in his chair. "Curious."

"Yes," she replied. "I dared step into the entrance and looked about. He was shaking hands with a man at one of the tables. It was a meeting. I'd have watched longer but the publican shooed me out the door."

"A pity," Barker said, glancing at me. "But you did very well. Could you describe the gentleman he met?"

"He was about thirty or thirty-five, well dressed in a gray cut-away coat and gaiters. Clean-shaven, brown hair."

"Light or dark?"

"Light, I'd say. Most women would find the man attractive."

"Did he seem well-bred?" I asked.

"How can one tell?"

"I suppose you can't. You just know." I turned to the Guv. "Hesketh Pierce, sir. I'd stake my reputation on it."

"Interesting," the Guv said, frowning. He turned to Miss Fletcher. "You did not stay beyond that time?"

"Actually, I followed him back to the palace."

"Satisfactory." Barker leaned back in his chair and regarded her steadily. "Miss Fletcher, I have been told that you are not presently comfortable in your business arrangements, in particular, your office. Is this true?"

"I don't know how you came by this information, sir," she replied, coloring.

"And you won't, Miss Fletcher, I assure you. Answer the question, please."

She was taken aback. Sarah Fletcher had learned that working for Cyrus Barker is not all beer and skittles.

"I would not malign Mr. Hewitt's good name, Mr. Barker," she said after a moment. "He has been very generous to me."

J. M. Hewitt was a friend of ours, a detective who often took cases that for one reason or another we could not. He was a good fellow, but he did have one weakness. Sarah Fletcher was that weakness. I was concerned that he might take advantage of the situation and had mentioned it to the Guv a few months ago. I had forgotten all about it.

"Does his generosity have restrictions?"

Her nose turned red. She wasn't comfortable having her private life probed.

"He has only been a gentleman," she said, smoothing her dress.

"Nevertheless, I understand he is pressing you."

"He is," she admitted.

"Have you considered moving offices?" Barker continued, tapping his finger on the desk. "After all, yours is at the very end of the court and few female clients are willing to travel deep into our narrow and dubious street."

"Of course, sir, but most 'To-Let's require a down payment and a month's rent, which is very dear."

"You are in a predicament, lass," he said.

She cleared her throat and looked away.

"I have an office to let of my own," he stated. "It is vacant and gathering dust. Would you care to see it?"

"Perhaps," she replied, being cautious. She was already in an uncomfortable situation. "Is it far?"

The Guv rose a finger toward the ceiling overhead. "One floor above us, in fact. Number five."

She looked up as if the roof would come down. "On what terms, Mr. Barker, sir?"

"Not onerous, I assure you. There is one stipulation, however."

Her eyes narrowed as she waited for him to continue.

"I like silence," he said. "You must purchase a large carpet. You are not given to humming, are you?"

"No, sir, I am not. However, I do have a typing service."

"Thomas bangs away on his typewriting machine every day. I barely notice when he uses it anymore."

Sarah Fletcher looked down at her shoes and swallowed. Then she looked up again. "And the cost? How much per month?"

Barker looked slightly pained. He is loath to discuss money. "Whatever you were paying before, I suppose. You may discuss terms with Mr. Llewelyn."

Her eyes went wide, and with good reason. That office nearly facing Whitehall Street was worth a good deal of money. Solicitors, clerks, military leaders, and even MPs would like an office so conveniently located. I didn't even want to think about how much the Guv could have charged.

"Would you like to see it?" I asked. "I could take you upstairs. I'll get the key."

I pulled it from a cubby of my desk. I thought there was a distinct possibility that she might become emotional. She seemed to be just holding it in. Whether from a male or a female, the Guv dislikes an obvious display of emotion. No noise, no discussing money, no sentiment allowed. There is a set of rules one must navigate to live in the orbit of Cyrus Barker.

"Come along, then," I said, shepherding her out for both their sakes.

I led her out into the waiting room, where Jenkins looked up from the pages of a penny dreadful.

"This door here leads into your stairwell," I said, "but it remains locked at all times. You enter number five from outside."

"Why isn't it seven-A and seven-B?" she asked.

"Barker and I have discussed this. I've looked at the earliest records and we have come to the same conclusion. Which is to say, we have no idea. At this point, it is unknowable."

We stepped outside and I unlocked the outside door, leading her into a very small foyer with barely enough room to turn around.

"It's a bit dusty," I admitted. "You might convince Mr. Barker to have it painted."

We climbed the stairs.

"That's a clever outfit, by the way," I remarked. "Did you purchase it in the East End?"

"No, I made it. That is, I dyed the dress and bonnet blue and sewed the cape. The pin I found in the pet—in Middlesex Street."

She'd nearly said "petticoat" in a man's presence. It would have been a scandal.

"As I said, clever. Here we are."

I unlocked the door and led us into a room which was identical to our own. In fact, we had used this one as our office when the one below was damaged in a bombing. It was empty apart from a large desk and chair in the center of the room.

Miss Fletcher stepped in and put both hands to her mouth. "I had not realized how big it would be."

"It's bare," I agreed. "When the bookshelves are filled and furniture put in, it will seem smaller."

"It's far too grand," she said, gesturing at the large room. "My agency is small. I could never use so much space."

The thought had not occurred to me. I looked about the room with a critical eye.

"There's another room behind this door, as well," I said. "I suppose it could be a flat. That's not a bad idea, in fact. The Guv has mentioned he wished there was someone around in the evenings to watch over the offices. Of course, you realize that there could be an element of danger in taking these rooms."

She was still taking it all in. I could imagine she was planning it all out in her mind's eye, fancying herself in such a position.

"Here you are," I said, holding out the keys. "By the way, how much was your rent with Hewitt?"

She named a trifling sum. I resisted the impulse to raise a brow, but I sensed he charged her little rent in order to have her about.

"I'll work out a contract this week," I continued. "Payment at the first of the month. We can discuss everything else later. That is, if you want the room."

"I do."

I left her there in the center of the room, blinking at her own good fortune.

Coming down the stairwell, it came to me. She had become a project to Barker. He was going to aid her, help her, and rehabilitate her, as he had with me and Mac and Jeremy. Probably Etienne and maybe even Ho. He had been gruff, even rude, to hide the fact that he was being a Good Samaritan. He doesn't like having his help acknowledged. It embarrasses him.

Although I would not number Miss Fletcher among my favorite people, if the Guv chose her I would do my best to help her.

"The office is very large for one small woman," I said to Barker when I returned to the office. "The thought occurred to me that it could be used as both an office and a flat. That way we would have someone on the premises at all times. A caretaker, if you will."

"Would she be safe on the premises at night?" he asked.

"No less so than during the day. The floor was blown out from under us two years ago while we were in the office. She has faced danger before."

Barker grunted, docketing the information. "Find out if she has any requirements."

"I noticed the stairwell needs to be painted," I said. "Female sensibilities and all that. Nor hers, I mean her clients'. We are fortunate that people can walk right into our offices from the street, while her potential clients climb a steep staircase to reach hers."

"Done. Can you think of anything else?"

"I don't know how much a caretaker makes per day. It might be simpler to let her the room in exchange for caretaking duties."

"A free flat and free offices, freshly renovated, in exchange for caretaking duties, which are negligible? Have you become her solicitor?"

I rose both hands. "Miss Fletcher is practically a stranger to me. I was thinking of your reputation. The first floor should be done as professionally as the ground floor, shouldn't it? You are a landlord now."

"Of course it should!"

"There you are, then," I said, nodding. "I'll find a painting contractor and get an estimate."

"Do it, lad."

I stepped outside and climbed the stairwell again. Sarah Fletcher was sitting on the edge of the desk, looking about.

"We'll hire a painter shortly. I'm to get a bid."

I turned to go.

"Mr. Llewelyn?" she called after me.

"Yes?"

"Thank you."

"Don't thank me," I replied. "It is Mr. Barker's decision."

I smiled as I went downstairs. Nothing is so discomfiting as kindness from a rival.

# CHAPTER TWENTY-ONE

S o," I said when I had returned to our chambers, "Jim Hercules is conspiring with Hesketh Pierce."

"So it would appear," Barker answered. He had lit his largest pipe, the size of a small ham, and was trying to fill the entire chamber with its smoke. I believe it represented Moses, but it's difficult to tell one biblical patriarch from another.

"What do you intend to do?" I asked.

The Guv opened his desk and took out a sheet of stationery. He scrawled a message, folded it, and handed it to me. "Give this to a messenger boy with a shilling. Have him take it to Kensington Palace."

"The chances are fifty percent he won't reach it. He'd be terrified."

"Tell him I demand he deliver it," Barker replied. "We'll see which prospect terrifies him more."

I stepped out and into Whitehall Street. Finding an urchin

is rather like catching a trout with a fly. One looks for the fish, lays out a line for him, and as he passes, you snag him on the hook.

"Ger' off!" the boy cried as I took hold of his arm. "Lemme go!"

I held up the shilling and he instantly stopped struggling. "Good. Now what's your name, boy?"

"Dicky Smiff!"

"Very well, Dicky Smiff. This is one to tell your friends about. I want you to take this note to Kensington Palace."

"G'arn!"

"No, I'm serious. I want you to find a guard and tell him to give this message to Corporal Dinsdale. Repeat that back to me."

"Um, take it to the palace. Find a redcoat. Tell him to give it to the bloke named Dinsdale. That'll be a shilling and sixpence."

"This is a shilling."

"I'm prolly gonna be socked by a guard. They don't like rabble like us there. Shilling and six or no."

I gave him the sixpence, wondering what he would do with the money. It was a large sum for so small a tyke. He could stuff himself with sweets or take it home to feed his family.

"Off with you," I said as we parted company. I went back inside our chambers and sat down at my desk. "Dinsdale, eh?"

"Indeed," the Guv answered. "He'll give it to Jim Hercules. It would be too suspicious to have an Abyssinian Guard receiving the message directly. I invited him for a friendly sparring match at our antagonistics school."

"How friendly?" I asked.

"That will depend on how forthcoming he is."

He looked at a slip of paper in his hand, his pipe clenched between his teeth, as he belched smoke. I recognized the paper. Sarah Fletcher had given it to him.

"Get your stoutest stick, Thomas. Miss Fletcher has given us the address of Kazimir Chernov. It is in Woodseer Street."

I spent a moment looking over a map of London in my head.

"Woodseer Street? That's about as far from the palace as a man can go, and I don't mean distance."

"We can't do anything about the location, lad," Barker said. "One can only go where the work is."

Outside, Barker hailed a cab. Normally, that is my duty. I believe he was on the scent and eager to find his prey. He certainly gave the springs in the cab some exercise.

"Brick Lane!" he bawled in my ear.

Cyrus Barker loathes anarchists. Socialists may rally, and Communists protest, but an anarchist simply destroys. It seems to be their only solution. Does the government need reform? Blow it up. Is the tsar intolerant? Assassinate him. Is a church too controlling of its parishioners? Burn it to the ground.

"They don't do anything by halves, these anarchists," I said. "It's all or nothing. Like hiring an assassin to kill a young man who hasn't done anything yet."

"It would certainly punish the current tsar, who had Sophia Perovskaya executed for planning his father's murder."

"I don't remember hearing of her before."

"You'd have been in school at the time. She was a nihilist, though no more than a girl. She was such a zealot that she was arrested numerous times before she was twenty-five. Each time she was released from prison she had become more revolutionary in her opinions. Finally, she planned the assassination of Alexander the Second. Afterward, she was captured, of course. The Okhrana knew her face too well by then, and Perovskaya had done little to hide her feelings. She never denied her role in the tsar's death as some of her compatriots did. She was the first woman in Russia to be hanged for terrorism."

"What makes a young woman do such a thing?" I asked.

"A tsar who kills all dissidents and Jewish peasants would do for a start. Saint Petersburg has become a crucible for anarchy, and the Russian government has exported it by expelling its dissidents."

"Thereby endangering the next generation of tsars," I remarked. "The spores have been released and now they will choke the heir."

"Not if we can help it, lad, if only for Jim Hercules's sake."

"He's up to some mischief," I said.

"Aye, but he's still our client."

The warren in Woodseer Street was a row of attached houses of red brick in a poor but respectable neighborhood. The properties had probably belonged to an absentee landlord or one who had no care about the property as long as the money was paid. The brick was chipped and green with mildew, and every bit of wood in the building was warped and cracked. One could grasp it and it would crumble in your hand. The people here were the lowest rung of society: young women without proper teeth, children on crutches, pale men who had one foot in the grave and swarthy ones who preyed upon the rest. It was a web. They were caught in it and they knew the spider was coming eventually. Some had grown weary of waiting.

Barker plunged in and I behind him. My nose protested immediately at the odor of cabbage and spoiled meat. Their bodies and clothes hadn't seen water in months. At some point the tenants had stopped trying to live. They were merely existing, alcohol and opium their only comfort now.

Barker seized a passing man by the shoulder. He was so shattered I heard the shoulder separate from the socket momentarily.

"Kazimir Chernov," the Guv growled in his ear.

"Second floor, t'other end," he replied.

"Have you seen him lately?"

The man shrugged and shook his head. I didn't know if he was drunk or merely apathetic. We continued down the hall.

"Stay vigilant," Barker said. "And show no mercy."

We were about a hundred yards down the length of the corridor on the second floor when a door opened and a man seized the lapel of Barker's jacket. My partner peeled the man's fingers off the fabric and then I heard the snap of the man's wrist. He screamed and dropped something at my feet. It was an open razor. Barker kicked it into a corner and continued onward. The scream was a warning to others to give us a wide berth. I tapped my pocket where I carried my Webley, just in case.

The men left us alone after that but the women came out to look at us. They smiled and winked and made low remarks and offers as we passed by. A hand slipped into my pocket, touched the cold metal of the pistol, and withdrew quickly. A greasy finger slid along my cheek. *This must be what hell is like,* I thought to myself. For all of us there.

"Chernov!" Barker rumbled at a man, who pointed at a room at the far end of the hall. My partner began to trot, and when he reached the far end he kicked in the door, which slammed against the wall. Barker walked in and stood in the middle of the room with his hands on his hips.

"Empty," he said

I looked about the narrow flat. There was a chair broken in pieces. Bedclothes were strewn about, and a pillow had left a dull stain on the wall. A pipe was broken in two and a hole was burnt in the blanket beside it. It was a wonder the entire warren hadn't gone up in flames like a tinderbox.

There was no fire in the grate, and though I felt no heat in the embers, there was a pot of beans hanging by a hook. It had congealed and cockroaches were crawling about it, trying to cling to life like everything else there.

"He didn't have dinner," I said. "It's here, uneaten. It looks like there was some kind of row. There's no blood, though."

Cyrus Barker lowered himself onto his haunches and studied the floor. Were there footprints in the dust? I couldn't tell.

"Look in that wardrobe," he said. "But be careful."

I crossed to the old cabinet. It had been new and gleaming once, more than half a century ago. It had been well tended for decades before someone died and abandoned it. Or perhaps fortunes had reversed and it was sold at a tenth of its original price.

It was purchased and sold again and sold again and somewhere in this bleak prospect found its way here.

The thought occurred to me that Kazimir Chernov could be hiding in that wardrobe, either waiting for us with a pistol or waiting for his eternal reward. I reached for the knob, inhaled, and threw open the door.

"Empty," I murmured. "There's an old carpetbag here, though. He wouldn't leave permanently without it. Perhaps he just escaped when he heard someone in the corridor."

"Someone was here, Thomas," the Guv said. "The chair is broken. Look! That framed print on the wall is crooked. The chair was thrown at it, no doubt."

"A row with a woman, perhaps?" I asked. "He could have thrown the chair in anger. I'd have considered it if she were cooking this slop for me."

"Aye, perhaps, but there's no second pillow. If there was a woman, she didn't live here."

"Why should she? She was probably one of the harridans from the hall."

"Thomas, what self-respecting woman would tolerate a lover with that?"

He pointed to an old dresser. The only piece in the room worth anything was a wooden picture frame inlaid with gold. It contained a yellowed newspaper photograph of a woman's face. I knew it could only be Sophia Perovskaya. She was a serious-looking girl, but then she would be. The article was in Russian, probably an announcement of her arrest or execution.

I bent down and stared at the image. "Were they lovers, do you think?"

"No," Barker stated. "As I recall, she had a coconspirator, her husband. Perhaps Chernov was a former classmate or a revolutionary who took a liking to her, which never fully ended. That is, unless it was as Morris hinted, and he was trying to associate himself with her in order to establish his standing among the an-archists with a heroine of the Revolution."

"That is possible, of course."

We stood and looked about.

"Is anything else peculiar here?" I asked.

"Just one thing," the Guv answered. "This black mark here on the floor. It was left by a polished boot. I don't believe Chernov gets his boots shined these days."

"You're right, sir," I said. "I doubt there is such a thing as a jar of shoeblack in this entire street."

We circled each other and looked about. I checked under the bed while he inspected the top of the wardrobe.

"A few shirts and trousers," he said, "and a threadbare suit. A Russian coat, vaguely military looking. I wonder if he was a former . . ."

He trailed off as he lifted a pistol from underneath the clothes. From where I stood, I didn't recognize it. It wasn't English.

"A Smith and Wesson Model Three, made for the Russian army."

"A pistol, a boot mark, a photograph, a broken chair, and a congealed pot of beans," I said. "He won't be back. He was taken. He wouldn't leave the pistol or the framed photograph behind. Who took him, do you suppose? Scotland Yard? Special Branch? The Okhrana?"

"Possibly," Barker said. "Let us go. We've seen all there is to see here."

We were jeered at by a long line of tenants as we left the room. Finally, we descended the broken steps and stood in Woodseer Street.

"I need a cup of tea," Barker said.

"I need a bath."

We found an ABC in Commercial Road, the great artery of the East End. The closer the streets came to it, the more respectable they were. Once inside, Barker ordered some Assam tea, since they did not have his beloved green gunpowder. I ordered coffee and when it came I regretted it. Tea shops serve bad coffee in order to show how delicious their teas are. This one tasted like burnt toast soaked in hot water, and this within a quarter mile of St. Michael's Alley and my favorite coffeehouse, The Barbados.

"Thomas, do you think it likely that the Okhrana has taken Chernov?"

"Yes, I do," I replied.

"As do I," the Guv answered. "We need to know where to look."

"I'll speak to Israel right away, then. He can put his ear to the ground and let us know if he finds anything."

"We should check the morgues," Barker said grimly. "The Okhrana have a penchant for torture, and I don't think they'd care that it is illegal in England."

"Do you think he's still in the East End?"

"I do," he said. "They will have caught him nearby, and could not have taken a struggling anarchist far."

I drank the flavorless coffee and studied my partner.

"Let us go back to the beginning," I said. "The delegation arrived from Russia a few days ago. Then Jim Hercules arrived in our offices and claimed that the tsarevich's life was in danger from an assassin. You refused the case, which I agree was a good decision. Then we took a stroll in Hyde Park and all hell broke loose."

Barker poured more tea. "If you're going to use strong language we must leave this tearoom."

"I did not curse," I protested. "I merely named a location. Anyway, why didn't you warn me that you released Bayles and sent him to threaten someone with a fake pistol?"

"I would think that obvious. You are not a member of the Knights Templar and therefore not privy to the information."

"Yes, but to all intents and purposes you are the Knights Templar. And I am your partner. Going about with no idea what may come next is not helpful."

"True, lad, but going about with no idea what may come is also part of being an enquiry agent."

I could not argue with his logic.

# CHAPTER TWENTY-TWO

When Mac learned we would have a guest within twenty-four hours expecting lobster and mussels, his heart nearly gave out. He is a never-say-die sort of fellow, however, and set out for the fish market, vowing not to come back empty-handed. As usual, he returned triumphant with a bucket of live lobsters and steamed three dozen oysters from a fish market in Brook Street. Before he left that morning Etienne Dummolard provided our oversize icebox with a cold salad, mixed vegetables, cheese biscuits, and a summer pudding with tayberry sauce. Rebecca pored over Mrs. Beaton's cookbook while Jacob wrestled a large pot from under the cabinet onto the stove. Rebecca would flee long before the murders began. It is a sad matter of Fate that lobsters should be so delicious with hot butter.

Corporal Alan Dinsdale arrived in mufti. I don't know why I assumed he'd be in his scarlet coat and busby. We were hardly

Kensington Palace, after all. Still, he looked a trifle diminished in his flat cap and ulster coat. Mac sailed out of the kitchen like a pilot boat in time to answer the door and then sailed back in again, having hung the coat and hat neatly on the hall stand.

The corporal was not expecting so fine a home and he was tongue-tied at first, but I consider myself a dab hand at jollying up a guest and making him feel at home. I began by getting a few bottles of ale from the cellar. Mac bottles them himself; a true Renaissance man is our Mac. Kensington Palace required dozens of staff, but we only need the one fellow. That's the last compliment I'll pay him, except to point out that it's not his fault that he is a prig.

Rebecca was quiet at dinner. It wasn't that she was sulking over some matter, no. She is intuitive, and she immediately understood that Corporal Alan Dinsdale was not present for an evening of male bonhomie. This was work. And anyway, she does not eat shellfish. They aren't kosher. She contented herself with the salad and dessert.

Barker and I knew our man and I searched throughout the house for metal nutcrackers, returning with three of them. Rebecca winced as we cracked the boiled claws. I think lobster goes best with champagne, but porter was probably more in Dinsdale's line. It would have been in mine as well if I hadn't wandered into the path of Cyrus Barker, Esquire. Not that he drinks champagne. Such French decadence would never pass his lips.

"Is the lobster to your liking, sir?" the Guv asked after sucking down a large oyster.

The corporal's mouth was too full to reply other than to nod. Dessert would follow eventually if Mac hadn't fainted in the kitchen.

When all was finished, we left poor Mac and Rebecca to clean every pot, pan, and dish in the house to Etienne's standard of cleanliness while Barker and I led Dinsdale up two flights to the Guv's chamber, a garret stretching the length of the house.

There the Guv offered him one chair and me the other. Then he placed a wooden chair in front of us, turned it around, and sat on it backward. He did not have a fire in the grate, and he opened some windows to let the night air pass through the garret, knowing the food and the heat would put the young man to sleep in a trice.

"Now, Corporal Dinsdale," said Barker said. "You must sing for your supper. I am going to ask you questions. Many questions. I shall often repeat myself, as will you. That is fine. It is part of the process. You were there by the palace, were you not, when Prince George's carriage was fired upon?"

"In it, too, sir," Dinsdale supplied. "The palace, I mean."

"Were you?" the Guv said. "Excellent. You seem an observant fellow. Now, Thomas here beat you to the punch, tackling the assassin, but only by a few seconds and because he was closer. I watched you leap from your horse and charge into the fray. You're a rugger, aren't you? What position?"

Our guest smiled modestly. "An openside flanker, sir."

"Good speed, fast off the mark, and keen. No manager could ask for more. Tell me, is there a duty roster for the day at the palace? A schedule of sorts, I mean?"

"Two, actually. One for the royal family and one for the guards."

"So if one schedule changes the other shall as well. Correct?"

"Exactly, Mr. Barker."

"Was Prince George's departure on the schedule?"

"It was."

"And was the schedule posted for all to see?" Barker asked.

"Not in the hall for visitors to see, but yes."

"Does the schedule list where a royal is going? Could any guard reading it know his destination?"

"Yes, sir. There's a lot to consider. Capes if it rains, which horses to take if the distance is long, that sort of thing."

"Very efficient," the Guv said. "Was His Highness intended to go alone?"

"He was, sir, but we were waiting, you see. The Russian had planned to tag along, but he's what my mum would call a sluggard."

"Corporal, you don't sound as if you approve of 'the Russian.'"

"My old man fought in Afghanistan, sir, and Granddad was in the Crimea. We're a military family and we have long memories. The royals may invite him, the newspapers may get all in a lather about his coming, but as Grandad always said, 'Smile, but keep your powder dry.'"

"That's good advice, Corporal," my partner said, nodding. "Your grandfather is very wise. Had the tsarevich changed his mind, or was he simply late?"

"I don't know, sir," he answered. "We were waiting for him and His Highness was none too happy. Princess Mary was waiting and he wanted to be there on time. He was already acting like a married man, I told my friend Alf. That's Alfred Winslow, the other guard who tackled the assassin. We needed to shove off as well. There'd be more places to go when we got back."

"There were a crowd of people standing about, as I recall. At least ten, wouldn't you say, Thomas?"

"Yes, sir, but bless me, that isn't a crowd," Dinsdale said. "When a royal leaves the palace, fifty people will come out of nowhere."

"Is the front gate leading into Kensington ever locked?"

"Only at midnight, when Hyde Park is officially closed. And early in the morning."

"Is the gate guarded or are the visitors restricted in any way?"

"Couldn't do it, Mr. Barker," he answered. "See, people are also coming and going from Hyde Park, so there isn't any way to restrict them if they can just come in from the other end."

"What about beggars, or protesters, or people who seem disturbed?"

"We can order them to move along. They can't protest within the grounds. Only in the street on the other side of the fence.

They can speak at the Speakers' Corner, of course, but there is to be no placards or trouble. If they make a disturbance, they'll have to deal with us."

"Did you notice Mr. Bayles among the crowd?" Barker asked. He'd risen from the chair and was standing with his elbow resting on the corner of the mantel.

"Not 'til he ups and waves his pistol," Dinsdale said. "They say he was a nutter, but he was pretty quiet. Old coat and dirty bowler. We get that kind day in, day out. Nothing noticeable."

"What were you doing the exact second you heard the pop of the prop pistol?"

"You're right, sir," Dinsdale said, turning to grin at me. "You do ask a lot of questions."

Barker smiled. "We're just getting started, laddie."

Mac appeared then with cups of strong tea. Very strong tea, to counteract the meal and the ale. We wanted this fellow awake and sensible.

I happened to notice Mac. He looked all in. Of course, he tried to hide it, but I knew him. I caught Barker's attention and nodded in our factotum's direction with the side of my head.

"Mac, you may retire for the evening," the Guv said.

"That's not really necessary, sir."

"Go to bed. We are perfectly capable of opening and closing the front door and bolting it after."

"Yes, sir," Maccabee said, too tired to argue. I heard him go down the stair. Normally he glides about silently, as if on skates. Now it sounded like someone was dropping shoes.

"Where were we?" the Guv asked. He had left the chair and begun to pace.

"The 'pop,' sir," I said.

"Thank you, Thomas. Corporal, you heard the pop."

"I'd just settled into my saddle and was inspecting Nell's bridle. She'll take her head if it ain't tight, you see. Anyway, I heard the pop and when I turned my head, I saw the look of fear on the prince's face. Bayles was shouting and there was a cloud of white smoke between them. I've seen my share of music halls and what a stage pistol looks and sounds like, but I wasn't thinking about it then. Brought my boot over Nell's side, landed on my toes, and run right toward him, I did."

"And then you saw Mr. Llewelyn."

Dinsdale took a gulp of the tea. We don't have dainty cups at the Barker household, or weak tea, either.

"Little fellow, but scrappy. Beg your pardon, Mr. Llewelyn. He took Bayles down at the knees. I wrested the pistol from his hand, still not aware it was a prop."

"How did he look to you, this would-be assassin?"

"A raving madman, sir, spitting in anger, eyes starting from his head. And then," the corporal said, "it was like one of them butchers in Leadenhall Market threw a bucket of blood all over us. Mr. Llewelyn, Alf, and me. I looked over and saw blood dripping from Mr. Llewelyn's hair and face. Then I looked at the assassin himself, with his head all blown apart. Made me green, the sight of him. I fought in the Sudan but I never saw anything like that."

"Did you hear anything before Mr. Bayles was killed?"

"I did, I think. It was like the sound a grasshopper makes when he's jumping. A kind of rattling sound."

"No audible shot from a gun, then."

"No, sir."

Barker finished his tea and so did we. The cups and saucers were stacked on the tray.

"Could you tell in any way from which direction the bullet came?" Barker asked.

"No, sir, I don't think so."

I strained to remember and likewise had no idea.

"The bullet did not fly from an obvious direction," the Guv continued. "You weren't sprayed with blood more or less than Mr. Llewelyn?"

"No, sir, and I know about ballistics."

"Have you arrived at any conclusions about the gun used to kill Mr. Bayles?" my partner asked.

"It wasn't a Martini-Enfield, sir. Too quiet. Same for an elephant gun or any other kind of hunting rifle. I reckon it's some sort of air gun, but they're just for plinking targets. Short-range. That means either the shooter was closer than we thought, or . . ."

"Or?" Barker pressed.

"Or it was some kind of new experimental rifle. That's all I can think of. Most rifles you can hear from far off. They are unmistakable."

Barker nodded and stood. "Just so. We are agreed on that." He began to pace again. "Did you see anything directly after the shot?"

"My eyes were full of blood, sir," Dinsdale replied. "Couldn't see nothing. I wanted to pull out my sword to defend myself, but there was no one nearby to defend against. Besides, it's useless, isn't it? A sword against a long-distance rifle."

"Indeed," murmured the Guv. "Continue."

"Then I heard a call from Alf, my mate, and the carriage bowls off as fast as the horses will pull it, which is standard protocol. I knew that something happened after that, but I don't really know in detail. The Russian came out and was chased back in, right?"

"Something like that," Barker answered.

"It's not fair. Prince George, third in line to the throne, is shot at, but our traditional enemy is kept out of harm's way. For all I know, this could all be a Russian plot."

I thought it likely as well, but it wasn't politic to say so. However, I decided it was time to put in an oar.

"Have you been all over the palace, roof to basement?" I asked.

"Oh, yes, we all have. We guardsmen get bored sometimes, so we look about. Sometimes we learn things. For example, the Prince of Wales likes to step out on one of the balconies to smoke in peace, but he carries a pair of opera glasses to watch the women pass. He has an eye for a well-turned ankle."

"Have you heard tale of a tunnel under the palace?" I pressed.

"There is a rumor but it's just rubbish. Some of our boys have searched for it, without any success. It's just an old wives' tale, I think. Or a soldier's idea of a prank. Besides, if such a tunnel existed, I'm sure the Prince of Wales would have used it by now."

Dinsdale laughed at his own joke. It would be churlish to repeat remarks about the prince when the watch he gave Barker was in my very pocket, but Prince Albert was known for his interest in the fair sex and his love of personal freedom. The Guv grunted. He had very decided opinions about how an heir to the throne should conduct himself.

"This schedule you mentioned," Barker said. "How easily would a member of the public—a bold member—be able to glance at the schedule?"

"He might see it, sir, if he was clever enough."

"Where is it kept?"

"Now, sir, that's palace business."

Barker nodded. The corporal had just risen in his estimation.

My partner offered our guest a cigar, but the soldier did not smoke. Then he crossed to a large jar full of his private blend and stuffed an ivory-colored pipe. He put it between his teeth and lit it. When he had it going he came forward and removed his jacket and straddled the chair again.

"Did you come into the palace after the shooting?"

"No, sir. I was a sight. I didn't want to be seen like that. A servant brought out some water and towels and then I went 'round the back to the servants' quarters to see if my beautiful uniform could be salvaged. It was done in, I'm afraid. Only my boots were able to be saved."

Barker puffed for a minute in silence. Dinsdale and I listened to the sound of the tobacco gurgling in his pipe.

"Let us begin again," the Guv said.

And so we did, from beginning to end. Every action, every word spoken, every thought or impression. The corporal was beginning to look fatigued, which is sometimes a good thing. People will say things when they are tired. We went through it, and then Barker began again. That's when it happened.

"You brought your horse around in front of the carriage," my partner remarked. "You didn't speak to His Highness, but you greeted your friend, Alf. Is that correct?"

"Correct, sir."

"And how did you feel?" he asked.

"Well enough," Dinsdale said. "I had a bit of a headache."

"Did you?"

"Yes, sir. It was the din."

Barker frowned. "What din?"

"The caterwauling," the corporal answered. "It was loud in the lobby, you see."

"I'm afraid I don't. What caterwauling?"

"A child was crying."

The Guv glanced at me. "A child in the palace? A royal child?"

"No, sir. A regular child there wandering around."

"Why was a child allowed in the palace foyer?" I asked.

"They were waiting for the tyke's mother."

"A second person unmentioned?" Barker asked. "Tell me about her."

"I only saw her for a moment, sir. It was a sad story. She was a widow. Had a Victoria Cross pinned to her breast and her dressed all in black."

"And why was she in the building with her child?"

"She'd been overcome, sir, in the heat of the day. She was heavy with child. Said she would have preferred to stay at home but she'd had her son there for weeks and he was fit to be tied with boredom. She took him to the park, but she began feeling faint. It was a warm day, as you recall. One of us took her into the palace. We have rules, but we're not savages."

"Describe the woman for me, Corporal."

"She was partially veiled, Mr. Barker. I could only see the bottom half of her face. Her skin was pale, her lips ashen. I think she was pretty, or had been when her husband was alive, poor blighter."

"She was heavy with child, you say?" the Guv asked.

"Very heavy, sir. Ready to give birth any day, I suppose."

Barker considered the matter. "What became of her?"

"Someone helped her to a water closet, I believe. I wasn't told it, but that's what I assume happened. There's a lot of rumors in royal service, sir, but not many facts."

Barker blew a smoke ring to the ceiling. "Describe the child."

Dinsdale shrugged. "A spoiled brat. He wore a sailor suit and a cap with a ribbon. The staff was having trouble keeping him out of everything. He was left with them, and a regular little savage he was."

"Did you see them leave?"

"No, sir," Dinsdale replied. "I went out and climbed onto Nell and then boom! Everything started."

The Guv stood. "You've been very patient, Corporal. I'll let you get back to the barracks now. I'm sure you must be tired."

"Thank you for the dinner, sirs. Best I've had in London."

We saw him down the stairs, into his coat and hat, and out the door. Barker led us to the library and we fell into the chairs. It was just past eleven.

"You rather tossed the fellow out, bum-over-brains," I told him.

"He was obviously all in, and there is a point beyond which pertinent information will be compromised. I got out of him what I needed."

"Do you really believe a woman with child is shooting at royals from the roof of Kensington Palace?" I asked. "You credit that theory?"

"I do. If you were an assassin, how would you transport an air rifle from the lobby to the roof of Kensington Palace and back again?"

"Under a voluminous dress? I'm sure the rifle would be as long as a broom, at least."

"I'll credit your cluelessness to the lateness of the hour. She carried it in pieces, perhaps hooked on a belt of some sort under her dress."

"Then La Sylphide is really a woman!"

"I'll stake my professional reputation on it."

"But how?" I asked. "How does a woman train to become an assassin?"

"We already know one fully trained."

I felt my face blanch cold and fell back in my chair. "Sofia Ilyanova."

"Aye, Thomas. Daughter of the late, unlamented Sebastian Nightwine and the murderer of my best friend, Andrew McClain."

"My word," I said. "What do we do?"

"Right now I need you to make a telephone call."

# CHAPTER TWENTY-THREE

Shortly before midnight there was a telephone call. I heard Mac pick up the receiver, and then come up the stairs. He never knocked; that was a constant when I was a bachelor. But now that I was married he could not simply walk in. So, his solution was to hover at the top of the stair and clear his throat, like a phlegmatic angel.

"Yes?" I called.

"You have a telephone call."

"Thank you, Jacob. I shall be down directly."

After he left, I buttoned my waistcoat and adjusted my tie.

"That should be Israel," I said to Rebecca.

I went downstairs and lifted the receiver. "Ahoy."

"Ahoy, yourself," Zangwill said. "I'm over at the Elephant and Castle. Come see what I've got."

"Just come here. You know Mac makes wonderful ale. Porter, stout, bitter. You name it."

"I'm already here and my Old Spotted Hen is in front of me."

"You're just afraid to beard the lion."

"Thomas, everyone is afraid to beard your bloody lion," Israel said. "You must accept that fact."

"He's not a cannibal, you know."

"I demand proof of that. Are you coming?"

"I shall be along directly," I said.

I left the house. Barker could work out where I had gone. The E and C is the busiest public house in Southwark. It was a coaching inn a century ago, but had grown like a mushroom and now featured six floors, two turrets, and a dome. Saying "Meet me at the Elephant and Castle" was like saying "I'll be in Hampstead Heath. Come find me." It took me near twenty minutes to locate my friend.

"Your beer's gone flat," Israel said. "Where've you been?"

"Be lucky I don't pour it on your head. I came as fast as I could."

"Now, now, I'm doing you a favor, remember?"

"Sorry," I replied, sitting down across from him. "I'm tired. What have you got?"

"People have seen a group of men going in and out of an empty building in Menotti Street, a former tailor shop. It's in . . ."

"I know where it is."

As Barker explained earlier, I once passed a test to become a cabman, just so I could please him by being able to name every street in London and to drive him somewhere if required. Menotti Street was near the Jewish burial ground in Bethnal Green, and was known for its population of Russian immigrants. I should have deduced the address myself.

"There were about eight of them, and they look rough," he continued. "The two people that told me said the men conversed in Russian, but no one knew them. I know it's not much to go on, and it might be a false lead, but it's the only thing I've heard that was out of the ordinary."

"What's the number?"

"Twenty-seven."

"Thank you, Israel."

"You owe me lunch when this is over," he said, smiling.

I nodded. "Very well."

"A beer, a dessert, and coffee."

"That's all?"

"No, no, Thomas. The lunch, as well."

"I'll have to check the budget."

"Hang your budget," he said. "You owe me."

"Oh, all right," I replied. "I'll keep you posted about what happens."

"No, leave me out of it," he insisted, holding up his hands. "I wasn't here."

"As you wish."

Once I was in Lion Street again, I headed up to Barker's garret and told him what Israel had said.

"Menotti Street," Barker murmured, staring out a dormer window into the darkness. "Of course. Mr. Zangwill has more resources than I give him credit. Not that the Okhrana is accustomed to hiding their movements. It is part of their power."

"When are we leaving?"

"Within the next half hour, if Mrs. Llewelyn will permit you."

"Permit me?" I scoffed. "I'm a grown man. I can make my own decisions."

He looked over his shoulder. I believe I saw skepticism in his expression. "No doubt. However, I think you should inform her that we are leaving."

I did. I'm sure Rebecca was not pleased, but she understood. Her only fear was that I would not return at all one of these evenings.

True to his word, we left within the half hour. We walked to a cab stand in the Old Kent Road, and found a cabman who conveyed us over Tower Bridge to the East End. Once in Commercial Road, very close to our destination, Barker called and the horse and cab rumbled to a stop where we alighted. Having located the street, we lounged against a wall and he pulled his watch from his pocket.

"What are we doing?" I asked.

"We are timing the beat of the local constable. I need to know his exact whereabouts."

It was black as pitch and so quiet I heard the constable's boots as he walked down Commercial Road. He gave us a glance and then a frown, but we seemed harmless enough. He continued on his way.

"Fifteen minutes, precisely," Barker pronounced when he went by again, consulting the watch one more time in that way of his. "A conscientious fellow. Now we know with whom we are working. Let us view the tailor shop."

Menotti Street was a row of attached houses from Regency days, cut up into flats, shops, and whatever else the landlords found capable of earning their keep. We saw a soiled "To-Let" sign in the window, but there was a light inside. It had to be the Russians, unless there was a gang of lawless tailors, fresh from prison, determined to take over the East End trade.

"Do you suppose they're all in there?" I said in a low voice when we found the address. The old shop was dusty, battle-scarred, and bedraggled. Oilcloth had been pasted to the back of the windows, but light still shined through.

"I doubt it," Barker answered. "The Okhrana is still guarding the tsarevich. If Chernov is in there, the light is a good sign. If he were dead, they'd have decamped."

"So, what do we do?" I asked.

"Take this."

He put something in my hand. I held it up to the puny light coming from the tailor shop.

"A police whistle?"

"Aye. Go down to the end of the street, then turn left and go onto the next. I want to see how many sparrows fly out. Count to twenty, then blow for all you're worth."

"Yes, sir."

The Guv pulled his repeater from his waistcoat pocket and consulted it again. How he saw anything at night in those dark spectacles is one of the questions about him I've never fully answered.

"You've got less than a minute," he said. "And when the constable comes running, hide the whistle and look uncommonly innocent. You're good at that."

The old streets there were narrow and there was a gutter channel running down the middle of the road. Every building was stained and the stone looked as if it had been battered with a hammer. I reached the end of the street and crossed to the next.

"Eighteen, nineteen, twenty . . ."

It's not an easy thing to do, using a police whistle. It takes some practice, and I've had it. I blew my lungs through that small cylinder of metal until my chest ached. Ten seconds later I heard an answering whistle from where I had come. Then a pounding on a door. Cyrus Barker is an expert at pounding on doors. Then I heard him bellowing.

"Scotland Yard! Open this door! Police!"

I tucked the whistle in my pocket and watched two men shoot out into the street I was watching. I leaned against a wall as they passed and ran squarely into the young constable, hurrying in answer to the whistle, bowling him over. I recognized Rachkovsky's men from when they had come to our offices. One of them was Olgev. The two ran off in different directions.

"Are you all right, Officer?" I asked, helping the fellow to his feet. He looked young and eager and was thin as a rail.

"Never mind that," he bawled. "Did you hear a whistle?"

"I did. In the next street."

It had begun to mist. The constable wore an oilskin cloak and he nearly slipped on the wet pavement. He turned into the next street and disappeared. I pulled my collar up around my ears, pushed my bowler hat down on my head, and followed him.

The yellow light spilling into the narrow street from the shop doorway reminded me of the molten steel in a foundry. All about it now seemed profoundly black as if this were the only light in the universe. I stepped into the doorway and took in several things: a door nearly knocked off its hinges. Barker sitting in a chair, with both hands on the brass ball of his walking stick. The poor constable trying to make sense of it all. In the middle of the room was a dirty cot, little more than rags, upon which a man lay. The cot was stained with blood. There was a poker on the floor near a fireplace, and many corresponding burns on the body of the victim, whom I assumed was Chernov.

"He is alive," Barker stated, holding a thumb to his wrist. "But unconscious."

"Who are you?" the constable demanded.

"Cyrus Barker, sir," the Guv said, handing him his card. "I am a private enquiry agent."

"I heard of you. I take it you, sir, are Mr. Llewelyn?"

"Guilty as charged," I said.

"We are friends of the commissioner," the Guv added.

The latter was a polite way of saying "Mind your step."

"What's this, then?" he asked, pointing at the cot with his truncheon.

"Let's say it was a misunderstanding. Some officials who are guests of our government thought it necessary to question this fellow, who is a known anarchist. The officials were not aware that torture is illegal in this country. That is, unless they know but do not care. What is your name, Constable?"

"P. C. Perkins."

"Well, then, Perkins. The men that did this ran out the back of the house."

"Was you the one with the whistle?"

Barker pulled his from the pocket opposite his repeater. It was attached to his watch chain.

"Mr. Llewelyn and I intend to give our statements, but this fellow needs medical attention immediately. How would you care to proceed?"

"I, well," P. C. Perkins said. He may be punctual, but he was no Isaac Newton.

"Mr. Llewelyn and I shall wait here until you return with a hand litter for Mr. Chernov. Then we shall proceed to 'H' Division and make our statements."

"Right," Perkins said.

"Or I can go to the corner and whistle for more constables," I said.

Barker nodded.

"Yes, that!" the young man said, with a look of relief.

"We'll both go," the Guv interjected. "Stay here, P. C. Perkins."

"You really shouldn't tell the truth," I told my employer when we were almost to the street. "It confuses people."

I looked over my shoulder. The constable stood in the doorway, concerned that he might be letting two criminals get away. Anyone could have a business card from the Barker and Llewelyn Agency. We print them by the gross. We reached the corner and lifted our Metropolitan whistles again.

"I'll bet I could get louder than you," I said.

Barker gave a wicked grin. "Lad, you're welcome to try."

We each took a deep breath and began to blow.

A quarter hour later Perkins and I were trotting down Commercial Road in the direction of the London Hospital. Chernov was in a bad way and we were not helping his condition by pushing the hand litter along rough cobblestones. It was fortunate for him that the hospital was about a half mile of where we found him.

Chernov was about five-and-forty. He had a prison regulation haircut and a long, thick beard. He looked, as a matter of fact, like Bayles, the fellow who was assassinated, at least as I could remember from the brief seconds I saw him. Chernov had been tortured with a red-hot poker, no doubt at the order of Rachkovsky. There were massive welts across his chest, limbs, and back, and two crisscrossed his face to form an X. He must have been in such pain as I could not even imagine. Perhaps it was a way for the Okhrana to recognize him should he ever return to Russia. If the anarchist survived, that is.

Barker had gone ahead by cab. No trotting along for my partner. Someone had to warn the hospital staff of the approaching litter.

We reached the hospital, Constable Perkins and I, hefting the hand litter and carrying it up the steps to the front door, where Barker met us. He was right to have gone ahead. The lobby was full. One man was screaming, his arm having been mangled in some sort of industrial accident. Elderly people sat in every corner, as if they had waited for months and become part of the furnishings. Tubercular children coughed under the protective arms of their mothers. It was heartbreaking, but it was a normal evening in Whitechapel, until Chernov was wheeled in with multiple injuries because he'd been tortured. It's not something one sees here in Jolly Olde.

Two orderlies lifted him off the cart and onto a gurney. Now that we were off the street, I could hear that he was murmuring. He groaned loudly when he was laid on the gurney, but then he returned to muttering under his breath. I attempted to follow after as he was wheeled down the hall, but one of the orderlies put a hand on my shoulder and pointed toward a chair. There is a spot just in front of the shoulder that produces pain if you press it correctly. He pressed it correctly. He'd been around the park a time or two. I sat. Barker sat down beside me.

"He was muttering when he came in, but I wasn't able to hear what he said," I told the Guv. "Couldn't make head nor tails."

"It may have been in Russian," Barker said.

"Perhaps."

"Did you see the men who ran out of the tailor shop?"

"I did," I answered. "They were definitely from the group of Okhrana agents in our office. One was Olgev."

The Guv frowned. "Did they recognize you as they ran by?"

"No, they heard the whistle and hared it."

"We owe Mr. Zangwill another debt of gratitude."

"So, what next? Do you intend to confront Rachkovsky?"

"That's a thought," Barker said. "I will consider the matter. He might assume his little game was foiled by Scotland Yard. The guards were gone by the time I kicked my way inside."

"You planned that intentionally."

Barker shrugged. "It was a ruse. It might have worked, or not. Rachkovsky could have been in there himself, armed and waiting for us."

"What do we do now?"

"Let us see how Chernov is progressing."

A half hour later a doctor came out of the wards and looked about. When he saw us, he came forward and stood in front of us.

"Are you gentlemen here about the man with the burns?"

"We are," Barker said. "His name is Kazimir Chernov and he is Russian."

"Who are you gentlemen?" the physician asked.

Barker handed him a card. "We are working with the Home Office and Scotland Yard."

"How did he come to be so injured?" he asked. "He was tortured in the most abominable manner."

"The Russian Socialists are at each other's throats. We assume he was one of them."

"I deal with battered wives and abused children, generally," the doctor said. "An occasional accident or someone who's fallen under a carriage. I've never seen a man branded before."

"What is his condition?" Barker asked.

"It is grave. There is no way to know if he will recover. It's really up to him. I've given him morphine. We are bathing his wounds with cooking oil."

"Excuse me," I asked. "Did you just say 'cooking oil'?"

"I did," he replied. "It works well on burns. A bit of a panacea. If you'll come back tomorrow, I'll have more information for you."

"Are burns his only wounds?" Barker asked.

"No, sir. He was beaten beforehand, by someone who knew what he was about."

Barker nodded, and started walking toward the door. I followed, and the doctor turned to leave, but then I stopped.

"I say," I called. "He kept muttering something over and over. Could you make out what it was?"

"Yes," the doctor said. "It was 'Sofia.'"

My blood ran cold.

# CHAPTER TWENTY-FOUR

We gave our statement in "H" Division, which was reasonably quiet at that time, and then went on to Barker's favorite spot in the East End, Ho's in Limehouse, a Chinese tearoom and restaurant. The tearoom is open around the clock, which begs the question: Why would someone want a cup of Chinese tea at three o'clock in the morning? The fact that Ho is a member of an organization known as the Blue Dragon Triad might explain some of it.

I had worked for Cyrus Barker long enough to feel, as he did, that Ho's tearoom was like a second home. A home full of spies, criminals, and rude Asian waiters, perhaps, but a home all the same. Like the Guv, I could go there and eat a bowl of rice and prawns and relax in a way that is not possible in the office or traveling about London on a case, never knowing what to expect. True, Ho's is one of the most unusual places in London, reached only through a tunnel under the Thames, but I had been there at dozens of festivals the owner hosted for the Asian community over the years. It was rare that a foreigner would be invited to attend a private party, but Barker was respected and I was tolerated because I was his satellite, and because I could nearly make myself understood in Cantonese and to understand them in turn. I had become a denizen, a regular customer, which was a privilege in the eyes of the Limehouse community and a detriment in the eyes of Scotland Yard. As any of my friends will tell you, however, I'd cross the street to stick my thumb in the collective eye of the CID.

I finished the final prawn, put down the bowl, and laid my chopsticks across it. Then I sipped plum wine from a cup the size of a large acorn. I won't drink tea unless forced, even the Guv's beloved green gunpowder tea. I'd heard the rumor that the leaves are thrown in the Pearl River on one end, steeped, and collected at the other by young female swimmers not wearing a stitch. Then the leaves are dried and rolled carefully into green pellets, like balls of gunpowder. The image of maidens frolicking in the water collecting leaves did not stop the tea from tasting like something an artist uses to clean his brushes.

"I disagree," Ho said to Barker. It was about three-thirty in the morning. The two had been arguing in a patois veering between English, pidgin, Mandarin, and Cantonese. I was not surprised by Ho's remark. He is almost always disagreeable.

"How so?" Barker rumbled.

"The Russian state visit is the perfect time to assassinate the tsar's whelp."

"Ho, we are trying to prevent the assassination, not encourage it."

"What has Russia done for you or me?" Ho asked. "Nothing, I tell you. They are a nation of drunkards."

"I have seen you in your cups many a time," the Guv said.

"Perhaps," he admitted. "But I am not a nation."

Barker settled back in his cracked captain's chair.

"You have been hired," Ho went on, "by a person of no official standing to protect the tsar's son without actually staying with him to protect him."

"Correct."

"And he will be traveling in an open carriage for all to see."

"Correct again," the Guv replied, nodding.

"And you will save him."

"If I can," my partner admitted.

Ho suddenly turned to me as if I'd said something. "Who is that *guailo* painter?"

"Which one?" I asked. "We have several."

"The one who is also an inventor."

"Ah, Leonardo da Vinci."

"That's the one," Ho said, shrugging. "He had an invention that flies."

"I think you're right. I've seen the sketch."

Ho smiled. He is not a beauty when he smiles. He's not a beauty at any time. "You build two of them. Then you fly around above the carriages until you spot someone with a rifle. Ha!"

He threw back his head and laughed and the waiter behind him did the same. His boss had shown the Westerners to be stupid again.

"Thomas," Barker said, "I want you to go to a public house in Mile End called the Potted Eel. You're looking for a man named Jack Carr. They call him Blackjack. Tell him I need to see him immediately. Tell him it is vitally important."

I stood at once, nodding, and headed out the door. The sooner I was off, the quicker I'd get in bed. After a ten-minute walk, I located the Potted Eel, not far beyond the late Andy McClain's mission. The establishment was no doubt one of the houses Andy brought his proselytizing to, by which I mean he'd had a knockdown with several patrons. I missed the old man.

The Eel had seen better days. The damp had gotten into every board in the place and at first I thought Barker was having me on. It looked not only vacant but derelict. Seizing the handle, I pushed open the door, which protested with a squeal.

Inside, a fat publican lounged behind his bar, cleaning his fingernails with a knife. Two men were playing at cards with a limp deck and another was passed out in his chair. A slattern with wild, witchlike hair looked annoyed as I entered.

"Here, beggar off!" she bawled. "We's closed!"

"I have a message for Mr. Jack Carr," I said.

"He's asleep," she answered. "Get out. Come back in the morning."

"I can't do that," I replied. "I need him in half an hour at Ho's in Limehouse."

The two men playing cards chuckled, as if I didn't know what I was asking.

"I don't care what you need, toff. Cut along or we'll slice you like mackerel. And you don't order Blackjack around. Who do you think you are, anyway?"

"It's not for me," I answered. "It's for Push. Cyrus Barker. He needs to see your leader. It's not just important. It's vitally important, he said."

No one had a response to that. In spite of his saying he didn't want to draw attention to himself, everyone in the East End knew the Guv. He cut a broad swath and had busted any number of heads even before I had come along. He wanted their respect, and got it. I, however, still had to earn it. No one was willing to do me any favors. One of the men, a bear of a fellow wearing a stained singlet with no shirt, got out of his chair and came toward me.

"That's a nice hat," he remarked. "Think I'll try it on."

I was all nerves from the evening's events. I pulled out my Webley and fired. The bullet knocked a pewter plate off the shelf behind him, skipped across the bar, and bounced into a corner. The bear looked stunned and sat down again.

"I like this hat," I answered. "It's mine, got it? Jack Carr, half an hour in Limehouse. Vitally important. Got it?"

I backed out of the room and pocketed the pistol once I was in the street again, then I walked back to Limehouse. It was the middle of the night. Most people had gone home. Some were getting ready to go to work. Those who hadn't either were stone drunk or plied a dishonest trade.

I entered the tearoom again through the long tunnel. Ho and Barker were still arguing, but then they did that all the time. Ho was the first mate once aboard Barker's boat, the *Osprey*. I imagine those must have been interesting times.

"And now you bring strangers to me in the middle of the night," Ho cried. "A gang leader. I try to keep a respectable tearoom here."

"Ha," I muttered.

He cursed me in several languages, but then I'd heard them all before. It wasn't as villainous as his tea.

At last our guest arrived. He did not appear to have any trouble finding Ho's establishment, though there was no sign to advertise it, only a battered door to enter through. He brought a half dozen men with him just in case. Jack Carr was an ugly man, though come to think of it I've never seen a gang leader who wasn't. He was shaved bald, and his black mustache and beard encircled his mouth like a ring. His beady eyes were bloodshot and puffy. He looked in a foul temper.

"Welcome, Mr. Carr," Barker said, sitting back in his chair and tenting his fingers.

"Push, you had no business waking a hardworking man from his sleep," he said.

I was still taking impressions. His men were very obviously second tier and therefore he was, too.

"My apologies, Mr. Carr," the Guv said. "And how are the Mile End Boys these days?"

"Thriving, sir, though times is hard. The messenger said you had something important to say." He turned to look at me. "You, you shot at my best plate!"

"That was your best plate?" I asked. "I wouldn't feed my dog off that plate."

"Mr. Carr. Blackjack. Do you have a group of Russians occupying a tailor shop in Menotti Street?"

"I do, yeah. They pay regular. I don't ask questions."

"Perhaps you should," Barker said. "They tortured a man tonight, burned him with hot pokers. A ghastly sight. They fled as we entered. We took the man to the London Hospital, where he died two hours ago. My reputation is far from spotless, but it is still better than yours. 'H' Division will soon be sniffing at your door. Prepare yourself."

"Why are you giving me the tip?" Carr asked, looking suspicious.

"I don't like their leader. His name is Rachkovsky and he is a visitor to London. He doesn't know the rules."

"I'll teach him his manners, then. He's not going to shock me with a fresh corpse."

"Find alibis for your men quickly."

"Yes, sir, I reckon I will."

"By the way, gentlemen," Barker said. "Rachkovsky and his men are staying at Brown's Hotel in Mayfair. They are privileged secret policemen from Saint Petersburg. They protect a Russian prince here for the royal wedding. I can't touch them. Scotland Yard, the Home Office, myself, we cannot punish them."

Carr frowned. He looked menacing enough, I supposed, but Barker could give him a shake he'd never forget.

"Secret police?" Blackjack repeated. "Like Special Branch? I hate Special Branch. Mayfair, got it. Why are you telling me this, Push? Do you think I'll owe you after this? Because I won't."

Barker shook his head. "Mr. Carr, you may do as you wish. I just know that you haven't done the thing for which you may be blamed, and I've learned where this man and his cronies are. Now hurry! By all means, go!"

The men didn't question him. Seconds were slipping away before they would be brought in by Scotland Yard for murder. Torture and murder, in fact. Those were grave charges and men were guilty, but not these men.

"You think that went well?" Ho said after they were gone. "The Mile End Boys, they are small. They are weak. They won't give you the vengeance you need."

"I don't need vengeance of any kind," Barker replied. "But if Carr and his hoodlums can teach the Okhrana some manners, I am not averse to that."

Ho stood and walked to the door. "I must be awake in a few hours and so must you. I have no use for Russians, or tsars, or anarchists or secret police or western gangs."

*Of course not,* I thought to myself. Ho's tearoom collected more than tips. It provided information of all sorts, some of which was sold to interested parties, and others used to gamble with.

"You had this information in your hands. You could have sold it. Instead, you gave it to the one person who required it. You never learn!"

Ho returned to his native tongue, whichever it was, and shooed us out the door. My partner took it philosophically and didn't mind the assault on his dignity. We walked through the long tunnel and up the stair to the narrow street. I passed by the bare wall that the weathered door was set into.

"Did you really shoot his best pewter plate? In the middle of the Potted Eel?"

"I did," I admitted. "It seemed the quickest way to get his attention."

"This is getting dangerous," the Guv said as we stepped into the cool night air. "I'm starting to wonder if you should stay home with your wife until this case is concluded."

# CHAPTER TWENTY-FIVE

The garden was in full bloom the next morning as if nothing could be occurring on this earth other than its beauty. Barker's half acre is not the sort of garden one sees at flower shows. It is a classic Asian garden and was designed to look austere, but even it is able to kick up its heels now and again. The plum tree was in full blossom overhead and a carpet of azaleas lay at our feet. The standing stones each wore a bright cap of green moss and tiny, insignificant leaves on our *pen-jiang* trees were being pruned with scissors, under the experienced hand of Rebecca, who had taken on the duty voluntarily. I had been entirely useless at the chore. The Chinese gardeners were shaving the bark from a young tree in order to make it look like an old one under the watchful eye of Cyrus Barker. I raked the white stones in circles around the much larger black rocks, standing like islands in the sea. Mac was inside doing whatever Mac does, and Etienne was experimenting in the kitchen with a dish that might soon be on the menu at his restaurant, Le Toison d'Or. As usual, Barker's prized Pekinese, Harm, orchestrated our movements from a rock by the bridge that spanned the stream that bisected his personal domain.

I stood and stretched. Raking stones is not as easy as raking leaves, and it is difficult to get the circles perfect enough to satisfy the Guv. I looked over and saw Rebecca with a look of distaste on her face, waving a hand in front of her.

"What is it?" I called.

"A mosquito," she answered. "Or a dragonfly. Something keeps buzzing by my ear."

I turned my head. The little grotto in the corner where the miniature trees are kept is mostly in the shadows. I was looking for something in particular and found it almost immediately: two or three very small rays of light coming from the fence behind her. The kind made by bullets. I cleared my throat and saw Barker turn his head.

"Darling, do me a favor?" I asked casually.

"Of course."

"Go over and stand inside the standing stones."

She looked alarmed but immediately crossed the bridge and stepped into the shelter of the trio of stones. I walked along in the other direction, circling the pond and passing our back door. I was walking by the large plate-glass window when it suddenly shivered and fell into bits. Running to where Rebecca stood, I crouched behind a stump. Inside the house, Etienne Dummolard began a tirade in mixed English and French, using words I hoped my wife couldn't hear.

"What's happening?" she called.

"Nothing important," I assured her. "A window broke."

The gardeners had flattened against the fence by the Moon Gate entrance, but Barker just stood there as if he was convinced no one would dare shoot at him.

The madness of it all was that it was early morning. The sun was shining, birds still sang in the trees, and outside one could hear the milk float trundling by, delivering bottles to the residents of Newington. No one would dare break the spell of a beautiful July morning, would they?

"Sir!" I called. "Have a care!"

He grunted, and as a concession, moved a yard closer to the fence.

"Thomas, I'm frightened," Rebecca whispered from inside the relative safety of the stones.

"It's going to be fine."

"She's shooting from the bell tower," Barker called.

"She?" I heard Rebecca ask.

St. Luke's to the east was not large but it had a bell tower wide enough that someone could stand in it. The rest of the Elephant and Castle district was no more than two stories tall as a rule, our house included. St. Luke's looked down over all.

"I don't see anyone in the tower!" I called.

We all went silent. One minute. Perhaps two. Time is relative when one is being shot at. Barker consulted his scarred old turnip watch. Then he crossed the bridge and went inside. The assassin could have been waiting just as we were.

It was my turn. I had to protect Rebecca, even at the expense of my life. I took her hand and crossed the bridge again, guiding her ahead of me. There was a terrible itching between my shoulder blades and I kept remembering Bayles's head exploding. For a brief second, my life flashed before my eyes. Well, not mine, but my wife's. A widow twice over. Who would marry her again? Not that I wanted her to marry again. I decided she could remember me fondly and do good works for the rest of her life. I needn't have bothered worrying. The assassin had abandoned the tower and we stepped safely into the back passage. Mac stood there with his sawn-down shotgun, which would have done little damage at thirty feet, let alone a quarter mile.

We went into the kitchen. Etienne was still cursing in voluble

French and was holding a round dish in his hand. The shattering window had caused his soufflé to fall. Glass had landed all over the breakfast table and the floor underneath. It is very expensive to make a sheet of window glazing so large, but Barker is a rich man and we had a glazier on retainer for such emergencies, which had happened enough times that it was less than an emergency.

Etienne ran into the backyard with a copper pan in his hand as if he would volley back any bullet heading his way. It excited Harm, who rushed about the backyard barking to protect his property. *Cave canem.*

I closed the door. It has a metal bar on the hinge side that can be brought down and locked into a bracket on the opposite wall. We had been too often intruded upon and I had demanded it be put in when I first brought home my bride. I'd have braced it now if Etienne and Harm were not running about the garden like savages.

"Thomas, what happened?" Rebecca asked. I could see the alarm on her face.

"I think you know what just happened," I said.

"Someone just shot at me," she said. "Someone tried to kill me."

"You were shot at, but no one tried to kill you, or you'd be dead," I reasoned. "Someone wants to frighten you."

"Someone is succeeding," she replied. "But why is someone shooting at me? What have I ever done to make someone shoot at me, besides marrying you?"

"Nothing," I said.

"You have a dangerous occupation, Thomas! More dangerous than anyone's, I think. A soldier expects to be shot at on the battlefield, but when he comes home he doesn't expect someone to be shooting at him and his family over the hedgerows."

"I told you how dangerous my work is before we married," I said. "In fact, once I even tried to talk you out of it for your safety's sake."

We were standing in the narrow passage. Etienne returned

with his pan and Harm followed him inside. I pulled Rebecca into the library.

"I thought you were exaggerating about the danger, that you were being overdramatic and romantic," she said.

"I was warning you, Rebecca. But I never suspected you to be shot at. From St. Luke's, no less."

She turned, crossed to the mantelpiece, and grasped it as if reassuring herself that it was real. She stared down at the fan of feathers and dried flowers that adorned the grate in summer. Then she turned back and looked at me.

"Mr. Barker distinctly said 'she,'" she said carefully, looking at me. "Do you think it was a woman?"

"We're not certain yet, but that is our current theory."

"Do you know who it is?" Rebecca asked.

I nodded. "I believe it is the daughter of one of Barker's sworn enemies, the late Sebastian Nightwine."

"What is her name?"

"Sofia Ilyanova," I said.

"A Russian," she murmured. "I should have realized. Why on earth is she shooting at me now?"

"Nightwine trained her as an assassin. He was a twisted man. I thought she had given it up after he died, but apparently not. Her father had expensive tastes and always required more money. Perhaps she is following in his steps."

"Wait," she said, lifting a hand. "Why would you think she had given up her training? Have you spoken to this woman?"

I sighed. It all had to come out now.

"I was shot a couple of years ago, and while I was unconscious, she kidnapped me. She chained me to a bed, dosed me full of morphine, and put some sort of herb concoction on my wound."

Rebecca stepped forward and I did not like the look in her eyes.

"Why did she do that?" she asked.

I stepped back and nearly fell into a chair. "It's complicated."

"Why would an assassin bother to attempt to heal a man she just shot?" she persisted. "That is, unless she fancied him. Did she fancy you, Thomas?"

"I honestly don't know," I answered. "She doesn't think like other people. She's half mad. Her father ruined her."

She stopped in thought and stepped over to the window, looking out.

"Come away from the window," I said. "It's dangerous."

"I should say it is, Thomas. A girl who fancies you is shooting at your wife. Why do you suppose she is doing that?"

"I really don't know," I said.

"Don't you? It sounds like jealousy to me."

"She's been shooting at me, as well!"

"Yes, to get your attention. To show you how she feels. She went off to wherever she was and when she returned you were married. She was hoping for a reunion, but her hopes were dashed."

"This is ridiculous," I said. "We did not have a great amour. She drugged me and put leaves on my chest and then she let me go, or rather, Barker saved me."

"He saved you?" Rebecca said frostily. "You mean that if he hadn't you'd still be there right now?"

"Of course not!"

"It seems to me you are in a better position than I. She's probably the one who shot at you, too. She must hate me."

"Believe me, Sofia does not love me. No doubt whatever feeling there was has curdled to hate and she is venting her spleen by taking potshots at me."

She looked up sharply. "You called her 'Sofia.' Had the two of you progressed to addressing each other by your first names?"

"At some point, I suppose. I don't remember. It's been so long."

"Were you lovers, Thomas?"

"Rebecca, I assure you we weren't. I was injured and drugged."

She put her hands on her hips and she was a terror to behold, all five foot two of her. "Does that mean you might have been if you weren't injured?"

"No!" I insisted. "She's just trying to rattle me."

She stepped forward and stared at me. "What does she look like?"

"Bizarre," I replied. "She's very pale and her hair is almost white. She wears kohl to darken her eyelids and brows. Her eyes are almost yellow, rather vulpine looking."

She stamped her foot. "I'll be certain to look up the word 'vulpine' when I have a moment between flying bullets. What of her figure?"

"What are you talking about?"

"Is she thin, is she stout? Does she have a nice figure compared to me?"

"Rebecca, no one is comparing her figure to yours! You are the one and only girl for me. I love you with all my being. I certainly don't have any feelings about her, save for anger and repulsion. If she had any for me, I never did anything to encourage her. My god, do you think I would desire an attachment to the daughter of perhaps the worst man I've ever met? He exuded menace. Nightwine twisted her, stunted her. He debased her and made her do his bidding."

"It sounds to me as if you're defending her," she remarked.

I moved forward and sat on the edge of my chair. "Rebecca, listen. I've done nothing to encourage the girl, then or now. I want nothing to do with her. I loved you then, even before we met again. I love you now. Please stop tormenting yourself. She won't hurt either one of us. She's here to kill Nicholas. She'll succeed or she'll fail. She's made her point, that you are vulnerable. Now she'll move on."

"Not before she's spoken with you face-to-face, Thomas," she said. "If you think otherwise, you don't understand women at all."

I sighed and drooped. "I don't want to understand women,

Rebecca. Just one woman, you. She can go jump in the Serpentine for all I care."

"I don't like this, Thomas. I don't like it at all. She has become obsessed with you. No one stalks someone and shoots at them and their family on a whim. Perhaps she hoped you would know it's her, only you were too thick to understand the message."

"Too thick?"

"Give me a pistol. I shall go out and shoot her back. No doubt she's hovering in the area looking for another chance. Will it be flattering to have two women fighting over you?"

"Rebecca," I said, standing.

She put both hands up, warning me. "I have a headache. I believe I shall lie down. Tell Mr. Barker if he wants to have his bushes trimmed he can get one of his gardeners to do it."

I watched her leave. What could I say to assure her? *Do I follow her? Do I not follow her?* This was not simply an argument about men and women. There was an assassin involved.

I fell back in my chair and stared at the ceiling. "Did you get all that, Mac? Or shall I bring Rebecca down again so she can repeat it?"

The door to Mac's chamber discreetly closed. I stood and looked at Barker's library. Actually, it was a communal library. Some of the books were mine. I reached for a title on Ceylon, on the second shelf from the bottom on the left. I opened it. There was an envelope in the middle of the book. I opened that as well, and unfolded a letter.

*14 May 1886*

*Dear Thomas,*

*I am sitting here on the veranda of a quaint little bungalow overlooking the Mahaweli and thinking of you. I hope Mr. Barker has recovered from his ordeal and your lives are no longer turned upside down as they were. I should be sorry,*

*I suppose, for the events I helped to facilitate, but then if it had not happened I should never have met you, and I am glad I did. Kidnapping you from the priory was a whim, but our time together during your recovery may have been the best moments of my life. I have given over my father's body to a Buddhist monastery for burial and am now free to live as I choose. I have money enough to last until I decide what that life shall entail. Your chastisement of me for the murder of Andrew McClain was the first regret I have ever had for a death at my own hand. I would like to think it was my last, and that I may in time forget the training that was forced upon me. And yet, I understand I am my father's daughter. I have always liked shiny baubles, and I'm not very good at penurious living. If I return to my old habits, you must share in the blame for not coming to rescue me from it. I should not need to make the only sacrifice. And yet, dear Thomas, you have given me a seed of hope. Perhaps I may live a normal life yet. Certainly, it was what my mother wished and prayed for. Ceylon is so peaceful, and it would be wonderful to live here forever, working with my hands by day and sitting on the veranda at evening's end, watching the sun go down. I wish you could be here to enjoy it. But don't worry. I do not expect you.*

*Sofia*

# CHAPTER TWENTY-SIX

Barker and I were approaching Craig's Court the following morning when I heard a grunt of displeasure from my partner's lips. I looked ahead and saw a man waving at us from the step of our offices.

"It's Colonel Waverly," I said. "I thought you'd sent him on his way."

"So I did, Thomas," the Guv replied. "It appears he's not convinced of our seriousness in refusing his offer."

"He did say he'd give us a few days to consider it, sir. Perhaps Philippa has been politicking. You should be careful or she'll be speaking to you again."

"Gentlemen, gentlemen," Waverly cried as we stepped down to the curb. "Hail fellow well met. Have you a minute to spare? The Home Office says you have insinuated yourselves into the tsarevich's good graces."

"Such as they are," I mumbled under my breath.

"Come, Colonel," the Guv said, motioning him into our chambers. "Would you care for a cigar?"

The remark was not said with enthusiasm.

I was pulled up short. I'd been around Nicholas too much and had been rude. Barker had shown decorum and politeness to a guest in his office. I would make an effort, as well.

"How are you, Colonel?" I asked as we shook hands.

"Never better, Mr. Llewelyn. Good to see you, boy."

Boy. Lad. There it was again. I suppose I should be flattered. I was eight-and-twenty now, and a married man, but then I was with two fellows whose experiences went far beyond mine. I believe the queen's equerry did not earn the rank of colonel in the diplomatic corps.

"A good Dunhill is a marvelous thing," our visitor said. I assumed it was a rhetorical remark.

"What can the agency do for you, Colonel Waverly?" Barker asked. "One does not often receive a visit from a royal equerry thrice in one week."

Waverly blew out the smoke. "First of all, to encourage you to reconsider and accept your ascension. I understand Baroness Ashleigh was going to mention it to you."

Barker glanced my way and I pretended to look at a scrape on my polished boots.

"Thank you, no, sir," he answered. "I'll accept no medal at this time."

"And you, young man," Waverly said, looking at me. "You refuse, as well?"

"I do, sir."

It was tempting and I thought of Rebecca's face if I returned that evening with good news, but I still could not accept.

"Very well, I shall press on," the colonel said, tapping off an inch of ash into the glass ashtray on the Guv's desk. "I've got to say you are more subtle than one would think by your appearance. The notes I have in your file did not mention this. I can

only conclude that the authors were not subtle men. Your remark only came to me that night after dinner when I was having
a cup of tea by the fire. A single word, sir. You said, 'I'll warrant
that . . .' You want a warrant. That is to say, a royal warrant."

I smiled to myself. The old duffer had mistaken us again. He
was grasping at straws, trying to understand why he had been
refused. Then I looked at Barker and realized that it was I who
had been mistaken; I who had not been subtle enough to read the
signs.

A full half of the facial expressions Cyrus Barker makes are no
expression at all, but I had become by default the world's expert
on reading him. He looked as if he were simply sitting in his
chair, mildly interested in what the colonel would say, but I knew
better. He was like a cat purring to himself.

"Of course, no detective has been given a royal warrant before," Waverly continued. "The idea is patently absurd. On the
other hand, why should a shortbread maker receive a warrant
when you have succeeded in saving two future monarchs in as
many minutes?"

Barker nodded.

"It is required that a warrant be given after five years of active
service to the empire," the old fellow said. "You saved the life of
the Prince of Wales six years ago, and according to deeper research on my part I was able to discover at least one time in each
year when you were of service to the crown. That terrible business with the Whitechapel murders a few years ago. I hear from
Scotland Yard that you were instrumental in bringing that case
to a successful conclusion."

It was Munro, I realized. That old dragon had actually
vouched for us. Either he had had a change of heart about Barker
since they shared the duties of the Templars or he found himself
unable to build a suitable argument against him. I felt generous
enough to imagine it was the former.

"Now, it will take some time, and you must attend a ceremony, but that is a formality. I have come to offer you the warrant. Please tell me, tell us all—the palace and the sovereign herself—that you will not turn down this honor."

"I will not," Barker said. "I accept your generous offer, sir."

The colonel gave a broad smile and seemed to relax in his chair. "Jolly good, then, sir. I congratulate you. You shall be able to hang your warrant sign within six months' time. Mind you, it cannot be too large and ostentatious. You don't know what arguments we had with a certain candy maker."

"Not too large nor ostentatious," my partner repeated. "I shall hang it on the wall by our front door."

"It need not be that small! One could hardly see it from White-hall Street," Waverly said, looking toward the bow window.

"True," he answered. "But anyone coming to Craig's Court for an enquiry agent shall spot it readily enough."

Waverly looked at Barker as if trying to penetrate his exterior, which was practically impossible. "I don't know about the detective business, but I'm sure you know what you are about."

The colonel drew in the smoke and blew a small but perfect smoke ring. Barker could blow one with the best of them, but allowed him this small flourish. Waverly stood and turned his chair in my direction and then sat down again.

"Mr. Llewelyn, I have come here all the way from Buckingham Palace expressly to see you as well. I've been to Lincoln's Inn to speak to an old acquaintance of yours and also to a few old cronies on the bench there."

"Cronies?" I asked.

"Yes, the Right Honorable Mr. Palmister Clay, QVC."

I nearly jumped from my seat. He was the bounder whose testimony had sent me to prison all those years ago. I had been his batsman before an unfortunate incident in which I was accused of theft.

"I needn't take you through the entire process, sir," Waverly said. "Although you might wish to hear it sometime, but the point is that Mr. Clay has recanted his testimony. All charges against you have been dropped. The government apologizes for your wrongful conviction and imprisonment. Of course, we cannot give you back those eight months, but there will be some compensation given in time."

Barker actually looked surprised as well, which meant he had no idea this had happened. For once, something was a complete surprise to him.

Waverly chuckled.

"He looks like a fish blowing bubbles, doesn't he?" Waverly asked the Guv.

"Close your mouth, Mr. Llewelyn," my partner said.

"I don't know what to say, Colonel," I replied. "This took me by surprise. I'll take it, and thank Her Majesty's government for me. I've been carrying that burden around for years."

"Yes, and I had a few choice words for your defending barrister, as well. His so-called defense was negligible. There is a vast difference between a servant holding up a coin and one putting it in his pocket. Even a layman knows better than that. I'd have spoken to the presiding judge as well but he is in a higher court now," he said, pointing to the ceiling.

"I don't know what to say," I answered. I looked at the Guv. "Sir, may I have an hour to speak to my wife and share the news?"

"Go, but come back quickly," Barker said. "We have work to do."

"Yes, sir. Colonel, you can't know what this means," I said, shaking his hand vigorously. "Thank you. Thank you for all you've done."

"Be gone with you, boy. Give your wife my regards."

I ran out into the street, waving my arms, and when a hansom finally arrived, I cried, "The City!"

Inside the cab, I held myself, much as I had held myself the day I was placed in a cell and left on my own. I wanted to do Catherine wheels and handsprings. It all came flooding back. Being caught, then beaten by Clay's cronies. The arrest, the charges, the trial. Then the treadmill and picking apart old rope for hours on end. I remembered the terrible food, the flea-ridden beds, the thump in the ribs from another inmate when no authority was in sight, merely for the joy of beating another human being. No books to read, no paper to write upon. No letters expected. The cruel notice of the death of my first wife, Jenny, from consumption. It was hell on earth. I served my time. Inexplicably, I was hired by Barker, and on our very first case together, I met a girl named Rebecca Mocatta, a girl of seventeen at the time, and my life began to start again.

The ride took forever, but I fell into one reverie after another. How did this happen? Would I awaken and find it was all a dream? I knew it was not much in the scheme of things. Those who did not know would probably find out, and those who knew already would never forget. But I was exonerated by Her Majesty's government, and most would begin to doubt that my disgrace was well founded, at least in their heart of hearts.

When I arrived in Camomile Street I slowed the cab and rode by once or twice, waiting to see if my wife was receiving a call from one of her set. She was, and I paid the cab and skulked about Bevis Marks Synagogue next door, waiting for them to leave. Apparently, some people are long-winded. At one point I wondered if they had been asked to tea, they were there so long. At last, I watched the two women leave, Rebecca almost pushing them into a cab. She went inside and I vaulted over the gate. That day I could fly.

When I threw open the door, Rebecca turned about, as if fearing her two guests had made a second attempt to storm the castle. Then she saw it was me.

"Hello, Thomas," she said. "What are you doing here in the middle of the day?"

Then she saw my face and I led her into the parlor. I left the door open so that our maid could hear. She was a spy for Rebecca's mother, looking for anything to complain about. There was a time when they separated from their daughter over me. Perhaps now they'd have less reason to despise me.

"What is it?" she demanded. "What is happening?"

"All charges against me from my time in jail have been dropped," I said in a rush to get it out. "I am exonerated and shall be compensated for my false incarceration."

She cried out with joy, and hugged me. Then we sat down and I told her the story from beginning to end, twice. She has a keen mind, Rebecca, and her remarks were sharp and to the point. Then we hugged again.

I saw the maid as she skulked off, possibly to call my mother-in-law. *Take that in the eye, Mrs. Mocatta.* I hadn't received such good news since Rebecca had agreed to be my wife, and many years before that.

We rang for tea, which was brought by a very stony-faced maid. Meanwhile, Rebecca lifted the teapot to pour.

"We must celebrate!" she said. "Can you stay?"

"I fear I must return for an appointment. We're still in the middle of the case."

Rebecca handed me a cup and studied me carefully. "I always believed you were cruelly used, almost the worst I've ever heard of. And now, exonerated! It's not just a triumph for you, but for the British legal system. Perhaps we should send flowers to Colonel Waverly."

"A wise choice," I agreed, "but I believe a box of Dunhills from Astley's would be more appropriate."

"I'll do that," she said.

We kissed again, and then I went in search of another cab. Who could believe it? Even I had trouble swallowing it.

"Was Mrs. Llewelyn pleased?" the Guv asked, after I returned to the office.

"Yes, sir. She was. And a warrant! That's wonderful!"

"Excellent. Thomas, I want you to send for Soho Vic," he said. "Leave the wallet here."

"Yes, sir."

"Jeremy!" he called to the waiting room. "Come here."

Reluctantly, I gave Barker his own wallet and waited to see what order he would give our clerk. My partner was having none of that.

"Off with you, Mr. Llewelyn. We don't have all day to dawdle."

"No, sir," I said, stepping out into Craig's Court and White-hall Street.

There are never messenger boys around when you need one, I noticed, and when you don't they're standing about with their hands in their pockets. Or yours. I spent almost five valuable minutes looking for one, while Jenkins strolled by as if he'd been given a duty far more important and interesting than mine. Finally, a boy slipped by like a salmon on the River Spey, but I hooked him at the final moment.

"Le'go, you tosser!" he cried.

I pulled some coins from my pocket uncounted and slapped them into his hand. He stopped struggling instantly.

"We need Vic. Now," I said.

"Go' it!" he replied, and was gone as he had come, slipping through the stream of slower-moving pedestrians.

My duty done, I hopped it inside to find out what the Guv had planned. Of course he wouldn't tell me.

"What time is the wedding, tomorrow, Thomas?"

"Twelve-thirty, sir, according to yesterday's *Times*."

"St. James's Palace?"

"Yes, sir. The Chapel Royal, to be precise."

"Let us set our watches."

We pulled our repeaters from our waistcoat pockets and stepped outside to synchronize them. It's easy when the most famous clock in the entire world is down the street. Mine was two minutes behind. It's the refrain of my life.

Half an hour later both Jenkins and Soho Vic were struggling to be the first in our office. Vic was once the bane of my existence, the blight on my escutcheon. He was the nominal head of the messenger boys in the area, and a crafty little fellow at seventeen.

"Wotcher, Push," he said, using Barker's underworld moniker. "What have you got for me?"

"I need you and your boys at the Speakers' Corner in Hyde Park as soon as possible."

"That'll take some doing," he replied. "How many do you need?"

"Fifty."

We blinked. I think Vic actually winced.

"Fifty?" he said. "You're barmy."

"I'll take my custom elsewhere, then, sir. Thank you for your time."

"I've only got about twenty lads, Push."

"Then get some from other gangs," Barker ordered. "Rival gangs, if necessary. I need them there by five o'clock."

"Five o'clock! That's only an hour and a half away!"

"Then you'd better stop arguing with me and get on with it. There is money to be made."

"Spoken like a Scot," Vic said. "Five o'clock. Hyde Park. Got it."

He wheeled and was gone. In the outer office, Jenkins was looking pleased with himself. There were two small pasteboard boxes on the corner of Barker's desk. I reached for one and got my hand slapped for my troubles. Really, a partner should not have his hand slapped by a mere clerk. It sets the entire world of commerce at naught.

"Let us walk along the route to St. James's and see what we may see, Thomas. Jeremy, you'll be there at the appropriate hour?"

"You can count on me, Mr. B.," Jenkins assured him.

I was less assured, convinced our clerk would stop for a pint or seven before his arrival, but that was just hubris on my part. For all his peccadilloes, when it came down to it he was always reliable. He even returned Barker's wallet to me.

We hailed a cab and turned west on the way to the palace. Then we rode as far as we could before we saw the road was being closed to vehicular traffic in preparation for the wedding the following afternoon. Already, a crowd was forming on both sides of the street.

"We are cutting it fine," I said.

"True," Barker conceded, "but I only came upon a solution last night."

"If we fail, the calamity would not fall upon our shoulders, sir."

"Perhaps not, but I would know and you would know. I did not open an enquiry agency in order to fail," Barker replied, a trifle tartly.

We walked along the outskirts of the crowd, looking overhead at the buildings. The street bristled with them, most at least three stories high or more. La Sylphide need not shoot from the roof. She could simply hire a room upon the parade route and then melt away afterward.

"I think she's half in love with me. Sofia, I mean."

"You're just working that out now?"

"I never once considered—I mean, she killed Andy McClain, not to mention who knows how many others."

"At the time, you were pining for Miss Mocatta, elusive as she was."

"Was it that obvious?" I asked.

"Let us say you would not be a good whist partner."

I looked up. So many windows. Too many windows to count, not to mention the roofs. The weather was warm. Windows would be opened. No one would wish to watch a parade through a pane of dirty glass. They'd want a good view. And in any of those windows could be a woman holding a mechanical weapon capable of vaporizing a man's head with a puff of condensed air.

Barker and I were stopped by the congestion of the crowd.

"This is impossible," I remarked.

"Let's head for the Speakers' Corner. It's our next stop."

Half an hour later, we arrived at the far end of Hyde Park on Piccadilly and walked to the Speakers' Corner.

First of all, it isn't a corner at all. It is an open area where all Her Majesty's citizens can come and hear someone speak on any subject for the common good. There is no stage, no podium, just a set of short steps one would use to mount a horse. People could come and state their views and the crowd was allowed to question, argue, or even call down the speaker. In fact, at that very moment a woman was giving an impassioned speech, while the crowd was doing all three.

"Violence shall find us all clapped in irons!" Eleanor Marx was crying. "All the good work the Socialist League has done in London will be sullied irretrievably if we turn to anarchy. Give Scotland Yard no reason to arrest us and we can argue about our government's egregious wasteful spending afterward!"

She was being hooted down. The anarchists weren't standing for her rhetoric. If anything she was too pretty, too intelligent, and too well-spoken. She sounded like one of them, the bourgeoisie. She lived in a beautiful home in the South of London. She'd never gone to bed hungry. She'd never spent a night on the street, or slept in a doss-house. The few times she'd been arrested, a solicitor had been there to post bail. She was a woman, and no anarchist wants to listen to a woman counseling them to calm down and be peaceable.

"It looks like Sofia Ilyanova may not be the only one to watch," I said, looking at the unruly crowd. "I hope Scotland Yard is up to the task."

"They'll have to be," the Guv answered. "We've got our hands full at the moment."

The meeting broke up. From where I stood Miss Marx did not look particularly pleased. As the crowd dispersed, I saw that there were over a dozen boys waiting for the next speech. More were coming from every direction, running, looking about, even breaking into fights. They belonged to various gangs with known grievances against each other.

"Give me my wallet, Thomas," the Guv said.

"Better you than them, sir," I said.

Soho Vic was waiting at the bottom step of the platform when we arrived. He saluted, but I suspected he was as nervous as I.

"How many did you speak to?" the Guv asked.

"About thirty, Push, but they are going to bring their mates. Everyone knows there's money to be made with you."

They began to arrive in earnest then, wondering what was going on. They were an even surlier crowd than the one Eleanor Marx had spoken to. The youths ranged in age from six to twenty. While many were still arriving, the group in front of us began hooting with impatience. I looked at Barker and he at me. Perhaps we need not wait another hour.

"'Ello, Mr. L. Here I am," Jenkins said, appearing with the mysterious boxes.

As I suspected he was plowed as a field. Our clerk could barely stand, but he was here and on time. That was what mattered, I supposed.

Barker handed one of the boxes to Vic. I heard jingling inside them. *Bells?* I thought. *Christmas bells. What was he about?* I was going to ask but my partner was already mounting the steps and quieting the crowd.

"Gentlemen," he boomed. "And ladies." The latter was directed toward a small girl in the front row. "I won't take up much of your time. Listen carefully. There will be a woman near the gate of St. James's in Pall Mall at noon tomorrow who means some sort of mischief toward the royal family. She should not be difficult to spot. Her face and hair are very pale and she is dressed as a widow. We do not know which building she will be hiding in but she must be found. Scotland Yard is occupied with the wedding. The Home Office will be searching the area building by building. They consider you a rabble of no consequence, but I believe the group of you are a match for both the Met and the Home Office any day."

The children laughed and many of them nodded their heads in agreement. To some it was novel to be spoken to by an adult as a group.

"In these boxes here are Acme Thunderers, the best whistles in England. You will each be given one. Whoever is the first among you to spot the woman in question, I will give fifty pounds." He reached into his pocket and held up a fifty-pound note for all to see. The crowd was going wild.

Fifty pounds! What could a family in the East End do with fifty pounds? It could feed them for a year. It could buy them clothes and shoes. It could provide them a better dwelling. Children could go to school. It was a sum so large that the children could barely imagine the amount.

"After she is found and one of you is the winner of this prize, the rest of you have two options. One, you can keep the whistle with my compliments. Or you can turn it in at seven Craig's Court in Whitehall for a pound note. Is that perfectly clear?"

"Clear as a pane-less window," one of the boys cried out.

"All right, gentlemen and lady," Barker said. "I will see you tomorrow. I wish you all good hunting."

A half hour later we entered our offices again. Within a minute Barker was in his chair, turned around away from me.

"Ah, Thomas. Sit down. We have much to discuss."

"We do?"

"Most certainly."

I sat, mystified. "Now, you've worked here several years and are approaching your second year as a partner. The question I would ask is, are you satisfied?"

"Satisfied, sir?" I asked.

"You are now unfettered and can do as you like," the Guv replied. "Some money is due you. You have your own house, a wife. What shall you do now?"

"Now?"

"Stop repeating the last word I say. The blot is off your record. You can return to university. You could be a professor, a barrister, even a doctor if you wish. You could dawdle for a few years and write another book of poetry. You could travel and see the world, take your wife to Rome or Athens. For a time, at least, the world is your oyster. So, what shall you do?"

I nearly repeated the last word again, but recovered myself.

"What do you mean, sir?"

"If it is your wish, I shall buy you out. You need not continue in so dangerous a situation. I'm sure your wife is keen for you to retire from enquiry work."

"But who would help you, sir?"

"Oh, I'd find another assistant, of course," he replied. "Mac has wanted the position for nearly ten years."

"But you need him at home. You've said so dozens of times."

The Guv nodded. "Aye, but you won't be living in Newington anymore. We both knew that would happen eventually, anyway."

We did, but it ached a little to hear it from his lips.

"I never asked to retire, sir."

"True, but you've never been in such a position before," he said. "All doors have been closed to you until now. Now they stand open for you. What shall you do?"

"I would never leave the agency," I stated. "It is my life."

"One can change one's life if one has the wherewithal. Consider the matter."

"Excuse me," I said, "but you are beginning to sound like the colonel."

"Am I? Discuss it with Mrs. Llewelyn and get back to me. Take a day to consider it."

"No need," I replied. "I'm not going anywhere. Who wouldn't want to work in a place with a royal warrant?"

# CHAPTER TWENTY-SEVEN

As promised when we met, Barker and I brought Jim Hercules into our bar-jutsu school for a private bout that evening. We had dinner at the Clarence and met in our antagonistics school at seven o'clock. He looked about our little establishment with approval.

"Good solid mats, mirrors, barbells, medicine balls, Indian clubs . . . You've got it all here, gentlemen."

"If you're going to do a thing," the Guv replied, "don't scrimp on details."

"You can change there in the locker room, Mr. Hercules," I said. "And there is a water closet in the back."

"You can just call me Jim, sir," he said before retiring to the locker room. "I don't stand on ceremony."

"Are you boxing today, Mr. Llewelyn?" Barker asked while our client was changing.

"He didn't come here to box me, sir, and I don't have anything to prove. You are the one with the reputation to uphold."

"Andrew taught you how to box, if you recall," the Guv said.

"I do. But not to a professional level."

"As you wish."

I doubted Jim practiced boxing regularly. He was relying on latent skills. My partner outweighed our guest by a stone at least and his fighting style was unknown to Jim, a combination of English and Chinese boxing. While Barker was fully versed in the Marquess of Queensbury Rules, he rarely used them since Brother Andrew had been a bare-knuckle champion. Still, Jim had shoulders like cannonballs and lean hips. He could move quickly and he was a few years younger than the Guv. It would make for an interesting match.

Jim came out of our small locker room in a pair of silk drawers and boxing gloves. I began to doubt that he was out of shape. His stomach looked like it could stop a bull. He was in his element and would put up a fight. His limbs were smooth and relaxed. He looked like a panther on the prowl.

Barker went to change while Jim began to punch a hanging bag. The rhythm of his punches was as steady as a steam engine. I reckoned that just one would tear off my head. I told myself this would be a friendly match but I began to wonder if that was wishful thinking.

Barker returned wearing a pair of loose black trousers and canvas shoes. He'd traded his spectacles for a pair of goggles with gray lenses. His body was a mass of tattoos, scars, and burns. There was a dragon on the inside of one forearm and a tiger on the other. A slash of scar tissue dimpled his shoulder and a triangle surrounded with Chinese calligraphy was on his left breast. There was a circular brand mark on his biceps. I could see that Jim Hercules found him interesting as an opponent.

"Mr. Hercules, you wanted to spar with Andrew McClain's boxing partner. Here I am."

Hercules nodded and then surged forward, but it was only to tap gloves. Both men stepped back and came in again to begin. Barker managed to lay over a halfdozen punches at Jim's head. He was testing his opponent's strengths and weaknesses. So was I. Hercules had almost six more inches of reach. Also, the Guv preferred to box bare-knuckle, but such a fight would be brutal. Men have died in bare-knuckle fights, which is why they were now illegal. Barker wasn't comfortable with his hands restricted in regulation sixteen-ounce boxing gloves. He had dozens of techniques, but only when his hands were free.

A blow by Jim caught him in the shoulder, which then scraped across his head. A fist tried to reach his stomach, but could not get past Barker's elbows and thick forearms. Then Hercules gave him a solid punch on the nose. Cyrus Barker stepped back and held a glove to his face to see if claret had been spilt. It hadn't. The fight continued.

A dozen blows were traded and parried, with no obvious damage to either party. Then Hercules snaked a fist in and tried another blow at Barker's head. The Guv parried it with a casual flick upward, then struck a spot the ex-boxer didn't expect in the tender skin under his arms, where nerves crisscross leading to the arms and hands. It wasn't expected here, but then Barker wasn't trained in England, and only learned boxing after meeting Brother Andrew. Hercules jumped back and shook his arm, grimacing, but was soon back for more.

I was half concerned one of them would kill the other and half wishing I had the foresight to sell tickets. This was some doings any sportsman in London would attend, if it weren't clandestine. Hercules connected with a hook punch to Barker's head and a minute later received a blow to the chin which snapped his head back.

Jim began to circle him, looking for an advantage. Barker

was not the sort to move about. His feet were solidly planted. This didn't work to his advantage. Hercules caught him in the kidneys and the Guv hissed through his teeth in pain.

"Warning!" I cried.

"Yes, sir," Jim said.

He danced around, then aimed another punch at my partner's head. Barker rose his gloves just high enough that Jim got under and slammed a fist into his stomach. I knew it was a mistake. I've delivered fifteen kicks in a row to the Guv's stomach and he never bats an eye. It was like punching a skillet. It also set him up for another blow. Barker's right hand dropped to his belt and I knew what was coming. The Guv's arm hinged at the elbow, came around in a circle horizontally, and caught our guest on the cheek with the edge of his glove. Jim's eyes rolled up into his head and he swayed sideways and fell onto the mat. Barker shook his hand. It was a risk he had taken. That move can easily break bones in the hand.

Hercules lay crumpled on the ground while I came over to inspect him, it being my duty to examine those who fought my employer and to scrape them off the mat afterward.

"You haven't killed him, I'm glad to say," I observed. "It's difficult to get paid after you kill a client."

Barker sat on the mat, looking sore and exhausted. "Check his pulse."

It took me a minute or so to find it. "Steady enough."

"Let us get him in a chair."

I lifted and dragged him to a chair. His eyes still hadn't aligned.

"Are you with us, Mr. Hercules?" I asked.

"I'm here," he said.

He was stout, I had to give him that.

"Tell me, sir," Barker said. "When were you going to tell me you were working for your government? Or is it ours?"

Our client smiled, revealing the blood in his teeth.

"Smart," he said. "Didn't I say he was smart, Mr. Llewelyn?"

"You did."

"That was a thing of beauty: that punch. I've never seen anything like it. When did you learn to box?"

"In Canton, under the tutelage of a doctor named Wong."

"I'd like to meet the man."

"I'll ask one more time," Barker demanded. "Which government are you working for? American or English?"

"Both, actually," Hercules admitted. "I was recruited by the Military Information Department after I was hired by the tsar. The Home Office is still concerned about Russia as a longtime enemy, while the United States is concerned about a possible attack across the Bering Strait, to a territory called Alaska. Apparently they've had a gold strike."

"You've been supplying them both information."

"I have. I've watched the tsar and his family for years. I go back to Washington every summer to report and send dispatches to the Home Office every month or so. No one knows the MID and the Home and Foreign Offices are using information supplied by a Negro."

"I'm sure you were a fine asset."

"How'd you guess I'm a spy?" Jim asked.

"I am naturally suspicious," the Guv said. "I had an operative following you just in case."

"The devil you say. I can spot a man a hundred yards away."

"I assumed that," the Guv continued, "so I sent a woman."

Jim Hercules burst out laughing. "Don't that beat all? Perhaps I was too smart for my own good when I hired you."

"If you intended to hoodwink me, yes, you were. Now, sir, I've been patient. Please tell me why you enlisted my services."

"The truth?"

"The honest truth, Mr. Hercules."

Jim bit the laces on his gloves and slid his hand out, then untied the other lace. "The god's honest truth was just as I said it was, I just didn't tell you all I know. No one, sir, no one cares about that boy. The Okhrana doesn't. They hope he is assassinated so the grand dukes will fight between themselves for power and line their pockets in the process. Scotland Yard is concentrated on keeping the public safe. The Home Office wants the wedding over and done with and the palace has more than enough ambassadors and sovereigns for three royal weddings. Nobody cares about Nicky but the queen herself, me, and the two of you. I'm occupied with keeping my friend calm and out of trouble and Her Majesty is hosting a family reunion. That leaves the two of you. Are you up to the task?"

Barker looked at him for a moment. He still hadn't changed and a towel was thrown over his shoulders. "You have no family of your own, do you, Mr. Hercules? No wife or children?"

"I am a lifelong bachelor. I didn't plan it that way, but there you are."

"And Nicholas's father is tsar of all Russia and disappointed in the son he had."

"That is true, Mr. Barker," Jim admitted. "He thinks his son is weak and spoiled by his mother."

"You are a second father and mentor to him and he comes to you for advice. Often you are the only one he will listen to. Likewise, Nicholas is the son you never had. You came to care because no one else did. You saw the man he might become if he were being properly looked after."

"He's a dark horse, but if I can keep him alive through this damned wedding, he might prove himself yet."

"Is the Military Information Division aware of your friendship with Nicholas beyond the news you send along?"

"No. If they knew, they'd order me out of Russia at once. Then who'd protect that boy? I've got to care about something. The U.S. ain't my home anymore, and all I have to do all day is see to the safety of the imperial family. I'm not bragging when I say I do a pretty good job. But this, this wedding, this assassin, it's too much for one person. I came to you because he needs help and I needed people I could trust. I need you fellows to do the very best you can."

"We will," the Guv said. "That I promise you."

I nodded.

Hercules stood up, a little wobbly on his pins.

"You've got a fine right hook," he said.

"And you'd have given Andrew a fine match, sir," Barker said. "He would have liked to meet you."

"Thank you, Mr. Barker," he answered. "I have to go wipe my eyes. I've got sweat in them."

When he was gone, I turned to my partner.

"Do you believe him?" I asked.

"I don't know him. But he's openly admitted to being a foreign spy."

I sat on a bench, picked up an iron dumbbell, and began curling it.

"He'd have to be a very good actor to put on a scene such as the one we just witnessed," I said.

"Aye, but the man was recruited because of his talent, as well as his position."

"True," I said.

Curl four, curl five, curl six.

"Either he's telling the truth or he's lying."

Barker rose a brow. "Brilliant logic, Mr. Llewelyn. And?"

"And there is no way we are able now to say which it is. We'll have to decide later, unless we find the answer first."

"He said one thing in his favor," the Guv remarked. "He did not think of America as his home. I suspect he is considering throwing over his duties as a spy and becoming a Russian citizen."

"To protect Nicholas?"

"I assume so. We can't know at this point."

Hercules came out in his suit, the jacket thrown over one shoulder.

"Thanks for the match, Mr. Barker. I ain't never seen boxing like that. I may have to find an Asian in Saint Petersburg willing to teach me some Chinese boxing."

"You are welcome to visit our school should you ever return," the Guv said.

"I'd like to think that Andrew McClain would say I had talent, but you beat me handily."

"Every boxer must understand that there are men who can best him. It is humbling, which is never a bad thing and encourages more training. I have my limits as well."

"I must get back, gentlemen, but there's something new afoot that you should know. There's going to be a ball tonight. Nicky suggested the royal family give one and they were caught out. They felt they could not refuse him."

"A ball," Barker said, with a look of distaste on his normally expressionless face.

"Worse," Jim said. "Far worse. A nightmare, in fact. It is to be a masked ball."

Barker shook his head. The government had lost all reason, kowtowing to the son of the tsar, scurrying to meet his every whim.

"The task has been given to Lord Haslemere, whose life will likely be tossed on its ear. Can you believe the chaos, the cost for a costumed ball? I didn't hear about it until last night."

"I suspect it's all so Nicholas can have a tryst with his mistress behind the elephant palms," I said. I turned to my partner. "We must prepare."

"I believe there is a domino mask in the back room, Mr. Llewelyn. That and a proper evening suit is all that a gentleman requires. Unless you prefer to go as Harlequin or Pierrot."

"No, sir," I replied.

The Guv was speaking about the lumber closet, which contained fifty hats as well as cloaks, coats, boots, gloves, and even a false beard or two. But those were for professional purposes. A masked ball was frivolous.

"I was able to convince Nicholas that the two of you might come in handy at the ball," Hercules said.

"Handy?" the Guv asked, turning to me as some kind of translator.

"Helpful," I answered.

"Ah."

"Of course, he told the Okhrana that it was his idea, not mine."

Barker smiled, which always looks like a dog baring his teeth. "Have you used this connection to the tsarevich before?"

"A time or two," Hercules admitted.

"Would you say that the gentleman is suggestible?" I asked.

"He's little more than a youth," Barker growled. "And is here in this country without a proper wet nurse."

"Oh, he's got one," Jim Hercules replied. "It's called the Barker and Llewelyn Agency."

"That's grand," my employer said, a bitter tone in his voice.

"Well, gentlemen, you did accept the case. Or enquiry."

"Where will the ball take place, sir?" Barker asked.

"At Lord Haslemere's house by Regent's Park."

An impromptu masked ball with the tsarevich conniving with his mistress and an assassin lurking in the shadows. Just another typical day at the Barker and Llewelyn Agency. Warrant pending.

# CHAPTER TWENTY-EIGHT

I'm not a great believer in the aristocracy. It seems rather arbitrary. Why should one fellow sell potatoes on a street corner in Whitechapel while another wastes his days in a castle because his great-grandfather played cards and wenched with King Henry VIII? It doesn't seem to be a matter of breeding. I've seen the most noble faces on young women in Poplar and I've seen countesses that looked like—well, I shall be gentlemanly. Let us say they did not present physical traits someone would appreciate three generations hence.

One could build a case that I'm envious. The old Llewelyn line strutted around Wales for a few hundred years, giving themselves airs. The problem was I arrived several centuries too late.

"I feel ridiculous," I told Barker, raising my domino mask up over my forehead.

"You look ridiculous," he replied. "But then, Nicholas did not arrange this ball for our benefit."

"He did not arrange it at all. He merely snapped his fingers and here we are. It was arranged for him."

"Semantics, Mr. Llewelyn. Keep your eye on the crowd."

"To what end, sir? Everyone is wearing a mask. Should there be an attempt on Nicholas's life, what do I say? 'Arrest that peacock'? 'Detain the second half of that donkey'?"

Very well, my speech tends toward hyperbole. Most men wore evening kit, as we did, with some sort of mask. Every phylum of animal was represented, and a like number of gods and mythical creatures. The men looked uncomfortable even while their identities were shielded. That morning they argued in the House of Lords. This evening, they were posing as a giraffe.

The women's outfits were historical fantasies going back to ancient Egypt. Cleopatra was neither as lithe nor as young as she appeared in art, and as for Helen of Troy: her face was more likely to stop a clock than launch a ship. However, the women appeared to be enjoying themselves immensely. Someone whispered that the more esteemed costume shops had been picked as clean as a Christmas goose in an orphanage.

I'd have worn something more elaborate than a Harlequin mask, but my purpose there was not to draw attention to myself and to search for any danger to the tsarevich. Scotland Yard was in evidence and were even more conspicuous than we were. Some guests assumed the bobby uniforms were some rich wag's idea of a joke. So far, a sword had been taken from a gladiator, and Dick Turpin had his flintlock pistol confiscated.

"Do you believe there will be an attempt on his life tonight?" I asked the Guv.

"Who can say? But if it happens and we were not here, or worse yet, unable to stop an attempt, what good are we?"

"We'll get on, or we won't," I said. My partner has said that to me on more than one occasion.

"That's the spirit, lad."

Barker wore spectacles in a deep green that gave him an insect-like appearance, a mantis in an evening suit. However, they were merely spectacles and no one could say that he was attempting to represent any particular subject. But then, if anyone expected him to come dressed as a penguin or Genghis Khan, they did not know Cyrus Barker.

"What sort of family has a ballroom in their home?" I asked. "The entire street I was rose in could fit in this one room."

"I'm certain Her Majesty's government will have something to say about the expense, as well," Barker murmured. "The costumes cost more than you realize. I believe the jeweled necklace about Anne Boleyn's throat there is genuine."

The mansion was immense and I shuddered to imagine the price of land hard by the Regent's Park. There was an enormous staircase that the guests ascended to be viewed in their elaborate ensembles. The walls were decked out in gold, which continued the echo of another time. An octet played selections from Schumann and Chopin. The orchestra wore breeches and powdered wigs. I wondered how much they were paid to play here. In fact, I wondered how much everything cost altogether, in the thousands of pounds, perhaps, all to satisfy the whim of a bored young royal.

Barker was wealthy, true, but he didn't spend it ostentatiously. In fact, much of his income went to supporting charities such as the Sailors' Home and General Booth's Salvation Army. He was not especially frugal, as was the reputation of Scotsmen. If he bought a pair of boots, they came from Maxwell's, the best bootmaker in London. Nothing was ever threadbare. If anything was deemed unsatisfactory by Mac, he would order whatever was needed at a shop that had the Guv's size on record. Goodness knows where he found the spectacles.

I wondered if there was anyone present to keep the young tsarevich in check. I did not see the Okhrana, for example. He was taking a risk being here in a room full of masked people. I'm not saying anything derogatory about Scotland Yard. They are second to none, but if a person wants to hide a pistol badly enough, a way shall be found. Murder will out.

They entered then, the four of them: Nicholas, Prince George, Prince George of Greece and Denmark, and Grand Duke Sergei. The tsarevich was dressed as d'Artagnan, and the royals were the Three Musketeers. Before I even had time to take it all in, Barker groaned beside me.

"What is it?" I asked over the music.

"Prince George's costume is nearly identical to Nicholas's," he said. "We shall have to protect two men, not one."

"Do we risk separating?"

"It is not, strictly speaking, our duty to protect the tsarevich, as it is to stop the man who shall attempt to kill him."

"Who's that?" I asked, pointing to a man dressed in cardinal's robes with a red mask that had whiskers attached to it. Was it Richelieu? Did he know ahead of time that Nicholas and his cronies—if I may call His Highness a crony—had chosen Musketeer costumes?

The waltzes gave way to the formal dances, which always remind me of a chapter from Jane Austen: two rows of people, separated by gender, facing each other, ready for a musical cue. One row contained baboons, tigers, gods, and ogres, stuffed into their near-identical evening kit. The other looked like a Covent Garden Market on Sunday morning, pastel dresses looking like bouquets of flowers in every color imaginable. Fairy-tale heroines. Bo Peep and Red Riding Hood.

I came closer, skirting the dancers, looking from face to face. Then I felt a hand on my elbow and turned, ready to defend myself, but as it turned out, they were one man short and needed another gentleman in the dance. I attempted to protest, but it was too late. I was drawn in and squared off against my partner in the dance, an older woman impersonating Elizabeth I.

I joined in. Step forward, step back, bow. Step forward, circle around your partner, and step back again. I held the little woman's fingers overhead and she made a small hop and turned about. We changed partners for a moment then returned again. We took each other's hands and lifted them so that other couples could dance between us. When we came through ourselves, we changed partners.

My new partner wore a historical French dress of the last century, with a bosom compressed by a tall corset. Her dress was sumptuous, her hair in elegant ringlets, and her eyes covered with a mask of red lace. She was either a fictional or historical figure and I knew I should realize which one. Then it came to me. She was Milady de Winter, Cardinal Richelieu's spy, the one who seduced d'Artagnan. As it came to me, she smacked me between the eyes with the tip of her fan.

"*Vous petit cur,*" she whispered. "You lied from start to finish. Sergei tells me you are nothing but a filthy detective sent to spy on us."

All this while we were dancing forward, backward, circling, separating, and coming together again.

"Guilty as charged, I must confess, mademoiselle," I murmured to Mathilde Kschessinska, "though it broke my heart to do it."

"I should shoot you."

"You would only draw attention to yourself, and that is no way to sneak off with the tsarevich. That is your plan, I take it? An hour or two alone with Nicholas?"

"Nikolai belongs to me, my pet. He'll never marry that scrawny German woman your queen is throwing his way. No, he is mine! I will be tsarina, and I won't be stopped by a contemptible beast like you!"

There we were, arm in arm, dancing along between two rows of people, and she was spitting at me like an angry house cat.

"I fear you'll never be tsarina," I told her.

"If I cannot have him, monsieur, no one shall."

We stepped apart and she was gone, submerged in the crowd. I tried to follow after her, but I could not. The dance continued. I turned and faced my next partner.

She was dressed as Marie Antoinette in a flouncy dress with poufy hair. Her face was pale and her cheeks and lips rouged. In a macabre touch, she wore a necklace of garnets, the jewel of death. Fitting for a woman who would eventually be beheaded. She was young, I could see. My age at most.

We bowed and began to dance. Forward and back. Around and back. I took her hand and rose it. Our faces were but a foot apart.

"Hello, Thomas," she said.

It was Sofia Ilyanova.

I stumbled, nearly fell, and was immediately overrun by volleys of couples aimed at us. We were separated and a minute later she was gone. I pushed my way through the crowd of aristocrats to Barker's side.

"That Richelieu is Hesketh Pierce," the Guv said, disappointed.

"She's here, sir!" I interrupted. "Sofia Ilyanova. I just saw her. She's dressed as Marie Antoinette."

"Where is she?"

"She disappeared, sir."

"Damn and blast!" he cried. "Well, look for her!"

I did. We both did. He told Scotland Yard and Pierce and we were all searching for her, but she had indeed disappeared. Vanished like a creature of the air, a sylph.

"I don't see how she got out of this room," I told the Guv after we'd searched for twenty minutes. "One would think a woman dressed as Marie Antoinette would not be difficult to find."

"She changed her clothing, Thomas. She brought a second costume with her, possibly even a man's evening kit and a mask, since everyone is looking for a woman. You are certain it was Nightwine's daughter?"

"Oh, it was her all right," I insisted. "She spoke to me. She called me by my name."

"There was no attempt on the tsarevich?"

"None," I admitted. "He's danced with a dozen girls and is now drinking champagne with his cousins. He's surrounded by a full thirty people hoping to fling their daughters at him, but he doesn't seem to care."

"Why should he?" the Guv asked. "He's got a mistress. I'm doing my best to keep them apart."

I glanced at Nicholas. He wore a doublet, a wide-sleeved shirt, breeches, and a pair of black boots that folded over at the knee.

"Look at him," I said. "Doesn't he realize what danger he is in?"

"I think it likely this lad doesn't have any idea," Barker replied. "Let's keep it that way, shall we?"

"But I don't understand. Why didn't Sofia kill Nicholas when she had the chance? She could have done it easily. Do you think she came tonight merely to speak to me?"

"Perhaps. Who can say? She may have come all the way to England to see you. If she'd wanted to, she could have killed Nicholas in Saint Petersburg."

I turned and looked about. The Musketeers were still carousing. The dancing continued unabated. No one was aware that a person responsible for several deaths around the world had danced among them, unnoticed.

Just then I turned and saw Mathilde Kschessinska walk up to the tsarevich and speak to him. My stomach tightened.

"My word, is there any security at all here tonight?" I said, pointing her out to Barker. "We should stop her."

"No," Barker growled, charging toward the tsarevich.

I looked ahead of him in time to see Mathilde's hand retrieving a pistol from a pocket of her dress. Time seemed to stop. Her hand was in the air, her finger on the trigger ready to fire, ready to kill Nicholas. Ready to make us a disgrace among our peers.

No warrant. Possibly no expunging of my record. Oh, and no future leader for Russia.

Cyrus Barker ripped the pistol from her hand just as Pierce lunged forward and seized her by the shoulders. The Guv broke open the pistol.

"Empty," he said. "Hollow, like her threats."

Nicholas had blanched and ducked from the rose weapon. He now stepped forward again once he knew he was safe.

"Mathilde, how could you?" he demanded.

She began to scream at him in Russian. It was a monumental tantrum. I stepped up behind her to see the spectacle. Hesketh Pierce had lifted his absurd mask. He leaned over toward me.

"He ended their relationship this afternoon," he said. "Princess Alix has agreed to convert to the Russian Orthodox Church. The queen has had her way."

Pierce and two of his men literally carried the girl away, screaming and flailing as she went.

When they were gone, there was a pause. Then the band, in its powdered wigs, began again. Switch partners and dance.

# CHAPTER TWENTY-NINE

At approximately eleven o'clock that night Rebecca and I heard the telephone set ring in the hall below. She and I looked at each other. We'd been asleep and the house seemed so restful that the jangling seemed unusually loud. It continued to ring, two, three, four, five, before Mac finally answered the call. No doubt he'd been asleep as well, though the Guv read until late. He told me once he had the whole of Western culture to study in order to keep up with the rest of us. In reply, I said that one in fifty had paid as close attention as he.

Mac murmured into the receiver for a moment, then there was some sort of brief argument, and then I heard the phone set down in its cradle with some force. He ascended the stair to our landing and then continued up to Barker's chamber. There was another murmured argument, and footsteps moving above us. Then Mac came down in an ill mood and knocked upon our door. We both jumped up and put on our dressing gowns. Then I answered as if we hadn't yet retired.

"Yes?" I asked, opening the door.

"The Guv says to get dressed. Nicholas is missing."

I shut the door at once and began pulling clothes, any clothes, from the wardrobe in our rooms. My wife had grown as accustomed as any wife can to her husband getting up and out the door in the middle of the night, often involving work that can be dangerous. One is up to devilry at this hour and that is frequently what we were up against.

Barker and I found a cab in Newington Causeway.

"Sir," he said to the cabman. "Take us to Kensington Palace immediately. Time is of the essence. Put your horse in a lather and get us there now!"

"Right, sir," he replied. "Hold on to your seats, gentlemen!"

We climbed aboard and were soon heading to the Middlesex side of the Thames at breakneck speed.

"What do you know?" I asked.

"Very little, blast it. Jim Hercules said the tsarevich was last seen in the company of both Prince George and the grand duke. It was an impromptu party after the ball to celebrate George's last night of freedom."

We turned a corner on one wheel but righted ourselves after a few nail-biting seconds.

"Could it be a trick and the breakup just a ploy?" I asked. "Could the display with Mathilde Kschessinska have been a ruse? Could they have eloped?"

"Tonight?" Barker asked. His hand gripped the leather door so tightly I expected to pay for a new one.

"It's possible," I answered. "It could have been the plan all along. The ball was a subterfuge."

A few nervous minutes later we skidded to a halt in front of the entrance to Kensington Palace and alighted. I gave the man ten pounds and my partner and I ran through the long paths to the entrance. I thought we'd be stopped there, but who should be waiting for us but Jim Hercules and Hesketh Pierce of the Home Office.

"Come, gentlemen," Pierce said, a grim look on his face.

"Mr. Llewelyn has broached the theory that they may have escaped in order for the tsarevich to marry Mathilde Kschessinska," the Guv said. "What happened after your men took her away?"

Pierce mopped his brow with his handkerchief. He was no longer dressed as Richelieu. "The tsarevich insisted we release her," he growled. "This is a nightmare."

"Is it possible they escaped the palace grounds?" I asked.

"No. We are surrounded by guards. They were told to be particularly vigilant tonight."

Barker turned to Hercules. "Did it seem as if George was leaving them or that they would join him later?"

"I couldn't say, sir." He turned and looked at Barker. "Do you think you can find my friend?"

"Even if he doesn't want to be found?"

"Especially then," Jim said. "He's not very good at making decisions, if you had not noticed."

He looked at Barker as he had on that day he first walked into our offices. Impress me.

"Let us start in the shooting range," the Guv said. He looked at one of the guards. "Look for Prince George of Greece and Denmark. He seems the most levelheaded of the group."

Hercules led us down various sets of stairs and through empty halls until we reached an area I recognized. There he opened a door and led us inside.

"What purpose did this room serve before it was improvised as a shooting gallery?" the Guv asked.

"I don't know, sir," I said. "It was as you see it."

"I looked at a map of the building a few evenings ago," he continued. "This room had no name, just an $X$ across it, as one would use indicating a storage room."

"Interesting. I wonder what is in these barrels."

The Guv reached into a sleeve and extracted his dagger. He examined the barrel top on which the infamous pistol that had killed Pushkin had laid. He found the cork and began prying it out with the knife. It did not come easily and we all watched in frustration. Finally, the cork came free.

Barker bent over the barrel and sniffed. "Empty. There is no odor at all, save a slight mustiness. I believe it once contained water for the household. It is very likely all these barrels did."

He walked to the center of the room and looked about with his hands on his hips. "I presume that stack of barrels at the end there is your gallery. There is a rough circle out of chalk."

"That's it," I replied. "That's the target we were using."

"Does it look the same as when you were here last?"

"It's just a bunch of barrels with more of them on top."

"Aye, but the placement, lad. Close your eyes. Remember the way the barrels were set up, then open them again."

I hate remembering things. The very act of doing so pushed the memory further away. I sighed, closed my eyes, and tried to visualize what I had looked at when shooting with Nicholas, and then opened them again. Nothing. Well, almost nothing.

"That barrel on the top, to the left. It might be out of place."

"Mr. Hercules, could you please live up to your name and boost me on top of that first barrel."

Jim said nothing, but hurried to the barrel, knit his fingers together, and waited for Barker's boot. His face was stricken. It had happened just as he feared. The tsarevich was missing and in danger.

Barker stepped onto the barrel then. He inspected a dozen or so and when he thought it was taking too long, he began pitching them over onto the floor. The noise of the bouncing casks was deafening, but he gave them no heed.

"Here!" he boomed, his voice echoing in the long gallery.

We rushed over. The three of us scrambled up the side of a

barrel as best we could. It's amazing what a man can accomplish when it is absolutely necessary.

We jumped from barrel to barrel until we reached one at the far end. Barker was bent over it, a faint light illuminating his features. We circled the barrel and looked down. A ladder was affixed to the side of it, going down into a chamber below. The cask was stationary, part of the floor, and the rest of the barrels had been moved around to conceal it.

"There's your tunnel, Thomas," the Guv said. "Remind me to take your suggestions more seriously."

He plunged down the hole and we followed after him. I was the last. As I looked about, I knew exactly where we were.

"It's the end of the tunnel in the Goat Tavern! The walls are identical. Those barrels at the far end concealed the opening entirely!"

The four of us raced down the narrow passageway. Jim arrived at the end first, crouching through a low entrance and swarming up the side of one barrel. Then he turned and pulled the rest of us up. There were more barrels in the cellar of the Goat Tavern than in the shooting range, but we were able to push our way through them one by one. When we finally burst through and jumped down we saw that the small stockroom was lit by a single candle, no more than an inch in length, that probably would have guttered within a few minutes.

"They came through here," Barker rumbled, his voice echoing. "Only a noble would be so careless as to leave a burning candle in a cellar full of casks soaked in ale and whiskey."

We took the steps leading upward two at a time. I could see Hesketh Pierce's plebian face slick with perspiration. Then I saw something I should have expected. He had a pistol in his hand. I imagined my partner did as well.

"Idiot," I said to myself, pulling my Webley from under my waistcoat.

There was a door above us on the stair, a perfectly functioning door with a knob for a handle. It would have turned and opened easily. That didn't matter. Barker and Hercules kicked it into splinters. When we burst in I saw three things at once: the barman looking at us with surprise, both Prince Georges passed out drunk at the bar, and Nicholas and Grand Duke Sergei just opening the door of the establishment to step outside into the night.

Hercules, Pierce, and I trained our pistols, but Barker charged at the front door. Sergei looked back at us and I saw it then. Desperation. A plan to be accomplished at all costs. I knew at that very second it was he who had hired La Sylphide to kill his cousin, the future heir of the tsar.

At the very last minute my partner dropped and began to slide, one heavily booted foot in front of him. It plowed into them, knocking the tsarevich completely off his feet. Nicholas's arm had been around the grand duke's shoulders and as he fell he pulled Sergei down with him. There was a familiar buzzing sound, and a cry from Mathilde's protector, and then bullet fragments shot in every direction inside the Goat Tavern. Hercules was unscathed, but Pierce had one rip through his jacket.

We ran to the door, not really certain what we would find. The grand duke lay on the floor, bleeding from the shoulder. Barker lay on his back, his suit dusty and more the worse for wear than he. And Nicholas, the hope of all Russia, was asleep in Barker's embrace, as if in his own mother's arms. Either that or he was passed out drunk. The choice is yours.

I did something idiotic then, not for the last time, for certain. I stepped out into Kensington High Street and spread my arms. I knew she was out there, eyeing me from a hundred yards or more.

I waited for a bullet that never came. She did not spare me; she was probably disassembling her air rifle and would be on her way in a moment or two. Sofia, clad in black, would fade into the night as she had probably done a dozen times across Europe already.

Cyrus Barker was annoyed when I returned. I had needlessly put myself in danger while the future leader of all Russia was sprawled across him, tight as a boiled owl. Jim was trying to lift him, but he was deadweight. However, the Guv slipped out from under him, and between them, they set him in a chair, his face buried in his arms on the table.

"Drugged," Hesketh Pierce said.

He was bent over Prince George, the future king of Greece. The royal groom was drugged, as well. Sergei had not planned to give anyone an opportunity to save the tsarevich. I wondered if, in fact, Sergei had gone to Japan with his two friends when Nicholas was attacked.

"Have you a telephone?" Pierce demanded of the publican.

"No, sir."

"Drat," he cried. "I'm going across the street and call the Home Office, as well as an ambulance. You gentlemen stay here!"

"Of course," Barker replied.

We sat and waited. The two Georges and Nicholas were in the arms of Morpheus. Sergei moaned every now and again. We wrapped his shoulder in bar towels, but there was no way to make a tourniquet for a shoulder wound. Jim Hercules went to stand out front, not being welcome in the pub. Barker and I stood in the doorway. I resolved to stop frequenting the establishment, rarebit or no.

"Do you believe what happened this evening will stop an assassination tomorrow?" Jim asked.

"No," Barker said.

I agreed.

"I supposed not. I need to see if Pierce is done with the telephone. I have some calls of my own to make. I'll see you tomorrow, gents."

We watched him leave, a man uncomfortable with London. Possibly a man uncomfortable with the entire world.

"That was so close," I said to the Guv. "A foot to the right and Nicholas would have been as headless as Bayles."

"He is alive," Barker replied. "The distance doesn't matter."

# CHAPTER THIRTY

Telephone calls were made in the middle of the night. The Russian ambassador arrived in a closed carriage to convey Grand Duke Sergei Mikhailovich to a doctor's care. There would be no indiscreet visit to a hospital. We were intended to follow and wait, as unofficial members of the tsarevich's delegation. A hotel was readied and a Russian physician was waiting when we arrived.

"This has happened before, gentlemen," Ambassador de Staal said. He had come from his bed to oversee the process. "Russians being shot in your country, that is. It happens more often than you would expect, enough that we have written protocols for it."

We watched as the grand duke was examined. He had been shot high in the chest. The bullet passed through the flesh near his shoulder and had expanded after it exited. There was damage to the shoulder, of course, but he would recover. He'd been given a drug, but before it took effect, he asked to speak to us both.

"I've been in battle before, Mr. Barker," Sergei said. "But I ran a battery of artillery. I've never been shot before. It feels . . . strange. Somehow, both more and less painful than I anticipated."

He was in a hotel bed and a robe was thrown over his bare shoulders. A bandage across his chest had a bloom of red in the middle the size of a poppy.

De Staal entered and they had a brief argument in Russian. Then the ambassador frowned and sat down in a chair.

"I'd like to make a clean breast of it, gentlemen," Sergei said. "I'm the one who paid to have my cousin shot."

"Of course," Barker responded. "But why?"

"Does it really matter?" he asked. "My uncles and cousins want his title. He will make a weak leader at a time when we need someone strong to keep the rebels in check. But I suppose the real reason is obvious."

"You love Mathilde Kschessinska," the Guv stated.

"Madly," Sergei admitted. "She is my sun and I must revolve around her. You cannot imagine the hell my life is when I drive her to a rendezvous outside of Saint Petersburg for a tryst. I want to kill him. And yet, there is the Potato Club. We are royals together and we have larks, and as bad a leader as he might be, he's damned entertaining and he is my cousin. We grew up together. I bloodied his nose in a fight when we were seven, and when I was eleven he helped me to the palace when I fell out of a tree and broke my leg. We've been through a lot together. When he asked me to take care of his mistress, of course I said yes, but that was before I met her. She is so bewitching. I think I fell in love with her on the first day." He paused. "Could I have some water, please?"

I poured a glass from a tumbler and brought it to his lips.

"How do we know it is you who hired La Sylphide and not

Miss Kschessinska?" Barker asked. "You are gallant, and as you say, bewitched."

"There was no need for her to do so. She railed, of course, but that is just her way. She is beautiful and Alix is not. She is alluring. She is intelligent, even cunning. She is monumentally ambitious and she can influence and decimate men in a way no other twenty-one-year-old could. She knows what she wants and she knows every stratagem, and what she wanted was to be tsarina. I regretted the decision to hire an assassin almost immediately, but it was too late. I had no way to contact her. It never occurred to me that they would break up on their own."

"Do not tax yourself," the doctor said.

"Oh, get out, you imbecile. When I need your attention, I shall call you."

There it was. Breeding. He was every inch the royal. No lowly physician was going to tell him what to do.

"She had not yet lost, you see," the grand duke continued. "Did you know that wagers were made over whether she would become tsarina? The odds were in Mische's favor, but then Alix is German and no Russian can abide a German. Mathilde was the favorite, even if she is a Pole. She will become the prima ballerina of Russia. She seemed a sure thing, but a great number of men will lose their money over that bet. And now? Nicholas will have to pay for her for the rest of his life to keep silent what everyone already knows."

I gave him another sip of water. He was pale and there was a sheen on his face.

"It feels good to tell someone," Sergei said. "I never even told Mische how I felt and she never guessed. She has no interest in me, you see. I might as well be a coachman or a banker for all I mattered to her. And yet I convinced myself if I got rid of Nicky she would grow to love me."

"Who paid for the services of La Sylphide?" Barker asked.

"Didn't I tell you? My uncles financed it. They would pay for it, but they would never be the ones to suggest it. They are all cowards. When the end comes they will scatter across Europe like cockroaches."

"You believe the revolution will happen, then?" I asked.

"A spark will ignite the masses, and what is Nikolai but a spark? An incendiary. It would have been better for millions of people if he had died tonight."

"There would be war," I said.

"A skirmish or two. You see, the masses don't like the military. It will all go to hell now," he said. He sounded sleepy. The medicine was taking effect. "She'll never love me. She'll never forgive me, even though I shall be the one to take care of her for the rest of her life. I should have hired La Sylphide to assassinate me, instead."

Barker rose. "Let us leave him, gentlemen."

De Staal and I followed the Guv out of the room.

"You realize he has royal status and cannot be prosecuted by your government," the ambassador warned.

"We are not part of the government," Cyrus Barker replied. "We are private agents. What will happen to him now?"

"We'll spirit him away on a boat in a few hours. Once he is in Saint Petersburg and fully healed, he will return to his artillery battery."

"Will this be a battery that will face some of the heaviest fighting?" I asked, thinking of Uriah the Hittite.

"Gentlemen, he did just come within a horse's breadth of killing the future leader of Russia," the ambassador said. "And the tsarevich is still in danger. An open carriage and a long-range assassin? The boy should be quaking in his boots."

The Guv cleared his throat. "We will see what can be done. I have one idea, at least."

"What I don't understand, Mr. Barker, is why Sergei Mikhailovich should feel the need to unburden himself to you. How well do you know him?"

"I only met him one time and that was for—what would you say, Mr. Llewelyn, ten minutes at most?"

"And you are English," de Staal said.

We were Scots and Welsh, but we weren't going to quibble.

"Why confess to you, a perfect stranger, as opposed to me, the ambassador to his own country?"

"That's not difficult to understand, Baron de Staal," Barker replied. "I shall without doubt be the first one in the door tomorrow morning, telling Nicholas what his cousin conveyed to him through me."

De Staal looked away for a few moments, then looked back.

"I cannot argue with that," he said. "I do not necessarily believe it but I can't find an argument that will stand in its place. Very well, tell him. I will put Mikhailovich aboard a ship early in the morning. This will not be set before the public, do you agree?"

"I don't see how doing so would benefit anyone," the Guv answered.

"We are agreed, then," the ambassador replied, putting out his hand.

Barker hesitated, then reached forward and shook it. We turned and left the hotel.

"Interesting," I said as we stood in front of the hotel. It was perhaps two in the morning and the street was empty.

"Very well, Mr. Llewelyn," Barker said, in no hurry to reply. "What do you find interesting?"

"Mathilde Kschessinska's financial support will be on a boat in a few hours," I said. "Who is going to pay her billet at the Metropole? Where will she get food?"

"You fear for her well-being?"

"No. I think it's marvelous," I said. "I hope she falls with a loud bump. This entire tragedy is because of her."

"She has certainly caused enough trouble," the Guv replied.

A cab bowled by, but we felt no need to stop it. It was quiet and calm. The air was cool, with no breeze to speak of. London was shuttered for the night and I felt that we and the cabman who passed us were the only people in the City who were awake.

"In a few days when the tsarevich is on his way back to Russia," the Guv said, "remind me to search for relations of Joseph Bayles. They deserve some recompense for his death. The fact that he was mad and tried to kill Prince George is incidental. I sent the poor fellow to his death, merely to gain an audience with Nicholas."

"You couldn't know he was going to be killed," I reasoned.

"That is immaterial. Were he snug in his bed in Colney Hatch, he'd be alive now. I was culpable in his death, and it is not the first time. There is blood on my hands. A hazard of the enquiry trade."

We passed Nelson's Column and stepped into Whitehall Street again. We couldn't walk all the way to Newington and yet we let more cab horses trot by. Having attended a masked ball, met an assassin, found a tunnel, stopped the murder of the future tsar of Russia, and listened to a confession like a couple of priests, a quiet walk seemed just the thing.

"Did you suspect Sergei from the start?" I asked the Guv.

"Of course I did. Putting a mistress in the hands of a young and unmarried aristocrat with time on his hands was just the sort of decision that proves what sort of leader Nicholas will become. She is beautiful, or so you say since I never saw her. She is ambitious and surrounded by admirers?"

"A coquette," I replied.

"One cannot put all the blame on her shoulders, however. He could have accepted that Miss Kschessinska was not his property."

"Do you believe Sergei feels remorse?"

"I think he felt it even before he hired Miss Ilyanova," he said. "He felt it after he hired her; he felt it when he knew he could no longer stop the assassination, and I'm certain he felt it keenly when he sat with the two of them and Nicholas showed that he felt safe with his cousins, the so-called Potato Club. It must burn in the grand duke's soul. Or so it seemed to me when we were talking with him."

"It had nothing to do with politics at all, then," I said. "Not the Socialists or the Communists or the anarchists or the nihilists. Not even the Okhrana."

"The Okhrana was obsessed with Chernov. It clouded their judgment. If they weren't so quick to jump to conclusions, perhaps they would have captured Miss Ilyanova."

"No, sir," I said. "Remember Occam's razor. The easiest choice is often the correct one. I think that was their standard method of investigation. Rachkovsky is a menace."

"What disturbs me is that his methods are no different from the days of Catherine the Great or Ivan the Terrible. It is barbarism. But he was never a suspect in an assassination attempt on Nicholas. He was genuinely hunting the killer, whom he believed was Chernov. He wanted the man to confess, ingratiating himself with the tsar. Like Mathilde, he is ambitious."

"And William Morris?"

"He is a tired old man. His heyday was twenty years hence. He is a national treasure, I suppose, but he is out of fashion, or so I should imagine. A man with gout is not capable of climbing rooftops to assassinate anyone."

"I didn't claim he assassinated Mr. Bayles himself, only that he paid someone else to do it."

Barker pursed his lips. "I could imagine him doing such a thing as proof Socialism is still viable to the modern revolutionary. But it is too late. This is not 1860. The twentieth century is almost on the horizon. Now Miss Marx, there was a candidate. What did you say about her? She's too . . . ?"

"She's too perfect," I supplied. "It's intimidating."

"She is very capable," Barker agreed. "And she is driven. I imagine she is the first at a meeting and the last to leave. Lazy members lay their burdens on her shoulders. And she makes little money at it, and so must translate books to provide for herself and perform onstage in the evenings, which in itself must be exhausting. Yet she endures."

"Yes, but there are many Marxists in Russia and England, and she is the daughter of its founder," I reminded my partner. "If she had hired the assassin, it would strike a large blow and start the revolution."

"As I said, she would have made a good candidate," the Guv replied. "She is dynamic, articulate, and can even shoot a pistol. She has her father's mind and were she a man she would be an MP by now. Yet she is a single woman and therefore a slave to all."

"And what of Mathilde Kschessinska?" I asked. We stopped by the river on the Embankment under the globe lights and watched the water. "Perhaps Sergei will take the blame for her actions. That is something he would do."

"It is," Barker agreed. "However, she did not kill Nicholas when she had the chance. She postured and threatened, but that is all. She'll be dealt with at the appropriate time."

We watched a fish jump above the surface, snap up a mayfly, and slip back into the river.

"Did you consider anyone else?" I asked.

Barker mulled the question. "I considered Prince George of Greece, but could find no reason to suspect him. He's the most upstanding royal we've met during this case. He isn't tied to the Russian royal family and he is intelligent enough to give someone like Mathilde Kschessinska a wide berth."

I turned and looked away from the river, then froze. We were out in the open. I was a perfect target for Sofia Ilyanova's air rifle. Barker stared at the buildings across the river.

"She's asleep, Thomas. A sharpshooter requires rest. We should be asleep as well. Tomorrow will mean everything."

We found a late cab and went home. Mac met us at the door in full dress at nearly three in the morning. He held a finger to his lips. My wife was sound asleep on the sofa in the front room. All this danger and excitement and I assumed she had gone back to bed like any other night. I was neither the best nor the brightest of husbands. In fact, I feared I was among the worst and dimmest.

Barker gave her the briefest of tender looks for her steadfastness and left the room. I woke her gently and we went upstairs together.

# CHAPTER THIRTY-ONE

And so the fateful day dawned. Birds twittered in the trees of Newington. The entire city was preparing for a royal wedding. It had been declared a holiday and people were released to enjoy the pomp, the pageantry, and the spectacle. It was a truly wonderful day, one to tell grandchildren about in years to come.

After some deliberation, Barker and I agreed that Rebecca could be freed from her imprisonment in order to see the parade. She would have two bodyguards with her in case of danger: Mac, and Sarah Fletcher. We were paying for Miss Fletcher's services, but we knew it was an outing, an outing Jacob Maccabee was very much looking forward to. I was still mystified. What he could find to admire in Miss Fletcher eluded me, but then I compared every woman in London to my wife, and found them wanting.

Rebecca came out from behind her screen in a powder blue

dress that made my heart beat faster. I knew what it was like to look at a truly beautiful woman and realize that she was my wife. Oh, luckiest of men. This was what Sergei had tried to kill for.

"I wish you were coming with us," she said, adjusting her hair in the mirror.

"No more than I," I replied.

She turned to look at me. "You will be careful."

"I will. I promise."

We descended the stair. Mac was in the hall with Sarah Fletcher. I don't know which surprised me more. Miss Fletcher wore a dress in bright yellow, accented in white. Her straw hat had a matching band and she had white gloves and a parasol. There was an attempt at artifice on her hair, which I suspected was my wife's doing.

As for Mac, well, I gawked. He wore an ivory-colored suit with a tan waistcoat and a salmon-colored tie. His pocket handkerchief was folded to points and his boater hat was tilted at what for him must have been a rakish angle. He wore tan spats over white shoes. Both he and Miss Fletcher looked simultaneously nervous and happy. Rebecca took Sarah's other arm and waved to me as they left. The door closed behind them with a finality. It was suddenly deathly quiet. Harm waddled up in front of me and regarded me with his head cocked to the side. He seemed to be asking what I was still doing there. I reached to pet him, but he backed out of range, then wandered slowly down the hall and scratched at the back door. I let him do as he wished. Etienne had fed him and he had plenty of shade and water outside.

Barker came down then, with a creak of wooden stairs. He was dressed, as always, in a black cutaway and waistcoat with striped trousers. His tie was a deep red over a wing-tipped collar and he wore a pin in the tie. Only the pin changed daily. He had a wardrobe of near-identical clothing. Mine matched his, for the most part. I had ties in various colors, but nothing he would object to.

"Where do we begin?" I asked.

"Pall Mall to start, then we'll make our way to the Mall."

As it turned out, we had to be let down from our cab a few streets away. London was teeming with people. The wedding morn was fine, warm but not hot. People had come from as far as Inverness and Dublin in Britain and there were royals and diplomats from every nation on earth. It was a show of strength on Her Majesty's part. All nations bowed to her empire.

"How do you think Clubland feels about that?" I asked, pointing to a row of carts. I smelled them before I saw them. Sausages sizzling in onions. Fresh toffee. Meat pies and pasties. Potatoes roasted in bacon fat. Fish-and-chips.

Everything was at its best. There were swags of buntings between the buildings; banners and flags everywhere twitching in the light breeze. I imagined the gentlemen's clubs were full of elderly men trying their best to get away from the crowds of commoners.

"Do you see anything?" I asked as we craned our necks.

"No, but I'll wager she isn't far from here. The crowds provide anonymity."

"I'd shoot from the top of the building there," I said, pointing at the Queen's Chapel.

"Would you, Mr. Llewelyn?" the Guv asked. "That's good to know."

We pushed our way through crowds the length of Pall Mall until we reached the corner of St. James's Street and Pall Mall. We looked one way. Behind a gate was St. James's Palace, with the chapel across from it. The other way was a row of open shops and a large theater.

"Thomas, work your way around to the Mall and send as many urchins as possible this way."

"Right."

I did not run, but I hurried. I had to go back to where we left the cab, then cross to the Mall. The closer I came, the more amazed I was by the size of the crowds and the shouting. The anarchist protesters were there, but were kept under the watchful eye of Scotland Yard. Every item they carried was examined for a possible weapon. I was looking for a professional assassin with a revolutionary air rifle, while they were taking away a workingman's penknife. But then, either one could kill a monarch, I suppose.

"You there," I said when I passed one of the urchins. "Got your whistle?"

"Got it, sir," he replied.

"Mr. Barker thinks the assassin will be over in Pall Mall, by the palace."

"On the level?" he asked.

"On the level," I answered. "Pass the word. Here's sixpence for you. Have an ice cream."

"Fanks, mister!" he shouted as he ran off.

I sauntered along with my hands in my pockets, the only one aware that I had a pistol in the waistband of my trousers. The sun was bright and I was glad to have a hat. It would be over an hour before the parade was to begin up the Mall from Buckingham Palace, to the lesser St. James's Palace.

I passed our little party. Rebecca has an amazing ability to strike up conversations with perfect strangers that often turn into friendships. At the moment, she'd found a woman providing equal parts history and gossip. I'm sure the woman had repeated the news verbatim four or five times that day so far, but it was new to Rebecca, Mac, and Miss Fletcher. I joined them for a moment or two but everyone understood that I was working. I found two more boys with whistles and sent them west to Pall Mall.

The Mall itself was a terrible place for an assassin to work. It was an open drive with trees spaced along it. Buildings were distant in every direction and I could not imagine La Sylphide being able to hit a target, which is to say, the head and shoulders of a future tsar, all that would be visible to anyone on the Mall. However, when the procession turned into the drive, he would become a better target from any of the upper windows in the clubs on the north side of the gate. This was where Nicholas was in danger of being assassinated. Sofia Ilyanova was somewhere nearby, I knew it.

I reached the drive near the palace and turned back. There was activity, men in top hats directing members of the royal family into open carriages. I hurried back, circling around the outer ends of the crowds. The thought occurred to me that I might lose Barker entirely in the thousands of people packed into a few streets. Afterward, I returned to Pall Mall. When I turned toward the gate, Hesketh Pierce was right beside me.

"Morning, Llewelyn," he said. "Does Mr. Barker believe the shooting will come from here?"

"I believe so, yes," I answered. "It is the most logical place."

"We've gained access to the top floor of almost every building in this street. There were only a few venerable clubs who refused. They remember William the Fourth as a young upstart."

"If La Sylphide uses one of those clubs for her attempt on Nicholas, there will be hell to pay," I stated.

"Does Mr. Barker really believe the killer is a woman?"

"She has murdered at least one acquaintance of mine."

"That was before my time," Pierce said. "Mr. Barker!"

Pierce skipped forward and we found the Guv still standing on the corner as fixed and solid as the red postal box at his side.

"Is there anything you can tell me, sir?" Barker asked.

"Nicholas is in the first group of carriages, consisting of foreign royals and ambassadors of many countries. The first group contains the largest number of carriages, after which will be the bride and her attendants, followed by Prince George and the Prince of Wales, and lastly, of course, the queen herself. The Home Office is here, as well as Scotland Yard and the Queen's Guard. Really, gentlemen. This is well organized. You may go home if you wish. You caught the scamp last night.

His ship left this morning and he will never darken our shores again. You must be tired."

I was, in fact, but I needn't have asked if we would see it through. Of course we would. There was no question of us not doing all we could to help Nicholas survive long enough to marry and become tsar.

"Scotland Yard has their hands full with this crowd," Pierce commented, looking at the vendors doing a brisk trade.

"I'm sure Munro would like to send all the East Enders back to Poplar, but the poor can't afford any other entertainment than a free peek at Her Majesty. Such a sight they'd travel miles for."

"And have," my partner added.

"Why, Pierce," I said. "You're a secret Socialist."

He laughed at the thought and turned to speak to a group of constables standing nearby. Barker and I explored St. James's Street, which was laid out in a straight line to the gate.

There was a public house, unimaginatively named the St. James, a sweet shop doing brisk trade, a theater in the middle of a small performance, a tattered bookshop I felt the urge to visit, and shops to let. On the other side were mostly businesses. An assayer, a dentist, an estate agent, a solicitor, and another To-Let building at the very front.

"I'd investigate the first building there," I said. "It looks promising for an assassin."

"No, lad. It's too far west and there's a brick post holding up the gate. She'd have to lean out into the street to find a proper shot."

"Look there," I said, pointing across the street.

He turned. There was a small figure standing on one of the roofs. Very small indeed.

"It's the lone girl we saw during your speech. She appears to be sucking on a lolly."

"I reckon she must have climbed the drainpipe, the wee monkey," the Guv replied.

"I see one, two, no, three other children on the roofs. But men—I assume Home Office men—are shooing them down."

"As you told me, fifty pounds is a lot of money."

"I say twenty would have done."

"We promised fifty, and fifty it shall be. I gave them my word."

I waited for a cab to pass, then stepped into the street. I stood for a moment and then returned to the curb. "Someone could shoot from a hansom cab, sir. A straight shot if they aim high, which Sofia Ilyanova would do."

"Good thinking, Thomas," Barker said.

Off in the distance we heard a muffled cheer. The procession had begun.

"We're in for it now," I murmured, my stomach beginning to tighten.

"Remember, Thomas, we are not solely responsible for keeping the tsarevich safe."

"That's true, sir, and you made a promise to Jim Hercules that we would save Nicholas."

"It was a business arrangement, Thomas. Let us not forget that Mr. Hercules is merely a client. Do not allow yourself to be personally invested in the case."

"But Jim is a nice chap and for all his faults I rather liked the tsarevich. He is rambunctious."

"More foolhardy," my partner grumbled.

We heard a second cheer, closer this time. I found myself holding my breath and I exhaled. Barker was right. We would do what we could but we were not responsible for Nicky's complete defense

I looked about. Everyone had stopped moving. They all held their breath, as I did. People craned their necks for a good view. Children sat on their fathers' shoulders. Some were frustrated by their neighbors' hats. The food trade had suddenly fallen off. Even Barker was up on his toes, awaiting the first carriage.

A final cheer sounded, closer than before. I could barely see

the Mall, where the first carriages would turn on to Marlbor-
ough Road and into St. James's Street.

Minutes passed and then the first carriage rolled into view, a
resplendent white landau. I could not recognize the occupants
inside, but I'd bet Sofia knew which one it was. She was not the
sort of person to make a mistake. Or miss.

A second carriage arrived, a third. I realized it would not work
to shoot from a hansom cab. The aim was too low. The back vehicles were obscured by the white geldings in front.

"I can't see the tsarevich," I said. "There are too many blasted
carriages in the way."

I tried to step up on a pole, but a constable immediately shooed
me down. Then I heard it. The entire crowd did. Heads turned,
wondering what made the sound. One plaintive note. I looked up.
It was the little girl and she was pointing away from the gate. She
was blowing that blasted whistle so loudly, I feared for her lungs.

Then two whistles, then five, then ten. Sofia Ilyanova was
poised and she was about to shoot.

# CHAPTER THIRTY-TWO

I saw the girl point, but the exact location was vague. Most likely, I concluded, it was at the theater, which looked like a cross between the Lyceum and the Tower of London. There were turrets and sunroofs and chimney stacks thrust chockablock upon each other. It was the perfect place from which to assassinate a royal.

We were hemmed in by a thousand people cheering for the royal couple. Slipping through them proved to be difficult. Men gave way for the Guv, if they knew what's good for them, but they didn't feel the need to show me any respect. There were also women about with children, which made pushing impolite. So I struggled along in Barker's wake, which had pretty well been my life for the last nine years.

Then, a hundred yards ahead, I caught a glimpse of her, the merest glimpse. Her appearance at the entrance of the theater was met by a dozen whistles or more from boys hoping to find and even capture her. She stood at bay for a moment and when one youth tried to seize her, she put a boot in his chest and kicked him into the street. Then she turned and fled into the depths of the theater.

We reached the entrance less than a minute later and opened the door in time to see her vault onto the stage itself, in the middle of a performance, no less. Appropriately enough, they were doing *She Stoops to Conquer*. The audience was shocked. The actors onstage were aghast. Sofia Ilyanova, however, continued her trajectory without a care in the world.

I knew what would happen next. It wasn't my first case. We ran down the aisle, then jumped onstage. Barker barreled through the actors as if they were skittles, and the only thing I could think of to do was to call "Sorry" over my shoulder. I'm certain that didn't do much in the way of making amends for interrupting their performance, but one had to admit our little melodrama was far more entertaining than theirs.

We raced to the back of the stage and fumbled about in the dark until we found the outer door and pushed through it into the blinding sunshine. We skidded on cobblestones in an ancient alley and nearly hit the far wall. At the end, we saw her climbing into a cab, urging the driver to go swiftly at all costs. There were no passing vehicles at such a time. She must have had one waiting for her. She ran unencumbered, having left the air rifle on the roof in her hurry to escape.

We reached St. James's Street and followed after her, but we couldn't catch up. The cab she was in was gaining speed. Boys with whistles were blowing by the dozens, which made the cab horse skittish, though it continued to plunge through the crowd. Women screamed and men were knocked aside by the large wheels.

"What do we do?" I shouted to Barker. "She's getting away!"

"There!" the Guv growled. A cab was coming down the street as if it were any other day and it wasn't surrounded by a thousand people. Barker jumped on board and when it neared, pulled me up as well. I only hoped we could make up the distance we had lost.

The cab ahead was smart, with gleaming woodwork and a decorative lozenge-shaped window in the back. Ours was not as pretty, but our horse looked up to the task, a mottled brown gelding, probably getting old, but clean-limbed and game for a race. Its driver was taken aback by our sudden appearance, but he was not averse to our paying him.

"That horse there," Cyrus Barker bellowed. "Follow it! I believe it is heading to Victoria Station."

We fell back onto the seats and held the straps while the cab bit into the limestone bricks and began to roll forward.

"Hurry!" he called.

Ahead of us, Sofia's cab was just turning into Pall Mall. People jumped out of the way as we reached the very gates of the palace. The guards in their scarlet uniforms had rifles trained on the carriage ahead, but they knew firing them could result in a panic. A hundred yards behind them, foreign dignitaries were stepping down from their landaus.

Our cab reached the same corner seconds after and I was able to show by gesture to the guards that we meant no harm, but were following only the first cab, which turned into the Haymarket heading north. The traffic was brisk. People were on their way elsewhere and didn't want some bally wedding slowing their progress. When we turned, there were two vehicles between us. Barker thumped on the trap overhead with the ball of his stick. The driver snapped it open.

"Oy, there, you! You'll do my cab a damage."

"Get us to that cab we are following and I shall double your fare."

"Done!" he agreed. "Get a move on there, Biscuit."

The man cracked his whip in the air and we sailed into the stream of traffic. The street was wide and there were a dozen vehicles before us in a kind of panorama. It reminded me of a scene from Lew Wallace's book *Ben-Hur,* with chariots racing in a circle, and charioteers trying to kill each other at breakneck speed.

Our cab was gaining ground now. We had passed the one near us and were now one away from Sofia Ilyanova's hansom. Biscuit was a sound horse, and the cabman was expert at cracking a whip overhead without harming the animal. By then, of course, we were bowling along at a perilous speed. I'd seen racehorses run at a slower pace. I felt droplets of sweat or lather coming from the horse.

The driver was determined to squeeze between the cab beside us and Ilyanova's own, trying to earn himself that fare. As we took the long curve from Piccadilly to Grosvenor Place, the nervous cabman beside us realized that our man meant business. Our wheel was going to collide with his, and as any student can recite, two objects could not occupy the same space. He gave way, slowed his horse, and we shot forward into the coveted position.

The gleaming cab with the tiny window was just ahead of us. For a moment I speculated that if we could get alongside the cab I might jump the distance into her vehicle. I could. I might, if we got close enough. But it was foolhardy. There was too small a chance for success.

The cab was so close, it was as if the two had become one. *You're ours, Sofia Ilyanova,* I thought. *We've got you now!* I saw a flash of white in the cab, a pale face, and a single eye staring out that back window.

Then the glass shattered.

"Pistol!" Barker shouted over the roar of hooves. "Down!"

Then she fired. I flinched, even though the bullet would pass through my head before I could react. It did not pass through my head, however, nor Barker's. It struck poor Biscuit full between the eyes. He was dead in his traces, falling to the ground like a sack of grain. We were shot upward, like an upside-down pendulum.

For a second, I heard the cry of the cabman as he fell from his perch. Then I was tugged out of my seat and struck the roof. I saw the Guv's arms go up and his hat fly off as his shoulders hit the back of the cab. We circled the fulcrum of the dead horse and when the vehicle struck the road it splintered into pieces and came to an immediate halt.

The cab beside us and the one behind it were so close that they crashed over the shattered vehicle.

"Lad! How are you?" I heard Barker call.

I screamed. Not in pain, but in anger. I love horses. I always have. Not a week goes by that I don't ride my mare, Juno. I curry her, brush her, and feed her oats. I baby her and whisper terms of endearment in her ear. Rebecca has joked about being third in our relationship. I am a member of various organizations that protect cab horses from neglect. We have a bond, she and I, as I'm sure our cabman had with Biscuit.

The cabman pulled himself to his feet and staggered. His scalp was lacerated, but he gave it little thought. His horse was dead. His companion and sole means of making a living was gone. His hansom was shattered to bits. He, too, began to scream, there in the middle of the road, while cabs whizzed by us on both sides.

Something caught my eye then. A bit of pasteboard landed on the horse's flank, a rectangle of white against the dappled brown. It was our business card. Barker had dropped it. I felt a hand in my collar and another at my elbow, and a voice growled in my ear.

"Thomas, we haven't the time to grieve now!"

Barker pulled me to the side of the road, stopping once to let a vehicle fly by within inches of our faces. Once on the far side of Grosvenor Place he lifted his stick, signaling for another cab. It had been snapped in two. The Guv was hatless and his collar was open. Goodness only knows what I looked like.

A cab pulled to our side and we climbed aboard. Barker acted as if he was a mere spectator of the horrendous accident that had just occurred. We left the dead horse, the pile of wood that had been a respectable hansom two minutes before, and the heartbroken cabman.

"Victoria Station, driver!" Barker shouted. "Hurry!"

"Right, sir."

The cab waded out into the stream of traffic leading inexorably toward the station. I only hoped it was worth the effort, that we were not too late.

"Have you got all your limbs, Thomas?" the Guv asked.

"Yes, sir. My knuckles are bleeding."

He gave me his handkerchief and I wrapped it around my hand.

"She shot our horse," I said. "What sort of monster shoots a horse?"

"Try not to think about it, lad. Concentrate on the matter at hand."

I felt the cab slow and saw that we were coming toward the entrance to Victoria Station in Grosvenor Place. The wheels skidded on the cobblestones and the iron shoes of the horse clattered. We jumped from the hansom and as an afterthought, I tossed the entire contents of my pocket at the driver, enough for five journeys to Victoria Station at least. Then we ran through the crowd, dodging people and their luggage, looking for every bit of space we could squeeze through. I heard Barker's boots just behind me. People were queuing. The gate was ahead. I could see it, but fifty bodies stood in our path.

"Make way!" the Guv thundered. "Make way!"

He took my arm and before I knew what was happening, a darby had been locked upon my wrist. "I have a dangerous prisoner here! He must be on the train to Newhaven! Make way!"

Every eye within the line of sight was looking at the prisoner, every ear hanging on the clarion cry of Cyrus Barker.

"Make way, sir! Madam, move this bag, please! Thank you! Where is the ticket man? What is the holdup, by god? It is essential that I make that express!"

He was having a glorious time in his sudden role. I knew it was a role because he would never say "by god." It was blasphemy, as far as he was concerned. There was a hissing from the crowd and belatedly I realized it was directed at me. I began to struggle and snarl at the passersby. I, too, could play a role. Then we were at the turnstile and Barker had no money. He never had any. I carried his wallet, but I couldn't exactly stop and pay the fare for him. Again, so close and yet so far.

I did the first thing I thought of. I attacked Barker. In our struggle, I hoped to reach my pocket and slip a pound note or coin into his hand, but people surrounded us and everyone was focused on the government man with the dangerous prisoner.

A hand thumped me in the skull and I saw they were helping this unnamed official gain control of his prisoner. Hands grasped my coat and someone delivered a kick to my shin.

"Let this man through!" someone cried. "Let him through, I say! He must get to Newhaven!"

The hue and cry was taken up by the crowd. The next thing I knew I was being pulled through the turnstile and prodded in the direction of the stair. We clattered down and when we reached the bottom, Barker unlocked my wrist restraint.

"Go, lad!" he said. "Run like the wind!"

I was off like a shot, putting shoe leather to pavement. I ran so fast the slightest misstep could cause me major injury, but I didn't care. I looked about, hoping to catch a glimpse of the train. I was a rail enthusiast and knew every line of the Continental Express. One could not miss the striking color of the engine, a warm caramel color, its lining picked out in red and gold. But where was it?

"To the right, Thomas!" Barker bellowed from somewhere behind me. "To the right!"

I caught a glimpse of it, then damn and blast if it weren't starting to leave already. I ran faster and faster still, cutting across to the platform there. I reached the brake car at the end and began to gain ground, reaching for the handrail. My bowler flew from my head and I saw faces above me looking out at the madman running pell-mell down the platform.

I reached for the handrail and missed. Again I reached and again I failed. One false move and I'd fall between the cars and be run over. No, no; I couldn't let that happen. *Get it, Thomas! Get it!*

My hand slipped again and I began to realize I wasn't going to make it. Then I looked up and saw a face, a face with fierce yellow eyes and skin as pale as a Siberian winter. Sofia was still in her widow's weeds, a small black hat of feathers and plumes pinned to her white hair. She watched me with fascination, perhaps even dread. Then she bent down and lifted something. *The air rifle*, I thought. She slapped something against the window just in front of me. I blinked into a pair of hazel eyes. It was a child. A small child. Three, perhaps? Four?

I'd recognize a Llewelyn face anywhere.

I tripped and fell, tumbling head over heels, skinning hands and ears, scraping elbows, ripping trousers at the knee. Pain bloomed everywhere and blood splattered on the platform. I skidded into a brick wall and upset an ash can. Meanwhile, the express picked up steam and headed out of the station, bound for the Continent with an assassin aboard. One assassin and one child. One sallow-skinned, hazel-eyed, curly-haired child.

*Oh, Thomas,* I thought. *What have you gotten yourself into now?*

# CHAPTER THIRTY-THREE

L ad," the Guv said, bending over me. "Thomas."

I was crumpled in a heap by an archway among abandoned newspapers and ticket stubs from an ash can I had not only knocked over but crushed.

"Yes, sir."

"Are you injured?" he asked. "Can you stand?"

"I don't know."

Rolling over onto my back, I pulled myself up until I rested against the arch wall. Everything hurt, and not just physically.

"I saw her, sir," I mumbled. "The child she took to Kensington Palace was hers. Hers and mine, I suspect. He looked like me."

"Och, Thomas!"

I was overwhelmed. The pain in my body equaled the pain in my soul. This was going to hurt Rebecca deeply. I couldn't even imagine what she was going to say.

Railway porters rushed over to help me up. I hissed in pain but nothing was broken. They put me on a bench. The Guv handed me a handkerchief. One cheek was bleeding. One of my trouser legs was ripped and I could feel blood puddling in my shoe.

Oddly, I felt as if there had been some sort of cataclysm, like a train wreck or bombing. I could not understand that a man had fallen and the rest of the world was going by heedless. An hour from now, none of the guards would remember the incident.

"Thomas," Barker said. "This man is a doctor. He's going to examine you."

I lost the memory of the event entirely. At some point a plaster had been put on my cheek. Then it was just the two of us again.

"I lost her, sir."

"What could you have done, lad? Outrun a train? You gave it all you had, anything a man could do. You did well, but it was not to be."

"But we failed," I said. "She escaped. Escaped to kill again."

"I doubt she'll come back to England," he replied. "As for the rest of the world, we cannot save everyone. I will pass the information along to the Foreign Office and to various organizations to warn them. I don't suspect a single assassin will become an industry."

Everything throbbed. I felt brittle, as if every part of my body had been pulled out of socket, including my life. Rebecca was going to be inconsolable. I very nearly became emotional, but I mastered myself. I needed Cyrus Barker to take me home.

"Let us go, Thomas."

He took me by the elbow and lifted me up. People were watching us. It occurred to me that some of them still thought me an escaped prisoner as I hobbled like an old man, leaning on my partner's arm.

"This way," I heard the Guv say.

It must have taken fifteen minutes to cross the platform, climb the stairs, and make my way to the entrance of Victoria Station. Barker talked as we walked.

"The important thing, Thomas, is that we saved the life of the tsarevich. It strained our resources, but we succeeded, for good or ill. Perhaps Nicholas will learn from this crisis and shall be a more sober and conscientious leader of his country. A good leader might stem the tide of revolution and heal the rift."

I could think of no response. A horse appeared in front of me and I was helped into the cab. I recall listening to the sound of the wheels turning as we rode. We did not speak. We had said all there was to say.

"Thomas?"

It was Rebecca's voice. We were in Lion Street. Barker and Mac helped me out of the cab. She kissed me on the uninjured cheek.

"The library," I murmured. "Take me to the library. Rebecca, we need to talk."

They put me in a chair and withdrew. Barker began to make telephone calls. I noted Mac did not even listen at the door.

"What is it, Thomas?" Rebecca asked. "You're frightening me."

I told her the entire story. It was brutal. I was honest and it hurt. Afterward, she and Mac helped me up the stair and put me to bed. Then Rebecca packed a bag and left.

No, not left. Fled. She was not angry. Like me she was overwhelmed. I've never blamed her for what she did. I'd have done the same under the circumstances.

Did she go home to Camomile Street to think things through? Or did she go to her parents' house, where her mother and sister would have their hooks in her and divorce proceedings would begin immediately?

As I lay dazed, an image came to me: a pale hand on my chest. White hair against my shoulder. A feminine sigh. I don't know if I recalled it or invented it. I drifted off to sleep knowing everything would be worse when I woke again.

In the middle of the night, I reached out and touched Rebecca's pillow. It was empty and cold. I thought someone had brought a water bottle, but when I reached down, Harm was lying against the small of my back.

When I awoke the next morning, as expected, everything was worse. I got up, still fully dressed except for my shoes. I went downstairs and out the back door and took a cold bath. Then I returned and shaved and dressed. The wound on my cheek was not especially bad, but one of my eyes was red and swollen. In the kitchen I drank coffee and ate a roll. It was mechanical. I was following a set routine.

"Ready, lad?" my partner asked.

"Yes, sir."

We went to work just like every other day. I felt sorry for myself, which I have a talent for, but the Guv would not allow me to wallow in it. He was brisk and businesslike.

"We must decide how much to recompense the cabman for the loss of his horse, his cab, and his livelihood," he said. "Then we must find the wee girl who spotted Miss Ilyanova and give her family the fifty pounds. If she has no family, we must care for her and see that she is sent to a proper school. She did us a great service."

"Yes, sir," I said, and promptly forgot. Luckily he did not.

"We are sending a steep bill to the Russian embassy, and as God is my witness, I will screw every ruble from Baron de Staal's pocket. Jim Hercules shall not have to pay. I'll excuse him for not telling us about his relationship with the Home Office, but I will have a sharp word for Hesketh Pierce. Are you getting all this down?"

I pulled my notebook from my pocket and began to write in shorthand, but when I got to it later, it was gibberish. Oddly, I was wondering what Sofia was doing at that moment. The idea of her with a child, my child, in fact, was incongruous. Was it that, like Rebecca, she needed a child in her life? Was it a physical need? I had no idea and never would.

"Mr. L., you have taken a beating," Jeremy Jenkins said. Somehow our clerk's words were the first that had given me comfort.

"That I have, Jeremy," I said, sounding more cheerful than I was.

And so the day began. Very few people ever knew how close the tsarevich came to being assassinated that day. The newspaper mentioned a small commotion in Pall Mall, but claimed it was a runaway horse that bowled through the crowd, which in fact it was. The most believable lie is the truth.

We never darkened the door of the Goat Tavern again. We met Jim at the Cromwell Arms that evening, which did not serve the delicacy, and if they had it would be like shoe leather, if the chop I had there was any indication.

"Thank you, gentlemen," our client said. "I was certain Nicky's life was forfeit."

"It very nearly was," Barker admitted.

"I think otherwise. You stopped an assassination with a few street urchins and a box of whistles."

"More than a few."

"You stopped another attempt by knocking the tsar's son off his pins," Hercules added.

"With but a second to spare."

"You're not chiding yourself, surely?" Hercules asked.

"Perhaps, but I have nothing with which to compare this enquiry," the Guv answered, downing the last of his ale. "To whom do I send my fee?" Barker continued. "I'm sure you could not afford it. Will it be the Russian embassy? The American? The Home Office, perhaps?"

The corner of Jim's mouth tugged to the side.

"I reckon that was my due," he said. "I regret having hoodwinked you gentlemen, but it was necessary. I respect you, Mr. Barker, or at the very least, your right hook. I can see why McClain chose you as his partner."

"We stopped the assassination and named the man who was

responsible for it," the Guv said. "However, we were not able to capture the assassin. This will be reflected in the bill. There were a number of expenses in this enquiry."

"Yes, sir," Jim said. The smile had gone from his lips.

"Is there anything else you require from us?" Barker asked.

"Nicholas wants to see you, to congratulate you."

Barker stared. Or at least, I thought he stared. At first, I thought he would refuse the request. No one deserves to be shot, surely, but the tsarevich had done little to be worthy of endangering our lives.

"Very well," he said.

The three of us took a cab. Barker was at his most adamantine. Jim Hercules looked over at me for some kind of aid. However, it was not a time when I felt generous. I'd liked the fellow well enough, but I was disappointed that we had been tricked. Barker must have been suspicious from the first or he wouldn't have had Sarah Fletcher involved. It occurred to me belatedly that the girl in Hyde Park who had watched us from a bench was she.

At the front entrance of the palace, we alighted from the cab. I crossed over the very spot where this disastrous case had begun. I followed a path to the palace from which the servants had come with their pitcher and ewer.

"When is the tsarevich leaving?" Barker asked.

"In the morning," Hercules replied.

The Guv nodded. For a moment I thought he was going to say "good riddance to bad rubbish," but he didn't. Inside, we met the butler, Bingham, at his most solemn.

"We are here to see the tsarevich at his request," Barker said.

"Very good, sir. At the moment he is in the stable mews."

The thought came to me that one of the man's duties was to keep a running count and a location for every royal in the building.

"I know where that is," Jim drawled.

He took us out a side door, through a hedged garden, and into an anonymous hall. Corridors went on forever and I wondered how large the property was. Finally, we stepped outside and saw an outbuilding with shavings and straw. We went inside.

Nicholas was putting a white Arabian gelding through his paces. He circled the ring several times and then jumped him over a low hurdle. He was not a fine horseman. He lacked skill and command. Nicholas had tried every other form of entertainment in the palace and this was all that was left.

"Hello, chaps!" he called at our advent. "Be down in a few minutes!"

He circled and jumped until the horse's body had a sheen and its rider became bored.

"I'll be so glad to be back in Saint Petersburg," he called. "I miss the food and the young people. Too bad London could not be livelier. Your staid reputation is well earned."

He slowed the horse and a stableman ran out and took the reins before he climbed down into the ring. Nicholas pulled off his gloves and began to walk toward us.

"You could have knocked me over with a feather when I learned it was Sergei who had hired that assassin," the tsarevich said. "I thought he was a mate. We were members of the Potato Club, after all. Obviously, he's gone off his chump. He'll arrive at the Summer Palace any moment now and will be roundly interrogated. I sent him to watch over my mistress and he falls in love with her. What cheek!"

"What shall happen to him, sir?" I asked.

"He'll be all right. My uncles and cousins are too powerful to allow one of their lot to be sent to a Siberian prison, but he will be put in charge of an artillery division on the Afghan frontier. If he survives that, I suppose I'll have to forgive him. Sergei and I have known each other since he was in short trousers and I in nappies. Blood is thicker, and all that. However, when he comes back I've got a suitable punishment. I believe I shall send him back to Paris and make him look after Mathilde. They deserve each other."

He turned to the Guv. "You did well enough saving my neck in the tavern across the street. Sergei was nearly too clever for you, I think, Mr. Detective. I forgive you, however, for knocking me to the ground. Couldn't be helped, I suppose, but you bruised my elbow."

"Thank you, Your Imperial Highness," Barker said with frost in his voice.

"Bad form about losing the assassin."

"Bad luck, sir," I heard Jim Hercules whisper behind him.

Nicholas turned his head in annoyance. "Bad luck, then. And you! Thank you for the shooting lesson. It was enormous fun. Give Jim one of your cards. I'm sure you've each earned yourself a medal."

A man in a Russian uniform marched up to him, saluted, and spoke to him briefly in Russian. The tsarevich looked perturbed at the interruption. He rolled his eyes right in front of the poor man.

"Yes, in a minute!" Nicholas said, waving him away.

"What has become of Miss Kschessinska?" the Guv asked.

"I pressed Cousin George into service to take care of her. The two don't really get along, but he's going to Athens and can escort her to Paris on the way."

The military man interrupted him again and the tsarevich snapped back in anger.

"I must go, gentlemen," he said. "My grandmother wishes to see me before I leave London. Good day to you both!"

He turned and left, his boots clicking on the marble floor.

"He never learned our names," I remarked.

It was starting to rankle, and then a group of men hurried past. I saw a number of bruises on their faces and at least one sling.

"Good-bye, Mr. Rachkovsky!" I called after them.

# CHAPTER THIRTY-FOUR

Things rather fell apart after that. The Russian delegation left England and we had no new cases for a week. The days were hot in mid-July and there were no pockets of cool air to be found anywhere.

Without Rebecca, there was no reason to get out of bed in the morning, save duty. Mac took to rousting me out of bed again, and when I went downstairs the only face I found waiting for me was Etienne's, which I wouldn't wish on anybody. Barker was forbearing for several days, leaving me on my own for the most part. My old mantle of melancholy, which had been cast aside for two years, returned like an old friend and wrapped about my shoulders.

My insomnia returned, as well, and I took to walking at night, often for miles. At times I was numb, at others short-tempered. I was angry with God. We weren't on good terms. This wasn't fair, I reasoned. When I was beaten and kidnapped those years ago,

I'd been leading a monk's existence for years. Any relationship I began with a girl quickly fell apart and once or twice a year I'd see Rebecca's cab go by and I'd yearn. I wanted her from the very day I'd seen her on our first case, in which I invaded the Mocatta household to act as a Shabbes goy, ostensibly to light the fires in the house, but really to get information on a case.

Not fair, I'd said, but as the Guv often tells me, life is not fair this side of the veil, otherwise there would be no need for the other. As for Sofia, I could recall little of our actual time together. She came and went. She changed the ointment on my wounds. She chattered, but I cannot recall what it was about. We did not have long conversations. We did not have a relationship of any sort, though if I remember, her decision to kidnap me had not been part of her father's plans. I was someone to talk to; someone who needed her, and needed the herbs to heal me, whatever they were. She was broken by her horrible father, a beautiful young woman made a weapon of destruction against his enemies. It wasn't the tryst that Rebecca thought it was. Far from it.

One night I couldn't take it anymore. I was wandering aimlessly when I resolved to do something. It was time to screw my courage to the sticking place, to quote the Bard. I would go to Camomile Street to see if Rebecca was there, and speak to her. Surely she could not hate me forever, and either way, I would find out if she was alone or had gone home to her parents. Perhaps I had been a fool and she was waiting for me all this time to come and apologize. The more I walked the more convinced I was that this was the case.

I stood in front of Rebecca's house, my house, for about five minutes before I got up the nerve to cross the street and knock. Perhaps I hoped that she would see me, fling open the door, run into my arms, and say it was all a misunderstanding. No. She did not.

The door did not open when I grasped the handle. It was

locked, so I seized the knocker and rapped. One minute went by. Two. I listened and watched for light in the window. It wasn't completely dark inside, although the light was low. I rapped again; nothing.

Then I pounded on the door, a good thirty times at least. If there were anyone inside at all they would come, if only to tell me to clear off. Finally, someone did. It was our maid.

"Lillian, is Mrs. Llewelyn at home?" I asked.

She was as cold as a statue and just as formal. She opened the door part of the way and blocked me from entering. I could have kicked it in, but I didn't want to add assaulting our maid to my list of sins.

"She is not, sir," she replied.

"Could you tell me where she is?"

"I could not."

I narrowed my eyes. "You will not say."

She stared at me with something approaching loathing. "Very well, I will not say."

"Lillian, this is my house. My property. If she is in there, I demand to see her."

She stepped back, pulling the door open fully, raising an arm, bidding me to enter.

It was no use. She wasn't there. Her parents had her. There was no reason to burst in and look through all the rooms for her. Rebecca was not the sort to hide from me.

"Thank you, Lillian," I said. "Tell her . . . Tell her I am thinking about her."

After a few days of solitary walks I stopped into a pub and bought a half. The next night, it became three pints, and five on the third. On the fourth day, I wandered into a gin palace and had to go home by cab. Mac was disappointed in me the following morning.

"Hold still," he admonished. "Give me that razor, before you slice your head off."

Then he poured me into a suit. He did a reasonably good attempt at making me look as if I were not shattered.

Barker saw it all, of course, and said nothing. If a man chose to fall apart silently and there was not a pressing case at hand it was not his business. We rarely spoke to each other in the office.

After a week, however, he finally pulled me aside.

"Brighten yourself up a little, Thomas," he said. "You're looking morose and slovenly. It reflects poorly on the agency."

The agency, the agency; everything reflected on the agency. I was walking off a cliff and all he could do was discuss the ruddy agency. No, that's not fair, but as he always said, who said life was fair?

"Thomas!" a man said in the doorway to our chambers one afternoon, pulling me into a crushing embrace. It was Brother Malachi, my pastor, come to take me out to lunch. By that time I had nearly stopped speaking. It was easier. When we were settled at The Shades, Malachi rattled on about this and that and tried to comfort me, but it only made me clutch my melancholy closer.

One morning I awoke, actually able to shave myself, but I found a stranger in the mirror. I was gaunt, gray, my eyes rimmed with red. After numerous attempts to attach my collar button with nerveless fingers, Mac finally took pity on me.

"This can't go on, Thomas," he said.

He'd never spoken to me like that before. He knew my life was circling the drain. He reasoned that every time I crossed Waterloo Bridge in the middle of the night I dawdled and looked over the side into the Thames wistfully.

"There," he said, settling my suit jacket correctly on my shoulders. He straightened my tie and my pocket square.

"Smarten yourself up, lad, there's a good fellow," I muttered.

I went downstairs slowly. They were building stairs steeper those days, I noticed. The only way to keep from stumbling was to actually tap the heel of my shoe against the back of each stair.

Finally, I reached the bottom.

"Thomas."

I turned and looked at the front door. Rebecca stood there, surrounded by suitcases. My heart nearly stopped. She seemed impossibly beautiful. One would have thought she'd finished a tour of the Mediterranean. Her beauty hurt my eyes. I sat down on the bottom step and pressed a palm to each eye. Later that day, I would learn that Barker had called Philippa the night she left, and she had swooped down on Rebecca like an eagle, or perhaps an angel, and carried her off to Sussex. I love that woman, Philippa, for her service, for all she did for the Llewelyns.

"Thomas," my wife said again, bending over me.

She tousled my hair and a thought came to me then: something good might actually happen in the universe. It was the last thing I expected anymore. A seed of hope.

# AFTERWORD

## SERGEI MIKHAILOVICH

Grand Duke Sergei Mikhailovich of Russia remained the protector and provider for Mathilde Kschessinska for the rest of his life. After having his proposal refused by her, he never married. While his relationship with Tsar Nicholas cooled, his last act was an incredibly brave attempt to save the tsar and his family at their execution in Ekaterinburg, by flinging his body in front of them to try to save their lives. He was buried alongside the Romanovs.

## MATHILDE KSCHESSINSKA

In 1896, Mathilde became the prima ballerina of the Saint Petersburg Imperial Theatre, with the help and influence of the imperial courts. She gave birth in 1902 to a son, Vladimir, but would not admit if the father was Sergei Mikhailovich or his cousin, Andrei Vladimirovich. She amassed property in Saint Petersburg, and when the Revolution came, she moved to Paris, where she lived quietly until her death, a few months shy of her hundredth birthday. She left behind an autobiography of her personal life and triumphs.

## ELEANOR MARX

After a life spent editing her father's works, speaking at rallies of the Socialist League, appearing on the London stage, and translating various works, Eleanor learned that her lover, Edward Aveling, was secretly married. She poisoned herself with prussic acid and chloroform in 1898 at forty-three years of age.

## PRINCE GEORGE OF GREECE AND DENMARK

Aside from the Otsu incident, in which he saved Nicholas's life, George is best remembered for helping organize the 1896 Summer Olympics and for an unhappy marriage to heiress Marie Bonaparte, a great-grandniece of Napoleon.

## WILLIAM MORRIS

Morris died in 1896, leaving behind a legacy of novels, poetry, translations of Icelandic sagas, a fledgling green movement, a revived decorative textile arts industry, and a number of Democratic Socialist publications. He is considered one of the most outstanding and colorful figures of the Victorian Age.

## PYOTR RACHKOVSKY

Rachkovsky was chief of the Okhrana in Paris until 1902. He perfected a system of infiltrating anarchist organizations throughout Europe. He returned to Saint Petersburg to helm the Okhrana there during martial law and was influential in aiding and disseminating the infamous anti-Semitic text *The Protocols of the Elders of Zion*. He died in 1910, before the Russian Revolution.

## JIM HERCULES

Jim Hercules served in his position as bodyguard to Nicholas and Alexandra until the palace was overrun by Bolsheviks. Afterward, he dropped from public record, but it is believed he survived the revolution.

## NICHOLAS II OF RUSSIA (NIKOLAI II ALEXANDROVICH ROMANOV)

Nicholas II's life is one of the most tragic in history. Several ill-informed decisions during his reign contributed to the Bolshevik Revolution of 1917. A happy marriage with Alexandra Feodor-ovna (Princess Alix of Hesse) and family life with his children, Olga, Tatiana, Maria, Anastasia, and Alexei, were ended with their execution at Ekaterinburg on July 17, 1918.

# ACKNOWLEDGMENTS

I'm staggered by the number of steps that occur between writing "the end" and your reading these lines. There are so many
people who worked tirelessly to bring it to you.

First, I'd like to thank my agent, Maria Carvainis, for her time
and encouragement, as well as Martha Guzman at the agency for
taking care of so many important details. I'd also like to thank
my terrific editor, Keith Kahla, as well as the wonderful team at
Minotaur, including Hector DeJean and Alice Pfeifer. I appreciate you all.

Last, but never least, is my wife, Julia, who lends me her ear,
her wit, her enthusiasm, and her encouragement. I couldn't do
this without her.

# LISTEN TO
# **DANCE WITH DEATH**
## ON AUDIO

- •

## READ BY ANTONY FERGUSON

"With a good mix of English reserve and theatrical
bravado, narrator Antony Ferguson takes on a plethora
of Scottish, Welsh, English, French, American, and,
especially, Italian accents to tell this energetic story."

## —*AudioFile* on *The Black Hand*

*Visit MacmillanAudio.com for audio samples and more!*
*Follow us on Facebook, Instagram, and Twitter.*

 macmillan audio